Mr. Teacher

A Novel by

Ozzie Tollefson

SELBU PRESS
Hegins, PA
2013

Selbu Press, 62 Bridge Road, Hegins, PA. 17938
Copyright © July 16, 2012, Reg.#TXu 1-819-106
All Rights Reserved

Printed in the United States of America

Book cover design: Laura Sepesi
Cover illustration: Russell Moore, www.studio68.org
Cover photo of author: Janine Macfarlane-Johnson

ISBN-13: 978-0615817316 (Selbu Press)

ISBN-10: 0615817319

Acknowledgements

This is a book of adult fiction. Any resemblance between the characters in this story and actual people either living or dead is purely coincidental.

Let me start by thanking the teachers at the Appalachian Writers Workshop, who gave me the motivation to think seriously about writing: Gurney Norman, Dick Day, Barbara Smith, Jim Wayne Miller, Ed McClanahan, and Jeff Daniel Marion.

I also want to acknowledge Jim Webb, of WMMT in Whitesburg, KY, who encouraged me to write and perform 96 episodes of our serialized radio drama, *The Lone Driver*. Thanks a bunch, Wiley! And a big thanks to Peter Crownfield for printing 8 additional Lone Driver short stories in his *Echoes Magazine*.

Three friends have played key roles in bringing this novel to print: my editor, Judy Newton, my publishing consultant and cover design artist, Laura Sepesi, and Bob Feder, who kept me on track through the process. Thanks for offering your talents.

I am grateful to Russell Moore of Lockhart, Texas, for the exceptional illustration he did for the cover of this book.

A special thanks to author Michael Fedo for his literary advice and my cousin Atle Renå Reitan, who aptly served as my Norwegian consultant and medical advisor.

I must thank Gabe and Mary Ann Brisbois, who were always ready with an answer when I was stuck for a detail about rural life in Minnesota or aspects of Native American culture.

I wish to thank Brooks O'Kane for granting me permission to use WWII combat information I obtained from his father, S/Sgt. Robert W. O'Kane, in a video interview I did in 1995.

I greatly appreciate the time my good friends and kinfolks have given to reading the manuscript. Your thoughtful suggestions and cheerleading were invaluable.

And finally, I would like to thank my three sons, Greg, Eric, and Alan for their repeated nudging, "Dad, you should write a book!" Okay, gentlemen, here it is!

Ozzie Tollefson
May 26, 2013

This novel is dedicated
to my brother Leonard,
who helped raise me
and would have been
a very good teacher.

Leonard Tollefson
1918-1963

Table of Contents

Chapter I...The Choice

Ernie Juvland wasn't qualified to kill German and Japanese soldiers, at least that's what the U.S. Army said. Drafted in early March of 1942, three months after the bombing of Pearl Harbor, the 23-year-old farm boy was sent home after two months of basic training. A tall, strapping, sensitive young man, nervous and shy as a kid, the Army doctors gave him a medical discharge. "Diagnosis: adjustment disorder, with depressed moods."

It was a shock to Ernie, and his train ride home from an Army camp in Arkansas to his family farm in northern Minnesota was a slow trip, haunted by disappointment and worry. Dressed in his uniform, he sat next to an elderly woman all the way from St. Louis to Minneapolis. And she was a talker. "Are you going home on furlough?" she politely asked.

Ernie didn't feel like telling her all the details. "Yes," he said, "I'm going home to see my mother and younger brother." He heard the measured barking of the steam locomotive and looked out the window across the flatlands, hoping the lady wouldn't ask any more questions. *What would she think if she knew I wasn't mentally fit to be a soldier? Would she think I'm a madman?*

She went on, "We owe so much to our soldiers, so young, so brave, fighting for our country in dreadful parts of the world."

Ernie saw American flags hanging from porches in a little town on the Iowa prairie. A water tower was painted red, white, and blue. "Yes, I agree."

"And people complain about rationing and not being able to buy certain items. It makes me so angry! They have no idea about the sacrifices our boys are making." She patted Ernie's arm and said, "You must feel so proud wearing that uniform, sir."

"Yes, I am." Ernie felt tears coming. "I haven't had much sleep the last few nights; I'm gonna try to catch a few winks."

"You go right ahead, sir. Don't let me bother you."

He pulled the visor of his Army cap over his eyes, stretched out his long legs, and leaned his head back on the seat. But he couldn't fall asleep. The old train chugged through a rough stretch of tracks, jerking from side to side, and Ernie's thoughts rattled in his head like the clanking couplings of the cars. *What will my four older brothers think? They made it through training. They're fighting in the war. But I'm not fit. A medical discharge? What did*

1

those Army doctors find out about me? He blinked his eyes and felt a cloth moving across his face. He pushed his cap back and touched a hand holding a handkerchief. It was the lady next to him.

"I noticed your tears," she said. "Don't worry. God will protect you. God has always blessed soldiers going off to war."

Ernie thanked the lady and looked out the window. He saw a farmer pulling a mired tractor out of the mud with a team of horses. He thought of his own farm, his mother, his kid brother, Andy, and their horses. *Now what? I guess I'll be hitching up the team and working the fields. That's more like a prison sentence.* His brooding turned dark, as the train moved into the night. Gone from his window were the images of the outside world. All he saw was the reflection of his own face, tired, frowning, and pensive. He took off his cap and held it in his lap. He looked again at his face in the window. *I'm not a soldier. I don't know what I am.*

Ernie stayed home and worked the family farm for more than a year, constantly nagged by notions of failure. Bouts of depression came over him without warning or reason. He fought it, but the routine of farming kept him trapped. He needed out and he needed a challenge.

Perhaps he had inherited some of the restless nature of his father, who was always running off to find work somewhere, North Dakota, Montana, and finally California, where he disappeared when Ernie was seven years old and was never heard from again. Willie Juvland was a mystery to Ernie. What he knew about him came from his mother, who claimed he was a lazy man, full of unrealistic dreams and notions of superiority. He was a quitter, who ran off when the going got tough.

Ernie's mother was the rock; she had not given up when her husband abandoned the family. She raised her six sons to be men and kept the farm going during the tough times of the 30s and war years of the 40s. Ernie admired that, but her demonstrated grit made him feel guilty. Each time he considered leaving the farm, he wondered if he was no better than his father, a quitter.

He often talked to his mother about his high school baseball coach who taught history. This enthusiastic teacher encouraged his students, telling them they could be whatever they wanted to be, if they worked hard at it. His mother hated to see him leave the farm,

2

but she wouldn't stand in the way of something he really wanted to do, if it sounded reasonable. Ernie wanted to be a teacher.

He made a choice. In the fall of 1943, he enrolled in a yearlong teacher training program in East Grand Forks, Minnesota, and received his certificate, which qualified him to teach in a one-room country school. He did well, finishing at the top of his class. He was ready for a new life in a little rural school somewhere, but he knew it wouldn't be easy. He'd be all alone with 25 kids or more, grades first through eighth, teaching all subjects.

A gray sky spread over Wilmot County, just north of Moorhead, Minnesota, June 12, 1944. Orvid Skime, Jackson Township School Board President, had sent a letter to Ernie, requesting a meeting to talk about a job opening at their Dahl School. Ernie made the two-hour trip and found the Skime farm. Mrs. Skime told the young man that her husband was out plowing.

So on a blackened prairie field, Ernie Juvland went for his first job interview. He wore a new black suit, a white shirt, a gray necktie, and a black dress hat. He had spit-polished his shoes that morning, but the muddy field he crossed was not kind to his shiny shoes and the bottoms of his neatly pressed trousers. He had a ways to go to reach Mr. Skime, who was plowing with a yellow Minneapolis Moline tractor. The brightly painted tractor and the green leaves on the willow bushes around the sloughs were the only colors on the prairie that day. The rest was drab and somber, black furrows of plowed sod, a gray sky, and a tall, young man in a black suit and hat.

Orvid Skime had been cranky all winter and most of the spring until it was finally dry enough to get in the fields. A 50-year-old dirt farmer with Norwegian ancestors, thin, grim, his beaked nose pointed like a compass needle over the top of his tractor. Orvid was plowing under last year's flood-flattened cornstalks scattered this way and that, black and rotting like dead soldiers on a prairie battlefield. Last summer, that same corn grew tall and tasseled out in August. Perfect timing. He recalled walking through rows of tall corn in early September, stripping back the husks to admire plump, golden kernels. "Best damned crop I've had in years!"

3

Then the rains came. The Wild Rice River went over her banks. Heavy rains continued day after day, and silt-laden waters surged into farmers' fields, toppling cornstalks from acre to acre across Jackson Township.

The tractor purred along, as Orvid glanced over his shoulder to admire fresh sod curling off the slick moldboards of his two-bottom plow, laying to rest the mildewed, dead cornstalks. It made him feel better. He said to himself, "I won't have to look at this møkka anymore! If it doesn't rain, I'll be planting next week."

When Orvid turned at the far end of the field, he noticed a black car parked on the township road and a tall man coming his way. Ernie slogged through the wet field, feeling nervous about meeting the man on the tractor. This was all new to him, first time in his life applying for a job. All dressed up in his new clothes, he felt like an actor in a play. He even had stage directions. In the student teacher's manual he studied at the training school, the last section covered pointers on going for a job interview. He remembered some of it. "Do not sit down until the interviewer directs you to do so. Do not slouch in your chair. Keep your eyes focused on the interviewer and smile when appropriate. Show you are bright and eager to teach children. Be polite."

Orvid Skime let the tractor idle and looked down at Ernie, who handed up a manila envelope containing his certificate from the teacher training school and recommendations from his teachers. Mr. Skime didn't bother to read the paperwork; he folded the envelope and wedged it into the toolbox under his seat. He yelled out, "How come you ain't in the war?"

Ernie looked up at the man seated on the tractor and carefully chose his words. "I was discharged two years ago."

The farmer took a can of snuff from the top pocket of his bib overalls, opened the lid, took a pinch, and packed it behind his lower lip. "We heard you had a nervous breakdown."

Ernie was thrown off guard. "What are you talking about?"

"I'm saying, maybe your head ain't screwed on right."

"It was a medical discharge, sir."

Skime smiled out of the corner of his mouth and said, "Is that what you call it?" He looked down. "Too bad you got your new shoes muddy."

"That's okay. They'll clean up."

"You're a tall drink of water. How tall are you, anyway?'

"Six-four, I guess."

Orvid held out his can of snuff. "You chew snuse?"

"No, thanks."

The farmer shifted his weight on the tractor seat and looked back at the furrow he had just plowed. Then he fastened his eyes on Ernie. "Did anyone tell you why we might hire you?"

"No, I just heard your teacher quit. Did she get married?"

"Who told you that?"

There was something about this man that bothered Ernie. An edge to his voice, his replies came with a snap, like the crack of a whip. "I don't know. I just heard it from someone."

"Well, you heard wrong." He studied Ernie. "I'll tell you why we need a good man. We've got some rough boys in Dahl School, two older brothers, the Smieruds. They need a good, swift kick in the ass!" He waved his hand like he was shooing a fly and scoffed, "Ain't no woman teacher can do that!"

Ernie felt like he was being scolded. "I'll do the best I can."

"You're a big guy, anyways. Stop by the schoolhouse later. Let's say six o'clock." He spit a stream of tobacco juice and looked off in the distance. "Is that your car on the road?"

"No, I borrowed it from a neighbor of ours."

"I hope you like to walk."

"I don't mind."

"I guess you don't have a choice, if you don't have a car. We ain't made up our minds yet, but if we hire you, Tom and Carla Henning will put you up. You'll be doin' a lot of walking. They live a mile from the school."

"I can handle that."

"The Hennings are good, church-going people. Tom and I have had our differences over the years—nothing too serious. Now as for Carla, she's a real looker and smart, too. She's a good mother to their young son, Dale, and she's on the school board."

"Sounds good to me."

"Well, I can't make any money talking to you. I got plowing to do. I called a board meeting for later today. We'll go over your paperwork. Be at the school around six. You hear?"

Ernie walked back to his car, confused and worried. *Not a very friendly guy. He seemed to be mad at something. I wonder what he thought of me.*

Carla and young Dale Henning were cleaning the upstairs bedroom, where the new teacher would sleep. Carla was 39 years old, a pretty woman, bright blue eyes, and a round face with rosy cheeks. She had a nice figure that the neighbor men noticed and women envied—Betty Grable legs and full breasts that filled out her housedress. Her long, blonde hair, usually done up in a braid, reached well down her back. Carla was energetic, kind, and outwardly cheerful, but she often worried over trifles. Friends were known to say, "Carla, you think too much."

At times she wondered about the choices she had made and how things might have worked out differently. She brooded over growing old and could be unreasonably hard on herself. Carla felt she hadn't accomplished much of anything, and time was slipping away. She pondered that now, as she put clean sheets on the bed for the new teacher. She thought she might have become a good teacher herself, or maybe a nurse, but that never happened. Carla Henning was a farmer's wife.

Her husband, Tom, was the son of Torkel Henning, a Norwegian immigrant who homesteaded the land in the 1870s. When the old man passed away, the 160 acre farm was given to Tom, the oldest son, honoring 'odelspeople', a hardbound tradition brought over from Norway.

But it didn't come without a fight from his uppity sister, Wilma, who left the farm after finishing high school, attended secretarial school, worked for an insurance company in Fargo, and ended up marrying the boss. She and her husband wanted the farm sold. She wanted half of what Tom and his father had struggled to keep going during the drought and depression of the 30s. Tom fought his sister and won, but the battle left scars of resentment. He had not spoken to his sister in ten years. Wilma didn't come to Tom and Carla's wedding, and she had never seen their son, Dale.

From childhood, Tom had worked side by side with his father, watching him crook his back, pulling stumps and grubbing roots, clearing the woods for pastures and grain fields. He could not look at a doorjamb without thinking of his father, who had built the house they lived in and the barn where he milked his cows. In Tom's mind this farm was a monument to Torkel Henning, a poor dreng from Norway, who caught 'America Fever', crossed the ocean on a sailing ship, and built a new life in the 'Promised Land'.

6

Tom and Carla's son, Dale, would be eight years old in September, a mindful boy, well-mannered and trained to help with chores around the farm. While his mother put clean sheets on the bed, he stood on a ladder outside the bedroom window, cleaning it with a piece of cheesecloth. The late afternoon sun glared on the window and made him squint, but he could see the moving green reflection of his father's John Deere tractor pulling the grain drill and leaving a trail of dust behind. Tom Henning was planting wheat on a small field beyond the red barn and granary.

Dale yelled at his mother to inspect his work. She opened the window and said, "That's good. I've got to go to a board meeting over at Orvid Skime's place, but I shouldn't be long. Hand me the pail of water and cloth, and I'll do the inside." The pail was a gallon syrup pail with the initials 'DH' painted on the side with red fingernail polish. It was Dale's lunch pail he carried to Dahl School each day.

Dale was a bright boy, thin and tall for his age, but rather quiet. He was their only child now; his younger brother, Kent, died of polio at the age of five in January of 1942, a month after the bombing of Pearl Harbor. Unable to dig graves in the granite-hard, frozen ground, they kept his body in the unheated attic until the spring thaw. Against his parents' warnings, Dale often sneaked up to the attic to see his frozen brother lying on an old cot covered with a blanket. He would pull the blanket back and touch his brother's face, his small nose, his cheeks, and the dead boy's chin.

Once his father caught him sitting on an orange crate holding his brother's frozen hand. He took Dale by the arm, pulled him away from the body, and told the boy never to come up to the attic again. Dale promised he wouldn't and kept his word.

After Kent died, Tom furnished the boy's bedroom with a bigger bed, a desk, a bedside table, and a tall wardrobe. Last year's teacher, Martha Sampson, had been the first to rent the room, and now Dale and Carla were making the room spick and span for the new teacher. But who would it be? Carla told Dale they might hire a man teacher. She would soon find out at the board meeting.

Since Ernie had time to kill, he drove into the closest town, about three miles away. He saw the sign along the highway, **Welcome to Sparborg, Fertile Farms and Friendly Folks.** At the bottom was printed, **Population, 1,216**. He pulled into LaVoi's Standard Oil and asked the man in greasy coveralls to put on a dollar's worth. The man grabbed the handle, jerked it back and forth, and Ernie saw the yellow fuel rise in the glass top of the pump. Ernie noticed the price was a penny higher here than in his hometown. Gas had gone up to 15 cents a gallon.

He drove past the high school, where the Dahl School students would be bussed after finishing eighth grade. He passed The Town Café, a hardware store, and a clothing store. He drove by Buck's Tavern, a grocery store, the Farmers National Bank, a blacksmith shop, and came to the west end of the little town, which was only about seven blocks long. To the west was the great expanse of the Red River Valley, rich prairie farmland that spread for miles to the river and deep into North Dakota.

Off to the north he saw the backstop and benches of the baseball field. He parked along the third base line, got out, and sat on a long bench. He looked at the houses beyond the outfield fence, and looming above, he saw the top of the water tower, and the roof of a grain elevator along the railroad tracks. It was quiet, except for an occasional car or truck passing on the highway.

Ernie was thinking about his interview with Orvid Skime. *I hope I get this job. This is a nice, clean town. The boys I teach will one day play ball for Sparborg High School right here on this field. I'll come back here to see my boys play, if I get the job.* Ernie started thinking about his own baseball days. He was a first baseman and a power hitter. His coach became like a father to him, and he thought one day he might be a coach himself. As he looked out at the infield, a big crow landed between the pitcher's mound and home plate and started pecking at something on the ground, maybe a seed or a worm. He noticed the long, thick beak of the bird, jabbing into the packed dirt, again and again, seeking some treasure, something covered over, hidden from view.

Ernie started feeling sleepy. He went back to the car and rolled down all the windows to let the breeze pass through. He leaned his head against the back of the seat and dozed off. An hour later he woke up, hot, sweating, and surprised to see the big crow walking around on the hood of his car. The large bird stepped up to the windshield and started pecking at a squashed June bug caught under the windshield wiper. Ernie slapped at the glass and shouted, "Get out of here!" The crow looked up, pointed his beak toward

8

the windshield, tilted his head to the side, and stared with fixed eyes at the man behind the glass. The bird gave out a loud, "Caw!" Ernie slapped the windshield again and the bird flew away.

He drove back through Sparborg taking a side street, lined with big houses. He was admiring the fancy gingerbread trim around the gables and eaves, when he suddenly hit the brakes. A two-toned coupe came to a sudden stop in front of him. The driver talked out his window to a nicely-dressed, middle-aged woman, who led a tan dachshund through the ivy-covered trellis at the end of her sidewalk. Ernie didn't toot the horn nor drive around; he sat, waited, and looked at the lady's large house and yard, enclosed with a white picket fence. An American flag fluttered from a white pole near a black cream separator. The silver-colored milk bowl on top served as a planter, holding red and yellow flowers in full bloom. Ernie noticed a padded porch swing and two pink wicker armchairs up on the porch. The top of the varnished door sported a window with six small panes. A narrow driveway passed between her house and her neighbor's house to the backyard. It ended at two large doors of a garage, painted white with blue trim.

The driver blocking the street finished his visit with the lady and drove on. Ernie followed behind and drove out of town, back to Dahl School. He stopped and looked at the square building with its porch facing the road. There was a flag pole out front, but no flag was flying. The school looked lonely, like a mother waiting for her children to come home.

Ernie felt uneasy and worried. *I'll bet the school board is meeting right now. I wonder what Mr. Skime will tell them. Will they hire me? Maybe.* Ernie looked at his watch. He still had time to kill. He drove south of the school on the township road, looking at the mailboxes, small two-story houses, and farm buildings along the gravel road. These were the farms of first generation Americans, sons and daughters of Norwegian, Swedish, and German immigrant homesteaders, who settled here in the last years of the 1800s. The roofs sagged on some of the barns; others needed a new coat of paint. Little farms, 80 or 160 acres, the small grain fields were tucked between the sloughs, lakes, willow thickets, and groves of birch, oak, maple, and elm trees. These were not rich farmers. It showed in the weathered buildings, rotting fence posts, dilapidated gates, junked cars, and rusted farm machinery, left broken and useless, swallowed up by weeds and tall grass.

Ernie noticed a telephone line, but no power lines. There were no electric lights, no electrical appliances, no running water, no central heating, and no indoor toilets. None of that would come until after the war. They used firewood for heat and kerosene for light, a pump for water, and the outhouse for whatever. But the people in Sparborg had electricity, and that made all the difference between the lives of town folks and farmers of Jackson Township.

Ernie saw a lake off to the right and drove onto a dirt road leading down to the shore. The road meandered through a patch of hazelnut bushes, willow and poplar trees until it came out on a small beach. Two wooden rowboats lay turned bottom-up in the grass to the left. A large, white sucker lay bloated in the sand, its mouth gaping wide, covered with black flies. He thought of the pictures he had seen in newspapers of the Normandy landing just a week before, June 6, images of dead and wounded soldiers lying helpless at the water's edge. He watched the flies swarming around the dead fish and thought of his interview with Mr. Skime. *The first thing he said was, 'How come you ain't in the war?' He mentioned a nervous breakdown. Where did he hear that? I need to be careful. Don't act crazy, no matter what!*

A few yards out in the lake two husky boys were trying to dunk a smaller boy. The lad would come up for air, screaming and spewing water, only to be pushed under again. The boys abruptly stopped horsing around and glared at the stranger in the car. They sank down silently watching Ernie, their chins resting on the surface of the water. Ernie rolled down the window and waved to them. They didn't wave back, but he heard them laugh. *Why did they laugh at me? Are the big ones the two brothers Mr. Skime mentioned? They're built more like men than schoolboys.*

The three boys turned and swam into deeper water. More laughter. Ernie watched them swim toward a wooded point of land jutting out from the north side of the lake. They crawled up on the shore. The two bigger boys sat on a log and looked back at Ernie. The younger boy broke off a stick from a fallen tree. He lay prone in the grass, aiming his stick at the big boys on the log, pretending it was a rifle. Ernie could hear the kid making the sounds of a gun. "Bang! Pow! Bang! Ratta-tat-tat!" He was playing at war. His voice came over the water. "You're dirty Japs! Kill the dirty Japs!" Then the older boys got off the log and aimed their fingers at

10

Ernie, as if they were pistols. He heard them yelling, "There's a dirty Kraut! Kill him! Bang! Pow!" Then they laughed.

Ernie started the car and turned it around. *Don't pay them any mind. They're just kids having fun. Better get used to it.* He headed up the narrow lane to the main road and drove back to the school. He was still early, but he decided to wait. He got out of the car and walked around the playground and up to the school. It was a square, one-story building, about 40X40 feet, with a hipped roof and white clapboard siding. He noticed there were no power lines. No electric lights in the school, but he saw a telephone line.

Tan-colored shades covered the four windows on the south side of the schoolhouse, but he found one that was open enough at the bottom to see inside. He cupped his hands around his eyes for a better look. He saw four rows of desks, the bigger ones closest to the windows and smaller ones on the far side. To the left, a long blackboard covered the length of the wall behind the teacher's desk and swivel chair. Large portraits of Washington and Lincoln hung over the top of the blackboard with a small American flag in a bracket at the far end.

There were three doors on the far side. A wall telephone hung between two of the doors, and next to the phone was a large pendulum clock with an octagon face. The time was wrong. The pendulum was still. A huge, square wood-burning stove stood in the back of the classroom. Its stovepipe rose and angled off to a chimney on the far side of the room.

Ernie walked over to the boys' toilet and peeked inside. There were three holes on a bench and a long metal trough to the right for taking a leak. The place smelled of urine and feces. An opened bag of lime stood in the corner near the urinal.

The girls' toilet was nearby and beyond that stood the woodshed, the iron swing set with an attached sliding board, and the pump house. Ernie opened the door to the pump house and tried the handle of the red pump. The rod had been disconnected. *No water. Where do they get their water?*

Ernie sat in one of the swings and waited. He idly moved back and forth listening to the squeak of the chains in the hooks overhead. A chilly wind picked up, and Ernie heard the thin rope slapping against the iron flagpole. He got up and went to the car to get his suit coat. He was putting it on when he heard a car coming from the south on the gravel road. He put on his black hat, and spoke to the reflection of his face in the window of the car. *You have to act like a teacher. Don't look scared. Here they come.*

Orvid Skime drove a black Model A Ford, and riding with him was a short, round-faced farmer, who struggled to get out of the car. His trousers were pulled high over his sizable belly and held in place with a pair of blue suspenders. He waddled over to Ernie and introduced himself by his last name, "I'm Vic, the board treasurer and, let me see now, you must be Ernie." The squat man had a swagger and a confidence that made Ernie wonder. *Is this guy a showoff? He reminds me of W.C. Fields. I like him.*

Ernie stuck out his hand and said, "I'm Ernie Juvland. Good to meet you."

Orvid climbed out of the driver's seat, spit a brown stream of tobacco juice in the grass, and looked up at Ernie. "You want to be good to Mr. Vic here; he'll be writing your paychecks."

Ernie smiled and loosened a button on his suit coat. "Does that mean I'm hired?"

Mr. Vic was taking a piece of paper out of a brown envelope. "We didn't have much choice, Ernie. You were the only man to apply. Most of the boys are off in the war. I don't have to tell you about that."

Orvid Skime found something between his teeth with his fingernail. He removed it, looked at it before flicking it away, and then turned to Ernie with a frown. "I know we talked about this out in the field, but maybe you could tell us a little more about your discharge from the Army. Some of the families around here have asked about that."

Ernie didn't answer. He looked over at the schoolhouse.

Mr. Skime continued, "All we know is, you got good grades from the teacher's training school."

Mr. Vic added, "Yes, we also called your high school and they remembered you. Good student, captain of your baseball team, and never stepped out of line." He looked down at the paper he was holding. "We're going to hire you, young man, but I think everyone would feel better if you explained this 'adjustment disorder'. I hope you don't mind."

"Okay," Ernie answered in a voice that showed his irritation, "I had some problems adjusting to the Army. I guess they felt I wasn't cut out to be a soldier. I wanted to stay. It was my duty to serve. Look, I have two brothers in the Navy and two in the

12

Army right now. One of them just landed on the beach of Normandy, and my kid brother, just graduated from high school, he'll be going into the Army in two months." Ernie took off his hat. "But what am I doing? I'm dressed up in a suit trying to be a schoolteacher! How do you think I feel?" Ernie realized that he had raised his voice.

Orvid Skime was impatient. He took the piece of paper from Mr. Vic and brought it over to the front of the Model A. He wiped a patch of dust off the hood and placed the paper down, holding it with one hand. He took out a fountain pen from the top of his bib overalls and said, "We have a contract here. But before you read it, let me just ask you straight out—do you think you might be crazy?"

Ernie tried to control his anger. "Of course I'm not crazy."

Orvid Skime looked down at the contract. "Maybe it ain't right to ask you something like that, but you have to see it our way. These youngsters, our flesh and blood, some only six years old, will be alone with you inside that building. So here you are, fresh out of school, you've never done any school-teaching before, you ain't got kids of your own, and the Army sent you home because, well, maybe you ain't right in the head. Believe me, young man, that has me and my neighbors worried!"

"Okay," Ernie blurted out. "Then don't hire me. I'll go somewhere else!"

Mr. Vic turned on Skime. "Damn it, Orvid! Shut your gopher trap! You're talkin' like a man with a paper asshole! We've already decided to hire Ernie. Let him sign the damned contract!"

Orvid banged his hand on the hood. The contract flew off and fluttered into the grass. He picked it up and turned on Mr. Vic. "Well, maybe we spoke too soon about hiring this guy. What about the Smierud boys?"

Mr. Vic threw up his hands, "Here we go again!"

Orvid was quick to jump on him. "Now damn it, Vic, you're gonna listen! Those two drittsekkers just drove a nice teacher out of here screaming all the way. Now these bastards are in eighth grade, bigger than you and me, for Christ sake! If Ernie here thinks the Army was a tough row to hoe, wait till he spends a couple of days with those sons of bitches!"

Ernie turned, shook his head, and sat down in a swing and listened to the two farmers argue back and forth. Orvid was going

13

off on the Smierud boys and Mr. Vic was trying to get him back on track. Now Orvid was referring to Ernie as, "This crazy guy here." Orvid brought up his daughter Eunice, who was going into seventh grade, and yelled at Mr. Vic. "You'll be singing a different tune if one of those Smierud bastards tries to feel up my daughter! What's the crazy guy gonna do about that, eh?"

Back and forth it went until Mr. Vic lost his temper. He pushed Orvid against the door of the Model A. "If you talk like a child, I'll have to treat you like a child! You're like the man who sold his brain at a cattle auction!" He took the contract and brought it over to Ernie. He sat down in the other swing and handed the paper to the new teacher. "Don't mind Orvid, Ernie. Yes, indeed, he's a regular steam engine today, with the valves wide open!"

Ernie took a look at the contract, and then glanced up at Orvid, who was sitting in the Model A, digging in his can of snuff. Then he spoke to Mr. Vic. "Sir, I feel like getting in my car right now and driving home. I wasn't expecting anything like this."

"Calm down here! Just, calm down now. Orvid just takes some getting used to."

"I want this job, but I don't know if you want me or not."

"Listen to me. You have the job. There are three of us on the board, Orvid, me, and Carla Henning. We all agreed to hire you. We voted on it just before we came over here." Mr. Vic looked over toward Orvid, who was still sitting in the Model A. He lowered his voice. "Orvid Skime is a good man. But he's very strict, and these Smierud boys have him all worked up. They're his neighbors, and Orvid has been on the outs with the whole family for years. To make matters worse, Orvid has this little buttercup daughter, Eunice. Nicest young girl you would ever want to meet and very smart. She can play the piano and everything. Well, she started coming home from school crying almost every day. Orvid threatened to take her out of school at the end of April, because the Smierud boys were pestering her, lifting up her skirt and talking dirty. Orvid was in such a tizzy, the man didn't know if he was on foot or on horseback. He came stomping up to the school and threatened to kill both of those boys. I'm surprised he didn't bring his shotgun."

While Mr. Vic was talking, Ernie was half listening as he read the contract. The pay was 100 dollars a month, but 25 of that would go for room and board. He thought about the money. *I could actually send home 50 dollars each month to help out Ma on the farm.* "Okay," Ernie said. "Where's the pen?"

Ernie signed the contract and dated it, June 12, 1944. He gave a copy to Vic and kept a copy for himself. "So, you said I'll be boarding at the…was the name Henning? Where do they live?"

"Yeah, gee, we almost forgot. Carla Henning knows you're hired. She's the board secretary. She said your room is ready and you can stop in anytime. They live straight east one mile on the township road. They have a black mailbox set in a red cream can. It's on the left. You can't miss it, white house and red barn."

Ernie said, "Sounds good. I'm not sure when I'll move down here. I have farm work this summer. Maybe the end of August. What's the first day of school?"

Mr. Vic answered, "The day after Labor Day. I think it's September, the 5th. It's written on your copy of the contract."

Orvid had calmed down. He got out of his Model A and shook hands with Ernie. He handed him a piece of paper. "If you have to check with the Hennings, they do have a phone. If you call from around here, it's two longs and two shorts. But from out of town, use this number. Carla's got your keys to the school."

"Well, that's it," Mr. Vic said, shaking Ernie's hand. "We gotta get going. I ain't had supper yet."

"Me neither," said Orvid, "and I'll bet Eunice and the missus have left me with the milking." They climbed in the Model A and Orvid started the engine. He stuck his head out the window and called to Ernie. "I've just been wondering how come a good-looking young man like you ain't married." He waited for a reply. Ernie didn't answer. Then Orvid asked, "You ain't queer are you?"

Ernie just shook his head and turned away. He heard Mr. Vic yelling, "Shut the hell up, Orvid, before I break every bone in your head!" They pulled onto the gravel road and headed south, leaving a cloud of dust behind.

The new Dahl schoolteacher stood for a moment and looked around. *I've got the damned job! I did it. What did my coach tell me about playing first base? 'You'll never know what ugly throw is coming, but you'd better catch it and keep your foot on the bag.' I can do this. I am a teacher.* A lid from a grease barrel, lying in a round patch of dirt at the edge of the playground, caught his eye. Ernie stood on it and looked to the south. He listened to the slapping of the rope on the flagpole. It sounded like the crack of a baseball bat. He was standing on home plate.

At the supper table Dale Henning wiped the last of the gravy off his plate with a piece of homemade bread. He had quietly listened to his mother and father talk about the new teacher. Then he spoke up, "What's his name, Ma?"

"Mr. Juvland," she said. "Put your plate in the dishpan. Then you need to bring in a pail of water before you go to bed."

"Yes, Ma." He went to the counter with his plate and grabbed the water pail. At the door he turned and said, "It's going to be different having a man for a teacher."

His father spoke up. "Yeah, I hope it will be different. I hope he makes you kids behave better than Martha Sampson."

Carla objected, "Please, Tom. She's gone now."

Tom looked up from the cigarette he was rolling. "Are you telling me what to think now?" Carla didn't answer. He searched in his pockets for a match. "What did you do with all her stuff?"

"Dale and I took most of her things down to the cellar. There are still a couple of boxes, mostly books, up in the room. We figured we could leave that."

Dale was still holding the water pail, leaning against the doorjamb. "Pa, will Miss Sampson be coming back?"

"Never mind," Tom answered. He scratched a match on the bottom of his chair and lit his cigarette. "How come you asked?"

Dale looked at his father and said, "I never had a chance to say goodbye to her. I wanted to thank her."

Tom blew out his match and put it on his plate. "Thank her for what?"

"She was nice, Pa. We really liked her."

"You don't have to like your teacher. You respect her."

Carla was at the counter washing the dishes. "Dale, what are you going to do with that pail in your hand?"

"Sorry, Ma. I'm going for water."

Carla turned to him. "Good boy, and when you come back, you can help me wipe dishes." She watched him run out the door and turned to Tom. "I heard Mr. Juvland almost backed out."

"Oh, yeah?"

16

"Orvid started pressing him for details about his medical discharge; the poor man clammed up and was ready to leave."

"So what happened?"

"Betty Vic told me her husband had to settle him down."

"The way I see it, this is a personal matter between the man and the Army."

"That's what I say, but you know how people are talking. All that stuff about a nervous breakdown. And you know what Orvid is like."

"Yeah, I sure do. I've told you before—give that man one little bit of gossip, and you might as well have put it in the papers!"

"Shush, Dale's coming."

Dale carried the pail of water to his mother, and she lifted it on the counter. "Ma, why do you always make me go out for water before I go to bed?"

Carla wiped her hands on a dish towel. "I learned that from my mother. And who knows, it might go all the way back to Norway. She always wanted water in the house at night in case someone got sick. And if, God forbid, you had to call the doctor, he'd want water handy."

Tom left the table and went to the counter, "Hurry with those dishes, Dale. Roosevelt is supposed to talk tonight and you're gonna sit with us and listen."

Dale was wiping a plate at the counter. "Pa, I wanted to listen to *Green Hornet.*"

Tom turned to Dale, "Well, you'll miss it tonight, because we're gonna turn on the radio and hear what the President has to say about the war. I'm sure he'll be asking for more money."

That same evening, Ernie Juvland returned the car to the Inderdal neighbors, thanked them, and started out across the pasture to his mother's house. A few showers had passed in the afternoon and the grass was wet. He felt the moisture seeping into his new shoes. The summer sun was dipping low over the big slough on his left, leaving a path of orange light. A pair of mallards rose from the weeds and headed off toward the woods. He heard bullfrogs trumpeting from every corner of the slough, lonely bachelors calling for mates. Ernie hurried to beat the mosquitoes.

17

As he climbed the steps to the porch, he heard the voice of Roosevelt coming from the big floor-model radio in the front room. His mother sat at the table. The last shaft of sunlight came through the west window, caught her white hair, and reflected off her reading glasses. Fifty-four years old, strong willed, and smart, she had spread out the *Grand Forks Herald* on the table and was writing letters to her sons fighting in the war, using thin, lightweight paper prescribed by the War Department. She looked up at Ernie standing in the doorway. "I see you got your shoes wet." She turned back to her writing, as President Roosevelt concluded his 'fireside chat' by assuring Americans that the June 6 invasion was successful. His calm voice came over the airwaves.

I think that from the standpoint of our enemy we have achieved the impossible. We have broken through their supposedly impregnable wall in Northern France. But the assault has been costly in men and costly in materials. Some of our landings were desperate adventures; but from advices received so far, the losses were lower than our commanders had estimated would occur. We have established a firm foothold. We are now prepared to meet the inevitable counter-attacks of the Germans—with power and with confidence. And we all pray that we will have far more, soon, than a firm foothold.

Ernie and his mother were silent until Roosevelt finished his talk. She got up to turn off the radio and said, "Yeah, we'll see!" She had become a student of the war since the day her oldest son enlisted in the Navy, a week after the bombing of Pearl Harbor. With two sons on ships somewhere in the Pacific and one in the Army, who just landed at Normandy, her life was consumed with the long, bloody struggle. Her only son she didn't worry about had only one good eye. He was kept out of combat and guarded German prisoners in Camp Picket, Virginia. But now her youngest son, Andy, only 18 years old, would be going off to war.

Ernie spoke up, "Do you want to hear some good news?"

"Sounds like you got the job."

"Yes, I did, Ma."

"Good." She folded the newspaper and placed it under the lamp. "What are they gonna pay you then?"

"A hundred dollars a month."

"Good." She closed her Bible and carefully placed it on the *Montgomery Ward Catalog.* "Did they find you a place to stay?"

"Yeah, I haven't met them yet. Their name is Henning."

"Sounds like a good Norwegian name." She went back to her letter writing.

"I have to pay them 25 dollars a month. That's for both room and board. So I'm hoping I'll have maybe 50 to send you every month. That should help."

"Good. That's better than you'd make around here."

Ernie plunked down in a chair across the table from his mother. "Where's Andy?" he asked. She didn't look up from her letter writing. Ernie waited for an answer and then asked, "How did he get the car started?"

"The Inderdal boys came over with their team. They pulled it out on the road and got it started. The battery was dead."

"We ran it down trying to get it started this morning. Then I cranked, but we flooded 'er." Ernie recalled how frantic he was, all dressed up in his new clothes with a two-hour drive to his interview, and the Chevy wouldn't start. "Did Andy go to town?"

Mrs. Juvland finished the last of her letters. "Yeah, he and a couple of his buddies took off. I suppose they went out drinking."

"Can't blame Andy. He's got just two months of freedom."

Blackie, their old Labrador retriever, was scratching the kitchen screen door. Ernie got up to let him in. He sniffed Ernie's new pants and new shoes. Then he raised his head to sniff a pot of something on the Home Comfort kitchen stove.

Ernie's mom came to the kitchen. "I'll bet you're hungry."

"What's that on the stove?"

"It's deer meat stew. Want some?"

"That would be good, Ma." He went to the cupboard, took a bowl off the shelf, and handed it to his mother. She ladled out three big scoops of stew and took a loaf of bread out of the warming oven at the top of the stove. They both sat at the table.

Ernie's mother had a natural gift for storytelling. She told him how she had watched the Inderdal boys and Andy hitching the team to the front bumper of the Chevy. When it finally started, the engine backfired, scaring the horses and they took off lickety-split

19

down the road. Buddy Inderdal was on the hood of the Chevy trying to hold back the horses. He held the reins with one hand and gripped the hood ornament with the other. She said, "It was like a movie with Laurel and Hardy!" She laughed and Ernie laughed as he buttered a slice of bread. "He could have fallen off the car and gotten run over, maybe dragged down the gravel road. Uff da!"

Ernie was hoping his mother would swing into another story, but before long her mood changed. "I don't know what I'm going to do now with you gone and Andy leaving for the Army. I want to keep the farm until the war is over, and your brothers come home. I'm sure one of them will want to farm it."

"I wouldn't count on it, Ma."

"Yeah, I suppose. I guess they'll be different when they come home." She gave a heavy sigh and looked over at the stove. "If you don't want any more of the stew, put it in Blackie's dish." The dog heard his name and raised his head. "Come say goodnight to me, Blackie." The dog waddled on bad hips over to Mrs. Juvland. He sat in front of her and stuck out his paw for a shake. She took his paw in both hands and rubbed it. "Good doggy." She got up and said, "Ernie, I'm proud of you. You've been through a lot for a 25-year-old man. You'll be a good teacher; I'm sure of that."

"Thanks, Ma."

"Now I'm going to bed. Maybe I'll read for a while. It stays light so long these days. It's hard to go to sleep until it gets dark."

Ernie said, "Goodnight, Ma." Then he took the pot of stew from the stove and brought it to Blackie's dish. Ernie sat at the table and watched the dog finish off the stew. Blackie licked the dish and scooted it with his tongue across the linoleum floor.

Ernie climbed the stairs to his room. A kerosene lamp sat on a wooden barrel, but Ernie didn't bother to light it. There was enough light from the south window to see his way around. He undressed and put his suit on a hanger and hung it on a long pipe nailed to the rafters on the pitched ceiling of the bedroom.

Ernie lay on his bed and listened to Blackie playing with his dog dish down in the kitchen. He was hoping to stay awake until Andy came home. He was eager to tell him about getting the job at Dahl School. He thought over the day. *How did that happen? They think I might be nuts, but they hired me anyway. Did I fool them? I guess I did. I dressed up and acted like a teacher. I wore a costume and played my part. Can I keep it up? Can I keep pretending or will they find out how scared I am?*

He lay awake until the window grew dark. Blackie was quiet. The house was quiet, except for a bat he heard crawling on the outside of the window screen. Ernie thought about Andy and wondered if he'd be drunk when he got home. That was his last thought before he drifted off.

Then the dreams came. He was back in high school playing in a baseball game. He watched his friend Charlie in the batter's box, which was covered in thick mud. Charlie swung at a pitch and sent a line drive between the second baseman and shortstop for a single. Ernie stepped into the batter's box and began to sink deeper and deeper into the mud. He was up to his knees. He pounded the mud with his bat until it slipped out of his hands. It lay in the mud and he could not pick it up. It weighed a ton.

He woke up in total darkness and thought about the dream, hoping he wouldn't have another one. He listened for Andy, turned over on his side, covered himself with a patchwork quilt, and went back to sleep.

From somewhere deep in his brain came the sound of laughter. Big boys were laughing. He was in an outhouse and couldn't find his clothes. He was naked and cold. He peeked through a crack in the door and watched two boys fighting over his clothes, a black suit coat, and a pair of black trousers. Another boy appeared and put on his white shirt. The outhouse started filling with cold water. It was up to his waist and rising. Then he heard the sound of a tractor. It appeared from a broad field and was coming very fast toward the boys. Mounted on the front of the tractor was a long spear, like a knight's lance. It pierced one of the boys and lifted him kicking and screaming into the air. Ernie came out of the outhouse, covering his penis with his hands and began yelling at the man on the tractor. "Stop! Stop! You're killing the boy!" Two of the boys were tearing the clothes to shreds as the stabbed boy dangled, bleeding, impaled on the spear overhead. The roar of the tractor became louder. Ernie was standing on top of his bed, gripping the overhead rafters with his trembling hands.

Andy pulled into the yard and parked next to the house.

Ernie yelled, "You're killing that boy!" He stumbled off the bed and knocked the lamp off the barrel, sending it crashing to the floor.

21

Andy heard the yelling and came bounding up the stairs with a flashlight. Ernie had fallen to his knees by the bed. He was beating the mattress with his fists. The tractor had stopped and Ernie was beating on the gas tank with a baseball bat and yelling at the driver. "Get off that tractor!" Now, two of the boys wrestled Ernie into the swirling mud. He tried to hit them with his fists, but his punches were weak. They made no impact whatsoever. One of the boys had him in a bear hug and would not let him go. He was pushing Ernie's face into the mud. Ernie screamed, "Let me go!"

Still in the nightmare, Ernie broke free and got to his feet. He charged Andy, swinging wildly with both fists, slamming his kid brother's body with heavy blows.

Andy yelled, "Ernie! It's me! Andy! Wake up! It's okay!" Andy was strong. He dodged the punches and wrestled Ernie to the floor. He sprawled on top of him, pinning him down.

Ernie could not move. He heard Blackie barking and felt the dog's hot breath on his face. Something was holding his head to the floor. The tractor disappeared. The three boys disappeared. He heard his mother calling from halfway up the stairs. "Mercy me, Ernie, it's okay. Just settle down. You were dreaming again."

Ernie heard the word 'dreaming' and went limp. His heart was pounding; his breathing came in short gasps. He reached out and touched Blackie's front paw. He smelled the liquor on Andy's breath and felt the heavy weight of his body lying across him. "I'm okay," he said, and Andy climbed off his brother, helped him to his feet, and guided him toward his bed.

Andy picked up the lamp and put it back on the barrel. The globe lay shattered in pieces on the floor. Andy sat on the floor with his flashlight and began to pick up bits of glass.

His mother called from the steps, "Did the globe break?"

Andy answered, "Don't worry about it, Ma. We'll get another one."

Ernie was quiet for a minute. Then he lay back on his bed and said, "I'm sorry. It looks like they've started in again." His anger rose. "What the hell am I gonna do? This is just crazy!"

His mother said, "Do you have a headache? I can get you an aspirin and some water."

"No," he answered. "Aspirin ain't gonna fix me."

Chapter II...The Arrival

The summer of 1944 dragged on for Ernie. He and Andy put up hay, cultivated corn, cut firewood, and spent rainy days fixing fences, but the young teacher's mind wasn't on farming. He was thinking about Dahl School, living with the Henning family, and how he would handle the nightmares if they came again.

His mother followed the war. Each day she wrote letters to her sons, took them up to the mailbox, and brought back the *Grand Forks Herald.* She spread the newspaper on the kitchen table and studied the war maps, illustrating the advance of the Allied Powers in Europe with black arrows sweeping across France and Belgium, pointing toward Germany and the Rhine River. Where was her son, who had crossed the English Channel and landed on the beach of Normandy? She pored over details of the massive invasion involving 700 Allied ships and 4,000 landing craft. In the Pacific, she read about the air battle in the Philippine Sea, where more than 400 Japanese planes and three carriers were destroyed. The U.S. Marines were landing on the Marianas Islands. Saipan fell on July 7. She wondered about her two sons on Navy ships somewhere in the Pacific. Where were her sons on those maps?

From July 19 through July 21, Mrs. Juvland was glued to the radio, following the Democratic National Convention held in Chicago. She was proud to see Franklin Roosevelt nominated for a fourth term, an honor that was never before achieved. The President was not at the convention to accept the nomination; he had an important meeting in the Pacific with General Douglas MacArthur. She had nothing against Vice President Henry Wallace, but the conservative wing of the party apparently did. They succeeded in nominating their favorite candidate for vice president on the second ballot, a little-known senator from the state of Missouri, Harry S. Truman. Mrs. Juvland told Ernie, "The only thing I know about the guy—he can play the piano."

On August 15, 18-year-old Andy Juvland left for the Army. The youngest of the family, he had a baby face and sandy-colored hair. He was shorter than Ernie and more easygoing, well-liked in high school, he had a number of girlfriends.

After the evening chores, Ernie drove him to Thief River Falls, Minnesota, to catch the 11:15 train to Minneapolis. They had some time to kill, so Ernie bought a case of cold Grain Belts at

Knute's Place, and they sat on a bench along the Red Lake River. Andy had a cloth bag of oatmeal cookies their mother had baked that afternoon. Ernie took out a church key from his pocket and opened a beer for Andy and one for himself. He said, "Here you go, brother, and let's hope this wind keeps the mosquitoes on the other side of the river."

"I'll drink to that." Andy took a long chug and looked out across the slow moving water. "I hated to see Ma cry."

"Yeah, so did I. Now she'll have five letters to write." Andy offered his brother the bag of cookies. Ernie pushed the bag away. "No, they're for you. It's a long ride to Minneapolis."

"No, go ahead. She packed a couple of sandwiches and two apples." He opened the bag and handed Ernie a cookie.

Street lights from across the river made little rippled trails on the surface of the water. They drank beer, ate cookies, and talked about the war in Europe, the march toward Germany, and the goal of crossing the Rhine River. Andy wondered if the Rhine was wider than the Red Lake River they looked across. Ernie figured it was much wider. Andy reminded Ernie about the day he beat him in a race across the river near the place where they sat. Ernie laughed, "Yeah, but I gave you a head start, because you were my kid brother. I'd race you again and beat you, if you didn't have to catch the train."

Andy had questions for Ernie about Fort Snelling, his physical exam, and where they would bunk him, before they shipped him down for his basic training at Camp Joseph T. Robinson outside North Little Rock, Arkansas. It had been two and a half years since Ernie had made the same trip, but he remembered most of it. "I was glad when the physical was over, so I could put some clothes on. We stood in line naked for a whole afternoon. But at least you're going in during the summer. I went through Fort Snelling in early March. There was still snow on the ground, and it was colder than a son of a gun."

Andy opened another beer, "I'll bet it'll be hotter than blazes down in Arkansas."

"Most likely," Ernie took another cookie out of the bag. "I don't know how Ma's gonna get along now with you gone and me teaching school."

"I think you should find her a place in town."

"She doesn't want to move to town. She put her foot down on that. She told me to leave her with the car and she'd be fine."

"How about the milking?"

"Well, she isn't going to like it, but I think we'll have to sell the cattle before I leave."

"Oh, boy, that'll be a tough one."

"I know. What else can we do?" The cookies were all gone. They left the river and drove to the depot. Andy took four beers out of the case and put them in the cloth bag. The train from Winnipeg was right on time, 11:15. Ernie shook hands with his brother, told him to stay out of trouble, and watched him board the last car. He stood by the tracks until the train was out of sight. There was no one else on the platform to see Ernie's tears. *Take care of yourself, little brother. God, I hate to see you go!*

When Ernie got home, it was near midnight. He noticed a note from his mother on the kitchen table. *Rosie broke out of the cow pasture again. She got into the Inderdal's cornfield. You'll have to get up early and go look for her.* He heard his mother snoring softly from her bedroom. *How will she handle the cows when I'm gone? We have to sell off the cattle. No two ways about it. I'll call the trucker before I leave.* He folded his arms across the table, making a pillow for his head. He soon drifted off to sleep.

Dale Henning was out of bed before sunup on his birthday, September 1. He dressed, made his bed, went downstairs, and lit the lamp on the kitchen table. He noticed a square, blue envelope lying next to the lamp. Carla had left it there after Dale went to bed, hoping he'd find it in the morning. It was addressed to him, but there was no return address. He carefully opened the envelope and pulled out a birthday card. On the front was a picture of a boy swinging over a swimming hole on a rope hung from the branch of an oak tree. Inside was the greeting, **Happy Birthday to a very special boy!** Under it she had signed her name, *Susan Rollag*, in beautiful cursive script. Dale saw the way she had written her capital 'S', large and fancy. Under her name it read, *P.S. You are the nicest boy in my class!* Dale thought about that. What did she mean? He and Susan were the only two students in their class. Dale started feeling jittery all over—maybe she meant the nicest boy in the whole school! He carefully put the card back in the envelope and slipped it into the top pocket of his bib overalls.

He washed his hands and face at the washstand and looked into the mirror. He was thinking his face would have changed. After all, he was now eight years old. He and Susan were promoted to third grade, and their new desks would be one row closer to the south windows where the big kids sat.

He spent the day doing chores for his dad and mom. After helping his dad with the morning milking—Dale learned how to milk cows when he was six years old— he helped his dad carry the ladder down to the barn. Tom Henning went up on the roof of the barn to replace some shingles that had blown off during a storm. He barked orders and Dale jumped. The boy was going up and down the ladder bringing him tools, shingles, nails, and a quart Mason jar of cold drinking water. He listened to the hammer on the roof and the putt-putt-putt of the washing machine engine coming from the back porch.

His mom called from the kitchen door, "Dale, I need help with the wash!" In the summer Carla did the washing on the back porch, but in the winter she kept the machine in the kitchen and ran the exhaust hose out the back door. Dale was barely three years old the time he almost died from the exhaust fumes of the gasoline engine on the washing machine. His mom had the washer running in the kitchen on a bitterly cold January morning. Carla set out a bowl of oatmeal for Dale at the kitchen table and went upstairs to get his little brother Kent out of his crib. She dressed him, stripped the sheets off Dale's bed, and gathered some dirty clothes to wash.

Meanwhile, Dale was sitting in his long underwear eating his oatmeal and shivering. A cold draft was coming through the back door that was left ajar for the exhaust hose. Little Dale got up, pulled the exhaust hose inside, and slammed the back door tight. The kitchen soon filled with blue exhaust, and Dale started to feel sleepy.

Upstairs his mom smelled the exhaust fumes. She picked up Kent and ran downstairs. She could barely see Dale through the blue smoke in the kitchen. He had passed out, face down in his bowl of oatmeal. Still holding Kent, she scooped up Dale with her free arm and took them both outside. She put Kent down, and he crawled off in the snow. She laid Dale down and rubbed snow in his face. He gasped for air, and in a few minutes he was breathing fine. She had caught him just in time. Another five minutes with his face in the oatmeal and he might have died.

Dale helped his mom run the clothes through the wringer. She carefully fed them into the rollers and Dale caught them on the other side. Doing the wash always made him think of something he once overheard his dad tell another farmer. A pig got in the house one day, and they were trying to chase the big hog out the door. It ran between Carla's legs, hooked his snout on her long skirt, flipped her off her feet, and left her riding on the pig's back. His dad said, "We never had so much fun since grandma got her tit caught in the wringer!"

That same afternoon, 80 miles north of the Henning farm, a big cattle truck pulled into the Juvland farmyard. Ernie was leaving for his teaching job that day, but first he was selling off the cattle. There were four cows that were milking, four calves that were born that spring, a couple of yearling steers, and the bull. Ernie and one of the Inderdal boys helped load the stock, and Mrs. Juvland watched from her rocking chair on the front porch.

Ernie walked behind the truck as it left the barnyard and headed up the lane to the main road. He heard their hooves on the truck bed as they shifted their weight from side to side. He came up to the porch, where he and his mother listened to the wailing of the calves and the roar of the truck, heading for the highway, heading for the stockyards and slaughterhouse in South St. Paul, 300 miles away.

Tears rolled down Mrs. Juvland's cheeks, and Ernie felt his own eyes water up as he looked at his mother's face. She blew her nose on a handkerchief and cleared her throat. "It feels like it's over now."

Ernie didn't say anything. There was a brooding nature to his mother. He could see it in her eyes, as she followed the trail of dust hanging over the road behind the cattle truck. She had kept the farm going after Ernie's dad disappeared for good, working as hard as any man, putting up hay, pitching manure, splitting wood, and chopping out ice holes in the slough, so the cattle had water to drink in the winter. She trapped muskrats, weasels, beaver, and mink. She knew how to skin them, pull their hides on stretchers to dry, and then she sold them in town for groceries.

27

But it was the cattle that defined her farm. Ernie remembered the day he came home after his medical discharge from the Army. She was in the barn helping a cow deliver her calf. She was on her hands and knees in loose manure pulling on the newborn. The struggling cow lay on her side, kicking and bellowing. The calf was coming out backwards and stuck. Ernie offered to help, but she said, "You'll get your uniform dirty." She rolled up the sleeve of her dress and reached her arm inside the cow, clear to her shoulder, to turn a front leg that was stuck crossways. She knew exactly what to do and she did it. Ernie remembered her holding the wet calf in her arms and wiping the slime from its face.

The roar of the cattle truck was gone and the dust had settled on the township road. She looked up from her folded hands and said, "When you sell off the cattle, it's the end." Ernie listened without speaking. Her recollections came in the solemn tones of a eulogy. "In 1873 when my pa came over from Norway with his parents and younger sister, he was ten years old. They came on a ship into Ottawa, Canada, and made their way to Milwaukee. My grandpa had just enough money to buy a wagon and a team of oxen." Her voice began to break, "And those two steers pulled my family across Wisconsin and into southern Minnesota, where they went to work on farms. That was the beginning. We managed to keep 'er going for 71 years, but today is the end. The cows are gone."

Ernie couldn't think of anything to say that would console his mother. He went inside and washed up. He dried himself with a towel and still noticed the smell of animal sweat on his hands from pushing the cows on the truck. He washed his hands again. He went up to his bedroom, changed clothes, and finished packing a suitcase and two cardboard boxes of books and clothes.

On the wall over his bed he saw a framed Thanksgiving prayer given to him by an Ojibwa woman, a midwife, who had helped Ernie's mother bring him into the world. When he took it down, he noticed the square white patch on the wall, where the prayer had hung for almost 20 years. He sat on his bed and read the first line, **We give thanks to our Mother, the Earth, for she gives us all that we need for life.** He looked out his window at the pasture and fields beyond and thought of what he was doing—leaving the farm to teach schoolchildren. The words of his

28

mother came back to him. *'We managed to keep 'er going for 71 years, but today is the end.'* *What am I doing? I'm breaking our family ties with Mother Earth. Am I the cause of my mother's tears?* He carefully placed the framed prayer in his suitcase.

He heard Buddy Inderdal talking to his mother on the front porch. Then he heard him call, "Hurry up Ernie. You're gonna miss that bus."

Ernie called out, "Come on up and give me a hand." He waited for Buddy at the top of the stairs. "Grab those two boxes sitting on my bed. I've got the suitcase."

When Ernie came out on the porch, his mother didn't get up from her rocking chair. He put his suitcase down, took her hands in his, leaned forward, and kissed her on the brow. "I hate to leave you like this, Ma." He picked up his suitcase. "I might live to regret what I'm doing here today."

"Don't talk like that. This is something you really want to do. You go, now. Good luck teaching school and don't worry about me. I'll make do."

Blackie followed Ernie to the Inderdal's car and wanted to jump inside. "No, doggie, you have to stay. Go to Ma now."

When Dale and his dad came up from milking, Carla was busy in the kitchen fixing supper. There were four places set on the table, and that caught Dale's eye. "Ma, are we getting company?"

"We sure are. Mr. Juvland is coming. Mr. Vic just called. He's picking him up in town, and if the bus is on time, he should be here by seven. Hurry up now with the separating and feeding the calves."

Dale stood on a chair and held the strainer as Mr. Henning poured the milk into the big bowl on the top of the De Laval cream separator. He placed a ten-gallon can under each spout, one for cream and one for skim milk, and Dale began to turn the crank.

When the milk was separated, Dale took two pails of skim milk down to the barn to feed four calves that were born that spring. They saw him coming with the pails and ran to meet him at the trough by the fence. On the other side of the barn his dad was feeding three pigs in the pigpen. The slop was a mixture of skim milk, potato peelings, carrot tops, cabbage leaves, scraps of meat, and just about anything Carla had thrown into the kitchen slop bucket. Finally, Dale carried a pail of cream to the icehouse and poured it into a ten-gallon cream can that was set between blocks of ice packed with sawdust. When he was closing the door of the icehouse, he heard a car coming on the gravel road. It was Mr. Vic bringing his new teacher.

Carla and Tom came out to greet Ernie Juvland, but Dale stayed back. He skirted around the edge of the yard to the wood pile and sat down on the splitting block.

Tom and Mr. Vic helped Ernie bring his baggage up to the front porch. Dale noticed that Mr. Juvland was taller than his dad. He was wearing a white shirt, with the sleeves rolled up above his elbows. Dale saw his big arm muscles. Then he heard his mother call, "Dale, get over here. Come say hello to your new teacher."

Dale stood up with his head down. He noticed the chopped-off head of a chicken lying near the splitting block. His dad had killed the chicken for supper. One eye of the chicken was still open. The boy looked up as his mother approached.

"Dale, what's the matter? Don't be shy. Come meet Mr. Juvland." Carla took Dale by the hand and brought him up to Ernie and said, "He's being a little shy."

Ernie said, "No need to be scared of me, Dale." The boy kept his hands in his pockets. The first thing Dale noticed was Ernie's shiny shoes. Their minister had shiny shoes, but not as shiny as Ernie's. He looked at his strong arms and finally noticed his kind eyes. Dale thought his new teacher was nice, a tall man with a nice smile.

Ernie said, "Let me shake your hand, young man," Dale pulled his hand out of his pocket and shook hands with Mr. Juvland. Still Dale was silent. Ernie looked him in the eye and said, "I've heard you're a real good boy."

Dale wondered where he had heard that. It pleased him.

"Yes, he is, Mr. Juvland," Carla said. "And this is a big day for Dale. It's his birthday."

"Well, Happy Birthday, Dale!" Ernie reached out to shake his hand again. "So, how old are you?"

Dale looked down at Mr. Juvland's shoes, "I'm eight."

"Eight years old," said Ernie with a smile. "I guess you'll be going into third grade, right?"

"Yes, sir."

Ernie smiled and looked at Tom. "I like a young man who says 'sir'. You raised him right, Mr. Henning."

"You betcha," said Tom. "We want him to respect grownups."

Ernie remembered what Orvid Skime had said about Tom Henning, "We've had our differences." Looking at Tom, Ernie could understand—both stubborn. Tom stood with a straight back, as if to make himself seem taller. Ernie noticed his dark brown, penetrating eyes. They were the eyes of a proud man, who let you know he was in control. This was his farm, his wife, and his son.

Mr. Vic said, "Well, it looks like you're all set here, so I'm gonna get going."

Ernie reached out to shake Mr. Vic's hand. "I really appreciate your picking me up at the bus."

Mr. Vic patted Ernie on the back, "Don't mention it."

The sun had dipped down behind the big oak trees to the west and the mosquitoes were waiting in the woods and sloughs, preparing to attack. The weather was warm and they had not finished their summer of terror. One hour after sundown they'd come out—you could almost set your clock by it. Carla saw an advanced scout, circling Ernie's head. "Come on in, now," she said, heading to the kitchen door. "If we stay out here any longer, we'll get eaten alive." They waved goodbye to Mr. Vic as he pulled out of the yard. Then they went inside and sat down for supper.

That evening, Mrs. Juvland sat at the front room table listening to *Duffy's Tavern* on the radio. She was reading a letter from Andy, who was now in his second week of basic training at Camp Joseph T. Robinson, Arkansas.

Dear Ma,

How are you? I'm fine, but it's hotter than blazes down here. I hope you're getting along okay on the farm. Just be careful when you feed the pigs. Don't get in the pen with them or that big one might knock you down. Did the

Inderdals come for the horses yet? You told me they were going to keep them.

Thanks for sending me Ernie's new address. Sounds like he'll be living with a nice family. I wrote to tell him that training is a lot tougher than he said it was. Our sergeant is pretty rough on us. We have reveille at five. Us farm boys don't complain about that, but we've got a few city slickers from St. Louis down here and they really bellyache about getting up before sunup.

Okay, that's it for now. Time to go to the mess hall for supper. I'll bet they have SOS again. Do you know what SOS stands for, Ma? I'd tell you, but I'd have to use a bad word. Ha!

Write soon,

Andy

Mrs. Juvland studied the letter and thought of the day last week when the Inderdal boys came to get Bill and Roany, the two broncos that had worked so hard over the years. They were small horses that had come from South Dakota and were full of spunk, especially Roany, the mare. You could ride Bill, but Andy tried to ride Roany once when he was maybe 12 years old and almost got killed. He brought her to the front porch to make it easier for him to climb on her back. Once on top, she took off for the barn. Andy was hanging on to the hames of the harness for dear life. The barn had Dutch doors; the bottom one was open, but the top one was closed. The horse came to the door going full speed, went into a crouch, slipped under the top door, and peeled Andy off her back as clean as a whistle. Andy hit the top door head first, knocking him out. It was several minutes before he came to.

She got up from the table, went to the kitchen window, and looked outside. Blackie was snoozing in the grass near the pump. And past the barn and the Inderdal's slough, she could just make out the forms of Bill and Roany in the fading twilight, grazing in the pasture. She called to Blackie to come in. She filled his dish

32

with water and watched him drink. She sat at the front room table and wrote to Andy. She stayed up and listened to *Waltz Time* and *The Art Linkletter Show*. Then she went to bed. She listened for sounds from outside, perhaps the call of a calf coming from the barnyard. But the barn was empty and the cattle were gone, halfway down the road to South St. Paul. Olga Juvland was alone in her house, and her sons were scattered across the globe.

At the Henning's kitchen table, Ernie had stuffed himself with roast chicken, mashed potatoes, and corn on the cob. After the plates were cleared away, Carla appeared from the pantry carrying a chocolate birthday cake with eight lit candles on top. They all sang "Happy Birthday" to Dale and he went to blow out the candles. "Make a wish first," Carla said, as she went to the cupboard for a knife to cut the cake. Dale thought for a moment, bowed his head as if to pray, and then he blew out all the candles in one big puff.

"So what did you wish for?" his dad asked, as he stood up to reach for a package on the top shelf of the cupboard.

"I'm not telling," said Dale with a giggle.

Tom Henning placed a neatly wrapped present on the table next to Dale's plate. It was white with a red bow and a tag with a greeting. **Happy Birthday to our son, Dale. From, Ma and Pa.**

Dale quickly opened the package, handing the bow to his mother. "Wow," he said, "just what I wanted!" It was a baseball mitt. "Thanks, Pa."

"Well, I guess you earned it," said Tom.

Ernie asked, "May I take a look at it?" Dale handed his teacher the glove. "This is a very good glove. Take good care of it now." Ernie handed back the glove and got up. "Here, let me show you the one I used in high school." He went over to one of his cardboard boxes and took out his old baseball mitt.

"Gee," said Dale, "That's a big glove. I've never seen one like that."

"It's a first baseman's mitt. You need something big to pick up those wild throws."

Dale looked at Ernie. "Will you play catch with me tomorrow?"

Ernie was quick to reply, "You bet we can."

Tom spoke up. "Don't feel like you have to. You've got more important things to do, getting ready for school."

"That's okay. We'll have some free time," said Ernie.

After the cake, the table was cleared, and Tom went to the cupboard for a bottle of blackberry brandy and three small glasses. "I think it's time for a little nip," he said. "Let's go sit in the front room. It's cooler in there."

"Good idea," said Carla, taking off her apron. "The stove is still hot from all the cooking today."

Dale wanted to stay at the kitchen table and have another piece of his birthday cake, but Tom, Carla, and Ernie went into the front room. Ernie sat down in a rocking chair next to the big floor-model radio, and the Hennings sat together on the davenport. Ernie had many questions for them about the school, the students, and their parents. The conversation turned to Martha Sampson, the last teacher at Dahl School and the problems she had, especially with the Smierud boys. Ernie had been thinking about those boys, ever since Orvid Skime mentioned them. He listened carefully to what they said.

"She was too easy on them," said Tom. "It's as simple as that."

"Nicest young lady you ever wanted to meet," added Carla. "She had no problems the first month or so, but then the older boys started testing her, to see what they could get away with."

"She should have laid down the law right away," said Tom. "You see, Mr. Juvland…"

"You can call me Ernie," said the teacher.

"Okay, Ernie," Tom continued. "She had a car and that was a problem. I told her to lock it up when she got to school, but she never did. Ain't that just like a woman? She didn't listen. If she'd locked it up, she never would have had that problem with the snake."

Ernie sat still in his rocker. "What snake?"

Carla said, "Neal, the older Smierud boy, put a big black snake in her car. So she's driving home after school and feels this thing crawling up her leg."

Tom turned to Carla. "I thought I was telling the story." Carla didn't answer. Tom went on, "It's a wonder she didn't go in the ditch and roll. The girl could have killed herself."

34

Ernie shook his head and finished his brandy. "So she didn't do anything about it?"

"Nope," said Tom. "Not a darned thing! I think she was afraid to do anything."

Carla got up to pull the shades on the bay windows. "Some nights we could hear her crying up in her room. She took it all on herself. We tried our best to help her, but she started to feel like she was a bother to us."

Tom was rolling a cigarette. He poured a portion of tobacco from his pouch of Bull Durham on the paper. He grabbed the tab of the pull string with his teeth, closed the pouch, and put it back in his shirt pocket. "Then she started going over to Anders's place."

Ernie asked, "Who is Anders?"

Tom and Carla looked at each other and chuckled. "Well," said Tom, "he's mostly a mystery."

Carla said, "Anders Lund. He lives across the road from us. You can't see his house from the main road. It's set back in the thicket down by the creek."

Tom added, "He's a hard one to figure out, but I know one thing, you never see him in church, and he only goes to town maybe twice a month to get groceries. I guess you'd say he's a hermit."

"Martha liked him. She told us what a kind and brilliant man he was," said Carla.

Tom was quick to speak. "Yeah, that's what Martha thought. I'd say he's one of those college guys—book smart and tractor dumb!"

Ernie managed to smile. "How old is Mr. Lund?"

Tom got up to get an ashtray. "Oh, I don't know—somewhere around 60. He's as strong as a bear, I know that, big guy, almost as tall as you." He was looking at Ernie. "I told Martha, it was none of my business what she did outside of school, but I warned her about the guy. He's just different. He's been living down there, what, two years now, and most people don't know any more about him now than they did the day he moved in."

Carla continued, "Martha told us he's a real gentleman, retired professor from St. Hallvard College."

Tom flicked the ashes from his cigarette. "I don't know, Carla, he's just a weird old man. Maybe he's smart, I don't know, because I ain't had that much to do with him. I told Martha if she was looking for a boyfriend, she could do a lot better than old Anders. A sexy little thing like her, heck, she could hook a banker's son and be set for life!"

Carla was trying to defend Martha. "She just needed someone to talk to, and he gave her a lot of ideas about teaching."

Tom, laughed, "You don't know what they were doing when she went down there." Carla got up and shook her head. Tom added, "Well, Ernie, I'm sure you'll run into him sooner or later. You're smart and you might like the guy. I just think he's different. He ain't common like the rest of us."

Carla added, "We really don't know that much about Anders, but I still think he was a comfort to Martha. Those Smierud boys were driving her crazy, and she just didn't know which way to turn."

Tom leaned forward on the davenport and pointed at Ernie, "Look, I've never taught school and I have no training for it, but I'll tell you what. My best advice to you, Ernie—get in there and scare the hell out of those Smierud boys, right off the bat! And believe me, every family in this township will thank you from the bottom of their hearts. You gotta get tough with those two. You're a big, strong bull. If you have to knock them up the side of the head, there ain't one parent around here who won't back you up."

Carla interrupted, "Well, there's one. Old man Smierud."

Tom laughed, "Ha! Forget about that lunatic! Nobody gives a damn what he has to say. Someone is gonna haul off and shoot that bugger one day, if he don't drink himself to death first."

Carla felt she should say something. "I just think it's been tough for Ben Smierud to care for his boys after he lost his wife."

Tom scoffed, "Yeah, you stick up for everybody, Carla."

They were quiet for a moment, but Ernie had one more question. "Orvid Skime mentioned the problem with his daughter. What was her name? I forget."

Carla said, "Eunice." She looked at Dale sitting at the table beating his fist into his new glove. She lowered her voice. "Well, that's where this whole mess with the Smierud boys went too far. I don't want to talk about it right now." She glanced back at Dale.

Tom sensed the worried look on Ernie's face. "Look, you ain't gonna have any trouble as long as you show those boys you won't put up with any of their crap, especially Neal, the oldest one. From what I hear there might be hope for Bobby. But Neal is just one mean son of a bitch. If he ever lays a hand on my boy, I'll kill the no-good hundejokker!"

Carla was ready to change the subject. She wanted to know more about Ernie. He told them about his mother and his brothers off in the war. He felt very comfortable talking to Tom and Carla. They were good listeners and kind. Tom was stubborn and opinionated, a typical Norwegian, quick to show his wife who wears the pants in the family, but Ernie trusted him and took his advice to heart. Carla had a twinkle in her eyes and a broad smile. She reminded Ernie of a girlfriend he had back in high school, same laugh and same round face. It was obvious that she was several years younger than Tom, who seemed to be somewhere in his mid-fifties, maybe his mother's age. Ernie wondered about that.

They had talked for almost an hour in the front room, long enough for Ernie to feel sleepy. Maybe it was the brandy. Tom started to get up and said, "Well, I suppose…"

"Yeah," said Carla, "maybe it's time for bed. It's been a long day for you, right Mr. Juvland?"

"Yes, it has," he said and handed her his empty glass. "Thanks a bunch for the big supper. That was very good."

Before she could respond, Tom said, "Oh, she's a good cook, all right. That's why I married her."

Carla pretended not to hear him and went into the kitchen, where Dale was looking at pictures of bicycles in the *Montgomery Ward Catalog*. She put her arm around him and said, "Well, birthday boy, how about showing Mr. Juvland up to his room?"

"Yes, Ma," he answered and brought his plate and fork to the dishpan.

Carla lit a small kerosene lamp and handed it to Dale. "Be careful with that now. Grab it with both hands."

Ernie grabbed his suitcase and his baseball mitt and followed the boy up the stairs. Halfway up he turned and said, "Thank you so much for everything. I'm going to like it here."

Carla said, "We're happy to have you."

And Tom said, "Show those school kids you're the boss, Mr. Teacher."

It was hot in the room, but there was a slight breeze coming through the west window. Dale put the lamp on the table next to the bed and showed Ernie the wardrobe where he could hang his clothes. Then he said, "Goodnight, sir," and went across the way, past the head of the stairs to his own room.

Ernie stripped down to his shorts, pulled the blanket and sheet back. He blew out the lamp and lay in the darkness with his eyes wide open, thinking of the Hennings, Dale, his new home, and the Smierud brothers. *Tom said get tough with them. Can I do that? I might have to. Carla and Tom are nice people, but they're very different. Tom wants to show he's the boss. He might be a hard man to get along with. Everything is cut-and-dried with him. He has rough edges. Carla is like a dish of tapioca pudding, smooth, soft, and sweet.*

Ernie listened to them talking softly downstairs, but even though there was no door to the stairway, he still couldn't make out exactly what they were saying. He noticed the light went out in the front room, and he heard the door to their bedroom close. He listened for more sounds. Maybe their bed would start squeaking, but the house was silent.

While Ernie drifted off to sleep, old man Smierud had passed out with his head on the bar of Buck's Tavern. "Wake up, Ben." Buck's wife, Velma, grabbed the drunk's shoulder and shook it. "We're closing. Come on, buddy. Everybody's gone home and that's what you have to do."

Ben slowly raised his head off the bar, "Did my wife go home?" he muttered with his eyes still shut.

"No," said Velma, "your wife's been dead a long, long time. Come on, Ben, wake up and get a move on." She tried to lift him off the stool, but he fought her off.

"Take your goddamned hands off me! I wanna talk to my wife!" He swung wildly at Velma's head; he missed and fell to the floor, banging his forehead on the brass foot-rail. He yelled, "Shit house mouse! I hit my head!"

Velma shouted, "Buck! Get out here! Ben fell and hit his head!"

Buck came out of the back room. "Holy Moses, Ben! What the hell are you doin'?" He grabbed a rag from the bar, knelt down, and wiped the blood from his forehead. "Help me get him up, Velma, and let's drag him to the davenport in the back room."

Velma yelled at Ben, "You'll be okay, buddy! We're gonna keep you here to sleep it off. You ain't in no shape to drive home. I'm gonna call your boys."

Ben mumbled something about his wife. "It was the biggest goddamned fish anyone ever seen and you speared it, Hazel. Don't let anyone tell you different. The biggest fish and you got it. Goddamn right, you did, Hazel!" Buck had heard about the fish many times before and paid no mind to Ben's mumbling, as he dragged him across the barroom floor. Velma was digging out the phone book and she heard Ben mumbling, "I don't give a rat's ass what you say! It was the biggest fish! To hell with all of yous!"

Velma yelled after him, "Shut up about the damned fish! I'm gonna tell your boys you ain't coming home till the morning."

Neal and Bobby Smierud didn't hear the phone ringing. They were out in the shed with a lantern, looking for a paintbrush. Bobby was the younger at 15. Neal was two years older. He had been held back a couple of years. They were both going into eighth grade. Neal was taller and more muscular, ruddy-faced, shaggy hair, unkempt. Bobby was quieter, smaller body, and seemed controlled by his older brother. If you saw them together, you would notice one obvious difference. Bobby would give you a blank stare, but Neal would flash you a sly grin, like he knew something about you, that you might not even know yourself.

Neal found a one-inch paintbrush, and Bobby grabbed a quart of white paint off the top shelf. He pried the lid off the paint can with a screwdriver. He took a stick and lifted a skin of dried paint off the surface and threw it out the door. He tapped the lid back on the paint can and asked, "Can we bring the lantern?"

Neal said, "Hell no! We gotta work in the dark." He stepped outside and called to his brother, "It looks like the mosquitoes are gone. Let's go!" He stuck the paintbrush and screwdriver in his back pocket; Bobby grabbed the can of paint and they started down the road, heading for Dahl School. A big moon hung over the trees to the east, leaving long shadows trailing behind them on the township road. In low voices, they made their plans. They marched in lockstep, making sharp thuds in the gravel with each footstep, like the steady beat of a military drum.

First, Bobby smeared mud up and down the sliding board, and Neal used the screwdriver to pry loose the 'S' hooks at the top of the swing chains. They took the swings down, all three of them. They carried them over to the boys' toilet and threw them down the toilet hole. Next, they dumped a bag of lime all over the floor, the bench, and in the urinal trough. Neal swung on the door and ripped it off the top hinge. Then they went to the girls' toilet. They found another bag of lime and did the same thing. Neal whipped it out and took a leak all over the benches. Bobby tried, but didn't have to go. Neal waited and listened. "You're like a little girl. Can't you even make a dribble? What's the matter with you?"

They waited for a car to go by, and then they went to the south windows. Bobby opened the paint can, and Neal dipped in the brush. There were four windows. Neal painted one big word on each window. **THE TEACHER EATS SHIT!**

Neal turned to Bobby, "What the hell are you standing around for? Get it done, you little sissy!"

Bobby said, "I don't think I should."

Neal smacked him in the face. "You goddamn right you're gonna do it. Get going!" And he smacked him again even harder.

Bobby went around to the front door. He checked for cars, but the road was quiet. He lowered his pants and shorts and squatted down on the porch. He took a big dump in front of the door. Neal went to the woodshed and came back with a shingle to use as a trowel. He smeared the feces on the door knob, the panels of the door and porch railing. Neal laughed and they ran for home.

Neal found a pint of Jim Beam under the old man's bed. He brought the bottle upstairs to their room. They sat on the floor, drank whiskey, smoked a cigarette, and looked at pictures of naked women in a girlie magazine. Neal grabbed Bobby by his leg. "Are you gonna be my girlfriend tonight?"

Bobby pulled away. "Cut it out! I'm gonna tell Pa."

Neal laughed. He took the magazine and stretched out on his bed. "Okay, I guess I'll have to take care of business on my own. Goodnight, sweetie pie."

Chapter III...The Hermit

Ernie woke up rested. He smelled bacon frying in the kitchen, and Carla was waiting for him at the stove. "I hope you're hungry."

"It smells good," he said, taking the towel she handed him.

"You can wash up over here." She indicated the washstand. "Did you sleep okay?"

"Sure did. I like the bed, and it cooled off real nice." He washed his hands and face.

Carla brought a pan of scrambled eggs and bacon over to the table. "Are you going up to the school today?"

"Yes, I planned to."

"Reason I asked, Dale was up early and asked if he could go along with you. Tom said he'd leave it up to you."

"Sure. I'll put him to work. Then I'll hit him a few ground balls so he can try out his new glove. Is there a bat at the school?"

"Should be one in the cloakroom. Dale is with Tom right now doing the milking. He'll be happy to hear he can go along."

"He sure is a good kid, the way he helps out around here."

She poured Ernie a cup of coffee. "Yeah, his dad works him pretty hard." She went to the window and looked out. "It's been hard for him the last two years, since his brother died."

"Oh, gosh!"

"Yeah, he had polio. Kent was a year younger than Dale. They were a real pair. Dale was taller—we called them Mutt and Jeff." She sat down at the table across from Ernie. "This will be so good for Dale having you live here." She looked into Ernie's eyes. "I probably shouldn't say this, but sometimes Tom forgets that Dale is still a boy. He expects him to do the work of a hired man."

"Well," said Ernie, "that might not be all bad. He's teaching him how to be a good worker."

"I suppose, but sometimes it's really tough on the kid. Tom can be very impatient." She pulled her long pigtail around front and stroked the braided hairs. "I think you, being a teacher, will understand Dale a little better. I guess I'm saying—he needs a lot of encouragement."

"Well, that's part of my job."

Tom and Dale came in carrying the milk cans. Dale was happy to hear that he could go to school with his new teacher.

41

Work had slowed down around the Henning farm. They were between haying and harvest. Dale and Carla had helped Tom put up the haystacks, and in a few days he would get out the International Harvester binder, grease 'er up, repair the canvases, and make everything shipshape to start cutting grain.

Like haying, harvest was a family deal. Tom drove the John Deere and Carla rode the binder, tripping the bundle carrier to make straight windrows of tied bundles. Dale knew he'd be helping with shocking, setting three pairs of bundles up right, leaning their tops together in a shock of six bundles. But today, he'd be free to go to the school with his teacher. He was excited.

Ernie had two boxes of books and magazines he wanted to bring to the school. Carla offered to drive them up to the school.

Orvid Skime was pulling a wagonload of logs with his Minneapolis Moline tractor on the gravel road south of Dahl School. He was bringing the load to the schoolyard, where the logs would be cut into chunks and used for firewood. Older boys would help with sawing wood the first week of school. As he approached the schoolhouse, some writing on the south windows caught his eye. Soon he could make it out. **THE TEACHER EATS SHIT!**

Orvid spit out his tobacco juice and yelled over the roar of the tractor, "Son of a bitch!" When he pulled into the schoolyard, he noticed the three swings were missing. "Son of a bitch!" He turned off the tractor and stomped up to the porch. He was going to get on the phone and call Peter Mosby, the town cop.

He put his key in the door, turned the knob, and smelled something on his hand. It was covered with feces. "Goddamned Smieruds! They took a big dump on the front porch!" He heard a pickup coming. It was Carla bringing Ernie and Dale to the school.

As Carla drove into the schoolyard, Dale noticed the swings were gone. "What happened to the swings, Ma?"

Carla stopped the pickup by Orvid's tractor, and the three got out. Ernie started to lift one of his cardboard boxes out of the back of the pickup, when Orvid came yelling, "Goddamned Smierud boys have done it again! Leave that box in the truck there and come see what they did!" Orvid grabbed a grease rag from his tractor and led them to the porch. He pointed, "Look what those drittsekkers did this time!"

42

Carla asked, "What's that awful smell?"

Orvid yelled, "They smeared crap all over the place!"

Dale ran for the boys' toilet. He felt like throwing up. Orvid wiped the doorknob with the rag, opened it, and he, Carla, and Ernie went inside. Orvid smelled his hand and said, "This was supposed to be nice, Mr. Juvland. We're proud of our old schoolhouse. Now we got this!"

Ernie noticed the letters painted on the south windows. It took him a few seconds before he could read the ugly message. He went to the windows and examined the paint up close. He was stunned. "Do you have a razor blade? I want to scrape this writing off the windows immediately, before more people see this."

Orvid shouted, "No, you won't! We're gonna get those two hundejokkers up here right now. They're gonna clean this up!" He went for the phone and rang up the operator. "I'm calling the cop."

"Wait," Ernie interrupted, "how do you know it was the Smierud boys?"

Orvid looked at Ernie like he was the dumbest man he had ever met. "Look, Mr. Juvland, there is no one else in the whole country that would do something like this!"

Carla had to agree. "Yeah, Orvid, it looks like their monkey business. That's for sure. They dream up mean stuff like this."

Orvid was on the phone. "Pete, this is Orvid. Get your ass out to the school right now! The Smierud boys are at it again!" He listened and then he yelled, "I don't give a damn what you're busy with! Just get the hell out here and see the mess they've made. They even took a big, smelly dump on the front porch!"

Carla took Ernie by the elbow. "Let's go outside. I don't think you should be in here, the way things are. A bunch of us were up here last week cleaning everything, washing windows and scrubbing floors. We really wanted it nice when you stepped inside." Ernie was quiet. Images of the Smierud boys on their rampage were running through his mind. Dale was sitting in the pickup with his head down. Before Carla opened the door, she turned to Ernie, "I want to get you out of here. I don't like to see you depressed like this. My goodness, school hasn't even started, and already these hellions are up to no good."

Ernie looked over at the slide and saw the mud smeared on it. "Yeah, this bothers me, and I should help out here. I really want to scrape that writing off the windows. That's personal. They wrote that about me and I don't like it!"

Carla stopped him. "No. Orvid will want the cop to see that. And mark my word, Orvid will make those boys get over here and clean up the mess they made."

"Okay, I see his point, but it really makes me angry. Why did they do that? Man alive! I need to get a hold of myself here."

Carla reached for Ernie's hand. "Look, why don't we go to town? I have to go to the creamery with the cream and drop off the eggs. That will give me money for some school supplies for Dale and he could use a new pair of overalls. That shouldn't take me too long. Then we'll take you over to the Town Café and buy you coffee and a nice piece of Judy's apple pie. It's the best in town."

"No," said Ernie, "I think I'll go home. I need to get my head straight about this. I have to get my mind off that writing."

"Okay, suit yourself," said Carla. "We'll take you home."

"No, I think I'll walk. It's a nice morning and the walk might do me good. I need to forget what I've just seen. What's going on here? Holy Moses! Those boys don't even know me!"

"I'm so sorry. Please try not to let it get to you." Carla climbed in the pickup, "Dale. Are you all right?"

He quietly said, "I found the swings."

"Really?"

"They threw them down the toilet hole. They broke the door, too."

She put her arm around her son, "Don't worry—they'll make Bobby and Neal crawl in there and drag them out!" She turned to Ernie, "I feel so bad for you. This should have been a happy day for all of us."

Ernie nodded and watched them turn around and drive away. *Why did they write that about me? What kind of kid would do that? I want to kill them! Strangle them with my bare hands!*

Anders Lund was coming home from town with a supply of groceries and a long 4X12 inch wood beam. He drove a 1937 deuce and a half flatbed truck and sat up straight and dignified with both hands on the steering wheel, looking more like a French chauffeur driving a limousine than an ordinary man driving a truck. His reading glasses hung from a shoelace around his neck

44

and settled on his barrel chest. He was too tall to drive wearing his straw hat, which lay on the seat beside him. His gray hair, neatly combed, slicked-back with Pomade, nearly touched the top of the cab. His goateed chin was pulled in, tucked tightly against his neck, and his deep blue eyes darted around, as if he wanted to see everything, the gauges on the dashboard, the side mirrors, the ditches, the fences, and the willow thickets. He was a man of eager curiosity, alert and always looking for something he had never seen before.

He made the turn by Dahl School and noticed Peter Mosby's black Chevy parked in the schoolyard. He stroked his goatee and wondered why the town cop was at the school. On the road up ahead he saw a tall man standing by the side of the road near a slough watching a beaver working near his dam. Anders pulled alongside Ernie and stopped. "Can I give you a lift?"

Ernie started walking and said, "No thank you, sir. I'm enjoying the walk."

"Okay," said Anders. "It's a lovely morning, isn't it?" He started to move on, but he heard Ernie yelling, "Wait up!" Anders hit the brakes and waited for Ernie to appear at his window.

Ernie caught his breath, "I was just wondering. Are you Anders, the Henning's neighbor?"

"You have guessed correctly, young man. Anders Lund is the name." Ernie noticed he spoke with a slight British accent, or maybe it was just good diction. They shook hands.

"I'm Ernie Juvland, the new teacher. I'm boarding at the Hennings."

"I figured as much. I heard they hired a male teacher." He took his straw hat off the seat and hung it on the brake lever. "Well, Mr. Juvland, would you like a ride?"

Ernie said, "Sure." He climbed in and closed the door.

They were silent for a while, and then Anders said, "I'm curious. How do you like our pleasant little township?"

"Fine," said Ernie. He paused and realized what he had said. But he decided not to mention the scene he had just witnessed at Dahl School. "People have treated me fair and square." He looked over at Anders and saw him smile. "The Hennings are a really nice family. I'm glad I landed there."

Anders said, "Very good." And then it was silent until they reached his mailbox with big letters spelling, **HIMMELEN**.

45

Anders climbed out to get his mail. Ernie noticed how big this old man was, how straight he carried himself, and the confidence he exuded in all his motions, as he went around the front of the truck, opened the mailbox, took out his newspaper, and returned to the driver's seat. "I was thinking," he said, "are you busy right now?"

"No, not really."

"It shouldn't take too long, but I could use some grunt labor from a strong man."

"I'd be glad to help."

"Very good," said Anders, as he eased the truck around the corner and started down his lane. "I'm working on an addition to my shack. I've finished putting in the studs and I'm about to raise the ridgepole. Do you know what a ridgepole is?"

"Sure. It's the top beam on the roof."

"Correct. I have the beam in the back of the truck and could use a little help putting it in place. The bolt holes were pre-drilled for me at Nystrom's Sawmill, and I'm just hoping I measured correctly. It might take some jockeying about to fit it in place."

"Sure," said Ernie.

When they came to the bottom of the gully where the creek ran through, Anders slowed down to a crawl. "Here's my little corner of paradise, young man. A place where I am free from the cares of the world. Welcome to Himmelen!"

"Himmelen," said Ernie. "I don't know that word."

"It's Norwegian for 'Heaven'," said Anders, as he got out of the truck, grabbed a box of groceries from the back, and went up the stairs to his house.

Ernie had never seen anything quite like Himmelen. It was all made from weathered lumber, with a sloping, lean-to roof. It rose over the creek, among the branches of poplar and birch trees, perched on a dozen telephone poles ten feet off the ground. It was a 30X40 foot single-room house. Attached to the west end was an addition under construction. The wall studs were in place, but there was no roof.

Anders put his groceries away and returned to the truck. He and Ernie dragged the ridgepole off the flatbed and carried it over to the new addition. To get it to the top, Anders used the winch on the front of the truck. When it reached the top, he locked up the winch and climbed the ladder. "Swing it around," he told Ernie, "and grab the far end." Anders grabbed the other end. They carefully guided the beam between a pair of open studs and placed the heavy timber on the floor.

They used the winch again to raise the ridgepole to the top, where Anders bolted it into place. The holes lined up, which greatly pleased Anders. The whole operation took about two hours and Ernie's shirt was wet with sweat. Anders looked up at the beam, firmly in place. He slapped Ernie on the back and said, "Thank you, young man. I never could have done it by myself."

"Glad to help you out, sir. Anytime."

"Are you thirsty?"

"I might be. I worked up a pretty good sweat."

"Let's go in and have ourselves a drink." Anders led the way. They went to the edge of the new addition and Anders opened a window of the house. "I'm going to knock out the bottom of this window for a door. For now we'll have to climb through."

Ernie followed Anders through the window and the first thing he noticed were books, hundreds of them, stacked on shelves and sitting in piles along the walls, and scattered on a large, oak library table. "Pardon the mess," Anders said.

Ernie said, "My gosh! Have you read all these books?"

"Yes, most of them. Some I've read twice and there are a few with a bookmark somewhere around page 17." He led Ernie through the back door which opened onto a screened-in porch. "Let me show you my poor man's dumbwaiter." Ernie watched him open one of the window screens and grab a rope. "Take a look," Anders said, and Ernie looked down. The rope was attached to a galvanized bucket sitting in the stream below. Anders pulled on the rope and brought up the bucket, removed a bottle of wine, then lowered the bucket back down into the creek.

Anders went to a cupboard drawer and returned with a corkscrew. Ernie looked down at the lazy creek and followed its course until it disappeared around a bend. "I can see now why you built your house on stilts. How high does the water rise here?"

Anders poured out two jelly glasses of wine. "Last September, it came up close to the floor we're standing on. I couldn't get out. Most of the outside stairway was under water. Fortunately, I had parked my truck up on the road. But the stream is gentle here, almost flat. Swift rapids might have carried my shack away with me in it." He handed Ernie a glass of wine and said, "Here's to the success of our new teacher."

"Thank you, sir." Ernie sipped the wine. "That tastes good. I don't know a thing about wine. What kind is it?"

"I make it from dandelions." Anders took a seat in a huge overstuffed chair. "Sit down, friend. Try the swing. I find it very comfortable." Anders had made the swing from a large piece of binder canvas and suspended it from the ceiling with a one-inch rope. Ernie liked the way it felt—he was enveloped. He spun around and kicked himself back and forth. "Enjoy yourself," said Anders. "That's what it's there for."

Ernie took another sip of wine. "This is really nice sitting here. I'm glad you're my neighbor."

"Well, we're happy to have you in our pleasant little community to enlighten our youngsters."

"I've never taught before, so it won't be easy."

"I'm sure you'll do a fine job."

Ernie wondered if he should tell Anders about the latest Smierud escapade. But he decided to hold off. "The Hennings told me the last teacher had trouble handling the older boys."

"Ah, yes, dear, precious Martha Sampson. She used to visit me, often showing up in tears. I tried my best to comfort her, you know, tried to get her to look on the positive side of things. She was young, 19 when she started and petite. I understand she was just fine with the younger students. It was a few older boys, who knew how to rattle her. I wouldn't worry about it, young man; I'm sure you'll get off on the right foot and be an excellent teacher."

Ernie accepted a refill on his wine and settled back into the swing. Anders wanted to know about Ernie's home life and how he ended up being a teacher. Anders was an exceptional listener. Ernie had always felt his life was rather unremarkable, but Anders's interest made him feel better about being just a farm boy.

Anders talked about his own teaching experience and how he was happy now to live alone in a house he had built, away from petty college administrators. He said, "St. Hallvard College gave me the boot. After twenty years, I think they felt I had become a threat to their insular, controlled institution of well-behaved Lutheran scholars and their equally obedient staff." He sipped his wine. "I suppose I could have stayed, you know, slavishly professing their scripted dogma, but that became unbearable. I'm a freethinker, and I encouraged my students to question most everything, except perhaps, gravity.

"The First World War had changed me. As an old infantry rifleman, I was in some bloody trench warfare and came home shell-shocked and angry. I became vehemently anti-war and engaged my students in lively discussions on the stupidity of armed conflict. When the present war began and American boys started dying by the thousands, they saw me as an unpatriotic pariah, teaching their students a bunch of rubbish. But I felt compelled to teach pacifism, until they showed me the door and told me to preach my Gospel of Gandhi elsewhere.

"I told my students to take a hard look at what we had achieved as a so-called civilized social species." He laughed, "Ha! We've done very little to tame our baboon instincts. In fact, we've perfected the tooth and claw. Bully for us! We've used our big brains to invent more powerful, more effective tools to kill each other. Voltaire said it best. I quoted this piece so many times to my students I believe I still remember it." He thoughtfully recited.

Men must have somewhat altered the course of nature; for they were not born wolves, yet they have become wolves. God did not give them twenty-four-pounders or bayonets, yet they have made themselves bayonets and guns to destroy each other.

Ernie was puzzled, "Who wrote that? You mentioned a name."

Anders nodded and said, "Voltaire. It's in *Candide.* Lot of good stuff in there."

Ernie shook his head, "There's so much I need to read."

"You will I'm sure. You're young and that's the joy of living—to discover something new every day of your life."

"So, did they fire you because you were against war?"

"Well, there was more. I also turned against organized religion, and when you're a professor of humanities in a Lutheran college like St. Hallvard, that is damnable. It does not mean that I reject the notion of a God. One cannot deny there is some kind of order in the Universe and I'm interested in that, but it's what civilizations have done to pervert the profound beauty of that mystery, using it to spread fear and gain power. When we take a cold, hard look at the history of civilizations, we discover that organized religions have left us a legacy of social divisiveness—pulling humans apart, rather than bringing them together in harmony. And that, my friend, I find appalling!

"But don't get me wrong! I have a deep respect for anyone with faith in a personal God. That is a private matter, and who am I to take issue with that? Whatever works for you is not my business. Life can be fearfully dangerous, and we all need comfort at times."

He filled his glass again and offered Ernie a refill, which he turned down. "As for my philosophy, I've chosen to live alone. I dwell among the trees with the birds and squirrels. I'm 60 years old, and it's taken me many years to realize that the most important thing in life is to live for right now, to develop a profound appreciation for the present moment. I try to avoid the two Rs, rehash and rehearse. I cannot change the past, and no one knows what the future has to offer. I have my books, my old Royal typewriter, plenty of writing paper, I have my garden, and I hunt ducks, pheasants, geese, grouse, and deer. I go about all of these tasks knowing deeply, that what I am doing at this very moment is really what counts, like talking to you, right here, right now. And I make a pretty damned good dandelion wine, if I say so myself."

Ernie had to agree. He got up, handed Anders his glass, and said, "I don't think I've ever met anyone quite like you. I could listen to you all day, but I really should be going. The Hennings will wonder if I fell off the edge of the Earth."

"Okay. Suit yourself. I enjoyed our visit and thanks for helping me with that beam. Like I said, I couldn't have done it on my own. Watch the ice on the steps going down."

Ernie looked at the steps, "Did you say ice?"

"Only joking, Ernie. I once knew a bartender who always said that, even on the hottest day of the year. He was a character!"

Ernie smiled, "Okay, thank you for the wine and the visit."

"My pleasure, young man."

Ernie felt good as he walked up Anders's dirt road, heading to the Henning's farm. It was partly the wine, but it was mostly this remarkable man he had just met. *His easy manner and intelligence. How content he is. He's chosen a simple life, surrounded by the wonders of nature. Good for him.*

50

Carla and Dale were sitting on the front steps when Ernie came into the yard. Dale was carefully putting notebook paper in his new two-ring notebook. Carla waved and shouted, "We were worried about you!"

"I was over at Anders's place. He needed some help raising the roof beam on his addition."

"I'm curious. What do you think of our hermit neighbor?"

Ernie wondered how to answer her. "Well, let's put it this way—he gave me a lot of things to think about. War, religion, nature, you name it. He's quite a guy."

"He's different, that's for sure. We all wonder what he does all day down there by himself. It must be lonely."

"I don't think so. He seems very content."

"I suppose," she said and put her arm around Dale. "You should take one of your new crayons and print your name on the front of your notebook."

He got up. "Good idea, Ma." He scurried into the kitchen.

Ernie sat down on the steps beside Carla. "You know—that writing on the windows really upset me. How did things pan out?"

Carla took in a deep breath. "Yeah that." She took a moment to collect her thoughts. "I'm so sorry that had to happen. We stopped by on our way back from the town. Orvid was there unloading logs. He and Peter Mosby had gone over to the Smierud house and dragged the boys out of bed. The old man wasn't home. The boys said he was in town."

"Were they the ones?"

"Yeah, they had white paint on their overalls, and Peter found the paintbrush on their back porch."

"So what are they going to do with the boys?"

"I guess Peter told them if they got into any more trouble, they might end up in reform school. Anyway, Orvid has them over there right now, scraping the writing off the windows." She placed her hand on Ernie's knee and looked into his eyes. "I'm so sorry those rascals gummed up the works. We want you to be happy here. You're important to us. Our children need a man they can look up to. Many of them have older brothers and dads who are off in the war. And it's frightening to them, the black-out drills, sitting in the dark or putting blankets on the windows, the sounds of bombs on the radio broadcasts, the newsreels at the movies. All

51

this killing. The children need to feel safe. They need a strong man to assure them that everything is going to be okay."

Ernie looked down at her hand on his knee. Then he patted it and gave it a little squeeze. "I'll try to do my best."

Carla got up and straightened out her dress. "We know you will." She grabbed a basket off the porch. "I have to pick corn for supper. We still have a few ears left on the row we planted late. We're gonna eat early." She looked off beyond the barn and saw Tom bringing the cows home from the pasture. "They'll be doing the milking early. It's Saturday night, and you know what that means?"

Ernie got up. "Well, if you're anything like my family, it means you're going to town."

"You betcha! Us farmers always go to town on Saturday night. It's almost like a religious thing."

Ernie chuckled and went up on the porch.

She stopped him with a shout, "Hey, I almost forgot! There's a letter for you on the kitchen table. The *Pioneer Press* is there, too."

"Thanks," he said, and went inside. Dale sat at the table with a pack of 16 crayons, drawing a picture in his notebook. Ernie sat down by him. "What are you drawing there, pal?"

"I'm not good at drawing," he said, covering up the page with his hands.

"May I see what you've drawn?"

"It's not very good," he said, lifting up his hands and revealing a picture of an airplane dropping bombs. Below were three tanks. Dale pointed to the tanks, "These are the Germans."

Ernie pulled the drawing closer for a better look. "I think you're very good at drawing."

Dale smiled and said, "Thanks."

Ernie moved the drawing back to the boy and said, "Do you ever draw pictures of cows?"

"Sometimes. They're hard to draw."

"How about barns?"

"Barns are easy."

"I think you should draw a barn and some cows," Ernie said, picking up the newspaper that was lying at the edge of the table. He saw a picture of a formation of B-17 bombers, high overhead with a dozen black puffs of flack spread out across the sky. He turned to Dale, who had taken his red crayon and was drawing a barn. "How about a tractor, son? Put your dad's John Deere in there, too."

"Okay," he said, reaching for a green crayon. "This is my first box of 16 crayons. Ma always said all I needed were eight. But now that I'm in third grade, she said I could have 16. See, there are two green ones. I'll use the dark green for Pa's tractor."

"Good idea," said Ernie, laying down the paper and picking up the letter. It was from his brother Andy. He noticed the return address, *Camp Joseph T Robinson, North Little Rock, Missouri.* He opened the envelope and read it to himself.

Dear Ernie,

How are you? I got a letter from Ma with your new address. She said you'll be living with a nice family. Have you started teaching yet? Don't let the big boys pull any tricks on you. Ha Ha! It's hot down here in hillbilly country. They talk funny, and they call us guys from Minnesota and South Dakota, 'Yankees'. I thought they were talking about the New York Yankees. There's a St. Louis guy in the bunk next to me. He's a Polack we call Ski. He's been to many Cardinal games at Sportsman's Park. He even got an autograph from Stan Musial. We get the Cardinal games on the radio in the barracks. It looks like they could be going to the World Series again.

Training is a lot tougher than you said it was. We do a lot of marching and our sergeant makes sure all our clothes are folded just right and we have to make up our bunks just right. We laugh about that, but we have to do it or we get in trouble. I guess they're teaching us to follow orders.

Yesterday we had our first day on the rifle range and I did real good. One of the older sergeants, he walks with a limp he got from a bullet in Africa. He said, "You

53

have a good eye, soldier. Keep it up." Maybe I shouldn't be too good, because they'll put me in the infantry. We get some news from the war. They will most likely ship us out to France when we finish training. So many are getting killed over there, they need replacements and I guess that's what we'll be. I'll be through with basic sometime before Christmas and then they'll give us a 10 day furlough. Sure will be good to get home and have some of Ma's cooking. You remember what Army food is like, right? Okay, it's almost ten o'clock and that means lights out. All for now. Write soon and tell me all about teaching school.

Your brother,

Andy

After supper everybody cleaned up and dressed for going to town. Tom and Carla climbed into the front of the pickup, and Ernie and Dale sat on a couple of orange crates in the back. As they passed Dahl School, Tom slowed down. Ernie could see Orvid standing in front of the school watching Neal and Bobby Smierud. They were on their hands and knees scrubbing the porch floor. Dale poked Ernie and said, "There they are, the Smieruds." Ernie got a good look at them and felt a tightness in his stomach. Tom didn't stop, but Orvid turned and waved. He had a big grin on his face. The Smierud boys went back to their work.

Tom parked the pickup in front of Oseberg's Grocery Store. Carla went inside to do the grocery shopping, Tom walked across the street to Buck's Tavern, and Ernie and Dale walked down to the Prairie Theater to see a movie. Ernie bought two bags of popcorn from the high school kid, who had moved the big popcorn machine out on the sidewalk in front of Tubby's Pool Hall. Dale looked up at the marquee over the theater. It announced, **ROY ROGERS in CARSON CITY KID!** They went inside and Dale wanted to sit down front.

Before the picture show started, the man from the post office came forward to sell U. S. War Bonds. Dale asked Ernie if he was going to buy one. Ernie checked his billfold and said, "I don't have the money on me. But if I did, I would buy one." The postmaster ended up selling two bonds, the lights dimmed, and they heard the theme music for *The March of Times*. Ernie saw the Third Infantry Division landing on the southern coast of France, August 15. The announcer called it, 'Operation Dragoon'. German resistance was low except for Camel Red Beach at the town of Sain't-Raphael. There were pictures of B-24 bombers making strikes on enemy machine gun bunkers. Dale covered his eyes with his hands as one American LLT landing craft was hit and started to sink. He grabbed Ernie's arm and said, "What happened to the soldiers? Did they drown?"

Ernie leaned over to the boy and whispered, "I'm sure many of them did." The graphic combat images flashing on the screen made Ernie think about his brothers fighting in the war.

The music changed and the sports news came on. The announcer spoke in an excited voice, "The Cooper Brothers of the St. Louis Cardinals teamed up as battery mates again trouncing the Chicago Cubs 11 to 1." Ernie poked Dale and whispered, "That's my team, the Cardinals."

Dale said, "My dad hates the Cardinals. They beat his Yankees in the World Series. When was it?"

"Two years ago, 1942." They watched Walker Cooper hit a home run, and the announcer said, "The Cardinal catcher blasted his ninth home run of the season and went four for four, raising his batting average to .331. And brother Mort Cooper on the hill shut down the Cubs for his 18th win of the season. The Cardinals are now in first place with a 17 game lead at 87 wins and only 29 losses. It looks like Billy Southworth's Cardinals are heading for another World Series." For a moment Ernie forgot about the war.

The feature started, *Carson City Kid*. Ernie had seen it before, but he didn't give away the surprise, when it turns out that Roy Rogers was, in fact, the Carson City Kid. Dale liked the horseback chases and the shooting, but he didn't like the mushy scenes with Roy Rogers and the dancehall singer, Dale Evans. They both laughed, when they were standing behind a rail fence saying goodbye, and Trigger, Roy's horse, stuck his head between the two of them. Dale said, "I'm just glad they didn't kiss."

Outside the movie theater, there were several farmers standing around on the sidewalks and sitting on doorsteps talking about the weather, the crops, and the war. Ernie and Dale made their way up to Oseberg's Grocery Store. Ernie noticed a poster on the window. Uncle Sam, in his star-studded top hat, pointed at Ernie. **I WANT YOU FOR U.S. ARMY!**

They found Carla sitting on a long bench visiting with three other farm women. They were talking about canning, their 'victory gardens' and complained about how hard it was to get the kids to help out with pulling carrots and radishes. They talked about how big the cabbage heads were that summer and how the price had gone up on Mason jars and lids. They talked about a woman who had her ninth baby. Carla said, "Yeah, I heard she was p-g again, but I didn't know she had it. Poor woman."

Carla introduced Ernie to her friends, and they were all pleased to meet the handsome new teacher. Carla pulled on Dale's shirtsleeve and said, "Dale, go over to the tavern and get your dad. I think it's time we head for home."

Dale frowned, "Can Mr. Juvland come with me?"

"No," she said, "you're a big boy now. You go ahead."

"Aw, Ma! I know they're gonna tease me in there. One guy always calls me 'Snot Nose'." Dale turned to Ernie, "Don't you want to come with me?"

Ernie tried to explain, "No, son, I really shouldn't go in the tavern. I'm the teacher here now, and it wouldn't look right."

Carla added, "He's right, Dale. You know how people talk. Hurry along now and get your pa." Dale shook his head and slowly started across the street.

Ernie put three boxes of groceries in the back, and Carla opened the door. "We'll all sit in front. Maybe you could hold Dale on your lap."

Ernie nodded and followed her into the cab of the pickup. Ernie was aware of her leg touching his, as he listened to her voice which had dropped down almost to a whisper. "Tom enjoys playing cards with his buddies in there. If they're in the middle of a hand, it could be a long wait."

Ernie looked out the side window and watched a boy on the sidewalk across the street. He had turned his bike upside-down and was spinning the front wheel. Carla said, "Dale wants a bike, but we told him he'd have to wait another year at least. He wants it to ride to school, which is fine when the roads are good, but when it rains, the ruts are pretty bad. And in the winter, you can't ride at all."

Ernie spoke up. "Here they come." Tom held Dale's hand as they crossed the street. Ernie noticed a slight wobble in Tom's stride. Sure enough, when he climbed behind the wheel, Ernie knew he had a lot to drink. He fiddled with the key and jerked the gearshift back and forth, trying to find reverse. He barked at Carla, "Move your damned leg!" To make room, Carla pressed her leg even tighter against Ernie. Dale climbed in and settled on his teacher's lap.

Carla put her arm around Tom's shoulders and whispered, "Are you all right to drive?"

He snapped at her. "What the hell do you mean?" Then there was silence as they drove out of town and headed home on the county road. Tom drove slowly, weaving from side to side and Ernie began to wonder if he should say something, maybe offer to drive.

Tom blurted out, "Open these damned windows! I need some air in here!" Ernie rolled down his window and the breeze and dust met him in the face. As they drove the last mile on gravel road, Ernie was worried about the ditches, and with each swerve, the pickup came closer and closer to the edge. Then Tom slowed the truck to a crawl. He pulled far to the right and hit the brakes. Ernie looked out the window. Another foot and they would have rolled into the ditch. Tom was fumbling with the door handle. It opened and he stumbled out. Soon they heard the guttural growls of Tom throwing up by the back tire. Carla sighed. Tom crawled back in wiping his mouth on his sleeve. "I have to fix that leak in the exhaust pipe. Can you smell the fumes? It makes me sick."

They drove home in silence. Tom pulled up close to the front porch and turned off the engine. As he opened the door, he said, "Ernie can help with the groceries. I'm going to bed. I guess I ain't as young as I used to be." They watched him struggle up the steps of the porch and stagger inside.

After the groceries were put away, Carla asked Ernie if he wanted a bite to eat, maybe a piece of rhubarb pie. He was tired, but he accepted the offer. He sat down at the table and looked at Dale's notebook, which was still lying open to the picture he was drawing. There was the red barn, one cow with stick legs, a bowling ball head with pointed ears, and his dad's green John Deere tractor. And high in the blue sky was a black airplane with a carefully drawn Nazi swastika on its side. It was dropping a bomb on the barn. The crayon drawing fixed on Ernie's mind.

Carla wanted to talk about Tom. She sat close to Ernie and spoke in whispers. She wanted Ernie to know what a hardworking man he was and how tough it was for him to lose Kent to polio. He worshiped the little boy, and it often hurt Dale to be compared with his kid brother. Kent had a lot of gumption. He was quick to learn and liked doing chores with his father. Dale was different. He was shy, and Tom often yelled at him for being 'soft' and acting like a 'mamma's boy'.

Ernie was becoming aware of Carla's melancholy, her frustrations, and her deep need to talk to someone who would listen. Ernie was thinking how quickly he had become involved with this family. Carla rambled on about giving up on being a nurse and how disappointed her mother and father were when she told them she wanted to marry Tom. She met him at a barn dance. He was 15 years older, but he owned a farm, free and clear. He promised to put her through nursing school. That sounded good to Carla, a hardworking girl, who had helped her dad on his farm for 12 years after high school. Soon after they got hitched, Tom got her pregnant. That was the end of her dream of becoming a nurse.

Ernie thought he shouldn't be hearing this. Was he encouraging this woman to pour out her heart, by patiently listening to her express all these pent up feelings? He finished his pie and said, "I'm very sorry. I don't know what to tell you."

"I'm boring you, right?" She took his plate and fork, got up, and carried them to the dishpan on the counter.

"No," said Ernie, "it's not that. I just think these are matters you should discuss with your husband. In fact it makes me feel a little uncomfortable listening to you tell me these problems, which are really family matters. They're personal."

"You're right. I guess I feel that you're our family now, and I can tell you anything, really."

"That makes me uneasy. Try to understand, I'm your son's teacher and I'm renting a room from you and Tom. Maybe that's where we should leave it."

She turned around, leaned against the side of the counter, and looked at him. "I'll bet you're tired. I'm sorry. I guess sometimes I just need to talk." She walked over to close the outside door. She came back to the table and slid Dale's notebook

58

closer for a careful look. "Oh, did you see this? Dale drew a picture of our farm. Did you ask him to do that?"

"Yeah, I made the suggestion."

"Oh, my," she said. "Why did he have to put that plane and bomb in there?"

"Well, like you said before, it's on his mind. It's frightening to these children. In fact it scares me, too."

"I know. I hope it ends soon."

"Don't we all," Ernie said, heading for the stairs. "Well, it's been quite a day, and now I'm ready for a good night's sleep."

"I don't blame you, Ernie. I opened the windows up there. It should have cooled down by now."

"Thanks," he said. "Thanks for everything. Thanks for being so kind. And don't worry about all that other stuff. You'll figure it out."

"I hope so. Goodnight, Ernie."

"Goodnight," he said, as he climbed the stairs. The bedroom was cooler. A gentle breeze was coming through the west window. He lit the lamp on the table next to the bed thinking he might read something to make him fall asleep. He stripped down to his shorts and pulled the blanket and top sheet back. He saw two cardboard boxes in the corner. Martha Sampson's name was written on the side of each. The book on top was the standard schoolbook, *The McGuffey Reader, Grade Four*. He took it to the bed and lay down without covering himself.

Ernie was familiar with the McGuffey series from his classes at the teacher training center. He opened it to a story titled "Knowledge is Power". It was about a young lad, talking to an old man about how excited he was to be learning all sorts of things through his reading. The old man cautions the boy. "When the power of a horse is under restraint, the animal is useful in bearing burdens, drawing loads, and carrying his master; but when that power is unrestrained, the horse breaks his bridle, dashes to pieces the carriage that he draws, or throws his rider."

"I see!" said the little man, "I see!" Ernie laid the book on the table. *Good advice. I must always stay in control.*

The events of the day played over in his mind until he finally fell asleep. A single mosquito sneaked into the room through a small rip in the screen. Skirting the glow of the kerosene lamp, it flew to Ernie's ear and went inside. The sleeping man did not hear the mosquito; he heard something else. He heard the roaring engines of a squadron of German bombers high in the sky over a red barn. The planes hung in the air, dropping bombs. Ernie saw the planes and raced toward the barn. A bomb exploded close by and catapulted him into the air. He landed in thick mud near the barn door. The scene was shrouded in smoke, and the roof of the barn was on fire. Ernie heard Dale crying, "I can't move! I don't want to die!"

The boy's screams were coming from inside the barn and Ernie called back, "Hold on Dale! I'm coming to get you out!" But he could not move. He could not pull his feet out of the mud.

He heard a woman's voice coming from somewhere. Was it Carla? The voice calling, "Ernie, Ernie! Dale is okay. He's here. He's fine. Wake up and you'll see him standing by the stairs."

"No, no! I have to save the boy. I have to save the boy!" Ernie struggled, "Dale, hide, hide! The soldiers are coming to get you! They have bayonets on their guns. They'll stab you!" Ernie had fallen off the bed. He rolled around on the floor, kicking and swinging his arms wildly.

Carla pleaded, "Wake up, please! Wake up—you're having a dream! Dale is here!" She used all her strength to control his thrashing about. She managed to hold him down with her knees.

Something was pressing into Ernie's back, as he struggled on the floor to free himself. He rolled on the braided rug and ended up on his back. He was weighted down with something warm and soft. He could not move. He smelled Jergens Lotion. Carla had sprawled full length on top of Ernie, her breasts pressing against his bare chest. She wiped the tears from his face and cupped his head gently in her hands, speaking softly, "It's okay. It's okay."

Ernie opened his eyes and looked into Carla's tender face, dimly lit by the kerosene lamp. He heard Dale's plaintive voice, "Is Mr. Juvland sick, Ma?"

Chapter IV...The Letter

The next morning Tom Henning sat at the kitchen table drinking his coffee and looking out the window, watching the autumn sun bring light to the farmyard. Near his coffee cup was a piece of brown paper he had ripped from a grocery bag and a yellow pencil. He had started to make a list of jobs, *Fix fence by cornfield.* That was all he had written. He was sidetracked by Ernie's nightmare the night before. The shouting had jarred him awake, and when he tried to roll out of bed, he stumbled and landed flat on the floor. The confusion had mixed badly with beers from his night of drinking.

Now, the coffee had a funny taste, and his stomach didn't feel right. He tried to piece it all together as the sunlight sparkled on the dewy grass and spread across the yard to the splitting block by the woodshed. The nightmare had scared Dale out of his wits. Carla sat up with him until the boy was able to fall asleep. Tom remembered his wife coming back to bed and recalled whispering to her in the darkness, "I don't like this one bit."

She was silent for a moment, and then she answered, "He has a lot on his mind, the poor guy."

"Yeah, but are we gonna have to put up with this every night?"

She was quick to reply, "He had a bad dream. That's all."

"But what about Dale?" He waited for an answer, but Carla was silent. "Just, think about it. This big guy is in the next room ranting and raving. Maybe he breaks into Dale's room. What if he hurts the boy?"

She waited a moment. "We shouldn't even be down here whispering about the poor guy. What if he hears us?"

At the kitchen table Tom remembered the last thing he said to Carla. "I think you should bring Vic and Orvid over here and question Ernie. Let's hear what he has to say. My God, woman, we don't know anything about this guy. We could have a crazy lunatic living right under our roof!"

Tom got up from the table and put his coffee cup in the dishpan. He grabbed two milk pails and a cream can and went out the door. Upstairs, Ernie heard the screen door squeak. He got off the bed and went to the window. He watched Tom walking down to the barn to do the milking. He dressed and quietly moved toward the stairs. Carla was waiting for him at the bottom. "I'll bet you're ready for a cup of coffee, and I'm gonna fix up some pancakes."

"That sounds very good," he said and made his way toward the kitchen table, where he sat down and glanced at Dale's drawing, which was still lying there, next to the newspaper. There was the red barn and the plane overhead dropping a bomb. He turned and saw Dale coming into the kitchen.

Carla was cheerful. "So, what are you doing up so early, young man? We were gonna let you sleep in." Dale looked down as he passed Ernie. He reached for his cap hanging on a nail by the door, grabbed his rubber boots, and went out on the front steps. Ernie watched him through the screen door, thinking he must have scared him badly with his nightmare. With his boots on, Dale stood up and ran down to the barn.

Carla brought Ernie a cup of coffee and sat down across from him. "How do you feel now?"

"Okay, I guess. I was finally able to get back to sleep." Ernie sipped his coffee. "I just feel bad that I caused such a commotion."

"I don't want you to worry about that. You're part of our family now, and we want to help." She glanced out the screen door and turned to meet Ernie's eyes. "Does it bother you to talk about it?"

"About the dreams?" he asked.

Carla reached across the table and placed her hand on his. They looked at each other in silence and then she spoke in a soft voice, "Tom is very upset. We talked in bed last night. He wants to bring Vic and Orvid over here. He wants you to tell them what's going on. You have to understand Tom. He wants everything under control. No surprises. He's worried it will happen again."

"I can understand that. Okay then. Do you want to hear the whole story?"

"I think that would be best and now might be a good time."

"The dreams started—I guess it was the sixth week of basic training down in Arkansas. We were stabbing dummies in a cold rain. We were running through mud and stabbing these dummies with our bayonets. I guess it really bothered me. I didn't have any trouble out on the rifle range, because I had hunted ever since I

62

was a little kid, and shooting at a target was easy as pie. But there was something about that bayonet going into that stuffed dummy that really bothered me. I guess I have a good imagination—the dummy became real to me, like a live person. In my mind I saw blood gushing from the open wounds. I thought I heard screaming. That was the strangest part, hearing the screaming and knowing it was just in my mind."

Carla brought her hands to her face.

"I started having these bad dreams and they were always about stabbing someone with a bayonet, a knife, or even a pitchfork. The last dream I had before I was sent home was really a bad one. I slept on the top bunk. They told me I stood up and was jumping around screaming my head off. I remember the dream vividly. I was stabbing a German soldier in the face with the sharp end of a tree branch I had broken off. The blood was squirting out of his eyes and splattering me in my face. At some point I fell off the top bunk and grabbed a light fixture that was hanging from the ceiling, ripping it out. They told me there were sparks shooting out of an electrical wire, and then the whole barracks went dark. The short had blown a fuse. There were 80 men in their bunks, and I guess they heard me screaming and started running for the door. The nightlights were out, and these guys were stumbling around in total darkness. They told me it was mass confusion. They had no idea what was going on. I finally woke up with a flashlight shining in my face. Two big guys had pinned me to the floor."

Carla pulled a handkerchief from her apron. She wiped her eyes and blew her nose, "You poor man."

"The next day a medic came to get me. He took me to the clinic and brought me into an office. There were three doctors, you know, headshrinkers sitting behind this table. They ordered me to sit down and then the interrogation started. And that was almost as bad as the dreams. I have never been arrested, but I've seen it in movies how suspects are grilled by cops, and that's what it felt like.

"They asked me all kinds of questions about what I was like as a kid and did I have a girlfriend and how did I feel about my mother and how did I feel about my father, who left home when I was little. They were very interested in my father. I kept telling them I hardly knew the guy, because he was never around. I was maybe seven the last time I saw him. They wanted to know if that bothered me, not knowing what happened to my father. I told them my mother and older brothers took good care of me and I didn't even think about my dad. He was gone—out of my life. That was it, plain and simple.

"I remember they had me crying once, because they really made me feel like I was stark raving mad. They asked me if there was any mental illness in my family. Well, that really threw me for a loop! I told them, 'No. We're just regular farmers.' They showed me these pictures. It was some kind of a test—I was supposed to tell them what I saw and I remember one doctor saying, 'You're seeing things in these pictures that we've never come across before.' I overheard one doctor tell another, 'Too bad. Take a look at his G.C.T. scores. The kid is really smart.' That made me feel better. But they sent me back to the barracks, and that was the last I saw of the doctors.

"Two days later our sergeant pulled me out of line after barracks inspection. The rest of our company fell out, but the sergeant asked me to sit down at the center table. He handed me a folder and said, 'They're sending you home, Ernie. Put on your dress uniform and clear out your foot locker. There'll be a bus coming to take you to the train station. Your discharge papers and tickets are in the folder.' So, that was that."

Ernie continued, "I tried to argue with him. I was begging to stay. I asked about a clerk's job. I remember telling him I took typing in high school. The sergeant laughed and said, 'We've got plenty of guys who can type, son. We need infantrymen, combat soldiers ready to go to the front.' I guess he shook my hand and thanked me." Ernie managed to smile. "It was a long train ride home, that's for sure. As soon as I boarded, I opened the folder and read through all the paperwork. It was a medical discharge for 'adjustment disorder, with depressed moods'." Ernie paused for a moment and then said, "I wasn't fit to serve my country."

Carla wiped her eyes. "I'm so sorry."

"Yeah, it was a bad deal. But I didn't give up. When those doctors told me that I wasn't fit to kill Germans, I made up my mind right there, that I could make something out of my life. I started thinking about my old baseball coach. I wanted to be a teacher, just like him. And damn it, that's what I did!"

Carla managed to smile, "You bet you did, and you'll be a good teacher, too. I know that. I can feel that in my heart and I'm going to talk to Tom, and I don't think Vic or Orvid need to know a thing about all this. You've told me, and that's good enough in my book."

"I'm glad you feel that way. It's a load off my mind." Ernie looked at his watch, "Are you going to church this morning?"

Carla was at the cupboard taking out a large bowl. "Yeah. Are you coming along?"

"No, but I'd like a ride to the school. I have more stuff I want to bring up there."

"Sure." She had started mixing pancake batter. "But first I'm gonna feed you. Do you like apple pancakes?"

"I like anything you fix up." Ernie went upstairs and started sorting out books and supplies into two boxes. He made his bed, closed the window, and carried the boxes downstairs.

They were all very quiet at breakfast. Tom didn't say much. Dale kept his head down as he ate his pancakes and never looked at Ernie. He was still thinking about his teacher's nightmare and wondering if it would happen again. After they finished up, Ernie helped Carla with the dishes; she washed and he dried and put the plates and cups in the cupboard and utensils in the drawer.

Ernie rode in the back of the pickup on the way to the schoolhouse. He asked Dale to jump in, but he shook his head, crawled in the cab, and sat between his mom and dad. Ernie thought about that as they bounced along the township road. *The kid's confused. I must have scared the heck out of him last night. Does he think I'm a crazy man?* Ernie leaned his head around the side of the pickup and could see the white clapboard schoolhouse up ahead. *I can't worry about bad dreams. I need to get ready for school.*

The Smierud boys had cleaned the porch and Ernie felt good about putting his key in the door for the first time. Everything inside smelled of strong soap. The bright sun on the windows did not find one solitary speck. The blackboard and chalk tray were cleaned, and the erasers were dusted and placed in a neat row. Ernie took the keys that hung from a string next to the big pendulum clock on the north wall. He wound the clock with one key and set the time to 10:45 with the other.

Ernie sat down in the swivel chair behind his desk and noticed an envelope with his name on it sitting on top of the register book. He opened the envelope and read the letter.

Dear Mr. Juvland,

Welcome to Dahl School. On behalf of the students, parents, and the school board, I want to tell you how happy we are to have you as our teacher. Our children are the most important blessings in our lives. We know that you will keep them safe in our little school and teach them well. Please remember, we are all here to help you. May God be with you each day as you begin your teaching career.

Sincerely yours,
Carla Henning, Secretary,
Jackson Township School Board

Ernie noticed his hands were shaking as he held the letter. He took out a new spiral notebook and pasted the letter on the first page. He took a black crayon out of the drawer and wrote on the front of the notebook, **Mr. Juvland's Logbook, Personal.** Then he took a pencil and wrote, *Sunday, September 3, 1944. Sunny day. Opened school for the first time. Good feeling. Make plans to get ready for the students. They will be here in two days.*

Before he put his logbook away, he remembered a suggestion one of his teachers at the training school had told him. "Keep track of your mistakes. Write them down." He turned to the last page and with the black crayon he printed at the top, **MISTAKES.** He looked at the blank page and thought about the days to come. He said out loud, "So far, so good."

Ernie walked around the room opening windows to let in the fresh morning air. He took his key ring out of his pocket. It had one big key for the door and two smaller keys, one for the middle drawer of the teacher's desk and one for the science cabinet. He opened the glass doors of the science cabinet, which stood in the southeast corner of the room. The shelves were dusted and the flasks, beakers, and glass tubing were all cleaned. He sorted through the items, one microscope in a wood box, a reagent bottle of hydrochloric acid, some iron filings, copper chips, tongue depressors, and a magnet.

Ernie locked the cabinet and walked over to the big wood burning stove. He pulled out the metal tray for ashes at the bottom. It was empty and cleaned. He took down the big water pan from the top of the stove. It needed cleaning; he noticed brown drippings from cocoa jars that had spilled over last winter. Ernie remembered from his own days in country school how the kids heated their cocoa jars in the water-pan-humidifier on top of the stove. Next to the stove were a two-burner kerosene stove, the washstand, and a ten-gallon crock with a spigot for drinking water.

Ernie went into the cloakroom and saw the benches and hooks for coats and scarves. The wood box was in there along the wall. It was empty now, but would be kept full by the older boys all winter long. Ernie remembered how he and a couple of his pals back in country school would pile the wood all the way to the ceiling, so high the teacher wasn't able to pull out the top chunks.

Finally, Ernie walked into the library, which was a side room about 12X16 feet. There were two windows on the north side and shelves on the side walls. Under the shelves on the west side was a long counter the length of the room. Ernie noticed the cut marks from coping saws the boys had used during industrial arts classes. The library also doubled as the woodworking shop. On the counter were a paper cutter and a hectograph, an 11X14-inch box containing a smelly gelatin that was used to make copies of tests, maps, word lists, poems, etc. Ernie had learned how to use the hectograph in teacher training school.

There were maybe 40 books in the library plus a set of *Encyclopedia Americana, 1919 Edition.* Twenty-five years old and the 'Q-R' volume was missing. Ernie opened an *Atlas of the United States,* the binding was held together with black friction tape. The page with the map of Minnesota was ripped out.

He found an open ream of yellow construction paper and used the paper cutter to make nametags for the student desks. The names of his students, grades first through eighth, were neatly printed in the register. There were 24 in all. He used a black crayon to write each name on the nametags and carefully pasted them to the desks, starting with the first grade desks along the north wall. He finished with the sixth, seventh, and eighth graders in the big double desks near the south windows. He put Neal and Bobby Smierud in the desk nearest the front, a mere four feet from his own desk. Ernie had students in every grade except fourth. He had only one boy in the fifth grade and he thought he would include him with the sixth graders.

He placed the register in the middle drawer and closed it. He tried to lock it with the key, but the drawer would not close tightly. He moved his chair back and got down on his knees. Something was stuck in the back of the drawer, keeping it from closing. He pulled out the drawer and looked inside. He saw a white business envelope stuck in the back of the slot. He removed it and examined the address. **Martha L. Sampson, Teacher, Dahl School, RD #2, Sparborg, Minnesota.** There was no return address. Ernie placed the letter on his desk and sat down. He noticed the envelope had been neatly opened with a scissors. Ernie was puzzled. *Martha Sampson? Last year's teacher. She left this letter. How come? It must be some school business. Maybe so. It's addressed to the teacher. Okay, now I'm the teacher. It could be something I should know about.*

He pulled the letter out of the envelope. Clipped to the top was an index card with a brief, hand-written message. He began to read. *Dear Miss Sampson, I am enclosing the report of your recent examination. You had mentioned that you wanted a copy mailed to your work address, when the lab work was completed. I hope you are well. Please do not hesitate to call if you experience any further complications. Best wishes, C.W. Chandler*

Ernie moved the note to the side and read the report.

Charles W. Chandler, MD, 23 Hoffman St., Crookston, Minnesota

The patient, Martha L. Sampson of RD #2, Sparborg, Minn., was examined in my office at 9:00 pm., on Friday, May 5, 1944. She indicated that she is a teacher. Patient stated that she had been raped between 4:30 and 5:00 p.m., that same afternoon. She knew the person, but refused to divulge his identity.

Patient is a small woman, 19 years old. She was dressed in a plaid skirt and white blouse. Her light brown hair was neatly combed. She was noticeably distraught. Her eyes were red, and it was obvious that she had been crying.

Examination showed bruises on both wrists and a large bruise on the upper right arm. Her underwear showed blood stains and some dirt. Vaginal examination showed lacerations on the left labia minora. The hymen appeared to be broken as evidence of penetration.

Lab report: The swab used for the vaginal canal examination revealed the presence of spermatozoa. Lab results for evidence of venereal disease are pending. If those tests return positive, I assured the patient that I would contact her immediately.

Patient was advised to report the incident to the police and to call if there was any further bleeding or other untoward symptoms.

Ernie placed the letter back in the envelope and pushed it far to the back of the drawer. He closed the drawer and locked it. He gripped the key in his hand and exhaled, "God have mercy!"

Labor Day was sunny and warm, a bit of Indian summer had come to the North Country. The leaves of the maple trees and sumac bushes had started to turn. They were bright red against the white birch trees along the shores of Brisbois Lake, named after Jean Luc Brisbois, an early fur trapper, who had come down from Canada, married a local Ojibwa woman, and settled on the lake which bears his name.

Ernie and the Hennings arrived early at the lake to set up for the annual Labor Day Picnic. Tom Henning was cleaning the barbecue grill, which was a 55-gallon steel drum cut in half, with two oven grates on top. It was a monster, large enough to make three dozen hamburgers with room left over for pork ribs, hotdogs, and chicken legs. Carla and Dale were covering the picnic tables with tablecloths made from 50-pound flour sacks, and Ernie was over at the softball field raking the base paths. He dragged a large tree branch that had fallen down by home plate and patched a hole at the bottom of the backstop with a piece of chicken wire.

As he worked on the backstop he thought about Martha Sampson and the doctor's report he found. *Who was the guy? Where did it happen? Why did she leave the report in her desk drawer? I wish I hadn't read the damned thing.*

Families began to arrive around one o'clock, and Ernie met many of the parents. Except for a few younger students, the older ones were shy about talking to their new teacher. He watched them in knots of three and four, staring at him and whispering behind their hands. It bothered him. *What are they saying about me?*

Carla came over to Ernie and said, "I noticed most of the kids are a little self-conscious about meeting you. Don't worry about that. Before we eat, let me take you around and introduce you to the older ones."

Ernie answered, "That's a good idea," He followed Carla from table to table, shaking hands and making small talk. When they finished making the rounds, Ernie felt better. "These are really nice people," he whispered.

"We're glad you feel that way," she said. "Now it's time to eat. Here, grab a plate and let's load up."

Ernie was hungry and he piled on potato salad, scalloped corn, two hotdogs, and lime Jell-O with whipped cream. Carla led the way to a table off to the side. Ernie said, "I've been looking around for them, but I haven't seen the Smierud boys."

Carla shook her head and looked across the table at Ernie. She answered in a low voice, "They never come to the picnics. It's because of their pa. Ben Smierud is on the outs with most of the farmers here, so he keeps to himself. Like I told you before, he really went downhill after his wife died." Carla put down her fork and looked out across Brisbois Lake. "There's another reason why Ben doesn't come here." Carla thought for a moment, not sure how to say it. In a soft voice, ready to break she said, "Hazel Smierud drowned out in this lake."

Ernie looked up. "Oh, Lord! How did that happen?"

"Yeah, that was a bad one. In the winter, Ben used to take her out there on the ice to his little dark-house, to spear fish. She speared one of the biggest northerns ever to come out of this lake. Ben was in the dark-house sitting by her. He wanted her to bring it up and get it out of the hole all by herself. She was a little woman, and he thought it would make her feel proud—that she could do that all by herself. The way people tell it, she got the fish up. Of course the darned thing was flipping and flopping around; it knocked over the little stove and the stovepipe came down. Ben had the door open and was helping her get the fish outside, but the floor of the dark-house was icy, and she slipped into the hole."

70

Ernie had stopped eating. His eyes opened wide.

"Ben stripped down and went in after her. I don't know how she had the strength to do it; she swam up against the ice, but she was about five feet from the hole. Ben managed to find her and pulled her over to the hole, but he couldn't get her up. She was too soaked in her clothes and very weak. She had on winter boots, and just think how cold that water was. He had to give up. He let her go and she sank to the bottom. He barely made it out of the hole himself. The poor man almost died trying to save his wife.

"Another fisherman came over from his dark-house. He saw Ben outside in his long underwear, frozen stiff like cardboard to his body. He was swinging his ax over and over, chopping that big fish to smithereens." Carla took in a breath. "Uff da! Ben never got over it. He blames himself, even to this day."

Ernie was riveted. "Did you know his wife?"

"Hazel Smierud was one of the kindest persons I have ever known. She took care of Ben, and he didn't drink all that much when she was alive. But when she died, Ben just went to pieces, and now the boys are on their own. When they go to town, he sits in the tavern and drinks, while Neal and Bobby buy what little groceries they can afford. I'm sure they eat a lot of mush. His farm went to pot. His manure pile got bigger than his barn. He sold off the cows and gave up. He does odd jobs, digs graves, does janitor work when he can find it, but what little he makes usually goes for booze. It's a very sad deal."

As Ernie listened to Carla's story, he kept thinking about the Smierud boys. All the advice he was given made him determined to be tough on the boys. He could not ignore what they had written about him on the windows of the school, just because of this family tragedy. He knew he had to take charge, right on the first day, tomorrow. Ernie thought about all the problems around him and he hadn't even spent one day with his students.

He wondered if he should tell Carla about the letter he found. *I won't do it now, maybe later. What would she think if I told her I read it? Maybe I won't tell her. Maybe I should try to get in touch with Martha Sampson and give her the letter. I don't like it lying there in my desk. I should put it with her box of things. I wonder about the guy who raped her. Did he come here to the picnic? Is he that guy playing with his little girl, or that guy over by the grill, or that guy leaning against the backstop?* Ernie's eyes swept around the picnic grounds and studied the face of every man he saw. *Is he here? Maybe so. Maybe not.*

By five o'clock the Jackson Township farmers had gathered up their dishes, serving spoons, water jugs and headed home. There was milking to do. Ernie and the Hennings stayed after to clean up. Tom and Carla were folding up the tablecloths and picking up trash. Ernie and Dale were taking a break on a bench over by the softball field. Ernie had been hitting ground balls to Dale and they both needed a rest.

Ernie slapped the boy on his knee and said, "You're getting good with your new glove. I never thought you'd get that grounder you dove for. Did you scrape yourself?"

Dale smiled, "No, but I got dirty." He wiped the dirt off his overalls.

"Hey, playing ball is all about getting dirty."

"I guess," said Dale and he pounded his fist into his glove. "As long as Ma doesn't mind."

"Your mother is very kind, isn't she?"

"Yeah, I only remember once when she spanked me."

"You don't have to tell me what you did, but I am curious."

"I wasn't being mean or anything. We were over at the minister's house in town and I wiped my nose on some nice curtains hanging in their front room window. I was little—I had a runny nose, and the curtains were handy. The bottoms were just even with my nose."

Ernie laughed, "Well, if that's the worst thing you ever did, that's not so bad."

"Yeah, but Ma had warned me three or four times before. She said I had a bad habit and she had to break my habit. That's why she spanked me."

"Did you ever wipe your nose on curtains again?"

"No, but I think about doing it sometimes. Ma knows that, so when we go visiting she still tells me, 'Don't wipe your nose on their curtains!'"

Ernie looked over to where Tom and Carla were putting things in the pickup. "I guess I should ask you something. Did I scare you the night I had that dream?"

"Yeah, at first you did. I thought it was the Boogeyman."

"I'm sorry. I have these bad dreams once in a while."

"So do I, and the Boogeyman always shows up."

72

"Do you ever fight him?"

"Once I kicked him in the pants. He flew out the window."

Ernie slapped Dale on the back, "Good for you, champ! We all need to show the Boogeyman who's boss." Ernie thought for a moment. "If I ever have another bad dream, I want you to stay away from me. I might think you're a little Boogeyman."

"Okay," said Dale.

They looked up to see Carla coming over. She yelled, "Okay, big man and little man, we're all packed up and ready to go." Ernie and Dale climbed in the back of the pickup. Carla and Tom got in front and they headed for home.

Tom and Carla were silent until they were nearly halfway home. Then Tom cranked his window up to the top and ordered Carla, "Roll up your window."

"Why?" She was surprised. "It's hot in here."

He barked, "Just roll up your damned window and listen to me! I have something to say, and I don't need them hearing it."

"Okay, what did I do now?"

"You're getting mighty chummy with the teacher there, and I don't think it looks good to the neighbors."

Carla looked out the window.

"They all saw you sitting alone eating, and I don't like it."

Carla was annoyed, but she spoke in a deliberate way. "What am I, Tom?"

"You're my wife and the mother of my boy."

"Aren't you forgetting that I'm on the school board?"

"So what?"

"Okay, I'll explain. Ernie is an employee of our school district, and along with Vic and Orvid, I represent the district."

"Ha! You're making it sound like you're the governor!"

"You can think what you want to, but I'm proud of what I'm doing—serving our community. I felt it was my duty at the picnic to introduce Ernie to the parents and students."

"Big deal! He could have done that on his own. He's a grown man. He didn't need you leading him around by the hand."

She rolled down her window. "I have nothing more to say,"

Tom said, "Just remember. I've got my eye on you." He rolled down his window and drove on.

73

Chapter V...The First Day

Early Tuesday morning, before the sun topped the trees to the east of the Henning farmyard, Dale was taking a bath in the big galvanized tub, which sat by the kitchen stove. "How come we're leaving for school so early, Ma?"

Carla had finished packing lunches for both Dale and Ernie and was setting the table for breakfast. "Mr. Juvland wants to get there before the kids come. Make sure you clean your ears."

Dale took a washcloth and dug into his ears. He heard his teacher walking around in the bedroom overhead. He climbed out of the tub, dried himself with a big towel, and dressed in his new school clothes, bib overalls, a white shirt, and black socks.

Tom came up from the barn and spoke to Dale, "I'll let you get by this morning, because you're going to school early, but starting tomorrow, you'll have to milk your two cows before you leave for school. You're eight years old now, so just get used to doing the morning milking, even on school days."

Dale didn't answer. He looked at his mother. Carla said, "I don't know. He's still pretty young to make him do that."

"Like hell he is," Tom snapped. "And don't correct me in front of the boy!"

Ernie broke the silence when he came down the stairs dressed in his new black suit and carrying an old brown leather satchel with two small buckles to hold the flap shut. "Good morning," he said. "My-oh-my, Dale, you sure look all snazzy in your new school clothes!"

Dale thanked his teacher and they all sat down to eat.

After breakfast, Tom and Carla stood on the porch and watched their son and his teacher start up the lane to the main road, heading for school. Carla reached for Tom's hand and said, "I just hope it works out okay for Ernie."

Tom pulled his hand away and reached for his pouch of Bull Durham. "You worry too much about the man. He'll be okay, so long as he puts his foot down right away."

Dale carried his gallon lunch pail in one hand, his new two-ring notebook in the other, and Ernie carried his satchel. The sun glistened off the dew on the tall grass and ragweeds in the ditches. The milkweed pods were opening and showing their white fluff, the cattails at the edge of the sloughs had darkened from early frost, and the Indian tobacco stood out in dark brown clumps. Canada geese flew in a V-formation overhead, honking their way south, and a beaver in a nearby slough slapped his tail and slipped smoothly into the dark waters, leaving concentric rings, which moved out and disappeared in the weeds at the edge.

Ernie was excited. *I'm a teacher now. Think of that—the first one in our family to hold a professional job.* He thought of his brothers off at the war and he thought of his mother, alone now on the farm. *I wondered how she'd feel if she were here today.*

Just past the half mile mark, they came over a small rise and saw the school up ahead. Dale was lost in thought, but then he spoke out. "Pa said he'd buy me a bicycle next year."

Ernie smiled and said, "Then I'll have to ride on the handlebars. How about that?"

"No. You're too big and your feet would drag on the ground." They laughed and Dale continued to talk about bicycles.

The last quarter mile, the road followed the fence line of Ole Gangstad's pasture, and charging toward the three strands of barbed wire, came Ole's big Black Angus bull. Ernie and Dale moved to the other side of the road and tried to ignore the beast, as he snorted and dug in the dirt with his front hooves in a menacing way. Dale stopped talking about bicycles. He quickened his steps and reached for Ernie's hand. The bull followed them to the end of the pasture, huffing and glaring behind the barbed wire.

They were the first ones to arrive. Dale put his lunch pail under the bench in the cloakroom and went into the classroom to find his desk. He put his notebook inside the desk and noticed Susan Rollag's nametag on the desk in front of his. He asked Ernie why he put him in the back of the room. Ernie said, "You're there because I know you won't start any monkey business."

Ernie took a stool from the library and brought it out on the front porch. Dale went down to the swing set. The first to arrive were Orvid Skime and his daughter Eunice, riding in the Model A. Eunice had curly brown hair, wore glasses, and was dressed in a yellow blouse and tan skirt. Physically mature for her age and tall. If Ernie did not know she was starting seventh grade, he would have sworn she was a high school girl. She smiled at Ernie and offered her hand to shake. "Do you remember me from the picnic yesterday? I'm Eunice."

Ernie shook her hand and said, "Good morning, Eunice."

Orvid had his arm around his daughter's shoulders, "This is my big girl. You take good care of her now. You hear?"

"I certainly will," said Ernie. "They tell me you can play the piano. I'm hoping you can play the songs for our programs."

"I can do that," Eunice answered. "I played for our Christmas Program last year."

"And she didn't miss a note," Orvid added.

"That sounds good," said Ernie. "I've put names on all the desks. You're with Janice Millrud in the back seat near the science cabinet."

Eunice nodded, "Janice is nice, and she doesn't copy off."

Ernie appreciated that inside information, "Well, I'm glad to hear that."

"I hope you didn't stick her near the Smieruds." Orvid interrupted.

"No," said Ernie. "I have them in the front seat, right in front of my desk."

"Good," said Orvid.

More students began to arrive, some riding with their parents, but most of them on foot, carrying their lunch pails and notebooks. Ernie sat on his stool on the front porch and greeted each of them. A few of the parents stayed to visit, but by 8:30 they had all gone home.

Ernie shouted for Dale, who was talking to Susan by the door of the woodshed. "Hey, Dale, get up here, please! It's 8:30. Time to ring the bell!"

Dale hurried to the porch. Inside the door was a half inch rope dangling from a hole in the ceiling. He gave it several pulls and the big bell, high in the cupola, began to clang.

The playground cleared, and Ernie took his stool and followed the last two stragglers inside. He put his stool back in the library and stood behind his desk. "Please rise," he said. "Face the flag and place your hand over your heart."

They began, "I pledge allegiance to the flag of the United States of America, and to the Republic for which it stands, one nation, indivisible, with liberty and justice for all." Then Ernie led his students in reciting "The Lord's Prayer". They bowed their heads. "Our Father which art in Heaven…"

When they finished, Ernie said, "Remain standing please and let us pray. Dear Heavenly Father. We thank Thee for our

76

good parents, the food they give us, and protection they provide. We thank Thee for our schoolhouse and the opportunity to learn to be good citizens. Help us to learn our lessons well, to be kind to each other, and grateful for Thy gifts. Bless each student and help me be a good teacher. We ask this in the name of the Father, the Son, and the Holy Ghost. Amen."

Ernie added, "We'll usually sing a song after the prayer, maybe 'God Bless America' or 'America, the Beautiful', but I want to teach the words to the younger students first." He sat down and opened the register book. "You may be seated. I put nametags on your assigned desks. It looks like you've all found your places. Please answer 'present', when I call your name."

Ernie began to call the roll of his 24 students. Some snickered when he mispronounced last names. He had trouble with 'Myklebust' and 'Bjornerud'. When he came to the end, two were missing, Neal and Bobby Smierud. Ernie wondered about that.

Ernie put the register book in the middle desk drawer and saw again the envelope addressed to Martha L. Sampson. The students were very quiet. Ernie carefully printed **MR. JUVLAND** on the blackboard. Some of the students opened their notebooks and wrote it down. Ernie explained, "All of my grandparents came to America from Norway, so 'Juvland' is a Norwegian name. A 'juv' is a canyon. I guess the name came from a farm family that lived in a canyon or on the edge of a canyon." He also reminded the students that the 'J' letter in Norwegian is pronounced like the 'Y' sound. Most of the older students knew that.

Ernie explained, "We won't have regular lessons this morning, because I need to go over classroom rules, our weekly schedule, and if we have time, I'll assign monitor jobs. Before we start that, I want you to know something about me and my family, and maybe we can learn some geography along the way." Over his desk hung a globe from a clothesline, which he lowered from a pulley in the ceiling. "Why don't you all quietly come up here? The younger ones may sit on the benches and the older ones may stand behind. I want you all to see the globe."

From his desk he took out a sheet of wax paper covered with red stars. Ernie talked about the war and asked the students if they had a father, uncle, or brother, who was fighting overseas. Many did. Then Ernie talked about his two brothers on ships in the Pacific Ocean. He turned the globe to show the large blue area of the Pacific. He placed one star near the Midway Islands and another star near the Admiralty Islands north of New Guinea. He placed a star in Belgium for another brother, who had landed on the beach of Normandy. He turned the globe to the United States and placed a star on Virginia, where a fourth brother guarded German prisoners at Camp Picket.

Dale raised his hand and asked, "Why isn't that brother fighting the Germans?"

Ernie said, "Good question. He lost an eye in a shooting accident when he was about your age, Dale. He had only one eye and the Army didn't think he was able to serve in combat." Ernie peeled off one last star and hesitated, "And finally, I want to tell you about my youngest brother, Andy. My mother and I expect him home for Christmas before he's shipped off to Europe. Right now he's here in Arkansas at Camp Joseph T. Robinson."

The room was quiet as Ernie pasted the last star over Arkansas. Then the front door slammed, so loudly it startled the students. Ernie heard loud footsteps stomping through the cloakroom. Soon two big boys appeared at the back door to the classroom. Ernie didn't have to ask who they were. It was Neal and Bobby Smierud. They stood by the washstand shifting their weight from one foot to the other. They looked down at their feet, and Ernie heard one of them whispering something, which caused the other one to smirk and look up at Ernie.

In a commanding voice Ernie said, "Okay, students, I plan to tell you more about the war, because there's a lot of world geography we can learn from it. Let's put the globe up for now, and you may all go back to your seats." Ernie felt an anger rising from deep inside him as he pointed to the Smierud boys and raised his voice. "You two boys go out on the porch and wait for me. I have a special way of dealing with students who show up for school an hour late. And don't even think about running home, because I'll come after you. Now, get out on the porch!"

The smirks left Neal's face and Bobby frowned as they turned to walk back through the cloakroom. Ernie waited to hear the front door open and close. "Okay, please open your notebooks and write down our daily schedule of classes. I've written everything here on the board." He turned toward the little desks. "I want my three first graders and five second graders to take your notebooks over to the big desks. Okay, seventh and eight graders, after you've written down the schedule, I want you to help the younger students print the schedule in their notebooks. I also want you to print the days of the week for them. Leave two spaces below each day so you can help them practice writing the days on their own." There was a flurry of activity as the students set about their tasks.

Ernie's anger was growing. He could not remember experiencing anything quite like the rage he had for those two boys out on the porch. He took off his suit coat and hung it on the back of the chair. He rolled up his sleeves and said, "I'll be right back."

Outside the Smierud boys were sitting on the porch railing. Ernie burst through the door and yelled, "Okay, off that railing and get up against that wall! Put your hands by your sides and look at me! You'll keep your mouths shut and listen to every word I say!"

They reluctantly eased off the rail and sauntered over to the wall. Neal gave Ernie a smirk and said, "What did we do?"

That did it. Ernie felt a power he could not control. He sprang at them. He grabbed each by the front of their shirts and shoved them against the wall. Ernie towered half a foot over them as he darted his eyes from one to the other. He felt Bobby shaking under his grasp. He yelled into their faces and with each point he made, he slammed them against the wall, so hard their heads bounced off the clapboard. They struggled to get free, but they were no match for the strength in Ernie's arms and his steel grip.

Ernie raised his voice to a scream. "This is for opening your yap!" Bam! "This is for being an hour late!" Bam! "This is for writing that dirty comment on the windows of our school!" Bam! "Was that meant for me?" Bam! "Was that meant for me?" Bam, Bam! "This is for taking a dump on this porch!" Bam! Neal tried to kick him in the shins, but Ernie answered with a knee to his groin. He felt a button rip out on Bobby's shirt, but he held fast. "Now, here are a couple more for the way you treated Miss Sampson last year!" Bam, bam, bam! He let go and cuffed each of them across the face with his open hands. It felt good to Ernie. He wanted to hit them in their faces with his fists, but he stopped.

Ernie stood back and caught his breath. The boys had given up running away. They were limp and shaking, hoping it would end, but Ernie wasn't done yet. "Now we're going to see how tough you are. I hear you're a couple of tough guys. Let's see if you can take one in the gut! Stand up straight and tighten your stomach muscles." Ernie picked Neal first. He held him against the wall with a firm grip on his shoulder. Then with a swift roundhouse swing, he rammed his fist into Neal's gut just above his belt. The boy grabbed his stomach and buckled over. Then Ernie gave Bobby a shot. They both staggered to the railing of the porch. They bent over it and started coughing. Ernie grabbed both of them by the back of their shirt collars and straightened them up. "Now, get inside and stand against the blackboard!"

Ernie walked through the cloakroom. He straightened his tie, tucked in his shirt, and entered the classroom at the back door. Bobby and Neal stood against the blackboard with their heads down. The students all turned around and stared at their teacher. Ernie's mind was racing. *What did I just do? It was all a blur. Was that me hitting those boys? No. It couldn't be. I'm not like that. It was like a different person inside me came leaping out. Now what? They're all looking at me like I'm a madman. Better take control. Better start saying something. Say anything. They're all waiting.*

In a strong, but controlled voice, Ernie began, "You all have horses on your farm, right?" Most of the students nodded their heads. A few raised their hands. "Well, we had horses on our farm, two hardworking broncos named Bill and Roany. They came from a ranch in South Dakota. When we got them, they were wild. And you all know what you have to do to a wild horse before you can hitch him to the wagon, right?"

Marvin, one of the sixth grade boys, raised his hand and said, "You have to break him. I watched my dad do that to a horse he bought for me."

"You're right, son. Your dad had to break that horse. So that's what I was doing. I was breaking a couple of wild horses."

A few of the older kids snickered. "No!" barked Ernie. "You don't laugh! This is serious business!" Ernie walked up to the front of the room and stood between Bobby and Neal. "Look at your classmates, boys." Neal lifted his head slowly; the smirk was gone. Bobby had tears running down his red face. Ernie put an arm around each of their shoulders. He pulled them close to him and said, "I want you both to look at your classmates and say, 'I'm sorry.' Go ahead now and say it."

In low voices, they both said, "I'm sorry."

"Good," said Ernie. "Now there's your seat right in front of my desk. I am not going to separate you. You're going to sit together and you're going to learn together."

Neal and Bobby Smierud settled into their double desk and Ernie sat on the edge of his teacher's desk. "I once had a teacher—he was also my baseball coach—maybe the best teacher I ever had. We were a rowdy bunch of farm kids and weren't quite sure what to expect from this man. On the first day of his history class, he looked at us and made this speech. He said, 'It's going to be nice in here.' He went on to explain to us that being nice is being good to each other, being kind and helpful. We don't make fun of each other, because that's not nice. We don't disobey and we don't break the rules, because none of that is being nice. We can't change the world, but we can decide how we're going to behave right here in your schoolhouse. And that starts with being nice!"

Ernie got off his desk, took a step forward, and put his hand on Bobby Smierud's shoulder. "Now, was I nice to Neal and Bobby this morning out on the porch? No, I wasn't." He looked down at Bobby. "My actions were not nice, right boys? But my intentions were all about being nice. You see, as your teacher, I will do whatever is necessary to make things nice in here. That's why your parents have brought me to your school."

Ernie sat down behind his desk and wondered if he'd done the right thing. *They all told me I had to put my foot down. Start off showing the Smierud boys who's boss. I think I scared them out of their wits. Am I gonna get in trouble? I hit them pretty hard. We'll see. They're quiet now, but it ain't over yet.* Ernie looked down at his logbook. He opened it to the back page. He made his first entry, *Sept. 5. Made my first mistake. Lost my temper with Smierud boys. I could have seriously injured them. Stay controlled.*

For the rest of the morning, Ernie explained the weekly schedule. Except for the first graders, the students were accustomed to the routine of the school day. For the basic subjects, arithmetic, reading, language, science, history and geography, each class would come to the front and sit on a bench for recitation. About 10 or 12 minutes were allotted to each class, so all the grades, first through eighth, would be heard over a period of an hour and a half. Ernie scheduled arithmetic first, followed by reading.

Lunch was at high noon, followed by recess until the bell rang again at 1:00 p.m. Ernie scheduled language, which included penmanship and spelling as the first class in the afternoon. He planned a half hour recess from 2:30 to 3:00 p.m. The last period of the day was a mix of the other subjects. On Monday and Tuesday they covered science. On Wednesday they covered history, and Thursday was set aside for geography. Friday was a choice of art, music, or industrial arts. The boys did woodworking projects, and the girls did sewing, crocheting, and some cooking.

After lunch, Ernie passed out geography and history textbooks. Finally he asked third through eighth graders to write a short essay in their notebooks. By that time they had all learned to write in cursive, so Ernie warned them not to print. They were to tell about themselves, sort of a short, one-page autobiography. When they finished, they were to place their assignment in an old roaster pan on his desk. The kids called it 'the cooker'.

The first and second graders were called to the benches. Ernie asked them to talk about their farms, what animals they had and if they had a pet dog or cat. They could also talk about their moms or dads. Ernie was especially interested to hear if any of their dads, brothers, or uncles, were fighting in the war. He sent the second graders back to their seats to write sentences about the things they had discussed, and Ernie asked the first graders to draw pictures of pets, farm animals, barns or maybe their houses.

Ernie was amazed by how the time flew by. *How the heck am I going to teach them everything I want to cover? There just isn't enough time in the day.* When 2:30 rolled around, Ernie took the students out for recess. He gathered them down by the swing set and went over playground rules. The students scattered to join in games, to swing, or go down the sliding board.

Ernie looked around and he didn't see the Smierud boys. Then he found them sitting alone on the porch steps. Ernie walked over and said, "Let's stand up, boys." They stood up, but kept their eyes down. "Now," said Ernie, "we're going to shake hands like men." He offered his hand and they offered theirs. Ernie looked in their eyes and said, "Sorry I had to rough you up, but you had it coming. I'm not mad at you. I'm here to make men out of you." They didn't answer, but Ernie noticed that Neal's smirk was gone.

Ernie started to walk away, but he stopped and turned to Neal and Bobby, who had sat back down on the steps. "Are you just going to sit there? Why don't you get up and do something?"

Neal scoffed, "You want us to play with those babies?"

"Okay," Ernie offered. "Why don't we do this? Let me go in and get my glove, a bat, and a baseball. Then we'll have some fun." Ernie didn't wait for them to reply, but went in to get the equipment and was back outside in a jiffy. He gave Bobby his first baseman's mitt and he gave Neal the bat. They followed him to home plate, where Ernie explained, "Next year you guys will be in high school. So, I'm going to give you a little batting practice to get you ready. The younger students will be playing softball, but you guys are ready for some hardball."

Then he called the rest of the students together. "Everybody, listen up! I'm going to give Neal and Bobby a little batting practice. We're using a baseball and I don't want anyone hurt. This is what we'll do. Eunice, would you like to help the younger students inside with some songs? Pick some easy ones out of the songbooks sitting on top of the piano."

"Sure," said Eunice. "I've done that in Sunday school."

"Good," said Ernie. "Take the first, second, and third graders inside and get going. The rest of you bigger kids can stay outside and watch batting practice, but I want you behind the backstop, so you don't get hit. You'll all learn from our practice."

Neal took the bat and Bobby crouched behind the grease-barrel-lid home plate. Ernie paced off 20 long strides and made a scratch mark in the dirt with his shoe. He turned around and threw a few easy warm-up pitches. Then he heard the roar of a tractor coming on the road from the south. He saw Orvid Skime's Minneapolis Moline tractor followed by his black Model A Ford.

When Orvid pulled into the schoolyard, Ernie noticed he had bolted the saw-rig to the front of the tractor. The frame was made of angle iron, and mounted on the business end was a big, 30-inch circular saw blade with no protective shield. He parked the tractor behind the woodpile, and Orvid's wife parked the Model A next to it. Ernie walked over and said, "Hello Mrs. Skime."

"Call me Chub. That's what they all call me." She looked over at the kids sitting behind the backstop. "Where's Eunice?"

Ernie smiled at her and said, "Listen. Hear that music?" The sound of the piano was coming through the open window on the south side, and they could hear the voices of the children singing, "Home, Home on the Range".

"Well, I'll be darned," said Chub. "Is that my girl playing?"

"Sure is," said Ernie. "Why don't you go in and see how she's doing? She's going to be my music teacher."

"Well, I might just do that." She walked up to the porch and went inside the school.

Orvid had turned off the tractor and stood near Ernie, listening to the music coming from the school. He pulled out his can of snuff and said, "I told you she could play the piano good."

"Yes, you did, Mr. Skime, and I'm happy she'll be able to help me when we start working on the Halloween songs."

"Well, that's okay, but first things first, young man. I can only spare my tractor for one day, so we'll have to saw wood tomorrow, and I'm gonna need about four big boys to help me out." Orvid added, "And don't give me the Smieruds."

"Okay, I know how you feel about those boys," said Ernie, "but stick around and you might change your mind."

"Oh, yeah?"

Ernie nodded and walked back to the pitcher's mark. "You might want to get behind the backstop, Mr. Skime, because I've heard Neal here can hit wicked line drives down the first base line." Orvid stepped back a few steps and sat down on a log that was sticking out of the end of the woodpile.

Neal was digging in at the plate, batting left-handed. Bobby crouched behind the plate and banged his fist into the glove. Ernie wound up and whistled a fast ball right under Neal's chin. Whap! The ball hit Bobby's glove and knocked him over on his rear end. Neal stepped back and shouted, "What do you think you're doin'?"

Ernie laughed along with the kids behind the backstop. He yelled back, "I thought I'd start you off with a little chin-music!"

Neal stepped back in the batter's box and said, "Take it easy, okay?"

Ernie wound up and whistled another one belt high, over the middle of the plate. Neal gave it a vicious cut about the time it hit Bobby's mitt, knocking him over again. Neal missed three more fastballs, and then he swung at a curve ball that landed in the dirt in front of home plate.

"I see two problems, Neal, and I think we can fix them." He put down the ball and walked up to Neal from behind. He reached around the boy and grabbed the bat over Neal's grip. "First off, you're swinging too late. You have to start your swing when the ball is about 10 feet out in front of the plate. Do you see where the grass begins?"

Neal said, "Yup."

"Good. That's where you have to start your swing. And here's another thing. You're not swinging level. The arc of your swing goes up and down like you're hitting a golf ball. The pathway of the bat should be level, so when you bring your bat down and turn your wrists back, the barrel of the bat should be level with the path of the ball. Let's try it. I'll guide you." Ernie still had his arms wrapped around the boy, gripping the bat over his hands. They practiced the swing several times and Ernie shouted to the other students watching from behind the backstop. "Are you all watching this? It's the same thing with softball. Keep your eye on the ball and start your swing before the ball reaches the plate. Drop your hands, turn your wrists back, and give it a smooth, level swing."

Ernie walked back to the pitcher's mound. "Okay, Neal, remember what I taught you." Neal pounded his bat on the grease barrel lid and Ernie wound up. He threw another fastball. Whack! Neal sent a sizzling line drive heading foul directly at Orvid Skime. The man didn't have time to duck his head. He fell off the log backwards, ass over teakettle and landed on his knees.

"Hey, boy! What the heck are you trying to do? Kill me?"

Ernie laughed first, and then everyone started laughing, and finally even Orvid broke into a smile as he picked up his cap and walked back to stand with the students behind the backstop. Ernie said, "Okay, I need a couple of kids to get way back there at the edge of Mr. Dahl's wheat field, because, I think Neal's ready to put the ball in play. Just remember, Neal, start your swing early, and keep your bat level as you swing through."

For the next five minutes Neal put three or four balls in play. Then it was Bobby's turn. He gave the glove to his brother and grabbed the bat. He had the same problems that Neal had at first, but with patience and his teacher's help, he was soon hitting the ball squarely, sending line drives clear to the wheat field. While Ernie was waiting for the ball to be thrown back in, he checked his watch. It was 3:45. "Holy smokes!" he said. "I guess we got carried away. It's almost time for dismissal. Okay, everyone inside, get a drink of water and I want you in your seats, nice and quiet when I come in. Okay?"

Ernie took the bat from Bobby, and Neal handed him the glove. "Good work, fellows," said Ernie. "You followed directions and we got some good results. You're both very strong and if we work on your batting and fielding this year, you'll be ready next year to play high school baseball. I've played with kids, even juniors and seniors, who didn't have half your power. You're a couple of bulls! Think about it."

As the Smierud boys walked up to the front porch, Bobby turned and yelled, "Thanks! That was fun."

Orvid spit out some tobacco juice and approached Ernie, "How come none of the other kids got to take a turn? You spent all your time with those two buggers."

Ernie looked up toward the school and said, "You can't ignore those two boys. That's a big part of the problem. They have no mother, their father drinks a lot, and the rest of the kids are so afraid of those two, they don't even want to be near them. So what do kids do when they're ignored? They do things to get attention. So that's what I was doing just now. I was giving them some positive attention to make them feel good about themselves."

"Yeah, but are you gonna ignore the other kids?"

"No," said Ernie, slightly annoyed. "Their time will come. Today was Neal and Bobby's turn." Ernie paused for a moment. "I maybe shouldn't tell you about this, but I'm sure you'll hear about it soon enough. The Smierud boys showed up an hour late this morning, and I decided to punish them. I took them out on the porch and roughed them up. I slammed them up against the wall and I even gave them each a pretty hard punch in the gut."

"Now we're talkin'," said Orvid.

"Yeah, you might think that, but if that's all I did to them, it won't amount to a hill of beans. If you punish a kid, unless you follow it up with a careful explanation and some positive instruction or activity, that punch in the gut will do more harm than good."

"Yeah, I suppose." Orvid was not completely convinced.

"And I'll insist on a little help from you, Mr. Skime, because tomorrow it's your turn."

"My turn? What's that about?"

"I'm going to send Bobby and Neal Smierud out to help you saw wood, along with two other boys. Just be nice and try to carry on what I've started today. That will be good for those boys, and you can teach them how to follow directions."

"But I'm not the teacher."

"Mr. Skime, when it comes to these kids, we're all teachers."

"Yeah, we'll see," said Orvid. He opened his mouth about to argue with Ernie, but he closed it. "Tell my missus I'm ready to go." He spit another stream of tobacco juice and climbed in the Model A.

When Ernie walked into the classroom, all the students were sitting quietly in their seats. Mrs. Skime was standing by the piano, and Eunice was still sitting on the piano bench. He was tired, but very happy, so happy he felt his eyes getting wet. His very first day as a teacher had gone well. He heard Mr. Skime tooting the horn of the Model A, and he looked over at Chub. "Someone's waiting for you," he said with a smile.

"Yeah, let him wait," she said with a huff.

"These are good kids, aren't they, Mrs. Skime?"

"Yeah," she said, and patted Eunice on the head.

Eunice didn't look up at her mother. She kept her head down, as she thumbed through the pages of the songbook. Ernie noticed that something was bothering the girl. He asked her, "Did any of the kids give you a hard time?"

She shook her head, and Ernie thanked her for helping out. He spoke to his 24 students, "Before I dismiss you, I just want to tell you how proud I am of you. Now, tomorrow is a big day. I'll be assigning monitor jobs, dusting erasers, cleaning the blackboard, helping out washing hands, and the big job is getting water from the Grundvig farm. Also, Mr. Skime will be sawing wood most of the day. He'll need four big boys to help him out. So, I have picked Peter, Wendell, Bobby, and Neal. Bring your work gloves tomorrow and work clothes, and I want you to remember, boys, Mr. Skime will be your teacher. That big saw is a dangerous thing, so you must be very careful. Follow instructions and there will be absolutely no fooling around. Just like if you had a job, Mr. Skime is your boss, and I'll ask him to fire you if you goof off. Do you understand?"

The boys looked up at their teacher and nodded, "Yes."

"Good," said Ernie. "Now tomorrow I'll hand out your workbooks for arithmetic, spelling, and reading. We're going to run through the schedule there on the board starting with arithmetic. That's about it, but before you leave, I want the older students to take your writing assignment carefully out of your notebooks. Open the rings. Don't rip it out, because after I grade it, I'll want you to put it back in your notebook."

The students all filed by Ernie's desk and put their papers in the cooker. They went out through the cloakroom, to pick up their jackets and lunch pails. Ernie plunked down in his chair and muttered, "Uff da! What a day!"

Mrs. Skime was still standing at the piano, and Eunice was still sitting on the piano bench. When the room was cleared, Chub came over to Ernie and said, "You look all tuckered out!"

"Yes, I am," he said. He told her how grateful he was that Eunice would be able to help out with the music. Chub talked about how she wanted to go to college after high school and be a music teacher. While they talked, Eunice had gone back to her desk to get her notebook. She took out her paper, placed it in the cooker, and slipped out the door ahead of her mother.

Now he was alone. He looked out the south window and saw a half dozen of his students running for home. He looked to the back window and saw Dale, swinging his lunch pail at his side, heading for home.

He opened his desk and took out the register. He looked at the names of the Smierud boys. There was a column to mark them 'tardy'. But he didn't put a mark there. He took out his fountain pen, removed the cap, and put check marks in the 'present' column. He opened his logbook to the back page and under **MISTAKES,** he made his second entry. *Came close to hitting Neal in the head with a fastball. No more showing off the arm.*

He began to put his logbook and the register back in the drawer and again he spotted the doctor's letter to Martha L. Sampson. He held it in his hands for a moment; then he carefully put in the inside pocket of his suit coat. *I don't want to leave this here. I'll take it home and put it in one of the boxes with her other things. I wonder how she's doing.*

Ernie walked around the room, checking to see if all the windows were locked. As he came by the piano, he noticed an unfamiliar odor. He looked down at the piano bench, and there in the middle was a reddish-brown spot about the size of a dinner plate. He wondered what it was. *Did Eunice sit in something?* He went back to the washstand and soaked a sponge in the wastewater bucket and returned to the bench. He got down on his knees and carefully wiped the spot away. It was blood.

When Eunice came home, she ran upstairs, grabbed a pair of overalls, and a clean pair of underwear. She sneaked out the back door and hurried to the pump house, staying clear of her parents. She closed the door and found an old wash bucket sitting on a shelf. She placed it under the spout and pulled on the pump handle, watching the water gush into the bucket. Then she took off her tan skirt and her blood-stained underwear and dropped them into the bucket. She stood naked from the waist down, holding back her tears. Then she heard her dad calling from the back porch. She threw herself against the back wall, face first and frozen stiff. Orvid's voice grew louder as he approached the pump house. A splash of light hit Eunice in the back as he flung open the door. "What the hell are you doing, young lady?"

She cried out, "Go get Ma and close the door right now!"

Chub heard the yelling and came running. When she approached, Orvid grabbed her by the arm and pulled her to the open door. "Will you just look at your daughter? Stark naked in the pump house! Son of a bitch!"

Chub pushed Orvid aside and went to Eunice. She turned her around and held the shaking girl tightly. The mother's voice was gentle. "Shush, now. It's all right." She looked over her shoulder and yelled at Orvid, "Well, don't stand there with your thumb up your ass! Leave us alone!" She stroked the back of her daughter's hair. She saw the bloody water in the bucket and said, "Why didn't you tell me at the school?"

She continued to cry as her mother held her, "I didn't want anyone to know, Ma."

"Don't worry about it. You poor thing. Just get dressed now and I'll wash out your things. Shush, now. Stop crying. It happens to all young girls. I remember how I felt, too, and I'll tell you all about it after your pa goes to bed."

Chapter VI...The Scream

That night at the Henning's supper table, Tom and Carla asked Dale and Ernie a lot of questions about the first day of school. Dale told them about the Smierud boys, and how they didn't cause any trouble. He looked at his teacher and asked, "Can I tell them everything?"

"You can tell your parents about anything that happens at school. That's your privilege," said Ernie, as he excused himself and placed his supper dishes in the dishpan.

Carla got up to clear the table. She met Ernie at the counter. "You look tired."

"Yes, I am. I feel like I've plowed three acres with a walking plow."

"Well," said Tom, "I'm glad your first day went okay." He used his jackknife to sharpen a wooden match for a toothpick.

Ernie said, "Yes, everything went better than I thought it would." He grabbed his satchel and started for the stairway. "I have papers to grade."

"What?" Carla was surprised. "Papers on the first day of school?"

"Yup," said Ernie, "but I'm going to take a nap first."

"You do that then," said Carla, "and we'll try to be quiet."

Ernie climbed the stairs, opened the south window, and took off his shoes. He hung his suit coat and necktie on a hanger in the wardrobe, lay down on his bed, and listened to the sounds downstairs. Dale was telling Carla all about the school day. He heard the radio, switching from one station to another. It settled on the voices of *Fibber McGee and Molly*. The last thing he heard before he drifted off was Gildersleeve accidently opening Fibber's closet door.

When Ernie woke up, it was past nine o'clock and dark. He got up, grabbed his satchel, and went downstairs. Tom and Carla were in the front room. Carla was on the davenport reading the newspaper, and Tom was over at a table. The Bible lay open in front of him, lit by a kerosene lamp. He was writing down passages on a yellow piece of paper. Hildegarde was singing over the radio on *The Raleigh Room*. Carla said, "Did you get a good rest?"

"Sure did."

Carla put her paper down. "How about I make some fresh coffee?"

"No, that's okay. I'm just going to read some things the kids wrote. Mind if I work at the kitchen table?"

"You go right ahead, and let me know if there's anything you need."

Ernie sat down, opened the buckles on his satchel, and pulled out the papers his older students had written. He began to read Eunice Skime's paper. *I like playing the piano. My grandma taught me when I was very little. I miss my grandma. She was very nice. She died last winter. She caught a cold. Then she had newmonia.*

He crossed out 'newmonia' with a red pencil and wrote in 'pneumonia' over the misspelled word. He continued reading. He found a run-on sentence, and she had used 'good' when she should have used 'well'. Her last paragraph made him smile.

Maybe if I work hard I can go to college and be a music teacher. I like school and I like my new teacher. He is nice. I wish my pa was nice like him. My teacher is tall, dark, and handsome. Ha, Ha.

At the top of the page, Ernie wrote, *Very good, B+*.

He noticed the music from the radio had stopped. Carla came in and closed the door behind her. "Sorry to bother you. Here's the *Pioneer Press*. I'm done with it."

"Thanks." He looked up at her. "Something happened at the end of the day—maybe we should talk about it."

"Oh, my," said Carla. "Anything serious?"

"No, not really." Ernie leaned forward and talked about Eunice and the red spot on the piano bench. "This is something they never told us about in training school."

"The poor girl. It's good that her mother was there. I'm afraid this is going to happen. You have seventh and eighth grade girls who might get their first period without any warning."

"What should I do if it happens again?"

"Well, you being a man and all, any girl that age is going to be embarrassed. I'll tell you what. I'm home most of the time. You just call, and I'll come and take the girl home. That's the best we can do."

"Yeah, there's so much about this job I never considered."
He reached for another paper to grade. "Back to work."

"Oh, I forgot to tell you, something came in the mail today." Carla got up and went to the cupboard drawer. She handed Ernie a letter, addressed to *New Teacher c/o Carla Henning*. In the corner, Ernie saw the return address. *M.L. Sampson.*

Carla chuckled and said, "I guess she doesn't know your name yet."

Ernie smiled. "Yeah, I've been wondering about her." He put the letter in his satchel. "I'd better get back to these papers."

"Okay. Are you sure I can't fix you something, a sandwich or a piece of pie?"

"No, thanks." Ernie was reading another student's paper.

Carla stood in the doorway. Then she said softly, "Dale went on and on about you tonight. He really likes his new teacher." She waited for Ernie to reply.

He turned and smiled. "I'm really glad about that."

"I'll leave you to your work. Goodnight, Ernie."

"Goodnight, Carla, and thanks for everything."

It was nearly midnight when Ernie finished grading the last of the papers. Some were better than others, but a few of the third and fourth graders would need a lot of work on writing good sentences. There was one disappointment: Neal and Bobby did not turn in the assignment. Ernie thought about that as he put the papers in his satchel, blew out the lamp on the kitchen table, grabbed his flashlight, and quietly climbed the stairs to his bedroom.

He sat on the edge of his bed and took Martha Sampson's letter from his satchel. He used his flashlight to read.

Hello,

I'm Martha Sampson, last year's teacher at Dahl School.

You've probably heard a lot about me. I hope it wasn't all bad. It was my first year, and I made a lot of mistakes. I'm sure you'll do better than I did. For the most part they were very good kids, and most of the parents were nice to me. It was only a few who made it difficult.

Oh well, maybe I wasn't cut out to be a teacher. I've been working in a bank here in Bemidji, and so far, that's okay.

I left some things in the bedroom. You've probably seen them. Carla told me she put my books in a box. When I get a chance, I want to drive over there and pick up those things. There are some clothes, books and two letters that are important to me. Maybe I'll meet you when I come back.

Well, that's it for now. I wish you all the luck in the world.
Martha Sampson

Ernie read again, *two letters that are important to me.* He reached in his suit coat pocket and pulled out the letter he found in the teacher's desk, the doctor's examination report. He put it in one of her boxes, under some books, papers, and other letters. He undressed, crawled into bed, and pulled up the covers.

The words of Martha's letter ran through Ernie's mind, as he lay there, hoping to fall asleep. *Poor girl. Those older boys must have driven her crazy. And then she gets raped in May. Who could have done such a terrible thing?* He drifted off to sleep.

The rest of the week at Dahl school was loaded with activities. Orvid sawed the wood and the boys stacked the chunks in the woodshed, clear to the rafters. Neal and Bobby behaved themselves, and that pleased Ernie, but Orvid didn't see much change. "You can't take your eyes off those two bastards. If you do, well, they'll start some trouble. You can bet they will."

Ernie assigned monitor jobs, bringing in wood for the stove, going to the Grundvig farm for water, raising the flag, sweeping floors, washing the blackboard, and cleaning toilets. Even the first graders had to dust erasers. He assigned Janice Millrud to handle the health chart. Every morning she checked each student for personal hygiene. She asked a number of

93

questions, "Did you brush your teeth, wash your face, and comb your hair?" She checked for clean ears and fingernails, and if the student failed on any task, Janice gave the child a check mark. At the end of the week Ernie gave a star to students with a clean health chart.

Ernie opened his logbook and wrote down another mistake on the back page. *Forgot to tell Janice not to make fun of kids with dirty fingernails. Teach her to be nice.*

There were so many details to attend to, but Ernie slowly began to feel more comfortable as a teacher. He loosened up and found moments when he could joke around. He told them stories of his own days in country school. "I had a teacher in fifth grade, who drove us kids nuts. When we returned from the toilet, we had to report on the results. She made us write a number '2' on the blackboard if we did 'number 2' and a number '1' if we only managed a 'number 1'. I guess she wanted to know if all the internal machinery was working up to snuff." The kids laughed.

"Jimmy Bauer was a real rascal. He came back from the toilet one day and wrote a number '3' on the blackboard. Our teacher threw a fit, and Jimmy tried to explain. 'Hey, I went out there to do a number '1' and hoping for a number '2', but the toilet smelled so bad, I threw up.' So Jimmy gave it a number '3'." The kids were hysterical.

Mr. Vic stopped in on Thursday morning. Ernie had called him about the lack of books and supplies. Ernie took him into the library to show him what he needed. Vic listened patiently as Ernie went over a list he had made. "I know we can get books on loan from the county library, but there are certain books we should have here all the time."

Mr. Vic interrupted, "Yes, well, you have your history books, your *McGuffey Readers,* and your geography books."

"Those are textbooks," Ernie protested. "We need more than that. We should have, *The Adventures of Tom Sawyer, Treasure Island*, and how about *The Jungle Book*? We don't even have that!" Ernie picked up an encyclopedia and turned to the inside page. "Look at this. This set was published in 1919, the year I was born, for crying out loud!"

"I can understand how you feel, but we just don't have the money to buy books. Our budget is tight, and, heck, what does a new set of encyclopedias cost, maybe fifty bucks or more?"

Ernie looked at his list. "How about supplies? I'm going to need art supplies. I could only find one pack of yellow construction paper, a couple of jars of dried up paint, and two brushes."

Mr. Vic put his hand over Ernie's list. "Now, that you can take care of—you and the children."

"You want the students to buy their own art supplies?"

"No," said Mr. Vic, "I didn't say that. You've got the Halloween Basket Social coming up. That's where you get the money for supplies, chalk, ink, paint, paper, the whole shootin' match."

Ernie looked down at his list as Mr. Vic went on, "You went to country school, right? You remember the basket social. Didn't you raffle off an Indian blanket and set up a fishpond and Bingo the night of the program?"

"Yes, I remember all that," said Ernie.

"Okay, that's where you get the money for supplies." Vic started for the door. "Look, I'll talk to Orvid about a new set of encyclopedias, but don't get your hopes up. Like I said, we just don't have the money." He looked at the students, who were quietly reading and writing in their workbooks. "Listen, we want you to teach our kids how to read, how to spell, and how to add, subtract, and memorize their multiplication tables. That's it. Drill it into them, and that's all we expect from you. The other stuff, Tom, what's-his-name and that, will just have to wait until they get to high school." He shook hands with Ernie and was on his way.

At his desk, Ernie looked again at his list; then he looked out over his 24 students. They had their noses in their workbooks. The only sounds were the turning of pages and the scratching of their pencils. Ernie was thinking. *There has to be something more than this. Look at them. They're working like little machines. We're not machines. We think, we create, we invent. We have minds that need to be challenged. Where is the challenge in filling in blanks in a workbook? I want my students to think.*

During recess on Friday, some of the students were playing 'pump, pump, pull away', and others were playing 'Annie-over-the-woodshed'. As Ernie was hitting fly balls to the older kids, he saw Mr. Dahl out in his wheat field, checking the shocks to see if the grain was dry enough for threshing. Ernie had been thinking about engaging his students in exciting learning activities, and he suddenly had an idea. He walked over to ask Mr. Dahl if the kids could come out on the field to watch threshing. The farmer said it was okay, as long as they didn't get too close to the machinery. But he was puzzled. "These kids have seen threshing since they were babies. It's nothing new to them."

Ernie explained how he wanted to turn threshing day into a lesson. He told him it was a good opportunity for the students to learn about mathematics and simple machines like levers, pulleys, wheels, and inclined planes. He could teach them about seeds, sprouting, pollination, insects, and how the grain is eventually turned into flour and bread. Mr. Dahl listened and then said, "Well, I suppose. Just don't let them get in the way or scare the horses."

Ernie said, "I'll set the rules with the students. Don't worry. They'll behave. So when do you expect to start?"

Mr. Dahl spit out some wheat kernels he was chewing on. "If the weather stays nice, it could be Monday or Tuesday next week. Just keep in mind, I ain't responsible if a kid gets hurt." Ernie thanked Mr. Dahl and went back to the playground, his mind whirling with plans for threshing day.

On their walk home Friday night, Dale kept up a constant chatter, but Ernie was thinking about lessons he needed to plan. Dale wanted to know if Ernie had seen him catch a tough fly ball during the softball game. Then he talked about a Schwinn bicycle he had seen in the *Montgomery Ward Catalog*. His dad had told him a Monarch was cheaper.

Ernie wasn't thinking about bicycles; he was thinking about his job. *How can I make school exciting? Where do I find the time? I have 24 students on eight different grade levels. Then we have to rehearse for the Halloween program. That's going to cut into my lessons. And they tell me I have to excuse the big boys for potato-picking. How can they do that?*

He thought of a poster he had once seen in a tavern. It was a picture of an old grizzled cowboy, a tired, sad, broken man, and he spoke in a caption under his picture. *There's a lot of stuff they never told me when I signed onto this outfit!*

As Ernie and Dale approached the Henning's farm, they noticed old Anders coming up his lane. He took a newspaper from his mailbox and waited for Ernie and Dale. "Teacher and student on their way home after another exciting day of learning. Hello, Dale. Were you a good boy in school today?"

Dale nodded and Ernie said, "He certainly was." He reached out his hand to Anders. "So, how are you coming on your roof?"

"I'm all closed in and I've cut out the window for the doorway to the main room. I'm rather amazed that I accomplished all that in a week. I have a lot more to do, but it's weather-tight. Would you like to come down and take a look? I'd also like to hear about your first week of teaching. How about telling me over a glass or two of dandelion wine?"

"Okay," said Ernie. "How about you, Dale? Do you want to come see the addition Anders put on his house? Or should I say big tree house?"

"No, I want to get home. I'm hungry. I'm gonna have some cream and bread."

Ernie laughed, "Good boy. Make sure you put some cinnamon on top."

"I always put cinnamon on and a little sugar," said Dale.

"Okay, you run along and tell your ma I'll be home in a little while." Ernie watched the boy pick up the mail and head for the house.

"Okay, Anders, let's take a look at your new addition." They turned and walked at a brisk pace down Anders's lane. They climbed the stairs into the main part of the house, and Anders led Ernie through the new doorway into the addition. They looked up at the ridgepole Ernie had helped put in place the week before. After Anders showed Ernie where the new bookshelves and potbelly stove would go, they went back to the old part of the house. Ernie sat in the canvas swing-chair and spun himself around a couple of times.

Anders went out to the back porch and pulled the rope on his bucket of wine bottles cooling in the creek below. He uncorked a bottle, took two jelly glasses from the cupboard, filled them, and handed one to Ernie. Anders glanced at the newspaper and saw a picture of a bombed out building. A crying mother stood in the rubble holding a child in diapers. He sighed and raised his glass to Ernie, "Here's to a quick end to this bloody war!"

"I'll drink to that," said Ernie, taking a good swig.

Anders sat at the table and pushed the newspaper aside. He said, "So, friend, I want to hear all about your first week."

Ernie hardly knew where to begin. He explained the challenges of teaching on eight different grade levels and the lack of books and supplies. Anders listened patiently with a kind smile and nodded repeatedly as Ernie went on. "There are so many lessons I want to teach these kids, but there just aren't enough minutes in the day."

Anders interrupted Ernie, "Now, now, now. There is only so much a teacher can do in a one-room school. These parents don't expect you to teach everything. They went to country school themselves and they know the limitations. Teach the three Rs, Ernie, and they'll be more than satisfied."

Ernie was not convinced. "But I want to make learning exciting. I hate rote learning and drill. I hated it myself as a student, and I just don't want to bore these kids. And the school board doesn't want to spend any money. I showed Mr. Vic the library and the lack of books. He didn't see a problem with that. Do you know that we're using an *Encyclopedia Americana* that was published in 1919?"

"Well," said Anders, leaning forward, "maybe I can help you out there. Your students should have at least one up-to-date reference source. Find out the price and I'll see what I can do."

"No," said Ernie, "you shouldn't have to worry about that. This is something the parents have to provide!"

"In an ideal world, you are correct. But it's different here. You must remember, these farmers don't have a lot of money. Many of them lost their farms in the 30s. If Steinbeck had written about rural Minnesota during those dry years, it would have been, *Thirty Below and Nowhere to Go*. Some of them toughed it out and managed to recover. However, the fear of losing everything is still there, and it scares the hell out of them. You were a schoolboy back, what, 10, 12 years ago? I'm sure you remember. People were starving!"

Ernie nodded, "I know. My mother always managed to put food on the table, but sometimes it wasn't much."

Anders continued, "And keep in mind, they are very old-fashioned when it comes to education. They don't expect their offspring to go to college; they just want them to get a job and stay out of jail. Their own schooldays have formed the standard. You hear these struggling farmers say, 'If it was good enough for me, it will be good enough for my kid.' That's the way they think, and how can we blame them?"

Anders got up to refill Ernie's wine glass. "Your predecessor, poor Martha, had the same frustrations, but in the end, it really didn't matter to them. They saw her as a failure, because she couldn't make a few of the older boys behave."

Ernie thought about Martha's letter from the doctor, the rape examination report she left in her desk. "Yes, I've heard stories. Miss Sampson had a tough time."

"Correct," answered Anders, "and tragically, she met with an event that eclipsed any of her teaching problems."

Ernie was silent. He waited for Anders to say more. Ernie was puzzled. *Should I tell him about the doctor's report?*

Anders sensed his uneasiness. Then he spoke, "I suppose I should tell you something about young Martha's tragedy. But I am telling you this in the strictest confidence." They looked at each other eyeball to eyeball. "It's over. And for that young girl's sake, it should not be dredged up. Do I have your word that you won't ever tell anyone about this?"

"You have my word," said Ernie, without taking his eyes off Anders.

"All right then. I'm going to tell you of an event that was shamefully evil, something a young woman would not imagine possible, when she chose to become a teacher. Young Martha was raped."

Ernie closed his eyes, lowered his head, and waited. *Should I mention the report? But then I'd have to admit I read it. Should I wait and listen to what he has to say? No, I can't do that. I must be honest with this man.* Ernie looked up and said, "Yes, I know about the rape."

Anders looked surprised. "Really, now. That's interesting. May I ask who told you about it?"

"No one told me. I came on it by accident. I had trouble closing my desk drawer the first day I came up to the school. There was something jammed in the back of the drawer. It was an envelope addressed to Martha L. Sampson, Teacher, Dahl School."

"Did you open it?"

"Forgive me, but I had no idea what it was—there was no return address. I thought, since it was addressed to 'teacher' it had something to do with school business, and maybe that's why the envelope was left there. Besides it had been opened. One end was cut off with a scissors."

"So, you read it?"

"Yes, I did."

"And...?"

"It was a physical examination report from a Dr. Chandler in Crookston. Tests showed that she was raped."

Anders studied his wine glass. "Then she did go to the doctor." Ernie had nothing to say. "I recommended the doctor and told Martha that she needed to see him."

"So do other people know about Martha's rape? Why hasn't anyone told me about it?"

"Did you show the Doctor's report to anyone?"

"No. You're the first person I've talked to about this."

"Okay, for the sake of Martha, let's keep it that way."

"Fine. I won't tell anyone. But it's always on my mind. I mean—what kind of place have I wandered into?"

"I can understand that and I'm debating now if I should tell you more."

"Please, Anders. As a new teacher, I think I have a right to know what happened to the last teacher."

"Fair enough, I'll tell you what I know, but some of this is not pleasant."

"Go ahead. I'm listening."

"It was a Friday, late afternoon, the first week of May, and I was coming home from town. I stopped at the mailbox to pick up my mail, and I heard a woman scream, coming from the Henning's place. I noticed their pickup was gone, but Martha's car was parked next to the house. I sat there waiting, not sure if it was actually a scream or one of the calves bleating."

Anders fixed his eyes on Ernie. "A moment passed, and Tom came out of the barn. He saw me and stopped. Then he gave me a friendly wave and went up to the house. I watched to see if anyone else came out of the barn. I sat there until Tom was in the house, before driving home.

"I had barely put my groceries away, when I heard a car coming down my lane. It was Martha. She ran up the steps, burst through the door, and ran into my arms. She was crying hysterically. I smelled the faint odor of cow manure, and when I patted her hair, I felt a single strand of hay. I asked her what happened.

"She told me she had stayed after school to prepare for the yearend school picnic. She said, 'A man came in the classroom and attacked me!' I asked her who it was and she said, 'I never saw him in my life.' She broke away from me, still crying. She went over to the door. I thought she was going to run out. Then she banged with both fists on the door and said, 'He threw me on the floor behind my desk and raped me!'

"I asked her if she called the police. She told me she was afraid to, because the man threatened her, and besides the school phone is on a party line, and she didn't want anyone to know what had just happened. I got her to sit down, right here at the table. She put her head down on the table and continued to cry. I got her a drink of water and sat with her. Minutes passed and the crying turned to occasional sobs and gasps for air. When she was ready to listen, I told her she had to go to the police. She didn't want to do that. She didn't want people talking. I told her not to worry about that, and I offered to help the best I could."

Ernie asked, "So what happened?"

"First of all, I did not confront her with her obviously fabricated story. She was not at the school. I had just driven by there on my way home from town. Her car was not in the schoolyard. When I heard the scream, I distinctly remember seeing her car parked by the Henning house. You don't have to be Dick Tracy to figure out she was making up a story."

"So what did you do?"

"I gave her the address of Dr. Chandler in Crookston. He's a good man—I've gone to him myself, and I figured that would be far enough away from local gossip. She was very worried about people around here finding out. I told her she needed to get a complete examination for rape. I told her the police would need a doctor's report. I even told her that I would pay the doctor's bill. So, she told me she would. She left, but never contacted me again. The last thing she said was, 'I don't want anyone around here to know about this.' The following week she was gone; they brought in a substitute to finish out the term. I never saw poor Martha Sampson again, but I'm pleased that she went to the doctor." Anders paused. "May I ask what you did with the letter?"

"Well, I didn't want to leave it in my desk, so I brought it home to my room. I put it in a box of books and papers she left in my bedroom. I still feel guilty as hell that I read that report."

"You shouldn't. In the long run it was the right thing to do."

"I'm not so sure it was."

"Consider this. If that letter stayed stuck in the back of your desk, there is no telling who might have come across it." Anders walked over to the window. The last of the September sunrays had left the leaves on the poplar trees. The room had darkened. He turned to Ernie and said, "Well, I think we can assume that poor Martha never went to the police."

"How can you be sure of that?"

"If she did, the police would have the report in their file. And the way news flies around here, I'm sure I would have heard something."

"That's right," Ernie got out of the canvas swing and put his empty glass on the table. He walked to the door and said, "She plans to come back here. I just got the word."

"Really?"

"She sent me a letter and told me she was coming back to get her things."

"Okay. I think you will like her. She's a lovely young lady, very sensitive and kind."

"I'm glad you told me all this, Anders. This thing has really upset me. It's this mystery—who was the guy? It keeps running over and over in my mind."

"But we don't know everything. It is merely a perception. And when perceptions make that dangerous leap to truth, bad things happen, and often good people are hurt. Don't make any assumptions from what I told you. I heard a scream. I saw Tom come out of the barn. I saw Martha's car parked by the house. That's all I can tell you. There is nothing conclusive in any of that. It was my perception. Remember that."

"Yes, you're right." Ernie stood at the door. "It just makes me wonder."

Chapter VII...The Bible Reading

Ernie was afraid to fall asleep that night. He lay on his bed well past midnight, thinking that another nightmare might come. He had just gone through a hellish week, and now this, hearing Anders's story about Martha. Ernie mulled over flashing images of Tom at the supper table that evening explaining the Bible reading he was giving at the church service Sunday morning. It was from Leviticus, and Ernie had trouble making eye contact with him. His mind wandered as he looked at Tom's large, callused hands gripping the edges of the Bible.

Were those the hands that gripped Martha by the wrists, squeezing, like an iron vice? Then the scream. And Carla at the opposite end of the table, her tender eyes fixed on her husband, admiring his strong voice as he explained the Bible passages.

Dale across the table, his eyes darting between his dad and his plate of food. I wonder how the boy would feel, if he ever knew what his father had done. Wait a minute! There were two stories about Martha's rape, the one in Tom's barn and the one at the school. Anders said Martha did not know the man who attacked her at the school. Is that what she told the doctor?

Ernie got up and went to Martha's box of books and dug deep for the envelope with the doctor's report. He lit the page with his flashlight and read. *She knew the person, but refused to divulge his identity.* Ernie put the report back in the envelope and tucked it deep in the box. He lay back down and finally dozed off just before dawn.

When he awoke, his thoughts turned to schoolwork. *Saturday. I need to catch up. Workbooks to correct. They're up at the school. Need to plan for the Halloween program. Have to start decorating the classroom.*

He heard Tom down in the kitchen. The milk pails rattled and the door opened and closed. He went to the window and saw Tom and Dale walking toward the barn. Ernie dressed, grabbed his leather satchel, and went downstairs. There was still coffee left in the speckled blue enamel coffee pot on the stove. He poured himself a cup, cut himself a thick slice of bread, buttered it, and sat down at the table. He took a sheet of notebook paper out of his satchel and wrote a note. *Carla. Thanks for the supper last night.*

I'm still stuffed. I'm going up to the school this morning. Not sure when I'll be home. I have a lot of work to do. Ernie.

Ernie went on his way, up the lane to the township road. He started to feel better with each step away from the Henning farm. He started to notice the changes with the coming of fall. The grain fields along the way were all golden; some waving in the gentle breeze, but some had been cut. Shocks of wheat, oats, and barley stood in long rows on the stubble fields waiting for threshing. Mr. Dahl would thresh on Monday or Tuesday. Ernie needed to outline his lessons for threshing day. There was so much to do. The first week had been hectic and with the Halloween Basket Social in six weeks, it wasn't going to get any easier.

When he got to the school, there was one thing he had to do, before he put it off any longer. He pulled out a sheet of paper and began to write.

Saturday, September 9, 1944
Dear Ma,

How are you getting along on the farm? I hope the Inderdals are helping you out. I worry about you there all alone. I still think we should find you a place in town for winter.

Sorry I didn't answer your last letter right away. I just finished the first week at Dahl School, and I'm really tuckered out. I had no idea how much work this would be, and it isn't physical work like hauling manure or putting up hay. It's all mental. I have to be mother, father, and teacher to these 24 children and sometimes I have to be their best friend. It isn't easy. And here I am on my day off, sitting at school still working.

I've only had one bad dream since I moved in at the Henning's farm, but I worry about having another one. Last night I tried to stay awake, just so I wouldn't have a nightmare and scare the blue blazes out of the family, like the last time. They are very nice people and their little boy, Dale, is good company when we walk back and forth to school.

What do you hear from Andy? Let me know. I'm sure he'll get a furlough when he's through with basic. I'll bet he has really grown up. I've read in the Pioneer Press that the Allies are moving into Belgium, getting closer to the Rhine, but we're losing a lot of men. More and more replacements are being shipped over and I'm afraid Andy will be one of them. Poor kid.

I've been following the Cardinals in the papers. They've slipped a little, but they're still 12 games ahead of the Pirates. So it looks like they'll be back in the World Series. Well, I want to put this in the mailbox before the mailman comes. Write soon and let me know how you're doing. And forward any letters you get from my brothers.

Love,

Ernie

He spent the next hour at his desk correcting arithmetic and reading workbooks. He was surprised to hear a boom on the west wall behind the blackboard. It sounded like a ball. Then he heard it again. Someone was throwing a ball against the wall. He went outside and saw Neal and Bobby Smierud. Ernie yelled, "Hey, you guys aren't supposed to be at school. It's Saturday."

Bobby took a step forward and banged his mitt on his thigh. "Is it okay if we play?"

"Sure, that's okay," said Ernie, pleased that they asked.

Then Neal said, "Wanna pitch to us?"

"I'd like to," said Ernie, "but I have paperwork to do. You guys go ahead and don't mind me. Do you need a bat? There should be one in the cloakroom. Just remember to put it back when you're done."

The boys headed for the cloakroom, and Ernie went back to his desk. He looked at his to-do list and saw *blanket raffle*. He used the paper cutter to make 100 raffle tickets out of yellow construction paper. He planned to have one of his older students number and price them, maybe 25 cents each. The prize would be an Indian blanket, which he hoped one of the parents would buy and donate to the raffle.

In the bottom drawer of his desk he found a supply catalog. Northern School Supply Co., Fargo, North Dakota. He looked up construction paper and found the listing. **Assorted colors, package of 50 sheets (9X12) $0.22.** Ernie ordered ten packages. He turned to the page on chalk, white and assorted colors. He was distracted by the roar of a tractor coming from the east. He got up and went to the window for a better look. It was an old, black Hart Parr tractor pulling a big threshing machine.

He went outside and noticed the Smierud boys had stopped playing catch to watch the tractor and thresher approach. Ernie walked behind the rig as it crossed the playground and stopped in the stubble field south of the school. The driver let the tractor idle and climbed off. Ernie introduced himself to Harvey Millrud, "I'm Ernie Juvland, the teacher here. Are you going to start threshing today?"

Harvey didn't look at Ernie; he was pulling the pin on the hitch. "Monday. We'll start Monday. Dahl couldn't get a crew together today." He put the pin in the toolbox and started to climb back on the tractor.

Ernie shouted over the noise of the engine, "Did Mr. Dahl talk to you? He told me I could bring my students out here to watch you thresh."

"He never talked to me about it," Millrud scoffed. "Just make sure that your kids don't get in the way."

Ernie walked back to the school, where the Smierud boys were playing catch. Neal said, "Millrud is a no good son of a bitch!"

"Hey," said Ernie. "Watch your language!"

Neal was quick to answer. "Well, he is."

Ernie said, "What makes you say that?"

Bobby said, "He always threshes his grain first. Everybody else has to wait."

Neal added, "Other threshing crews draw straws. Not Millrud. He goes first, and someone always gets stuck in the rain. One year our wheat rotted in the field. Pa was gonna kill him."

"Well," said Ernie, "it's his rig, so I guess he figures he can do what he wants to."

Neal went on, "He's cheap, too. We picked mustard for him once. We worked for a whole day and he gave us a quarter. Not a quarter each. He gave us a quarter between us!"

Bobby added, "How about gophers? I trapped two for him and he gave me a lousy nickel. Millrud is stingy."

Ernie smiled and said, "Looks like you guys have to start a labor union." They walked up to the porch and sat down on the steps. He looked at Neal, then at Bobby. "I guess I should tell you boys, I think we're getting along okay, right?"

The boys looked at each other and then they looked back at Ernie. Neal said, "You scared the shit out of us!"

Ernie cut him off, "Hey! You can't use that word around me. I'm your teacher, remember?"

They laughed and Bobby said, "You're worse than our pa."

"Oh, yeah?" Ernie was smiling. He jumped to his feet and grabbed Bobby. He put him in a headlock and started tapping him on his head with his knuckles. "I'll show you how bad I am!" They all laughed and went inside the school. Ernie sat down behind his desk and the boys slid into their desk, side-by-side.

Ernie got out his list and said, "I've been thinking about the Halloween program. I've been trying to remember what we did when I went to country school. I have a book of plays here, but they all seem pretty dumb."

Neal said, "I ain't gonna be in any play. No, sir! Not me!"

Bobby said, "Remember that one Sampson did last year?"

Neal chuckled, "That was the dumbest thing."

Ernie asked, "What was it about?"

Bobby said, "It was about this little girl who wanted to be a witch for Halloween, but her mother wanted her to be a princess."

Ernie asked, "So what happened?"

Neal said, "Not much. It was just dumb."

Ernie thumbed through the book of plays and said, "Yeah, that one is in this book. I started reading it and you're right, it's really dumb." Ernie looked at the boys and started to smile. "I've got an idea. Maybe we should make up our own play?" The boys didn't say anything. They wanted to hear more. Then Ernie got an inspiration. "Have you ever seen an Abbott and Costello movie?"

Neal looked at Bobby, "Yeah, we saw that one last winter. They were in the Army."

Ernie said, *"Buck Private."*

Bobby said, "That's it. *Buck Private*. It was funny."

Ernie asked, "Do you listen to them on the radio?"

Neal said, "We used to, but we don't have a radio anymore." Neal corrected himself. "Well, we have a radio, but the batteries went dead, and Pa don't want to spend any money for new ones."

Ernie said, "That's too bad." He took out a sheet of paper and a pencil. "Reason I brought up Abbott and Costello, I think you could act like those guys and I'll help you write a play that we can do at the program."

"Not me," said Neal. "I'm not gonna be in any play!"

"Come on, Neal," said Ernie. "It'll be fun."

"I can't memorize my part," Neal said.

"We'll see about that. Now just listen to my idea. Neal, you're a little taller, so you'll be Abbott. Bobby, we'll put a pillow inside your sweater to fatten you up a little to play Costello."

Bobby started to laugh, "So what are we gonna do? Are we in the Army?"

"No, we'll do something completely different. How about if you're doctors operating on a patient? We could make a dummy for the patient, maybe take a couple of gunny sacks and stuff them with straw. We could put the dummy on my desk and cover it up with a sheet. Maybe stick a pair of boots on the end for his feet."

The boys had started to laugh. Neal said, "We should put some pig guts inside the dummy, and we start pulling out the guts."

Now Ernie was laughing. "I don't know. That would be pretty messy. And I don't know where we could get innards. Farmers don't butcher around here until freezing comes, right?"

Bobby said, "Maybe the guy has a motor inside him?"

Ernie leaned forward, "Now you're talking. So you start pulling out motor parts."

Bobby said, "We have an old pump engine on the back porch that's all torn apart."

Ernie said, "Ask your pa if you can borrow some parts."

Neal said, "We don't need to ask! We'll just take them."

The boys were out of their seats and excited. They hurried out the door and headed for home. Ernie leaned back in his chair and thought it over. *This is way too easy. It ain't supposed to be this way. Why have they done this big turnaround? Could it be all about fear? Were they that scared of me? Or do they like me?*

Ernie was puzzled and not totally convinced that their good behavior would last. He hoped he wouldn't have to rough them up again. That first day on the porch haunted him. He could not remember ever being that angry. It was the strangest feeling. He did not understand how he could have been so out of control, as if he were another person, but still in his own body.

Ernie spent the rest of the morning working in the classroom. He found the curtains for the Halloween program in the bottom cupboard in the library. He spread them across two rows of desks. They were like huge white sheets, four of them, two big ones for the main curtains which would be strung on a wire going across the front of the room from the north wall to the south wall. The other two were smaller. They were the side curtains to mask off the 'backstage' areas on each side. The curtains were musty and needed to be washed before the program.

Ernie was starting to feel tired. Loss of sleep was catching up with him. He heard the sound of Harvey Millrud's Hart Parr and went to the south window for a better look. Harvey had hooked up the big drive belt from the threshing machine to the tractor. He had cranked out the blower pipe for the straw, and it looked like he was ready for threshing on Monday. He went back to his chair, and making a pillow out of his arms on his desk, he laid his head down for a nap.

The next thing he heard was a voice coming from the doorway to the cloakroom. "I brought you something to eat."

Startled, Ernie looked up and saw Carla standing in the back holding a paper bag and a thermos jar. He stretched his arms over his head. "You caught me napping."

"Sorry to bother you. I thought you'd be hungry by now."

"As a matter of fact, I could use a bite to eat. I was feeling a little dizzy about an hour ago. Maybe that's what it was."

She walked to the front of the room, put the lunch bag and thermos on Ernie's desk, and sat down in a front row student's desk. He watched her pull her skirt up over her right knee to examine a bruise. She looked up and said, "Did you hear me stumble on the porch?"

"No." Ernie stood up and leaned across his desk. "Looks like you skinned yourself."

"Somebody left a bat on the steps. I put it away for you."

"Oh, gee. That was my fault. The Smierud boys were over here, and I told them they could use the bat."

"Neal and Bobby were here?" She sounded surprised.

"Yeah, I want to talk to you about those two." He opened a desk drawer and took out a first aid kit. "Maybe you should put some iodine on that scrape. There should be some Band-Aids in here, too." He handed Carla the box and watched her work on her knee. Ernie noticed her nice pair of legs.

Carla put a bit of iodine on her scrape. "Ouch! That stings!"

When she finished, Ernie put the kit in the desk drawer and said, "I was really tough on the Smieruds the first day of school."

Carla smoothed her skirt over her knee and said, "Yeah, Dale said you must have roughed them up pretty good."

"I didn't hurt them. But I let them know who's boss here."

"That's good. They need that."

"Since then, they've been nice as pie."

Carla nodded, "Good."

"They're almost too nice. It doesn't make sense they should suddenly change like that. Actually, I'm getting a little suspicious. Are they playing up to me, waiting for me to drop my guard?"

"I don't think you should worry about it. Big boys like Neal and Bobby understand one thing, brute force! It looks like that's what you showed them." She bent over Ernie's desk and laid out a cloth napkin and his lunch, a bologna sandwich and a bowl of potato salad. Ernie opened the thermos and poured himself a cup of black coffee. He ate his sandwich and thought about the big white curtains lying across the desk. "I was wondering if you could wash the curtains for the program."

"Yeah, I can do that. I'll take them right now as long as you have them out." Ernie got up to help her and she stopped him. "No, I'll take care of it."

"I can help you fold them."

"No. You just eat now. I'll handle the curtains."

Ernie watched her bundle up the curtains and carry them out to her pickup. Ernie finished up his sandwich and poured himself another slug of coffee. When Carla came back, he asked, "Did you notice the threshing machine out in the field?"

"Yeah, I just spoke to Harvey. He's waiting for his wife to give him a ride home. He told me they're supposed to start on Monday. We're next to the last on Harvey's list this year. I just hope the rain holds off." She looked up. "May the Lord be with us!"

"Did Dale tell you what we're going to do?"

"Yeah, he said you're taking the students out there to watch. Tom was wondering about that. You know, these kids see threshing every year, and it's nothing new to them."

"I understand that," said Ernie, a bit defensive. "I'm trying to turn threshing into a lesson. I'm working out ways to teach arithmetic, science, and even a little physics. And don't worry. I'll make sure the kids don't get in the way."

"Tom was telling Dale that they'd be better off sitting in their desks memorizing their spelling words or multiplication tables or reading. But that's just Tom."

"We'll be doing plenty of that, too. I just thought this would be a chance to teach in a more interesting way."

"I suppose," she said, not all that convinced. "Well, I'd better get going. Do you need anything from town?" She smiled, "How are you fixed for blades? They always say that on the radio."

Ernie laughed, "As a matter of fact, I could use a pack of razor blades. The one I used yesterday wouldn't cut butter."

"Single or double-edged?"

"Double." He took out his wallet. "Here, take this dollar."

"Put your money away," she said and waved goodbye. Then she turned at the door. "Supper will be late tonight and we won't be going to town. Tom and Dale are cutting the last of the wheat and they'll be working late. Which reminds me." She took a piece of paper and a pencil out of her skirt pocket and started to write. "Tom is running low on binder twine. I have to pick up a couple of bales at the elevator. He'll shoot me if I forget."

Ernie sipped his coffee and watched her hurry out the door. *What a remarkable woman. Everything about her is so pleasant.*

Carla had a twinkle in her eye, like his old hometown girlfriend, Lenore Swanson, who had waited on tables at Johnnie's Café in Thief River Falls. Ernie remembered sitting in the back booth many Saturday nights waiting for her to get off work. Then they'd park down by the river or up in the cemetery. She let him feel her breasts, but that was as far as he could go. Ernie had fallen in love and knew he would marry Lenore one day. Then this fat truck driver from Rugby, North Dakota, started stopping in on his way back from Duluth. He always sat at the counter, his big leather

111

wallet sticking out of his hip pocket, chained to his studded belt. He talked to Lenore about the bars in Duluth, his new car, and the money he made working overtime on long hauls.

Listening to him brag to his girlfriend made Ernie feel sick. One night, Lenore Swanson hung up her apron and took off with the truck driver. Ernie remembered calling after her, "Where the heck are you going?"

The last thing she said was, "See you in the funny papers!" He never saw her again. Two weeks later, Ernie left for the Army.

At the supper table that night, Tom asked Ernie if he'd like to come along to church in the morning. He said, "I'm reading the Bible lesson, and maybe you'd give me some pointers on how I could improve."

Ernie thought about that for a moment. There was something about this man, standing before a congregation of church-goers reading from the Bible that troubled Ernie. "I'll see how I feel in the morning. Maybe I could hear you run through it before you leave."

When Ernie woke up Sunday morning, he heard the cream separator whining down in the kitchen. He heard Carla say, "We'd better wake him up to see if he wants to go to church with us."

Ernie got up and looked at his black suit hanging in the wardrobe. Then he grabbed a pair of overalls and a work shirt, got dressed, and went downstairs. He sat down at the table and Carla placed a bowl of oatmeal and a cup of coffee before him. He thanked her and said, "I think I'll stay home this morning."

"Oh, yeah," said Tom. "I was hoping you'd come and hear me read."

"I'm sorry. Tomorrow's a big day, and I really want to spend the day planning."

"If you go to church," said Tom, "the Lord will help you."

Ernie thought that his own mother might have made the same comment. "I'm sure God would," he said.

"Well, suit yourself," he said. "But maybe you could listen to me practice my reading before we go."

"Sure thing," said Ernie.

"And don't be afraid to act like my schoolteacher."

"I'm sure you'll do just fine."

Tom went out the door with two pails of skim milk for the calves. Ernie and Carla talked at the table about canning. She opened the door to the pantry and showed Ernie the line of corn, beets, carrots, and string beans in quart-sized Mason jars sitting neatly on shelves. "I'm hoping to finish up this week. There'll be pumpkins, squash, and rutabagas to do. It's been quite a chore, and I'll be glad when it's done. But before you know it, there'll be potato picking, deer hunting, butchering, and sawing ice for the ice house. Uff da! The work never ends."

Dale came downstairs all dressed up for church, dark brown pants and white shirt. He held a green necktie in his hand. Carla slicked back his hair with her hand and said, "Maybe, Mr. Juvland can help you with your necktie."

"Sure thing," said Ernie, "but I'll have to tie it on myself first." When he finished, he said, "There you go. You look like a banker or a travelling salesman."

Dale giggled and Ernie excused himself. He went upstairs to make his bed. He opened his leather satchel and took out his logbook. He opened to the back page and read over the mistakes he had written down. He thought about them. *Not too bad for a first year teacher. They can't expect me to be perfect.*

He sat at the small desk under the window and started planning out his lessons for threshing day. He would give the older students the problem of figuring out how many bushels per acre the crop would yield. They needed to check the price of each grain, oats, barley, and wheat. They needed to find out what Mr. Dahl had paid for seed and ask if he had paid anyone to pick mustard. They needed to know how much Harvey Millrud charged for threshing. His students would tally the net profits of Mr. Dahl's harvest. He would ask the younger students to draw pictures and write sentences about what they saw. Ernie was getting excited.

After Tom got cleaned up and dressed in his suit and tie, he called Ernie down to the living room to hear him read the lesson for the day. Ernie sat in the stuffed chair and Carla and Dale sat on the davenport. Tom held the Bible and stood with one hand resting on top of the floor-model radio. Ernie noticed the Bible shaking in Tom's hand. "Okay," said Ernie, "nice loud voice. Remember the people sitting way back in the last pews."

Tom began, "Today's lesson is from Leviticus. Chapter 26, Verses 2-13." He cleared his throat and began to read.

Ye shall keep my Sabbaths, and reverence my sanctuary: I am the LORD. If ye walk in My statutes, and keep My commandments, and do them: then I will give you rain in due season, and the land shall yield her increase, and the trees of the field shall yield their fruit. And your threshing shall reach unto the vintage and the vintage shall reach unto the sowing time; and ye shall eat your bread to the full, and dwell in your land safely. And I will give peace in the land, and ye shall lie down, and none shall make you afraid: and I will rid evil beasts out of the land, neither shall the sword go through your land. And ye shall chase your enemies, and they shall fall before you by the sword. And five of you shall chase an hundred, and an hundred of you shall put ten thousand to flight: and your enemies shall fall before you by the sword. For I will have respect unto you, and make you fruitful, and multiply you, and establish My covenant with you. And ye shall eat old store, and bring forth the old because of the new. And I will set my tabernacle among you: and My soul shall not abhor you. And I will walk among you, and will be your God, and ye shall be My people.

"Thus ends today's lesson." Tom closed the Bible.

Carla clapped, "Very good, honey."

Tom looked at Ernie, "So what do you think, professor?"

"I think you'll do just fine," said Ernie. "The preacher better watch out or he'll lose his job."

"Thanks," Tom said, "I was nervous. I suppose it will be worse when I get up in front of the congregation."

Ernie said, "You'll do a good job, Tom. Don't worry."

Before they left for church, Carla told Ernie he would have to fix his own meals. She said, "We're going to the Vic's for Sunday dinner. It should be fun. Betty told me they bought two new reels for their View Master, one is on the Carlsbad Caverns and the other one is on the Grand Canyon. She said, 'It's so real, you feel like you can walk right into the pictures.' The Rollags are coming, too, so Dale and Susan will have a chance to see the pictures. I mentioned to Orvid we should buy a View Master for the school, but he thought it was a waste of money. No surprise there, eh? See you tonight."

Ernie waved goodbye and shouted, "Good luck on your reading, Tom!" as they pulled out of the yard and up the lane.

The sun was well over the trees to the east. It would be a warm, sunny day and Ernie decided to take a break from schoolwork and go for a walk. He went down to the gate next to the barn, and Tom's two big work horses came to greet him. They were Belgians, well-fed and friendly. Ernie rubbed their noses and pulled a few clumps of green grass to feed them. He thought about Bill and Roany, their broncos back on his farm, and wondered how they were getting along. These Belgians were surely a lot bigger.

Ernie walked over to the wheat field that Tom and Dale had cut the day before. Ernie had seen them when he came home from school. Tom drove the John Deere tractor and Dale rode the binder, tripping the bundle carrier. Ernie noticed Dale's straight windrows of bundles and made a mental note to compliment the boy on his good work.

It felt good being out in the field, and as if from habit, he picked up two bundles, one in each hand and started to shock. He had not done that in more than a year and welcomed the physical exercise. After a half hour of shocking, he walked back to the barn. He had never been inside before and was curious. The barn was empty except for a lone pigeon that watched him from a crossbeam overhead. The bird cooed and sounded like a mournful woman.

He walked along the stanchions of the cow stalls—there were eight of them. When he got to the back corner, he saw three feed sacks and a pile of hay. He stood still and stared at the pile of hay. *Maybe that's where he did it. But, maybe not. I must remember what Anders said about making assumptions.*

And four miles away, Tom Henning stood at the lectern before the congregation of the Bethany Lutheran Church and began to read. **Ye shall keep My Sabbaths, and reverence My sanctuary: I am the Lord.**

Chapter VIII...The Lesson

On Monday the day broke with a chill in the air, no clouds, no rain in sight. There would be threshing. When Ernie and Dale came out of the house ready for their trek to the school, Tom shouted at them from down by the barn. "You want a ride?" He had hitched his Belgian horses to the hay wagon and was ready to drive the team up to Mr. Dahl's threshing site.

Without answering, Dale and Ernie ran to jump on. They bumped along the road with their legs dangling over the side of the hayrack.

Tom stopped the team to drop them off in the schoolyard. He told Dale to be a good boy in school and then continued on to Harvey Millrud's threshing machine, which was ready for business, just beyond the playground.

Dale went to the swing set, and Ernie unlocked the door, went inside, and sat down behind his desk. As he listened to the children arriving for another week of school, he made final preparations for his threshing day lessons. At 8:30 Dale rang the big bell in the cupola and the children bustled into the classroom.

After opening exercises, Ernie brought the students to the south window, where they watched the farmers getting ready for a day of threshing. Two more farmers had driven their bundle wagons to the field, joining Tom. Ernie explained that horses were better to pull the bundle wagons than tractors, because it eliminated climbing on and off the tractor. When the farmer wanted to move from one shock to another, he didn't even have to handle the reins. He could just shout, "Giddyap," to his team, and they would move ahead until he yelled, "Whoa!"

Ernie pointed out the long drive belt that went from the pulley on the side of the tractor to the pulley on the side of the threshing machine. He asked them why it was twisted one-half turn. Even the older students were puzzled over the twisted drive belt until Ernie drew a picture on the board and explained, "By twisting the belt one-half turn, it changes the rotation of the pulley on the thresher. The tractor pulley turns in the opposite direction of the thresher pulley, but by twisting the belt, the thresher pulley turns in its proper direction."

116

He also talked about wheel ratio by using Peter's bicycle to illustrate how a larger drive sprocket would make the smaller sprocket turn the rear wheel faster. He set the bicycle upside down on his desk, and made a chalk mark on the rear tire. The students counted the number of turns the wheel made for one turn of the pedals. They discovered the bicycle sprockets had a three to one ratio. He asked the students to look for all the different sized pulleys on the threshing machine.

Next, Ernie turned to mathematics. He explained how grain fields and even whole farms were laid out in acres. He told them that an acre was just a little smaller than a football field from one goal line to the other. He wrote on the board, *4,840 square yards= 43,560 square feet.* He told them a good way to remember the size of one acre was to remember the number 'six'. He had them write two numbers in their notebooks, '66' and '660'. Then he had the older students multiply 660 by 66. He checked their work to make sure they came up with 43,560 square feet, the size of one acre.

Ernie continued, "Now you older students, we want to find out how many bushels of wheat Mr. Dahl will get per acre. That is called the 'yield' and a good yield would be about 40 bushels an acre. So what numbers do we have to know to figure out Mr. Dahl's yield?"

Ernie continued his lesson for another hour, going from the window to the blackboard to illustrate his points. At 10:00 a.m. he gave his students their last-minute instructions. "Now listen. There can't be any running around. Don't make any loud noises. I have promised Mr. Millrud that you would be on your best behavior and stay out of the way. Okay, grab your notebooks and let's quietly go out to the field."

Ernie led the way with the first and second graders holding hands. When they approached, the noise of the Hart Parr and the threshing machine excited the children. They sat in the field with their notebooks open. The lower grades began to draw pictures, and the older students were describing the operation in neat cursive writing.

The first bundle wagon approached from the east, loaded to the top with bundles of wheat. Tom Henning stood erect on top of the load and carefully drove his team close along the side to the thresher and brought them to a stop by the feeder house. This was a long metal extension to the thresher which served as the conveyer of the bundles to the knives which would cut the twine and the beaters which would push the opened bundle into the cylinder. Ernie had explained that the cylinder was the 'guts' of the machine. That's where the stalks would be threshed by more beaters until the kernels were separated from the hulls.

Tom moved to the back of the load, piled high, and started pitching the bundles onto the feeder house. When each bundle met the cylinder, the machine gave a groaning sound, whoooamp!

Ernie approached Harvey Millrud, who was standing off to the side, leaning on a pitchfork and watching Tom pitch bundles. He wanted to ask him a question about the half-bushel grain measurer at the top of the grain auger. As they stood there talking over the sound of the tractor and thresher, Ernie noticed a strange smell. He looked at the ground behind Harvey and saw a thin sliver of smoke. Ernie said, "There's something burning down there?" It was a string of lady finger firecrackers.

Harvey looked down and said, "What the hell?" In one motion he took his pitchfork and flicked the smoldering lady fingers out of the way. They sailed up in the air in a long arc, leaving a trail of blue smoke behind. But they went too far. They came to rest in the stubble under Tom Henning's horses. The firecrackers went off. Pow! Pow! Pow! Pow! Pow!

The children sprang to their feet, too startled to run. They stood and stared as the big Belgian horses leaped forward.

The team took off and Tom Henning lost his balance. He toppled head-over-heals backward from high on top of the load. He came down hard, his head and left shoulder smashing into the ground with a thud.

Ernie took off to catch the horses; they were heading for the road. They went into the ditch and came up on the road. The wagon tipped over, the hay rack came completely off, strewing the grain bundles in the ditch. The wagon was upside down with the wheels spinning in the air. The horses dragged the wagon down the road and Ernie followed, gasping for air in the cloud of dust.

A car approached from the south. Betty Vic was bringing coffee and a dishpan of sandwiches for the forenoon lunch. She stopped her car in the middle of the road and got out. The horses slowed to a walk and Ernie, still running at top speed, was able to catch one of them by the bridle. He dug his heels into the gravel. The horses dragged him for another 20 feet before they stopped.

Betty came running, "What the heck is going on?"

"Here, hold the bridle; I have to unhitch the wagon." Ernie unhooked the tugs from the singletrees. He unclipped the yoke at the end of the pole from the hame-straps, and the horses were free. He grabbed the reins and drove the team back to the threshing rig, leaving the wagon upside-down on the shoulder of the road. Betty climbed back in her car and drove to the schoolyard.

As he came closer to the rig, Ernie could see his students. They had gone back to the school and stood in a bunch along the south windows. The tractor and threshing machine stood idle. Orvid Skime came running toward Ernie. He grabbed the reins and blurted out, "What the hell were you doing, bringing the kids out here?" He was breathing heavily, spewing tobacco juice in Ernie's face as he yelled, "You're one stupid son of a bitch, you know that? Get up to the rig and face the music! Harvey is madder than a wet hen, and I don't blame him. Son of a bitch!"

A half dozen men stood in a circle at the side of the threshing machine, looking down at Tom Henning, lying motionless on the ground. Harvey met Ernie and yelled, "Goddamn it! I knew something like this would happen! What do you have to say for yourself now?" Ernie walked by him and approached the circle of farmers. Two of them parted and Ernie could see Tom, lying on his back. Dale was on his knees near his father's head, sobbing heavily.

Mr. Vic said, "He was knocked out, but he's come to. He said it's his back. I called Carla. She should be on her way."

Ernie kneeled down and put his arm around Dale. The crying boy pulled himself away and ran up to the school. Ernie moved close to Tom, whose eyes were closed. "I'm sorry, Tom." He placed his fingers on his neck and could feel his pulse. It was rapid, but steady. "Stay still. We'll get you some help right away."

Tom opened his eyes and looked up at Ernie. He managed to speak, "My horses?" And then he closed his eyes again.

"Your horses are fine, Tom. I caught them and brought them back. Don't worry about that. We're going to get you to a doctor. Just stay put and don't move. Carla is coming."

Tom Henning lay still. He closed his eyes and whispered, "I'm shot now. My father's farm is lost."

Ernie called off school for the rest of the day and sent the students home. Carla came with the pickup and drove it out to where the farmers had laid Tom Henning on a twelve-inch plank. When she got out of the truck, she ran to her husband, "I'm so sorry, Tom. We're bringing you to Fargo. I called Pop Andrews at the funeral home, but the hearse isn't available. I'm gonna take you in the pickup. I'll ask Ernie to ride in the back with you."

Tom managed to speak with his eyes closed, "Tell someone to get my horses home."

"Don't worry, dear. Someone will take care of that." Then she turned to Mr. Dahl, "There are quilts in the pickup." He went to get them. He and Harvey Millrud wrapped Tom in two heavy quilts, and secured him to the board with a clothesline. Ernie, Orvid, and Vic helped them carefully lift Tom off the ground and carry him to the back of the pickup. Ernie climbed in the back. He sat on a toolbox next to Tom's head, and Carla climbed into the cab. Dale crawled inside the pickup and moved close to his mother. Carla backed the pickup away from the farmers. They stood and watched as she slowly drove across the field, through the schoolyard, and up to the main road.

Ernie sat on a bench in the waiting room of St. Lukes Hospital in Fargo thinking about the Smierud boys and why they were nowhere in sight when he dismissed the rest of the students. Dale sat next to him, his hands folded in his lap and his head down. Ernie heard him praying in a whisper. They had been there all afternoon, waiting for Tom to come out of surgery.

When Carla finally appeared, Dale had stretched out on the long bench and dozed off. Carla motioned Ernie to come to her. She looked at Dale, and then stood on her tiptoes to whisper in Ernie's ear. "I don't want Dale to know. It doesn't look so good. He has no feelings in his legs." She turned away from Ernie and started back toward the door. She stopped, turned around, and whispered to Ernie, "I'm gonna sit with him tonight. You should take Dale home and fix him something to eat. Can you and Dale do the milking?"

"Don't worry about that. We'll take care of the chores." Ernie thought for a moment. "When you get a chance, tell Tom how sorry I am. It was my fault. I never should have taken the kids out there."

"Just take care of Dale, please. Get him something to eat. I'm not sure how much gas we've got in the pickup. You should maybe stop and put on a dollar's worth." She reached in her purse.

Ernie stopped her. "Don't worry. I've got money."

"No you don't," she insisted and handed Ernie a dollar bill. Ernie watched her turn, open the door to the hall, and disappear.

Dale was quiet in the pickup on the way home. Ernie stopped at the mailbox to get the mail and the *St. Paul Pioneer Press.* When he climbed back in, Dale said, "I know who did it."

Ernie didn't say anything as he turned into the Henning's lane. But Dale continued, "I'm not sure if it was Bobby or Neal, but I know it was one of them."

"Did you see them throw the firecrackers?" asked Ernie.

"No, but I heard them talking outside before school. They wanted to get back at Harvey Millrud. They hate him and call him bad names." Ernie had nothing more to say.

They brought the cows into the barn and did the milking together. Dale cranked the cream separator and Ernie heated up a can of soup. After the calves and pigs were fed, Dale cleaned up and went to bed. Ernie sat at the kitchen table and read about the war in the newspaper. He thought about his brothers and his mother alone on the farm and wondered if he had done the right thing. *Why am I here, in a strange house, in a strange community? Trying to teach school. It all seems so stupid now.* Tears came to his eyes. He shoved the paper aside, laid his head down on the table, and began to sob. He stayed there with his head on his folded arms until he fell asleep.

The phone woke him up—two longs and two shorts. He went to the phone, which hung on the wall near the door and said, "Hello."

"Ernie, this is Betty Vic. Just calling to find out how Tom's doing? Is Carla there?"

"No," said Ernie. "She's staying over at the hospital in Fargo."

"Oh, yeah? How's he doin'?"

Ernie lowered his voice, "Well, it doesn't look so good. Carla told me he has no feelings in his legs."

"Oh, gosh!"

"Yeah, I'm here with Dale. He took it pretty hard."

"Do you need any help over there?"

121

"No, Dale and I got the milking done. And we'll take care of the chores in the morning before school. He's only milking four right now, so that's not too bad."

"Yeah, you poor thing. Too bad this had to happen."

"It was all my fault—any way you look at it."

"Don't take it out on yourself. How would you know?" She broke off and was silent. They both heard a click and the sound of a radio in the background. Then Betty yelled, "Get off the damned phone. I'm talkin' here!" There was another click.

Ernie asked, "Did someone take care of Tom's horses?"

"Yeah," she said. "Orvid has them over at his place. They got the wagon off the road, but the hayrack is still in the ditch. The wagon is shot. I guess they'll have to get along with only two bundle wagons tomorrow. But they'll manage. You shouldn't have to worry about that."

Ernie thanked her and told her that he and Dale would be okay. He hung up, blew out the kerosene lamp, and went up to bed.

Threshing continued the next day, but Ernie kept the students inside and followed a strict schedule, arithmetic in the morning followed by reading, with each class taking their turns coming to the bench in front for recitation. There was no talk about the threshing lesson and no mention of the Halloween Basket Social. The students were quiet and obedient. All through the arithmetic lessons, Ernie kept his eye on the clock. Neal and Bobby Smierud did not show up for the 8:30 bell, and he wondered just how late they would be.

I have to get this off my mind or I'll go nuts. Over and over, I see Tom tumbling off that wagon. Even now, the roar of the threshing machine sounds like voices. There it is again. This time it sounds like someone laughing at me. I must turn off the sounds in my brain. Have to get tough with myself now. I have to do my job.

After lunch, he took out the bat and softball and called the students over to home plate. Ernie kept the first and second graders behind the backstop and sent the rest of the kids to the outfield. Ernie was ready to teach the little kids how to bat. "When we choose up sides for softball, everyone is going to play. That means everyone bats. And you younger kids remember, if you make an out, it counts the same as a big kid making an out. So we're going to teach you how to swing the bat." Three of the older kids, two girls and one boy, took turns pitching and Ernie got down on his knees behind each little kid to help the boy or girl hold the bat and swing. As soon as the little batter hit the ball, Ernie would yell, "Now run! Run like a deer for first base!"

Recess passed, and the kids had a good time. But back at his desk, the accident continued to play over and over in Ernie's mind, as the sound of the threshing machine and Harvey Millrud's Hart Parr droned across the stubble field and murmured in his ears. Ernie looked across the empty desk of the Smierud brothers during the afternoon lessons. It bothered him. *I need to talk to those boys. I made a good start with them and can't give up now.* By four o'clock they had finished threshing, the last wagonload of wheat had left for Mr. Dahl's granary, and Harvey Millrud was making ready to move his rig to the next farm.

Ernie stood on the porch and said goodbye to each of his students. He noticed Orvid Skime coming up to the school. He told his daughter, Eunice, "Go get Dale and you two wait in the car! I need to talk to your teacher."

He approached Ernie, and stood planted, with his legs spread apart and his arms folded across his chest. He fixed on Ernie's eyes and said, "I could say I told you so, but I ain't gonna bother with that. You'll have to live with it, one way or another." He took a step closer to Ernie, and then planted himself again. "A man broke his back yesterday and might not ever walk again. I just got a call from Tom's wife. We're gonna take Dale over to the Vic's until Tom can come home." He paused and looked down at the ground. "In a wheelchair, I suppose. We're gonna get someone to take care of their chores. And as soon as we can find another teacher, we're gonna tell you to pack up your stuff and get the hell out of here!" He turned and walked back to his Model A, leaving Ernie alone on the porch.

Inside, Ernie stood by the south window and watched Harvey Millrud roll up the long drive belt. He carried it to the top of the thresher and tied it down. Ernie watched him crank in the long, metal blower pipe and secure it to the top of the rig. Then he folded in the feeder house and fastened it tight. Ernie stayed by the window and watched Harvey back the Hart Parr up to the thresher, hitch it to the drawbar, and slowly pull the rig out of the field, through the schoolyard, and up to the main road.

Ernie went back to his desk, which was piled high with workbooks, and with the sound of the tractor fading away, he took out a red pencil and started to grade the students' work. When he finished, he opened his logbook to the back page. He wrote, *I let my enthusiasm get away with me. Stop and think before you act. Use caution in all activities with your students. Listen to the advice of parents. Stop being such an idiot. I will live with Tom's injury the rest of my life.* He closed his logbook and looked at his watch. It was five o'clock.

He went outside and walked over to the spot where the threshing machine had stood. He kneeled down at a pile of weed seeds the shakers of the machine had sifted out and left on the ground. He scooped up a handful and spread the seeds out in his open palm. He noticed the different colors, yellow, brown, black, and a few red ones. He remembered doing the same thing on his farm as a kid. He ran his fingers through the seeds and examined them carefully. He thought about this amazing machine, with a number of shaking grates that could separate the weed seeds from the grain. *These colorful seeds have been sorted out and left lying in a pile in the field. They've been rejected. But I'll use these seeds. The older students could identify them, if I can find a picture book of seeds. The younger children could use the seeds for an art project, maybe make a mosaic. I'll bet they could use a needle and thread to string them together for a colorful necklace.*

The ideas began to work on the young teacher's mind. He went to the woodshed and found an old flour sack. Using his hands, he scooped the seeds into the sack. When the sack was full, he carried it back to the school and put it in the corner next to the science cabinet. He sat down at his desk and looked around the room. He slammed his fist down on the top of the desk and said out loud, "Goddamn it! This is my school, and they ain't gonna kick me out!" He had one more thing to do that he couldn't put off. He buckled up his leather satchel, locked the front door, and walked up the lane to the Smierud farm.

Bobby and Neal saw him coming and lit out for the woods behind the house. Ernie saw them run away and stopped. He wondered if he should turn back and leave well enough alone. *No. I have a job to do. I have to take care of this right now.* He walked around to the back of the house and yelled for them. "Boys, I need to talk to you!" No answer. He yelled again, "I'm going to wait

124

here until you come out. If you're real men, you'll come talk to me. Cowards hide, but real men face the music!" There was still no reply. Ernie walked through the weeds to a rusted sickle bar mower. He put his satchel down by the iron wheel, and climbed onto the seat. There he sat, thinking. *I'll wait right here for them. They have to come out sooner or later.*

He looked around and didn't see any car except for a rusted Model T smothered in weeds over by the outhouse. On the back porch he saw the pump engine the boys had mentioned. He noticed an iron bed frame, a spring, and a mattress leaning against the wall. There were cardboard boxes and a pile of old clothes in a big chair, which had stuffing coming out of its armrests. Cats of different colors were coming in and out of a hole in the screen door. Off to the side Ernie saw an old Maytag washing machine, with a wringer on top. The lid was open, and weeds were growing out of the inside. He saw a circle of dirt around an elm tree with a dog chain tied to the tree. The dog was gone.

He sat on the mower for several minutes before Neal and Bobby came out of the woods. They stopped about twenty feet from Ernie and stood with their hands in their pockets and heads down. Ernie looked carefully and saw that Neal had a black eye. "Who hit you?"

Neal looked up, put a knuckle against one nostril, and blew a wad of snot out the other. He wiped his hand on his overalls and said, "We had a fight."

"You boys were fighting?"

Bobby moved a few steps closer, "Orvid Skime came over last night, and him and the old man got into a fight. He had Pa down and was punching him in the face. I went to pull him off. Then Orvid got up and started swinging at me and Neal. He got Neal pretty good."

Ernie got up off the mower and walked to the boys. He tilted Neal's head back to examine his eye. It was bloody around the edges. "Your dad needs to get you to a doctor. Is he in the house?"

Neal said, "No. He's in town."

Ernie put his arm around Neal, but the boy pulled away. They started for the back porch, but Ernie stopped them. "You did a dumb thing, boys, but I'm not going to give up on you." They stopped and looked at each other. "Did you hear me? We're going

125

to take care of this the best we can. You're going to learn from this mistake."

Neal yelled back, "We were just having some fun."

Ernie said, "But it didn't turn out fun, did it? You didn't stop to think. Now both of you are going to face up to throwing those firecrackers and it will start tomorrow. We're going to have a student meeting first thing in the morning. We're going to talk about this as a group. And we'll decide together what is best."

Neal said, "We won't be there!"

Ernie was irritated, "So, what are you—afraid to face your classmates?"

Neal said, "We won't be there tomorrow or ever."

Ernie walked up to them, "What are you talking about?"

Neal answered, "We're quitting school."

Bobby added, "We're both over 14. Pa said we could quit school."

Ernie thought for a moment, "Okay, you're right. They can't make you go to school once you're 14. But is that what you should do?"

They didn't answer their teacher. They turned, walked up the steps of the porch, and went in the house. Ernie yelled after them, "You'll regret it!" He waited for an answer. Then he picked up his satchel and walked back to the school.

From the road he could see three large cardboard boxes sitting on the porch, shoved up against the door. He went over and opened one of the boxes. There was a note from Anders, *For you and your students. Best wishes, Anders Lund.* It was a complete set of *Encyclopedia Americana,* latest edition. Ernie smiled, put the boxes inside the school, and walked home.

Ernie had a lot to think about as he did the milking that night. The yellow lantern light made shadows inside the barn, strange black images on the ceiling and walls. They appeared like distorted demons that had come to haunt him. They hovered about like warnings of bad things to come. When a cow moved, the demons moved, drawing closer to Ernie's brain, where the voices of the Army psychiatrists still echoed.

"Adjustment disorder with depressed moods." It was there in writing on my discharge papers. I remember scoffing at it, but maybe they were right. But I can't keep thinking about that. I have

126

a job to do. Right now, I'm milking a cow. Think about that. Keep your mind on what you're doing.

He leaned his head against the flank of the cow and listened to the squirts of milk against the bottom of the pail. The noise sounded like bursts of laughter. The cow had been in the slough, up to her waist in mud, and her tail was wet with mud and scum. She swatted her tail against the back of Ernie's head. He grabbed the wet tail and squeezed it between his left knee and the side of the milk pail.

I wonder if they would actually fire me. Orvid Skime has already made up his mind, but how could he make that decision on his own? Maybe Carla will speak up for me. Maybe there are other parents who think I'm doing a good job. But maybe not. Just like the Army. I wasn't cut out to be a soldier. Maybe I'm not cut out to be a teacher either.

Ernie spent the rest of the week following the regular schedule at school, but all the time the possibility of being fired loomed. He tried to be cheerful with his students, but it wasn't easy. Carla was still staying overnight at the hospital and they had not found anyone to do the chores. So Ernie continued to do the milking each night, four cows, and then the separating and feeding the calves and pigs. By the time he fixed himself something to eat and finished his schoolwork, it was always near midnight before he went to bed.

Saturday came and Harvey Millrud was setting up his rig on the Henning farm. The crew would be arriving soon. To avoid facing Orvid, Dahl, and Harvey, Ernie decided to go over to see Anders. When he came down the lane, Anders was sitting on the front steps reading the local newspaper. "Hello, Mr. Juvland. To what do I owe your visit on this fine autumn day?"

"Hello, neighbor," said Ernie. "I wanted to thank you for the encyclopedias. That was mighty generous of you."

"Don't mention it. Glad I could help out."

"Well, they certainly will help the students." Ernie paused. "If you aren't busy right now, I'd like to talk to you. Did you hear about Tom's accident?"

"Yes, I heard about it in town this morning. Terrible tragedy."

"And I suppose they're all blaming me."

127

"No, I didn't hear anything like that." He shook Ernie's hand and patted him on the back. "Come in, come in. I just put on a pot of coffee. Are you ready for a cup?"

"That's sounds good."

Ernie sat down at the table and Anders brought the coffee pot. "I hope you like it strong. Most people around here make coffee that tastes like dishwater. I like it strong."

Anders sat down and slid the newspaper over to Ernie. "I see where a couple of your schoolboys made the front page. Everybody in town is talking about it."

Ernie stared at the headline. **Local Teenage Boys Shoot up Town.** He looked up at Anders and said, "Then it was true. Some of my students were talking about it yesterday, but I just thought they were making up stories. I didn't give it a second thought."

Anders said, "I saw a couple of the stores. The windows were boarded up with plywood. They must have had one hell of a time. Like the wild, wild West."

Ernie read from the newspaper.

This past Thursday, near midnight, two Jackson Township teenage brothers, Neal and Robert Smierud, broke into Whiteley's Hardware Store in Sparborg by smashing a front window. They stole a rifle, two shotguns, a pistol, and several boxes of ammunition. They walked down Main Street shooting out store windows and street lights. Officer Peter Mosby was out of town visiting a brother in Detroit Lakes.

Front windows in the following stores were shot out with shotgun blasts: Rude's Clothing, Marchand's Drug Store, Kline's Bakery, Balfe Insurance Company, and the Town Café. They barricaded the front door of the Town Café and continued to fire round after round at windows across the street. The barrage continued until they apparently ran out of ammunition. When Wilmot County Sheriff Kahl arrived with his deputy, they forced their way into the café and found the Smierud brothers. Four hamburgers were frying on the kitchen stove, and the boys were sitting in the back booth, eating a lemon meringue pie and chocolate ice cream.

Chapter IX...The Strange Visitor

Carla came home from the hospital on Sunday morning. Vic gave her a ride over to the farm so she could dress for church. When she was ready, she came out of the house and approached Ernie, who was by the woodshed splitting kindling. "Are you sure you don't want to come to church with me?"

Ernie rested on the handle of his ax and thought for a moment, "No. I think I'll stay home. You need wood split for winter, and I don't mind doing it."

"You really don't have to do that you know."

"I don't mind," he said and gave another chunk a whack, splitting it clean.

"They're coming over this afternoon," she said.

"Who's that?"

"Vic and Orvid."

"So, are you going to give me my walking papers?"

"Well, if it was up to Orvid, you'd already be gone." She moved closer to Ernie and saw the sadness in his eyes. She shook her head and said, "I shouldn't have said that. I'm sorry." She reached out to hug him. She held him tightly and softly said, "I don't want you to go."

"I don't want to leave," he said. "I've got a job to do here—teaching these youngsters. I might have failed with Neal and Bobby, but I'm not giving up on the rest of them."

"I know you won't." She turned to get in the pickup. "Dale will be coming home with me after church. He misses you."

"Well, I miss him, too. He's my buddy."

She climbed in the pickup and closed the door. She rolled down the window and said, "I'll say a prayer for you."

"Thanks. I need it. And say one for yourself, too." She smiled and waved. Ernie watched her drive up the lane, and then he went back to splitting wood. Most of the chunks were poplar, which were dry and easy to split. The sun was well up and Ernie was working up a good sweat. He took off his jacket and sat down on the splitting block to rest. Across the pasture to the east he saw a young man in a red and black plaid shirt and a baseball cap approaching. He came striding up to Ernie and stood with his hands in his pockets. Ernie stood up and asked him what he wanted.

With a slight grin he said, "I'm supposed to work here."

That's all he said. Ernie figured he was maybe 19 or 20 years old. The stranger's eyes darted around from the barn to the house, to the woodshed—only glancing at Ernie, who wondered if there was something wrong with him. He had a twitch at the side of his mouth. And when he took off his cap to wipe his forehead, Ernie noticed that his head was shaved.

Finally he said, "I'm Timmy Burstrom. We live over there." He turned and pointed toward the pasture beyond the gate.

Ernie stuck out his hand, "I'm Ernie Juvland."

Burstrom shook his hand, "Yeah, I know. You're the schoolteacher. I know about you. Tom told me." He looked around the yard. "When's he coming home from the hospital?"

"I'm not sure." Ernie was trying to figure out what was wrong with this young man.

"Is Carla home?" Again his eyes darted around the yard.

"No, she's at church."

Burstrom smiled out of the corner of his mouth. "You wanna see something?"

"What's that?"

"Don't tell anyone. They might take it away from me." He reached in his back pocket and pulled out a stick of wood that had been neatly carved and polished smooth. He held it close to Ernie's face. It was a penis about ten inches long.

Ernie took a step backward and wondered if he should reach for the ax.

"Do you like it?" The young man showed a wide grin. "I made it myself. I like to whittle."

Ernie turned around and went back to the splitting block. He sat down and wondered what to say.

The young man grinned and said, "If Carla was here, I'd show it to her."

Ernie spoke up, "I don't think you should do that."

"Why not? She'd laugh. I like Carla and I like Dale, too."

Ernie watched Burstrom rubbing his wooden penis and grinning. Then he put the carving back in his pocket and his face grew serious. "They said you're a little funny in the head. Is that

130

right?" He waited for Ernie to say something. Then he said, "You seem normal enough to me."

Ernie managed to smile. "Yeah, I guess you could say that I'm pretty normal." He got up again and looked down toward the barn. "Did someone ask you to come over here?"

"No. I was over here for threshing yesterday. I found out Tom was in the hospital, and Carla and Dale would need help, so I came over. Have you done the milking?"

Ernie wanted to get rid of the young man—the sooner, the better. "Yeah, I did all the chores this morning."

"It must be funny to see a schoolteacher doing milking." He was grinning again.

"I grew up on a farm. I've done a lot of milking."

"Tom used to have a bull, but he sold it. I used to watch his bull jump on the cows. Boy, that bull had a big one, and it was pointed on the end. I remember one time, Carla was watching, too. She was standing right by me, and I asked her if she liked what the bull was doing. I was getting a lump in my pants. Do you know what I mean?" He grabbed himself by the crotch and began to cough and laugh hysterically.

Ernie had been leaning on the ax handle and now his grip grew tighter. "Look, I think you'd better come back later."

Burstrom took a step toward him and reached for the ax. "I can split that wood for you."

Ernie swung the ax out of the way, "No you don't!" They both froze and stared at each other. "I'll do the splitting myself." Ernie grabbed another chunk and put it on the splitting block. Before he raised the ax he turned to Burstrom and said, "I think you should get on home now."

The young man's face grew sad. It seemed to Ernie that he was about to cry. His voice was pleading, "Don't you like me?"

"You're just fine, but I think you should go back home." Ernie waited for him to leave, but he just stood there, with his head down and his hands in his pockets, scuffing the dirt with his shoe. Then Ernie said, "Please go now. I'll tell Carla you were here."

Burstrom turned and started running for the pasture. Ernie watched him scramble over the gate. The wooden penis fell out of his pocket. He bent over to pick it up and said, "You don't like me, teacher!" Then he ran full speed up through the pasture and disappeared behind a thicket of willow bushes. Ernie watched him

131

until he was gone. He raised the ax over his head and slammed it into an oak chunk, splitting it clean and leaving the ax stuck firmly in the splitting block.

He left it there and walked up to the house. Alcohol addiction ran through Ernie's family, and he was aware of his own craving from time to time. He was usually able to control the impulse, but not now. He needed a drink, badly. He found Tom's bottle of brandy on the top shelf of the cupboard. He took a glass and filled it to the brim.

He went out on the porch and sat on the steps. The brandy burned on the way down, but to Ernie, the burning was good. He looked around the yard, the red barn, the woodshed, the toilet, and the pump house. He remembered the first time Vic brought him to this farm. *All the way on the bus I was imagining what the place would look like. And when we pulled into the yard, it was everything I had hoped for. Now, three weeks later, it's all changed. It's like an ugly dust storm has hit this place. The buildings have lost their color. Two of my eighth grade boys have quit school and are probably sitting in jail right now. Tom Henning is in the hospital with a broken back, the last teacher was raped, and now I'm paid a visit by a crazy neighbor who carves wooden cocks. What's going on here? This place could drive a man crazy!* He gulped down the rest of his brandy, washed out his glass, went up to his room, and lay down on his bed.

He thought about Orvid and Vic coming over in the afternoon. He wondered what he'd tell them. *Sure it was my fault. I know about horses. I know how easily they can be spooked. I kept the children far enough back and told them they had to be very still and quiet. But then the lady fingers came flying through the air. Why did Harvey flick them out of the way with his fork? Couldn't he have just stepped back? They were just little firecrackers. It wasn't like they had thrown a stick of dynamite at the man.*

Over and over, the events played out in Ernie's mind. But the brandy soon kicked in. The tension slowly left the muscles of his legs, arms, and stomach. He was slightly dizzy, but relaxed. He slowly drifted off to sleep.

When he woke up, it was just past noon. He heard voices downstairs, different voices. Men were talking, and he heard dishes clattering. Mixed with the sounds, he heard the strange voice of Timmy Burstrom, saying over and over, "You don't like me."

He went downstairs and into the kitchen. He looked around for the strange young man, but he wasn't there. Orvid and Vic had finished eating, and Carla was pouring coffee for them. He noticed Dale through the open door, sitting on the front porch steps playing with his slingshot. It was all very strange to Ernie. All the movements had slowed down, even his own footsteps as he moved over to the table and sat down. He felt lightheaded and wondered if he was dreaming or actually awake.

Carla said, "We tried to be quiet. I'll bet we woke you up?"

Ernie said, "I slept too long anyway." He greeted Orvid and Vic, who sat across from him. He watched Carla move toward the stove. She seemed to glide without moving her legs.

"I kept your plate warm for you." Carla opened the oven door and took out a plate of ham, fried potatoes, and squash; she placed it on the table before Ernie. She brought out a pumpkin pie and started cutting it into six neat wedges.

The men ate in silence. Ernie heard the slap of Dale's slingshot coming from the porch. He looked out the open door and saw the boy. He was trying to hit a coffee can he had set out in the yard. Then Orvid spoke up. "How are you getting along, Ernie?"

Ernie was surprised at the kindness in his voice. He thought for a moment and realized this was the first time Orvid had called him 'Ernie'. He wiped some grease off his lip with a cloth napkin and said, "I'm doing okay, I guess." Then he added, "Considering everything that's happened."

Orvid took a bite of pumpkin pie. "Carla tells me you've been doing all the chores here by yourself, and still teaching school on top of that—you're a hard worker."

Ernie appreciated his tone of voice. "It's been okay. Somebody has to do it."

Orvid went on, "I saw you run after Tom's horses. You can run pretty damned good. I used to run like that, but not anymore."

Carla said, "I told Tom—the first thing you did was run after the team. He appreciated that."

"Yeah," said Orvid. "That was the right thing to do."

Ernie ate his fried potatoes and wondered where this conversation was going. *They're supposed to talk about firing me. Why are they talking about Tom's horses?*

Orvid cleared his throat. "I suppose you got the lowdown on the Smierud boys."

Ernie figured that would come up. "I saw the article in the local paper."

Vic asked, "Did you see the one in the *Fargo Forum*?"

"No, I didn't," answered Ernie.

Orvid said, "I heard it was in the *Minneapolis Star,* too."

Carla said, "Those rascals really put our town on the map!"

Ernie looked at Orvid and asked, "What's going to happen to them, do you think?"

"Juvenile correction, most likely." Orvid put down his fork. "They should lock them up in Stillwater, in a regular prison. Juvenile correction is a joke!"

Vic spoke up. "You did the best you could, Ernie."

Ernie took a deep breath and let it out. "You know, I thought I was getting through to them. And then they came with those firecrackers. I just don't know." Ernie noticed they had all stopped eating and were looking at him as if they were waiting for him to say more. "They had it in for Harvey Millrud. They told me about their dad's grain rotting in the fields, because Harvey always did Ben Smierud's threshing last."

Orvid interrupted, "Did they tell you about the tire iron stuck in a bundle?"

Ernie was surprised, "No. Someone did that?"

"Awhile back, old man Smierud had been on the outs with Harvey for a couple of years, and one night—he was most likely drunk—he took a tire iron and stuck it inside a bundle of oats."

Vic corrected him. "It was barley, but you always say it was oats."

Orvid went on, "Oats, barley, what's the difference? Let me tell the story. Next day, we were all there threshing over at Vic's place, and that bundle went into the rig and smashed the hell out of the knives and beaters, even the cylinder was shot to smithereens. It shut everything down for a week. We were waiting for parts from Milwaukee."

Vic piped up, "Racine. You always say Milwaukee, but I.J. Case is in Racine."

Orvid shot back at Vic, "Well, since you know everything, I'll just shut up!"

Vic smiled and said, "Sorry, Orvid. There's nothing more to say, except that Smierud and Harvey Millrud have been on the outs ever since. End of story."

Carla spoke up, "I feel sorry for those two boys. Their dad just went to pot after their mother drowned. I don't know. What can you do?" She looked at Ernie. "If you ever went over there, and saw the way they live. Ish! I just don't know where they even get money for food."

Ernie turned to her, "I was over there."

"Really?" asked Orvid.

"Yeah," Ernie explained. "I went over there one day after school—I guess it was Tuesday. They ran in the woods when they saw me coming, but they finally came out. I tried to explain how serious their prank was. They had no idea how badly Tom was hurt. I think they had a lot of regrets about what they did. I told them that I wouldn't give up on them, and then they told me they were going to quit school. I tried to talk them out of it. They told me they were over 14, and they could do what they wanted to do."

Orvid said, "I look at it this way. There wasn't much you could do with them."

Vic pushed his chair back and put his napkin next to his plate. "Well, I suppose..."

Orvid wiped his mouth with his napkin and said, "Yeah, we should get going."

Ernie got up and asked, "Orvid, the last time you talked to me, you said I was finished as soon as you found another teacher. Does that still stand?"

Orvid reached for his hat on the back of his chair and said, "I have my faults, Ernie. They can tell you. Ask Carla and Vic here." He slapped Vic on the back. "I have a temper. Eunice and Chub will tell you, too. I'm a stubborn son of a bitch and I shoot my mouth off." He started for the door and turned. "Most of it is just talk. So long, Ernie."

Ernie stopped Vic, as he started to leave. "I had to order some school supplies from Northern Supply. I paid for it with one of my own checks."

"Good enough," said Vic. "Keep the receipt when you get the order, and we'll pay you back with money from the Halloween Social."

"Okay," said Ernie. He followed the men out, waved goodbye to them, and sat down on the steps next to Dale, who was still shooting at the coffee can. "I've missed you. How've you been getting along?"

Dale looked up at Ernie. "Okay, I guess. I heard them talking to you in the kitchen. I'm glad you'll still be my teacher."

"So am I, pal. I'm pretty happy right now." Ernie put his arm around the boy. "Nice slingshot. May I have a look at it?" Dale handed him the slingshot. "You've got these nice thick rubbers. Where did you find those?"

"Pa got them from the garage in town. They're from a truck inner tube."

"I see that. They're the best. Have you seen the inner tubes they've been making since the war started?

"Yeah, they're no good."

"They're called Butyl Tubes. It isn't real rubber. It's a synthetic."

Dale put a stone in the pouch, drew back, and let fly. Ping! He knocked over the coffee can.

"Gee willikers! Nice shot, buddy!"

Dale smiled and went out to grab the coffee can, and then he ran down to the gravel pile behind the barn to get more stones.

When he came around the far corner, someone was waiting for him. It was Timmy Burstrom. "Hello, Dale." He had come up behind the boy and put him in a head lock. Dale tried to yell out, but Timmy's strong arm was pressing against his windpipe. "You be quiet now, Dale, or I'll have to hurt you." Still holding Dale around the neck, Timmy reached in his pocket and pulled out the wooden penis. "Do you know what this is, Timmy? It's a cock. I think your ma would like it." Dale fought to get free, but Timmy held him fast around the neck.

While Dale was struggling behind the barn, hidden from view, Carla came out of the house and sat down on the steps next to Ernie. She patted him on the knee and said, "I told you so, right? I told you they'd never fire you."

"I guess you did. Thanks. I have an idea you spoke up for me."

"Both Vic and I did. It took some talking, but Orvid finally came to his senses. I think it's because Eunice really likes you. What am I saying? All the kids like you!"

"Well, I feel a lot better now, and I think I'll go up to the school and do some work before milking."

"Oh, I forgot to tell you. I found us a hired man. He's worked for us before and he'll be able to do both the morning and evening chores."

Ernie looked at her, "You mean this kid Burstrom?"

"Timmy Burstrom? Heavens, no. How do you know him?"

"He came over here."

"When? This morning?"

"Yeah, right after you left for church. He said he was going to help with chores."

"He's supposed to be in Fergus. I guess they let him out."

"You mean Fergus Falls? The mental hospital?"

"His mother had him committed—I think it was the end of May. He's not right in the head, poor thing. But he doesn't hurt anyone, not that I know of anyway."

"Yeah, I could tell something was wrong."

"If I'm not around, and he comes over here, just send him home. Tom doesn't want him around Dale. Just between you and me and the fence post, Tom thinks he likes little boys."

Behind the barn Dale broke free and came running up to the house. His face was wet with tears and he was huffing and puffing. He flung himself down next to his mother. Carla hugged him tightly and said, "My goodness, sweetheart! You're shaking!"

Dale was sobbing but he managed to blurt out, "Timmy scared me. He's behind the barn."

Ernie sprang to his feet and took off in a dead run for the barn. But Timmy had a lead on him. He jumped over the gate and ran up through the pasture. Ernie stopped at the gate and yelled, "You stay away from here, goddamn it!" Ernie watched him disappear past the willow thicket. He caught his breath and walked back to the house. Ernie was thinking about the wooden penis. *I wonder if I should tell Carla. Maybe I'll wait and say something when Dale's not around. That weird bastard came back. He went after Dale. This guy needs to be locked up!*

Dale had stopped crying and sat holding his empty coffee can. He tossed it to the bottom of the steps.

Carla asked, "Are you sure Timmy didn't hurt you?" She waited for an answer.

Dale looked at the coffee can and picked up his slingshot. "No, he just scared me. He was talking about stupid stuff. I don't know what he was saying."

"Sweetheart, you must tell me if Timmy ever tries to hurt you in any way."

"He wasn't gonna hurt me. He was just saying dumb stuff."

"Okay," Carla said, "We'll make sure he doesn't come around here anymore. When I get a chance, I'll call his mother." Then she patted Dale on the back. "You have to get ready to go with me now. I need to get back to the hospital. I'm gonna take you over there and maybe they'll let you stay over in Pa's room with me."

Dale said, "Yes, Ma." He got up and went in the house.

When Dale was inside, Ernie moved close to Carla and whispered, "This kid Timmy is really screwed up in the head."

"I know," said Carla. "I don't know why they let him out of Fergus."

"When he was over here, he showed me a wooden penis he had carved. I think he needs to be locked up somewhere."

"Well, it doesn't surprise me. But his mother claims he's never hurt anyone." Carla had more to say, but she shushed up when Dale came back. She wiped her brow with her hand and thought. "Oh, I should tell you. The guy coming to do the milking is Kenny Torstad. He'll talk your arm off. You'll have to overlook that. He drives this old rattletrap car. You'll hear him coming if you're anywhere around."

"Well, I might be still up at the school. I want to do some decorating for the fall. Maybe pick some of those maple leaves from that tree behind the girls' toilet."

She scolded him. "Yes, Ernie, you mentioned that. Now, I don't want to sound like a mother, but I feel I should say something. It's Sunday, your day of rest."

"No, that's okay. I'll feel better up at the school, getting my work done."

"Well, I still worry about you. The least we can do is give you a ride."

When Carla dropped Ernie off at the school, it was two o'clock. When he opened the door, a blast of heat hit him. The room had been sun-baked for two days and it was hotter than blazes inside. He opened the windows, but there was no breeze. He decided to go outside and gather up some red maple leaves.

He was behind the girls' toilet when he heard a car pull into the schoolyard. He thought it was Carla—maybe she had come back to tell him something. He came around the side of the toilet and saw a very attractive young woman step out of a black Ford, maybe a 1939 or 40. She wore a tight-fitting white dress with lilac blossoms. She ran her hand through her curly brown hair and said, "Hi. I'm Martha Sampson. I taught school here last year."

What a surprise! She's come back. And she certainly isn't too hard on the eyes. "Hello, Martha." He wondered what to say next. "I got your letter. I'm Ernie Juvland, the teacher here."

"Yeah, I figured that's who you were." Ernie noticed how she tilted her head to the side when she spoke. She wore bright red lipstick. "I found out they wanted a man teacher. I guess they figured a woman wasn't tough enough for the job." She gave out a nervous giggle and reached for the gold locket hanging from her neck. She played with it as she spoke. "I read about the Smierud boys in *The Bemidji Pioneer.*"

"Yeah, they went on a crazy rampage. That's for sure." Ernie looked down at the red maple leaves he was holding in his hands. "They're locked up in the county jail now. I was thinking I should go over and see them, but I don't have a car right now."

She tilted her head to the side and squinted, "I guess it's none of my business, but why would you want to do that?"

"I don't know. I guess I liked them."

"Liked them?" She said, "Poof!"

"Well, I thought maybe I could help them straighten out."

"Yeah," she said with a chuckle. "I thought the same thing when I was here."

"So you're saying I was pretty—what's the word?"

"Naive?"

"That's it. Why couldn't I remember that word? Yes, I guess I was naive."

"We both were, I suppose. You know, I grew up in town. I was a town girl, and I just thought country kids didn't know enough to be mean to people."

"What town?"

"Bemidji. And I had it good. My dad is a history teacher at the college there. That's where I got my two-year degree." She glanced around the schoolyard. "When I was little all of my playmates were town kids, but I remember in high school, each spring, the farm kids would visit the school on Rural School Day."

"We had that in our high school, too."

"Well, then you know. These ragged eighth grade kids would come into town on the bus from all the one-room country schools around Bemidji. Many of them were Indian kids. I'll bet most of them had never used a flush toilet. Some were so poor, the boys had holes in their overalls, and they smelled like they had just crawled out of a barn. The girls wore dresses that didn't fit and were probably made by their mothers out of flour sacks."

Martha's face grew sad. "Some of the town kids made fun of them. That really upset me. These poor kids were so shy, so lost, you couldn't help but feel sorry for them. You wondered how in the heck they would ever make it in the world."

Ernie chuckled, "Yeah, I'm still wondering if I'll make it in the world."

"What do you mean?"

"I was one of those farm kids. I went to a one-room school north of Thief River Falls."

"Really? Hmmm."

"And that's why you wanted to teach in a country school—to help those poor kids?"

"Yes, it was that, and it was also my father. My dad is the greatest man in the world, and I wanted to be a teacher like him."

Ernie was thinking about Martha. He could understand how Carla and Anders felt deeply about this young woman—how their hearts went out to this bright, energetic teacher, who had come to Dahl School and apparently failed. And as he stood there with a handful of red maple leaves, he wondered if he would do any better. He said, "I'm gathering some maple leaves to decorate around the blackboard. Do you want to help me?"

"Sure. I can do that." They walked around behind the girls' toilet to the maple tree. Martha was very careful staying clear of the sticker bushes. She giggled, "I want to help you out, but I don't want to get a run in my stockings."

Ernie looked down and noticed her nice legs. "You don't want to do that."

Martha carefully squatted down in her tight dress and gathered leaves. When she couldn't hold any more, she stood up and carefully stepped over to the back wall of the girls' toilet. "Here's a little job for you." She pointed to a two-inch hole that had been neatly drilled with a brace and bit. "Boys will be boys, right? I found out about it from one of the girls. Just one of those things I never got done."

Ernie looked at the peephole and shook his head. "Yeah, I'll get a piece of tin and take care of that." He looked at the leaves Martha was holding and said, "I think we have enough. Do you want to come in the school?"

"Sure," she said, and led the way up to the school. Ernie watched her walk ahead of him in her tight white dress with the lilac blossoms. *Lovely figure. Yes, Indeed.*

Ernie put the red maple leaves on his desk and sat down. Martha sat on top of a desk in front of him and dangled her legs over the side. She wiggled around and tugged at the hem of her dress, pulling it over her knees. She ran her tongue over her upper lip and said, "It's funny seeing a big man like you sitting at the teacher's desk. If I were one of your students, you would scare the dickens out of me."

"I look that mean? Is that what you're telling me?"

She giggled and tugged at her dress again, "Now if I were one of your eighth grade girls, I would probably have a mad crush on you."

"I doubt that. I'm just an overgrown farm boy." He turned serious and looked into her eyes. "Is it hard to be back here?"

She tilted her head and looked out the south windows. "I wish you hadn't asked me that."

"I'm sorry," he said softly. They were both silent for a moment, and then Martha got off the desk, walked over to the door of the library, and looked inside. Without turning around she said, "I ran out of here in such a hurry, I might have left some of my things here. You didn't find anything, did you?" She turned to face him, "How about in the desk?"

Ernie wondered if she meant the examination report from the doctor. He didn't want to mention it. "You left some things at the Henning's place."

"Yes, I know about that. Maybe I could drive you over there when you're ready to leave, and I'll pick up those things."

"We can do that. There's no one home right now, but I know where your books are. Carla put them in two boxes, and they're still in my bedroom. She won't be coming back tonight; she and Dale are staying over in the hospital with Tom."

"Tom?" She looked surprised.

141

"Yeah, Tom's in the hospital."

"Really?" She walked back to Ernie. "What happened?"

Martha sat down on the recitation bench and listened to Ernie tell the whole story of the accident on threshing day. When Ernie finished she asked him, "Do they think he'll ever walk?"

"He has no feelings from the waist down, but Carla thinks they might do more surgery. The doctors at St. Lukes said they might even take him down to the Mayo Clinic in Rochester. Yeah, it's a terrible thing and I can't help feeling that I caused it. It was so dumb to bring the kids out there while they were threshing."

"You can't blame yourself." Then she gave out a nervous giggle. "I'm one to talk. I blame myself for everything that goes wrong." She got up and took a couple of leaves off Ernie's desk. "Do you have any thumbtacks?"

Ernie took out a box of tacks from the desk drawer. He wondered again if he should mention finding the letter in his desk. *No. That could wait. Maybe I'll tell her back at the Henning's place.*

Ernie and Martha spent the next hour decorating the classroom. Martha tacked up leaves all around the blackboard, and Ernie found some rolls of black and orange crepe paper to hang streamers across the front of the room. Martha opened the cabinet in the library and brought out a stack of 8X10 alphabet cards, 'A' to 'Z', each letter neatly written in both print and cursive.

Ernie asked, "Where did you find those? I didn't know we had them."

Martha arranged them in alphabetical order, and Ernie reached up to tack them in a neat row at the top of the blackboard.

The afternoon flew by for Ernie. He liked Martha and appreciated the help she gave him. When Ernie locked up the school and climbed in Martha's car, he felt a whole lot better about his job. *I have to keep busy. Can't think about the bad stuff that's happened. I must keep my mind fixed on each task at hand.*

It was almost five o'clock when they pulled into the Henning's yard. They stopped at the bottom of the stairs to Ernie's bedroom and Ernie said, "I'm glad I made my bed this morning or you'd scold me, right?"

She giggled and patted him on the arm. "Yes, I would. You betcha!"

He said, "Lead the way." Ernie was distracted. Her legs looked even better going up the stairs. "I put the boxes over here." He carried them to the foot of his bed.

She sat down on the bed and sorted through the things in the first box. She picked up her diary. "Did you read any of this?" She looked at him with a coy smile.

"No, I didn't." Ernie was beginning to feel uneasy. *Maybe I should leave her alone and go downstairs. My mouth feels dry. Maybe I'll go down for a drink of water. No, I'd better wait.*

Then she closed the diary and said, "Nothing exciting in there anyway." She rifled through the rest of the books and papers in the first box, and then she started on the second box. Ernie watched her thumb through the letters and papers. Then she found it. She held it carefully, blew in the open slit, and pulled enough of the doctor's report out to see what it was. Then she slid it back in the envelope and looked at Ernie, who was standing rigid at the head of the stairs. "How did this get here?" She looked back at the envelope. "I swear to God I forgot it in my desk. I remember Orvid Skime came barging in the school shortly after I read it. I know I stuck it in my desk."

Ernie said, "Yes, you did."

"And you found it?"

"It was jammed in the back of the middle drawer, and when I couldn't close the drawer tight enough to lock it, I pulled the drawer all the way out and found it stuck in the back."

She pulled the report out of the envelope and asked in a flat voice, "Did you read it?"

"Yes I did."

She got up off the bed and charged toward Ernie, "You're one nosey bugger, aren't you? Here! Read it again, if it gives you a thrill!" She flung the letter in Ernie's face. He let it fall to the floor and watched her stomp over to the window. She leaned on the windowsill and shouted, "You're not a very nice person!"

Ernie slowly walked near her. He saw her body shaking in heavy sobs. "I'm sorry."

She turned and scoffed, "I'll bet!"

"Really, I saw it was addressed to you, but I thought it had something to do with the school. I don't know, supplies or books or something—I had no idea it was personal."

She sneered, "Yeah, it was rather personal, wasn't it?"

"You're making fun of me. Please don't do that."

She stormed by him and grabbed the letter off the floor. "Do you have any idea how awful that was for me? Do you know how it hurts me that you read this thing?" She slapped the paper as if she hated it. She walked back to the window and started wailing again. "Why would you do such a thing? That was my letter—addressed to me!"

Ernie thought of leaving her. Maybe he should just let her cry by herself. He decided to try again. "As soon as I read it, I felt terrible. I was so sad for you—I still can't get it off my mind. It's been driving me nuts! I didn't want to leave the letter in my desk, so I brought it home and put it in with the rest of your things."

"Whom did you tell? Did you tell the Hennings?"

"No, I only told one person."

She had stopped crying, but sounded very tired, "Who was that?"

"Anders."

"Anders? You told Anders?" She took a deep breath. "That's interesting. Why did you tell him?"

"I needed someone to talk to."

"And what did Anders have to say?"

"He told me you had come to see him right after it happened."

She turned sarcastic. "So, you two men had a nice little chat over me, right? So what did you decide was best for the poor little schoolteacher, eh? I'm sure it was very constructive. Two brilliant men deciding my fate. Of course. How wonderful!"

"I think I should leave you alone." Ernie started heading for the stairs.

"Yes, please do."

"If you want anything, let me know."

She didn't answer. She slowly moved to the bed. She carefully put the doctor's report back in its envelope and placed it inside her diary. She lay down on the bed with her back to Ernie, who stood at the head of the stairs watching her. She slowly curled up with her knees against her breasts. She looked small, like a little girl.

Downstairs Ernie took a pint Mason jar to the pump and filled it up with water. He brought it over to the woodshed and sat

144

down on the splitting block. He drank it down with big gulps. He picked up the ax and started to split wood.

Martha dozed off, but not for long. She heard the ax smashing the chunks with sharp cracks and went to the window. Ernie had started to sweat. Martha watched him take off his blue shirt and carefully hang it over the door to the woodshed. She watched him swing the ax, splitting each chunk with one clean stroke. She saw the sweat on his chest and arm muscles glisten in the orange light of the autumn sun. She thought of all the things she had said to this man she hardly knew. She wondered if he was angry with her, or if he thought she was crazy. She remembered the way he looked at her as soon as she stepped out of the car at the schoolyard. He looked pleased.

She went to the wardrobe and opened the doors looking for clothes she had left behind. She saw Ernie's black suit, his white shirt, and grey tie. She moved her hand through the rest of his clothes, work pants, dress slacks, and shirts, looking for the dresses she had left. She went to the window and opened it. She caught Ernie's attention as he leaned on the handle of his ax. "Ernie! Can you come up here? I can't find my dresses."

He nodded and with one hand swung the ax over his head and set the blade deeply into the splitting block.

"And could you bring me a glass of water?" She watched him approach the house. "I feel better now."

When Ernie came to the top of the stairs, he saw her lying on the bed propped up on her elbow. She took the water and sat up with her legs hanging over the edge. She sipped the cold water and looked at Ernie, "I can really be a bitch sometimes. I let you have it with both barrels, eh? Right between the eyes."

"Look, I had it coming. That was your personal mail. I never should have read it. That just wasn't right."

"I don't know. I've been lying here thinking about that. I might have done the same thing myself. I think anyone would have." She studied his face. "Are you upset with me?"

"No, I'm not." He pulled a chair close to her and sat down.

She reached for his hand. "Do you think I'm awful?"

"Why should I feel that way?"

"I don't know. I guess I feel awful about myself." She took another sip of water and looked at her feet. She had taken off her shoes. Then she looked up at Ernie. "Would you do me a favor and sit on the bed by me?" Ernie slowly got up and sat next to her. She moved close to him and he put his arm around her. She wiped the moisture off the water glass and said, "I feel so damned helpless sometimes."

"You've had a tough time of it."

She managed to smile, "Yeah, it hasn't been easy." She reached for his hand, which was hanging over her shoulder. "I've been keeping it all inside of me. You and Anders are the only ones who know about what happened. I haven't told anyone, and it's really been hard for my boyfriend back in Bemidji. He can't figure out why I've been acting so strange and defensive. I just freeze up when he goes to kiss me, and he's such a good person."

She leaned over and grabbed her purse, which was sitting on the end of the bed. "You wanna see a picture of him?" She handed Ernie the picture. A blonde-haired young man wearing white swim trunks was standing next to the statues of Paul Bunyan and Babe, the Blue Ox. She said, "He's a lifeguard in the summer at Diamond Point Park. All the girls are in love with him, but he's mine, all mine!"

Ernie handed the picture back to her. He thought for a moment and then said, "Maybe it would help if you told him what happened."

"No, no, no! I can't do that. I don't want anyone to know about what happened. That's why I never went to the police." She stood up. "You must give me your word that you will never, ever tell anyone about this. You must promise."

"You have my word. I promise."

"And when you see Anders, tell him what I told you. Would you do that for me?"

They both stopped talking to listen to the loud noise of a car approaching. Ernie got up and started for the stairs. "I'll bet that's the guy they hired to do the milking, Kenny somebody."

"Kenny Torstad?"

"Yeah, that's it." Ernie listened to the car stop out front. "Do you know him?"

"Unfortunately. I had his son in school last year. He was an eighth grader, so you wouldn't know him." She had started putting on her shoes. "I don't want him to know I'm here."

"Okay, I'll go down and show him the ropes, and then I'll come back."

"Oh, he'll know the ropes all right. They had him working over here last year quite a few times. He's a real BS artist. Pardon the expression, but that pretty much sums him up."

They heard him shouting from the front door, "Hey, anybody home?" Ernie hurried down the stairs and opened the door for Kenny Torstad. It didn't take long for Ernie to realize what Martha was talking about. He was well-built, maybe 35 or so, and the guy would not shut up. He fired question after question at Ernie, and each time he answered, Kenny Torstad would snicker and say, "Yeah, I know. Somebody told me that." Ernie found him the milk pails and cream can and managed to get him out the door.

At the bottom of the porch steps, Kenny Torstad stopped and turned, "Is that your car?"

Ernie said, "No."

He started walking toward the barn with his eyes on Martha's car. He said over his shoulder, "I guess you don't want to tell me. It sure looks familiar."

Ernie found Martha's clothes, dresses, blouses and skirts hanging up in the cellar, and he helped her carry the two boxes of books, papers, and letters out to her car. She was eager to leave, but she gave him her parent's address and phone number in Bemidji. She also gave him the phone number of the bank where she worked. She told him to write when he had a chance. The last thing she said before she drove out of the yard was, "You're a very nice man, and I'm sure the kids all love you. Maybe we can get together again."

Chapter X...The Assault

The weather turned cold that night, and by morning heavy frost covered the stubble fields along the road to school. Dale was wearing his winter coat and Ernie wore his long olive drab Army coat. Some of the farmers had plowed, leaving stretches of black loam between the willow thickets and pastures. Three deer came out of the ditch, stopped on the road, and stared at the tall teacher and boy. Ernie and Dale stopped. The two does and one young buck trotted for a few yards; then they sprang to the ditch and leaped over a barbed wire fence, flashing their white tails in rapid bounds.

It was Monday, October 2, 1944, and Ernie had only four weeks to prepare for the Halloween Basket Social, scheduled for Friday, the 27th. To make matters worse, four of his older boys had been excused for two weeks to pick potatoes. Ernie wondered how they would ever keep up with their lessons and learn their parts for the program. But that was the law of the land. Students were let go during potato-picking season.

Halfway to school, Ernie stopped and opened his satchel. "Darn it! I forgot my logbook and I really need it. Dale, would you run back to get it? I'm sure I left it on the kitchen table."

Dale gave Ernie his lunch pail. He turned around to run back home, and Ernie continued on to the school. Dale found his teacher's logbook on the table and headed back to school. He was worried about walking by Ole Gangstad's bull alone, always feeling safer when his teacher walked beside him. He slowed down when he saw the beast up ahead. Then he heard a voice shouting from the road behind him.

It was Timmy Burstrom running hard. "You wait, little boy!" he yelled. Dale stopped in the middle of the road shaking. He looked ahead and saw Gangstad's bull pawing with his big hooves in the dirt by the fence. He looked back and saw Timmy coming closer. He had something that looked like a stick of wood in his hand. Dale started running toward the school, but Timmy grabbed him around the waist with his strong arms. He picked him off his feet and dragged the kicking boy into the ditch, only a few feet from the snorting bull.

Timmy pulled off Dale's coat. He held the boy to the ground and loosened the straps of Dale's bib overalls. "Don't try to get up or I'll throw you over the fence, and the bull will get you. Would you like that?"

Dale cried out, "Stop it! Please stop!" Dale lay struggling in a patch of thistles. The sharp barbs were piercing his hands and face. The bull dug in the dirt.

Timmy pulled Dale's overalls down around his ankles. He held the wooden penis in Dale's face and said, "Now I've got you! Guess what I'm gonna do?"

Dale struggled to get free. He grabbed for Timmy's neck. "No! Please! I'll tell my pa!"

Timmy laughed and said, "You better not, or I'll throw you to the bull." Dale was crying hysterically. Timmy rolled the boy over on his belly, pulled down his underwear and tried to push the wooden penis into Dale's rectum.

Dale yelled, "Stop! Please, stop! You'll hurt me!" The boy squeezed the cheeks of his buttocks tightly together. Timmy was trying to force them apart with his strong fingers. Dale was screaming loudly. Suddenly, Timmy let go of the boy.

He heard a truck coming. It was Anders on the way to town. Timmy stood up and stuck the wooden penis in his pocket. He yelled at Dale, "Get your pants on, quick!" Then Timmy climbed up on the road and started running. Anders stopped the truck when he ran by. Anders yelled, "Wait up!" But Timmy kept on running down the gravel road.

Dale managed to get his bib overalls pulled up by the time Anders stopped the truck. He yelled, "What's going on here, Dale?"

Dale turned his head away, so Anders would not see him crying. He looked down and said, "I had to take a dump."

Anders barely heard him. He chuckled and said, "Well, that's okay, lad. Would you like a lift to school?"

Dale kept his head down, "No, thanks. I'll walk." He slowly put on his coat, picked up his teacher's logbook, and watched Anders drive on. He crawled out of the ditch and stood on the road sobbing. He wiped his tears away and thought, "I can never tell anyone what happened." And Ole Gangstad's bull snorted and pawed the dirt.

When Ernie reached the school, Vic was sitting in his car waiting for him. He folded his newspaper and laid it on the seat next to him. He rolled down the window and yelled, "Good morning, Ernie. I've got something for you." He reached around to the back seat and brought out an Indian blanket. He passed it through the window and said, "Me and the missus drove down to Moorhead Saturday to pick it up. It's a real beauty! I think you should get the kids going on the raffle right away. What do we have now? Just four weeks before the program."

"Yeah, I made tickets. How about the price?"

"Well, last year they were two bits apiece, and I don't think you can go any higher."

"Okay, 25 cents a ticket. I'll get the kids going on that today."

"Yeah, and tell them there'll be a prize for the kid who sells the winning ticket. Last year I made a bird house that turned out pretty fancy. This year the missus is going to knit a pair of mittens; she picked up the yarn in Moorhead, red and white. She knows the Selbu pattern, which comes from Selbu, Norway, where her mother was born. She does a heck of a good job."

"That will be real nice. Maybe we should give a prize to the student who sells the most tickets, too. I'll pick something up for that."

"Sounds good. Well, I'd better get going—got plowing to do before the snow flies. We'll be getting flurries soon. Could get them today, the way it feels." He stepped on the starter, and all he heard was a click. She wouldn't turn over. Vic pounded the steering wheel with both hands. "Son of a buck! I never should have shut 'er off. And it's a brand new battery, too. It must be the generator going bad on me. Damn! If it ain't one thing, it's another!" He reached under the front seat for the crank.

Ernie handed the blanket through the window, "Here, hold this. Give me the crank, and I'll give 'er a whirl."

Vic handed him the crank through the window. "Just give 'er half turns. Don't whip 'er around, or she might kick on you."

"Don't worry. I'm an expert at cranking," said Ernie. It only took a couple of tries and the engine started. He went to Vic's window and exchanged the crank for the blanket. "Here you go. And thanks for picking up the blanket. I'll get the kids out there selling right away."

Vic had raised his voice to speak over the sound of the motor. "Yeah, tell them to sell in town, too. Those rich buggers can afford it better than us." He put the car in gear and then remembered something. He reached over on the seat and grabbed the *Fargo Forum*. "We picked up the *Forum* on Saturday, and there's an article on the front page." He held it in the window, and Ernie saw it. **Hearing on Wednesday for Teenage Shooters**.

Ernie glanced at the article and shook his head. "I still can't believe they did that. What on earth were they trying to prove?"

"Well," said Vic, "at least they're out of your hair. They're gonna be sent up. You can bet your boots on that."

"I don't know if I should feel so good about that." He stood back as Vic started to pull out. "Give 'er the gas, so she doesn't kill on you again." He waved and yelled, "So long!"

When Ernie reached the porch, Dale was waiting for him with the logbook. He was rubbing his eyes, and Ernie thought something was wrong with the boy. "Hey, buddy, you're all red in the face. Do you feel okay?"

The boy picked up his lunch pail off the steps, but kept his head down. "I ran all the way and I'm tired out."

Ernie put his arm around Dale and said, "Well, thanks for going back for my logbook. I can't believe I forgot it, but you saved my day!" The boy looked up and managed to smile.

Inside the school, Ernie took a bunch of thumbtacks and tacked the blanket over the south end of the blackboard. He stood back to admire it. At the very top was a blazing orange sun, with flares going out in all directions. Along the bottom was a blue lake shore and in the background were snow-peaked mountains. He went to the library and looked up Navajo Indians in the brand new *Encyclopedia Americana*. There was a paragraph on their blankets, with a picture. He brought the book to his desk and jotted down some notes in his logbook.

That morning after opening exercises, Ernie passed out raffle tickets and explained that there would be a prize for the student who sold the most. Then he asked the first and second graders to sit on the recitation benches, and he called the older students to come closer to the front of the room.

He took his pointer and stood next to the blanket. "The Navajo Indians are noted for weaving beautiful rugs and blankets. They take great care in making the pattern just right. If this blanket were woven by a real Indian, the weaver might have worked on it for many months. This blanket is what we would call a 'print'. The pattern was copied from a blanket done by a Navajo and printed on this material."

Ernie reached to the top of the blackboard and pulled down the map of the United States. "Now, do the Navajo live here in Minnesota?" The students looked at each other, puzzled. Ernie answered for them. "No, the Indians who live near here, like on the White Earth Reservation east of here are Ojibwa. The Navajo live way out here in the desert country of the Southwest." Ernie pointed to Arizona and New Mexico. "We're going to learn more throughout the year about the first people, who lived in our country thousands of years before Columbus arrived."

Ernie abruptly stopped and looked at Dale. He saw tears running down his cheeks. He walked over and put his arm around him. "What's the matter?"

Dale looked down and said, "Nothing." Then he said, "My ma knows a family of Indians. They're nice. They bring us gifts of wild rice every Christmas."

"Okay. I'd like to meet them sometime," he said. He left Dale, turned back to the blanket, and continued his lesson. "The Indians have a different religion than we have. They are not Lutherans, Methodists, or Catholics. They are not Christians like us, unless they've been converted. Their God is The Great Spirit or Mother Earth. They deeply worship the earth or nature and all that the land and the water bring us—the crops we grow and the birds and animals we hunt for food."

Ernie looked at the clock to see if he had time to tell the students a story. He decided this was a good time. He reached in his satchel and took out the framed prayer that hung over his bed. "I want to tell you about my connection with Indians. I was born in our farmhouse in my mother's bed. Lisa Olson, an Indian woman, who lived near us, helped my mother deliver me. My dad had gone somewhere and there was no doctor present, just my mother and Mrs. Olson. So the first human being to hold me was an Indian, and my mother made sure I never forgot that.

"I came home from school one day—I was maybe in the second grade—I told my mother that one of my classmates said Indians were dirty and they were always drunk. Well, my mother made me sit at the kitchen table. She gave me a stern look and said,

'I think it's time you learned something about Indians.' She told me how they have been badly treated, how their land was taken away, and she reminded me that if Mrs. Olson had not been there to help me come into the world, I might not be here today."

Ernie had caught their interest, so he went on. "I asked my mother if they believed in Jesus. She told me they had their own religion, which was beautiful and made a lot of sense, because they worshiped Mother Earth. Later that year, Mrs. Olson brought over a Thanksgiving prayer she had handwritten and placed in a frame." Ernie held it up so the children could see it. "And this is it. My mother hung it over my bed, and she made me read it so many times, I practically know it by heart." Ernie read in a soft voice.

**We give thanks to our Mother, the Earth,
for she gives us all that we need for life.
She supports our feet as we walk upon her.
She is there to catch us if we should fall.
It has always been this way since the beginning.
For she is our Mother, the one
who takes care of us.
It gives us great joy that Mother Earth
continues still to care for us.
So it is that we join our minds together to give
Greetings and thanks to this Earth, our Mother.**

The students were silent. Dwight was usually very shy. It surprised Ernie when he spoke up, "Mr. Juvland, maybe you should hang that prayer on the wall, so we can see it every day."

Ernie was pleased. "Good idea, Dwight. When I get a chance, I'll hang it over the blackboard between the pictures of George Washington and Abraham Lincoln." Ernie thought about how that would look, and felt it would be very fitting. Then he turned to use the pointer on the blanket. "Now remember that prayer and you'll see that message shown in all the parts of this blanket. We see the sun at the top. The sun brings us light and warmth. Nothing would grow without the sun, the flowers, the trees, or the crops your dads plant. So the sun brings us our food.

"Notice at the bottom, we see the blue water of the lake. There would be no life here without water. We are the water planet and we have all kinds of life. The warmth of the sun and water bring life. Now look at the snow on the mountain peaks. The snow melts in the spring and the water fills the rivers and lakes to help the fish and geese and ducks, which also help feed us."

Iris Vic interrupted Ernie, "Mr. Juvland, what is that blue line at the top of the lake? It goes right off the edge of the blanket."

"Good girl. I'm glad you noticed that. I just read about it in the encyclopedia. They call that the 'spirit line'. And it means that the line takes the weaver's spirit out of the blanket and into the world. Otherwise the spirit would be trapped inside the blanket. So you can see that just from this one blanket, there are so many things we can learn. We learn about the world from all the things we see around us. But we have to keep our eyes open and we have to be willing to ask questions. Just like Iris—she saw that line and wondered about it. That's why we're in school. I want you to wonder. Then we'll work together to find out the answers."

After the students went back to their desks, Dwight went up to Ernie and whispered, "My mother is half Indian, but we don't talk about it. Don't tell anyone that I'm part Indian. Promise?"

Ernie put his arm around Dwight and whispered, "I promise. But don't be ashamed. You should be proud of that."

Dwight said, "Thank you," and went back to his seat.

That day, the entire afternoon was spent making plans for the Halloween program. Ernie made a list in his logbook of everything they had to do in the next four weeks.

1) *Sell raffle tickets for the Indian blanket.*
2) *Select two songs the older students would learn on their Tonettes.*
3) *Select two songs the rhythm band of grades first, second, and third would play on sand blocks, rhythm sticks, triangles and tambourines. Eunice would accompany them on the piano.*
4) *Learn three songs to be sung by the entire school.*
5) *Find three short plays the students would rehearse and perform.*

Here Ernie stopped. He was thumbing through the book that had been left in the library, *Ten Short Plays for Children*. He

154

looked up and said, "I've been looking through this book of plays, but I think most of them are pretty dumb."

Some of the older kids started to giggle. Ernie smiled and said, "Does it surprise you that I would say that something written in a book is dumb?"

They giggled again and some nodded in agreement. "Okay," said Ernie. "Maybe I shouldn't have used the word 'dumb'. I think a better word would be 'inappropriate'. These plays aren't about anything that you can relate to or even know about. For instance, here's one, *Bobby Goes to the Opera*. Here's another one, *A Scary Day at the Zoo*. And then there's this one, *Mrs. Baldwin's Garden Party*. Do you see what I'm talking about? How many of you have been to an opera, a zoo, or when was the last time you had a garden party?"

Ernie had the kids laughing. Janice Millrud said, "I have to pull weeds in the garden and it's no picnic and it isn't a party."

"Right," said Ernie. "So this is what we're going to do for plays." Ernie stood up and grabbed a piece of chalk. "We're going to write our own plays, and they'll be about things we know about. Now what do we know about?"

The students started raising their hands and Ernie wrote down a whole list of things they had shouted out. Then he stood back and read them off. "Let's see what we have here. We have cows, horses, pigs, baby puppies, slingshots, deer hunting, butchering pigs, picking mustard weeds, trapping gophers, pouring water down gopher holes, fixing fences, digging toilet holes, pitching manure, dark-house fishing, making bow and arrows, shucking peas, catching fireflies, plucking chickens, making quilts, listening to the radio, splitting kindling, making snow-forts, drawing pictures on the frost of the windows, pumping water, picking blueberries, crab apples, and chokecherries, making haystacks, feeding calves, feeding pigs, milking cows, cranking the cream separators, and playing farm in the dirt."

Ernie stood back and said, "Holy cow! Just look at all the things we can write plays about. Now I'll help you, but I really want your ideas. Just remember this, in a play, something has to happen almost right away. It will be fun, right?"

The first week of October passed in a flurry of activity. By Friday night Ernie was exhausted, and he knew he would have to spend Saturday and Sunday afternoon working at the school, grading papers and workbooks, and helping those students who wanted to come to the school to rehearse their parts for the program.

That night, Ernie got the news on the Smierud boys. Carla had been to St. Lukes Hospital to see Tom and had brought home the *Fargo Forum*. Ernie read the article at the kitchen table. They admitted to stealing the guns and shooting out the windows of five stores in town. The Wilmot Country Judge Morris sentenced them to one year in the Bass Lake Juvenile Detention Center near Ely, Minnesota. After Ernie finished the article, he noticed his eyes had teared up. He wiped them with his handkerchief and wanted to take his mind off those boys. He asked Carla, "When do they think Tom can come home?"

She was busy at the stove making lefse. "It could be sometime next week." Ernie could tell from the sound of her voice that it was all starting to take a toll on her. She had lost her smile and her eyes were tired and sad. "We're getting a wheelchair from the hospital in town, so we don't have to go out and buy one."

"That's good," said Ernie.

"Yeah, and Kenny Torstad will be able to keep coming over for the chores. We'll make do, one way or another."

After supper, Ernie helped Dale with his homework. When they finished with his arithmetic problems, Dale said, "I have an idea for a play."

"Really?" Ernie was excited. "Tell me about it."

Dale laughed and said, "It's pretty silly." He opened his notebook. Ernie could see that he had written some dialogue. "Okay, it's about this farmer. He teaches his cow how to talk. And then maybe the cow can learn to do tricks."

Ernie laughed, "Smart cow. Then what?"

"Well, I was thinking, he sells the rest of his cows and turns his barn into a circus. People come from all over to see the talking cow."

Carla overheard Dale. She came over to the table and sat down. "Where on earth did you come up with that?"

He giggled, "I don't know. I just made it up."

Carla said, "That will be very funny."

"You bet," said Ernie, "and I'll help you figure out how we're going to do it." The three of them spent the next hour working on Dale's little play. Carla would use some old gunny sacks to make a costume for two kids to play the cow. And Ernie helped Dale with the rest of the dialogue. It was fun.

Carla took the last of the lefse and placed it on the table. Ernie buttered and put sugar on a slice for Dale, rolled it up, and handed it to the boy. Then he fixed a slice for himself. They munched on lefse, talked, and laughed. For a time they were able to forget the bad stuff that had happened. Ernie went to bed that night tired, but feeling good.

Dale was feeling better, too. He would not tell anyone about Timmy Burstrom, unless he did something bad again. He lay on his bed thinking. *If I tell Ma how it happened, I'd get Mr. Juvland in trouble for sending me back for his logbook. I'd never do anything to hurt my teacher. He's my best friend and he's always helping me. He even buttered my lefse.*

The next three weeks flew by for Ernie and his students. He was so involved in preparing for the Halloween program, he stopped following the St. Louis Cardinals. He might have missed the big news altogether if he hadn't seen the *Pioneer Press* lying on Carla's kitchen table. The headlines caught his eye. They read, **Cardinals are World Champs!** They defeated the Browns in the sixth game of the World Series, on October 9.

Winning the World Series did little to take Ernie's mind off rehearsals. He told his students they had to work extra hard on their morning and early afternoon lessons, because each afternoon, they would be rehearsing for the program from 2:30 until dismissal at four o'clock. The raffle tickets were selling like hotcakes, and Ernie had to make more tickets. His order of school supplies had arrived, so the younger students were able to make orange pumpkins for decorating the room. The students were working hard on memorizing their lines for the plays and the songs were coming along nicely.

Carla had more time to help out once Tom came home from the hospital. And Dale was happy to have his Pa there to talk to. He ran errands for him and helped him get around in his wheelchair. Ernie found it hard to talk to him. He still felt guilty about Tom's accident. Every time he saw the man, sitting in his wheelchair, he thought of that day and how bringing his students out to see the threshing operation was a stupid mistake. He could not blame the Smierud boys. When all was said and done, he was the cause of that accident.

157

Tom had grown quiet. He spent his days staring off into space. He only glanced at headlines of the newspaper, and even stopped reading the Bible. Ernie felt sorry for this hardworking man, so helpless now, confined to his wheelchair. Ernie found himself paying less attention to what Anders had seen that day— Tom coming out of the barn after he heard a scream. He began to doubt that Tom Henning had actually raped Martha. What Anders said was all about perception.

Three days before the Halloween Basket Social, Carla brought the clean curtains up to the school. Carla, Ernie, and two of the older boys strung the wire and hung the big curtains across the front of the room. She also brought a letter for Ernie. "This came in the mail for you," she said.

Ernie looked at the return address and saw, *M. Sampson, Bemidji, Minnesota.* He stopped to think. *Well, that was quick. I only wrote her a couple of days ago.* During afternoon recess Ernie sat on the front steps and read Martha's letter.

October 21, 1944

Dear Ernie,

How are you? I'm doing fine, still working at the bank. Thanks for the nice letter. It sounds like you're busy working on the Halloween program. Thanks for inviting me, but I don't think I'll be coming over to see it. I hope you understand. I want to see you again, but I'd feel sort of funny being at the school. With the parents there, some of them didn't like me very much. But I wish you and the kids a lot of luck. What do they say? "Break a leg!"

I've been thinking about the day I came to see you and how nice you were to me. I'm sorry about yelling at you. You must have thought a Halloween witch had flown through your window to curse you. Ha Ha. Seriously, it's been hard for me since I quit teaching at Dahl School. People keep telling me I've changed. It's hard because I can't tell them what's going on. I carry this awful secret and it drives me crazy sometimes. You should know what I mean, the way I was acting up in your room. But then you were so kind to me. You didn't get upset at all. I'm a little mixed up right now, but I want to tell you what a nice person you are and that I really like you. Do I sound like a silly little school girl? That's what I feel like sometimes. My mom thinks I need to grow up.

I just read what I wrote and tried to imagine what you would think about this letter. Then I almost scrapped it up. Does that make any sense?

Well, time to go. Don't work too hard and don't worry about the Halloween program. I'm sure all the kids will remember their lines and sing with happy voices. If it were a basket social somewhere else, I would make a basket and hope a tall, handsome man named Ernie would bid on it. I'd have to give you a signal (like a wink) to let you know the basket was mine. Is that cheating? Ha Ha. Do you remember the first time a girl winked at you?
Good luck with everything,
Martha
P.S. My boyfriend hasn't called me in two weeks. I don't know what's going on.

Ernie put the letter back in the envelope, folded it in half, and put it in his pocket. He went back in the classroom and checked the calendar on the wall. Tuesday, October 24. They had four more rehearsals. When the students came in from recess, they were all excited about rehearsing for the first time with the curtains. Ernie assigned the two tallest students, Iris Vic and Peter Brunsvold, to pull the curtains.

Ernie sat in the back by the stove. "Listen to me," he shouted. "We're going to pretend that your parents are sitting out here just like it's going to be Friday night. That means you have to be quiet behind the curtains." Ernie paused for a moment. "I still hear talking back there. We're not starting until it's absolutely quiet." The voices were still. "Okay, I'll come out in front of the curtain and give a little welcome speech to the parents and neighbors. Then Dale, you will come out with the flag and I'll ask the audience to rise for the 'Pledge of Allegiance'. You guys will say it from behind the curtains. I can't have you out front, because many of you will be in your costumes.

"After the 'Pledge', I will go back behind the curtain and sit on the side by the library to prompt you. And let's hope I don't have to give you too many cues. You should all have your parts memorized by now. Okay, Eunice, as soon as I go behind the curtain, you will start to play the first verse of "Pick, A-Pick-A Pumpkin". After one verse, Iris and Peter will open the curtains. That means all the first, second and third graders should have their pumpkins lit and all be in place. Okay, quiet now. Are you all in place? Good. Hit it, Eunice!"

The piano rang out in the little schoolroom and rehearsal had begun. There were plenty of mistakes and Ernie had to stop them several times to go over the rough spots, but by 4:15, they made it through to the end. Before he dismissed them, he asked them all to take their seats. Ernie sat on the edge of his desk and said, "Well, we got through it. Don't worry about the parts where you messed up. We have three more rehearsals, tomorrow, Thursday, and on Friday, there won't be any lessons."

The children shouted their approval. "I know that makes you happy. We are going to rehearse all day, because when we go on Friday night at 7:00 p.m., we want to be perfect. And whom are we doing that for? Answer me!"

The students shouted, "Our parents!"

Ernie shook his head. "No, it will be nice to show your parents that you've done a good job, but you know whom you are really doing a good job for?"

Susan quietly said, "We are doing it for you, Mr. Teacher."

Again, Ernie shook his head and said, "Okay, it will make me happy to see you do a good job, and I'm sure you will. But you are still missing the point." Ernie paused and looked around the room. Their eager faces made Ernie feel a strain in his voice. "You are doing this for yourself. This is your reward for working hard. It will be something you can look back on and say, 'By golly, I did a good job'. It will give you confidence, so when you're faced with something that's really hard to do, you will remember that night in Dahl School, when you did your best.

"Okay. It's way past dismissal time, and your moms and dads are going to think a wolf ate you on the way home. Go over your parts again tonight before you go to bed. Sleep tight. Don't let the bed bugs bite. Class dismissed."

The children scampered out to the cloakroom to get their coats and lunch pails, and Ernie plunked himself down in his chair, tired but satisfied. He heard the door to the library close. He looked over and Carla stepped out from behind the curtain. Ernie was surprised, "What the heck? How long were you back there?"

She sat on the desk in front of Ernie. She held the gunny sack cow costume for Dale's play. "I was working on the cow. I tried it on the kids and I think it's going to work out okay. They wanted to wear it for rehearsal and surprise you, but I told them to wait." Ernie got up and helped her stretch it out. It was made for two students, one in front and one in back. She held the head and Ernie held the back end. "Did you hear us giggling when I tried it on the kids? The kid in the back end had his head sticking up. It looked more like a camel than a cow!"

Ernie laughed. "This is just fantastic! Thank you. Thank you. We'll try it out tomorrow. This is going to be very funny."

Carla sat down and smiled at Ernie. "I was back there listening to your speech to the children just now. It made me want to cry. We are so blessed to have you, Ernie. I keep wondering, where did you come from? I believe you must have come from God. He has sent you to our school to help all of us, including me, a simple farmer's wife. I thank Him for your gifts and your kindness every night before I go to sleep."

Ernie was thrown off by what she said and how she said it. He heard a tenderness in Carla's voice and saw a warmth in her eyes that was new. He had been too busy to notice her growing affection toward him. Her attachment had slipped beyond a parent's appreciation for her son's teacher. Ernie had awakened something inside of her—something she thought was dead. He tried to cover his confusion with a smile and said, "You're more than a farmer's wife. You're a costume designer." He thanked her and started to gather his scripts and songbook to put in his leather satchel. "I'm tired," he said. "If you're ready, let's go home."

161

The last rehearsals went well and the raffle tickets were selling to beat the band. By Friday, the students had raised 48 dollars and 25 cents, and there was still more money they would raise from auctioning off the baskets, Bingo and the fishpond. By 4:30 the students had finished their last rehearsal and were ready to go home. The last thing Ernie said to them was, "Make sure you take a bath before you come back. We don't want you stinking up the joint!" Ernie had planned to stay. There were too many details to take care of, and he had only two hours before the cars and pickups would start rolling into the schoolyard for the Halloween Basket Social.

Ernie went behind the curtains and started checking to see if all the props were in place. Then he heard a student's voice coming from the back of the room. "Excuse me, Mr. Juvland."

Ernie peered around the curtain and saw Dwight Alstad, the shy fifth grade boy, who had told him his mother was half Indian. "Dwight," said Ernie. "Did you forget something?"

The boy came forward. "I wanted to thank you for hanging that Indian prayer on the wall. I told my Ma and it made her happy. I also wanted to ask you something about the program. It was going to be a surprise, but Eunice said I should ask you first."

Ernie was puzzled. "A surprise?"

"Yes, you know my pa is in the war." He looked down at his shoes.

"Yes, someone told me that. He's a Marine, right?"

"Yes, Ma isn't sure where he is right now. Maybe on a ship going to some island where they'll have to fight."

Ernie put his arm around the boy. "It must be hard for you, your little sister Jane, and your mother. I have brothers in the war and I know how you must feel. But what about this surprise?"

"Well, Eunice and I have been practicing a song about my pa, and I'd like to sing it tonight, if it's okay with you."

"That would be nice. We'll have you sing at the very end."

"Thanks. I'm really nervous. And I just told Eunice that I was scared to do it. I sometimes throw up when I get scared."

"So what did Eunice tell you?"

"She told me not to worry. She told me she gets nervous every time she has to play in front of people." Then he looked up at his teacher. "She said I should talk to you."

162

Ernie said, "Let's sit down for a minute." He brought Dwight over to one of the double desks near the south windows. They sat together and Ernie put his arm around the boy. He thought maybe he should tell him about the trouble he had in basic training, how stabbing the dummies made him so nervous he started having bad dreams. But he changed his mind. He said, "Think of your dad on that ship with his buddies going to some island and they have no idea what is going to happen. Now that is something to be scared about! You bet!

"But think about what scares you right now, singing in front of the folks tonight. That's nothing compared to what your father is going through. And also think how proud he would be of you, standing up and singing a song for him. And remember how proud your mom and your little sister Jane will be hearing you. And you can count on me. I'll be right there to help you. And if you throw up, I'll get the mop and clean it up myself."

The boy started to laugh. "I'll try my best not to puke on the people in front."

Ernie laughed, "That's the spirit. You'll be just fine." They both got up and walked together to the front door. The teacher and student shook hands, and Ernie stayed on the porch and watched the boy run for home. *Damned war! And what a thoughtful lad wanting to sing a song for his pa. That man should be here to see his proud son perform. But no, a bunch of dictators and generals and politicians have taken his father thousands of miles away. Tonight, while this boy sings, his father is ordered to risk his life in a contest where winners live and losers die, an ugly game played by powerful world leaders sitting behind desks. Anders is right. There is no glory in war. It's just plain stupid!* Ernie watched the boy until he was out of sight, and then he went back to work.

He made a last minute check of everything. It was six o'clock when he came back with two pails of water for apple-bobbing. He walked up to the piano to make sure Eunice had her script and music sheets in the right order. He went in the library to check on all the props. He checked all the pumpkins to make sure the candles were in place. *Matches? What did I do with the box of matches? Right. They're in my desk.* He took the box and put it inside the biggest pumpkin. He started to feel dizzy and weak. He needed something to eat. He went to the back of the room and took an apple out of a sack by the bobbing tub. He brought it back to the library. He sat on the long counter and ate the apple.

The front door banged and a strong voice yelled out, "Anybody home?"

Ernie came out of the library and saw a plump, middle-aged man dressed in a gray suit and black hat holding a large cardboard box. "Hello," he said. "Where do you want your books?"

Ernie was a little confused, "I don't think I've met you."

The plump man walked past Ernie and put the box on the library floor. He took off his hat and stuck out his hand, "I'm Carl Swanson, Wilmot County School Superintendent, and I'm guessing you're Ernie Juvland."

"Yes, I am."

Mr. Swanson said, "I brought your library books from the Wilmot County Library. I'll be back around Thanksgiving to pick these up and bring you a new batch." He looked around at the curtains and said, "Looks like you're having a big shindig tonight."

"Yes, we are. I'm just taking care of last minute details. Would you like to stay and see our program?"

"Sorry, this is my last stop of the day and I'm ready to get home and put my feet up. I've been to twelve country schools today and I'm bushed!"

"Wow! Twelve schools! You've put some miles on."

"Yes, I have. I've got just enough gas in the old jalopy to make it home."

Well, it was nice meeting you, Mr. Swanson, and thanks for the books."

"You bet. Next time I stop by, we'll have a talk. I want to know how things are going for you. First year teacher, right?"

"Yes, I am. And I've been learning something new every single day."

"That's what I like to hear. Hey, good luck with your program." He put his hat on and went out the door.

Ernie didn't bother checking the box of books. He leaned against the doorjamb of the library door and listened. *Voices again. Voices and laughter. It's coming from somewhere outside.* He went to the window and saw Mr. Swanson's car pulling out of the schoolyard. *Must have been the motor. Why did it sound like someone laughing? I can't think about that now.* He felt weak and

164

needed to lie down to rest before the crowd showed up. He bunched up the cow costume for a pillow and lay down on the counter. *Just close my eyes for a minute. So tired. So tired.*

The dream came softly at first. Martha was there in her white dress. They were wading in water, trying to get to a giant ship. There was a rope ladder going up the side of the ship, and they were climbing up to the top deck. The ship was moving and they were alone.

Martha began to shiver in her wet dress. She took it off and wrapped herself in a black sheet. She fastened the sheet at her neck with a large safety pin. Now the ship was going through a jungle. Overhanging branches from trees were hitting them. Then Japanese soldiers jumped out of the trees and landed on the ship. They carried swords and were cutting their way through the vines and branches trying to get to Martha. Ernie started to scream, "No, no!" She lay helpless on the deck of the ship wrapped in her black sheet. Ernie found a rifle with a bayonet and jabbed at the soldiers.

He had fallen off the counter and was stumbling through the door of the library. "Stop it! Stop it! I'll kill you!" Ernie was swinging his arms wildly. In his dream he was tangled up in vines trying to get to Martha. He felt cloth in his hand. He knew he had reached Martha. A sword had gone through her belly and blood was gushing out. "No, no! You bastards! You've killed her!" He pulled out the sword and tried to use the black sheet to stop the bleeding. He tugged on the black sheet, but it would not come free.

Then from somewhere he heard a familiar voice and he felt the sheet being pulled out of his hand. He heard a hissing sound and opened his eyes. There was a light coming from somewhere. It was a gasoline lantern sitting on a front desk. Then he saw Vic standing over him.

"Holy smokes, Ernie, wake up! What the heck are you doing on the floor? Look what you've done to the curtain!" Vic tried to pull the curtain out of his hands.

Ernie was shaking violently. He looked around and said, "Is Martha here?"

"Martha? You mean Martha Sampson? Jeepers Creepers, Ernie! What's going on with you?" Vic went down on one knee. "Ernie, you've got to get up. Carla and Tom are outside; we need help getting Tom's wheelchair up the steps. People will be coming soon. You can't be on the floor there. Moses! Look at the curtain!"

165

Ernie started to get to his feet. His mind was whirling. Then it all came back to him. *Was the county superintendent still there? No. There's the box of books on the floor, and I remember he left. Uff da! That was a close one. What if Mr. Swanson would have seen me sprawled on the floor?* Ernie saw the main curtain lying on the floor. He had pulled the hook-screw for the curtain wire out of the wall. Vic helped him to his chair. Ernie grabbed him tightly by the arm and said, "Look! Nobody can know about this. Promise you won't tell anyone."

"Okay, okay, but we've got to get that curtain back up. Where's the ladder? I'll go get it."

"It's out in the woodshed." Ernie stood up and saw Carla standing in the doorway.

She looked at the curtain on the floor. "Holy smokes! What happened here?"

Ernie said, "I don't have time to explain it right now. I had another dream. I'm okay, but please keep it under your hat."

"My lips are sealed." Carla looked up at the hole in the plaster where the hook came out. "You know, maybe it's good that happened. Can you imagine if it came down during the program?"

"I never thought of that." Ernie was starting to feel better. Vic returned with the ladder, and Ernie said, "Thanks, buddy. Before we hang the curtain, let's get Tom inside."

Vic and Ernie lifted the wheelchair up on the porch and Dale pushed Tom into the cloakroom, where they took off their coats and Carla hung them up.

Ernie climbed the ladder, and using a hammer and nail, he made a new hole for the hook-screw. When he had it snugly in place, Vic handed him the curtain wire and he fastened it to the hook. "That should hold okay now."

Vic went over to the gas lanterns and started to pump them up. "Maybe you can stand on a desk and get the lanterns hung. There's a hook in front and one in back. Do you see them?"

"Okay." When the lanterns were in place, Ernie looked around and said, "I think everything is done now."

"Yeah," said Vic, "I just need to put a couple of kerosene lanterns in the toilets. That should do it."

Tom shouted out, "Well, I'm ready for the big show!"

Chapter XI...The Basket Social

Ernie had a few last words for the students behind the curtains. "Okay, please listen. Do you hear that sound out there?" They all froze and listened to the chatter of the parents, former students, bachelor farmers, and other older folks who didn't have children of their own attending Dahl School. "The room is packed and they're all eager to hear you do your best."

Pricilla, a little second grade girl, tugged at Ernie's suit coat, "Teacher, I have to go bad."

"Okay, I should have thought of that. Anyone who has to go, slip out by the side curtain now and get right back. Mr. Vic put kerosene lanterns in the toilets, so you should be able to see. But be careful. Don't fall down the hole or you'll miss the show." The students let out with nervous giggles.

When they came back, Ernie was ready to begin the program. He looked into their stark faces. He thought some of the little ones would make perfect Halloween ghosts. Their faces were white with fear.

"Okay, everyone get in your places. Pick-a-Pumpkin kids, get your pumpkins out of the library and line up. Peter, I put a box of matches in one of the pumpkins. Light each of the candles as soon as the children are in place. Okay, Eunice, "I'll give you a nod when I've finished my little speech." Ernie looked down at the script he was holding in his hand. It was shaking so badly, he could hear the papers rattle. "Okay, I'm going out front. Dale, follow me with the flag and stand by my side. The rest of you, stay quiet and good luck. I know you'll do a very good job!"

Ernie and Dale carefully slipped out where the curtains joined in the middle, and Ernie could not believe the size of the crowd. Every seat was taken and folks stood two-rows-deep along the windows to the south, along the back wall, and along the wall to the north. He could see farmers' heads stretching out from the back door to the cloakroom, and little toddlers were sitting on the benches, close enough to tickle Ernie's knees. They slowly grew quiet. Every face pointed toward the front. Dale held up the flag and said, "Please rise for the 'Pledge of Allegiance'." The crowd rose, the older folks struggling to get out from their desks.

After the 'Pledge', Dale slipped behind the curtain, and Ernie raised his voice, "Thank you all for coming out. When I saw those snow flurries this morning, I was a little worried about the weather, but the Lord has blessed us with a clear night for our festivities. I've met most of you, but if you don't know it by now, I'm Mr. Juvland, the teacher here, and I'm proud to show you the program your children have worked very hard to prepare. They are wonderful boys and girls, maybe a little nervous right now."

Ernie held out his hand to show them it was shaking. "And their teacher is a little nervous, too. But before we begin, I would like to thank all the people who have helped us with the program, especially Mrs. Henning and Mr. Vic, and I can't forget Eunice Skime, our talented musician, who will play the piano for our program. Eunice, would you stand up? Eunice is in seventh grade and she has really become my music teacher, and that's good because I can't play. I tried to learn 'Twinkle, Twinkle, Little Star', but it hurt the dog's ears. He started howling in pain. How about a hand for the helpers!"

There were a few chuckles and everyone clapped for the helpers. Ernie continued, "There are two more people I would like to introduce. You might have noticed the young man in uniform standing by the windows. I met him earlier. He is Private William Backlin, and his little sister Priscilla goes to school here. In fact she is standing right behind this curtain, ready to sing. Private Backlin is home on furlough and will be shipped overseas in another week. We want to remember him and all of the other servicemen and servicewomen in our prayers and let us also pray that this war will soon end, so all our loved ones can come home."

Ernie took a deep breath. "There is another gentleman you all know, but I believe he should be recognized. That's Mr. Elmer Gustafson. He's the man who built this school back in 1907." Everyone turned to look at a small, bent over man in his 80s standing by the back door. There was a good round of applause for the soldier and the old carpenter.

Ernie started to chuckle, "I don't know if you heard what I heard from behind the curtain. One of my students said, 'Come on, let's get the show on the road!'" Everyone laughed. Ernie smiled and turned to Eunice, nodded and slipped behind the curtain. The music rang out from the old upright piano and the curtain slowly opened. There in a row, were ten first, second and third graders. They held their pumpkins below their chins and the flickering light of the candles lit their faces in a soft, yellow glow. They sang.

Pick a pick a pumpkin from the pile.
We can make his eyes
and a great big smile.
Pick a pick a pumpkin round and clean,
Then we'll be ready for Halloween!
Halloween, Halloween,
Then we'll be ready for Halloween!

They were off and running and Ernie felt good. At the end of the song the curtains closed, the kids blew out their candles, and put them back in the library. The fifth, sixth, seventh and eighth graders lined up with their Tonettes. The curtains opened and they played, "Swing Low, Sweet Chariot". They took their bows and the little kids marched in a line and stopped in front of the older students, holding their rhythm sticks, drums, sandpaper blocks, triangles, and tambourines. Eunice played the intro to "Dancing to the Sound of the Tambourine".

Kick up your heels and let's make a scene,
Make a funny hat and paint your face green.
Don't care what people think,
When you act like rinky-dinks,
Cause we're dancing to the sound
of the tambourine.

Ernie sat on his stool backstage and slapped his knee in time. Everything was working out just fine. The kids were having fun and their parents were loving it. Next came a short play the students had written about three gossiping women making a patchwork quilt stretched on a frame and propped up on the backs of four chairs. Two little boys were hiding under the quilt making comments about what the women said. They acted like little old ladies and imitated their voices.

Next, two girls sang a duet in harmony, "Way Down Upon the Suwannee River". Following the song came another original play about two older boys pouring water down gopher holes to flush out three little gophers.

After the play the first, second, and third graders sang another Halloween song.

169

October brings us Halloween,
A spooky time, it's true,
When Jack-O'Lantern's flaming eyes
Seem like they're watching you!

The black cat's howling at the moon,
A witch goes flying by;
And in the distance you can hear
A goblin's mournful cry.

October brings us Halloween,
A spooky time, it's true,
Be careful or, before you know,
A ghost will scare you... BOO!

While they sang, Ernie was in the library getting Marvin and Clyde into the cow costume for Dale's play. They were reaching the end of the program and Ernie said to the boys, "Now, the program is going great! Just remember what we rehearsed and no monkey business when you get out there. Do you understand that?"

Both ends of the cow said, "Yes, sir!"

Peter stepped through the middle opening of the curtain. Eunice banged out a half dozen loud chords on the piano and Peter yelled out, "And now, ladies and gentlemen, direct from the Ringling Brothers and Barnum and Bailey Circus, allow me to introduce Master Dale Henning and Bertha, his amazing talking cow!"

The curtain opened and there stood Dale, dressed in a tuxedo, red vest, and a stovepipe hat Carla had made out of—what else? A piece of stovepipe! He held a silver baton in his hand and said, "Ladies and gentlemen, I present to you, Bertha, the amazing talking cow!" The cow came out, very lively, but she had trouble seeing. She butted into Dale and almost knocked him over.

Dale tapped the cow on the head with his baton and said, "Steady there, old girl. Now, remember all the lessons I have taught you. First of all, who is the President of the United States?

In a loud voice the cow said, "Clem Kadiddlehopper."

The folks laughed, and Dale bopped the cow on the head again. "No Dummy! Our President is Franklin Roosevelt."

The cow said, "Sorry, I thought it was Mickey Mouse."

170

A voice came from the back end of the cow, "I thought it was Daffy Duck."

Dale bopped the cow on the head with the baton again. The audience loved it, but Ernie was wondering where their shenanigans was going.

"I want you to get serious, Bertha. You're giving me silly answers, and you know better. Now, who were the two young brothers from Dayton, Ohio, who invented the first airplane?"

The cow thought for a moment and said, "Amos and Andy."

Dale said, "No!" He bopped the cow on the head.

"Abbot and Costello."

"No!" Bop on the head!

"Bob Hope and Bing Crosby."

"No!"

"Jack Benny and Rochester."

Then Dale did his finest imitation of Jack Benny. He said, "Now, cut that out!" He gave the cow three more bops to the head. "Now, one final question and you'd better get this one right, or we'll all be in trouble. Give me the name of our teacher."

The cow said, "Betty Boop," and the audience went wild. The curtain closed and the cow stumbled toward the wings followed by Dale. When they went by Ernie, he slapped Dale on the back, and said, "I'm going to kill you guys! Just you wait!" Dale knew he was only kidding because Ernie had a big smile on his face.

The audience was still laughing and some of them started to clap, as Ernie walked out in front of the curtain. He held up his hand to quiet them down. "You didn't know my real name is Betty Boop, did you?" More laughter. "Let me assure you, that's not the way we rehearsed it."

Ernie looked around at the smiling faces and said, "We have come to the end of our program, but we want to close with something very nice." Ernie looked down at his notes. "In honor of his father, who is on a ship this very minute on his way to some island in the Pacific, Dwight Alstad has asked if he could sing a song." Ernie looked up and said, "Marine Corporal Robert Alstad, this is for you, 'The Soldier's Farewell'." The curtain opened and young Dwight stepped forward. Behind him were all of his schoolmates, their hands folded and their heads bowed. It was so still in the room, all Dwight heard was the hissing of the gas lantern hanging over his head. Eunice played the introduction softly, and the shy young boy began to sing.

Ah, love, how can I leave thee?
The sad thought deep doth grieve me,
But know, what e'er befalls me,
I go where honor calls me.
Farewell, farewell, my own true love!
Farewell, farewell, my own true love!
No more shall I behold thee,
Or to my heart enfold thee;
In war's array appearing
The foe's stern boats are nearing.
Farewell, farewell, my own true love!
Farewell, farewell, my own true love!
I think of thee with longing;
Think thou, when tears are thronging,
That with my last fain't sighing,
I'll whisper soft, while dying-
Farewell farewell, my own true love,
Farewell, farewell, my own true love.

Ernie stepped forward and shook Dwight's hand, "Thank you, Dwight. That was beautiful. And now in closing, your wonderful sons and daughters would like to sing one of my favorite songs, 'America, the Beautiful'."

O beautiful for spacious skies,
For amber waves of grain,
For purple mountain majesties
Above the fruited plain!
America! America!
God shed His grace on thee,
And crown thy good with brotherhood
From sea to shining sea!

The students of Dahl School joined hands and stepped forward to take a bow. The audience rose to give them a standing ovation. The curtain closed and the kids went berserk. They were jumping up and down, hugging each other, and wildly laughing. Ernie gave hugs and handshakes to all of his happy students.

172

Orvid Skime was the first parent to approach Ernie, "Didn't I tell you my Eunice could play the piano good? I just hope she doesn't get the big head now." He came up close, tapped Ernie on the chest with his finger, and said, "She still has to feed the chickens you know."

Ernie looked to the back of the room, and saw Dale with his mom and dad. Carla gave him a big hug and Tom reached over to shake his hand and pat him on top of his head. The cow was back there as well. Marvin and Clyde had put the costume back on and were parading around. Some of the younger children were laughing and petting the cow. One father lifted his three-year-old boy up and set him on top of the cow. He said, "Giddyap, Bertha! We're going to the rodeo!"

Peter Brunsvold and Iris Vic were setting up the fishpond. Iris was in front collecting a dime from each student who went fishing for a prize behind the side curtain. Attached to the fishing pole was a string, and on the end of the string was a spring-loaded clothespin. Iris had to help some of the smaller students throw their lines over the curtain where Peter sat with a bag of prizes for the fishers, a pencil, an eraser, or if they were really lucky, they might catch a lollipop, a cookie, or a candy bar.

But it wasn't long before there was chaos in the fishpond. Ernie was over by the window talking to Private Backlin, when he heard a bloodcurdling scream! Then he heard Iris yelling at Peter, "You dirty rat, you! Just you wait! I'm gonna get you back!"

Ernie worked his way through the crowd to question Iris. "Hey, hey, hey. What's going on here?"

Iris said, "Please, Mr. Juvland. I want you to paddle Peter on his behind! Look what he did!" She held up her fishing pole for Ernie to see. There dangling on the end of the line was a dead mouse!

Ernie went behind the curtain, trying to keep from laughing. He put his arm around Peter, ushered him into the library, and closed the door. Trying very hard to wipe the smile off his face, Ernie spoke in a stern voice. "Listen, Peter, I let you run the fishpond, because I can trust you. Now why would you play such a nasty trick like that on Iris?"

Peter said in a whisper, "I didn't do it to be mean. It's hard for me to explain. Well, I kind of like her."

173

Ernie put his arm around him. "Okay, I figured that. I see you two together all the time. But I think you should express your affection in a nicer way. Write her a note or something."

"I can't do that, Mr. Juvland. She'd just laugh at me and probably show it to a bunch of girls!"

"Okay, I'm sure you'll find a way of showing Iris how you feel about her. Just take this advice: a dead mouse isn't going to do the trick!"

Peter looked up and managed to smile. "Yes, sir."

"Now get back in the fishpond and remember, no more monkey business!" When Ernie opened the door to the library he heard the girls giggling and squealing. Iris was shouting with glee, "I got him in trouble! I got him in trouble!"

Ernie heard Vic's booming voice. "Okay, does everyone have a Bingo card? And if you need more corn, we have a couple of kids up here who can help you out with corn! Yes, you can't play the game without some corn." He stood up front and his wife, Betty, who sat at a desk beside him with a milk pail full of little tile pieces. Spread out in front of her was the big BINGO chart.

"Okay, is everyone ready? Your first number is 'FREE'. Yes, Indeed. You will find it in the middle of your card. Yes, put a kernel of corn on 'FREE'."

Some of the people laughed, and a woman over by the window said to the lady sitting next to her, "He does that every year and thinks it's funny. Tell you the truth, I think it's getting old!"

One of the farmers back by the stove said, "Come on Vic, stop joking around and let's play Bingo!"

Vic was laughing. "Well, I just had to add a bit of levitation to the situation. Okay, I'm getting serious now. Here we go." Vic reached into the milk pail and pulled out the first tile piece. "Under the G—54."

While Vic and Betty were running the Bingo game, Carla and Chub Skime had carried the little-kid-table to the front of the room, where they neatly arranged all the baskets. The standard basket was a shoebox decorated with colored wrapping paper and usually tied together with a ribbon and a fancy bow. Ernie had told all the girls, even the little ones, to make a basket of food that would be auctioned off. Some of the mothers also made baskets, and some of the former Dahl School girls put one together, hoping their high school boyfriend would win it.

After several rounds of Bingo, Vic, Betty, and a few students gathered the cards and corn and put everything in the milk pail. Then Vic walked over to the table which displayed more than a dozen baskets. "Okay, pipe down out there. Pipe down!" Most of the folks stopped talking. "Yes, they give me these jobs because I have the loudest voice in the county."

Betty said, "Yeah, you don't need to tell them that, honey. Everybody knows you're a loudmouth!" The folks laughed.

"She should know," said Vic, "because I'm always yelling at her." He picked up a basket wrapped in bright red paper, with a yellow bow. "Now, gentlemen, don't be shy. This is your chance to share a lunch with some lovely lady. And who knows, it might start a beautiful romance.

"And keep in mind, all the money we raise here tonight will help Mr. Juvland buy school supplies for your children. And we need the money. I should tell you, the last order for paper and some other things, Mr. Juvland paid for that out of his own pocket. And that ain't right! So gentlemen, don't be a bunch of tightwads, and somebody out there, what do you give me for this beautiful basket? I would bet my best milk cow that this basket was made by a vision of loveliness!"

Dale had talked to his mother about bidding on a basket, but he didn't tell her about the inside information he had on Susan Rollag, the third grade girl who had sent him the birthday card. That morning out on the playground, Dale found out that Susan had made a basket. She had one of her girlfriends tell Dale that her basket would be wrapped in blue paper and covered with gold hearts. Dale did not see the basket on the table, but he figured maybe it was way down at the bottom of the pile.

The bidding went on, and Vic was enjoying the spotlight showing off his auctioneer's voice. "I have 25, 25, 25...who'll give me 50? Do I hear 50 cents for this fancy basket made by some vision of loveliness?"

Dale stood in the back by his mother and father. In his pocket was a one dollar bill Tom had given him to spend at the social. He did not play the fishpond, nor bob for apples, and he didn't play Bingo; so he still had that sweaty dollar bill in his pocket. He was saving it for Susan. Finally, he saw it, the blue box with the gold hearts. Vic held it high over his head. Dale looked over at Susan, who was sitting in a double seat with her mother. Susan looked back at Dale and waved at him with her fingers.

"Okay, gentlemen, who's going to start the bidding on this lovely basket? Just look at these exquisite gold hearts. I'll bet the girl who made this basket is looking for a boyfriend. Who will start the bidding?"

Dale tugged at his mother's skirt. "You do it, Ma. I'm too scared. Say 25 cents, Ma, please."

Carla looked down and said in a whisper. "No, Dale, you have to be a man now. Go ahead."

In a voice that cracked, Dale said, "25 cents."

Vic didn't miss a beat, "I hear 25 from the nervous little man in the back. Do I hear 50, 50, 50?"

A bald head rose from the bunch of farmers standing in the back doorway of the cloakroom. A gruff voice blurted out, "50 cents!"

All the heads turned to the back. It was old Willard Hoppstead, a bachelor farmer, who lived just down the road. He stood well over six feet and on the ends of his long arms, where callused hands the size of shovels. He wore bib overalls, a white shirt with black armbands, and a broad, flowered necktie of many colors. He had big fluffy eyebrows that had not been trimmed in years. They hung over his deep set eyes like a thatched roof. He was skinny, and noticeably uncomfortable, a quiet man, more suited to a barn than social gatherings. He stroked his necktie with his long fingers and stared at Dale, waiting, waiting.

Finally the young boy shouted, "75 cents."

In an instant, Willard Hoppstead answered in a louder voice this time, "One dollar!"

Dale took the wet, wrinkled dollar out of his pocket and looked at his mother. "Ma, Ma, can I have a quarter?"

Carla glanced around for her purse. She thought, "Where did I leave it? Is it in the library?"

Vic boomed out, "Do I hear one dollar and twenty five cents? One-twenty-five, one-twenty-five, one-twenty-five?"

Dale poked his dad's arm, "Pa, can I have a quarter?"

Vic was looking back at Dale, "How about it, young man, do I hear one-twenty-five?"

176

Tom Henning took his son's hand and whispered, "Sorry, Dale, I told you just a dollar. That's final. Besides, Willard will just keep bidding. He's well off, you know."

Vic pounded his fist on the table. "Going once. Going twice. Sold, American! It goes to the gentleman by the back door! Bring me a buck, Willard, and come get your basket."

The gangly old bachelor farmer walked to the front of the room and paid Betty Vic with a crisp one-dollar bill. Then he held the basket, which looked like a tiny pill box in his enormous hands. He stood staring out at the crowd, not knowing what to do next.

Then he saw Susan Rollag's mother getting up from the double seat beside her third grade daughter. "Willard," the mother said, "she's over here."

He walked down the aisle and Susan didn't look up. She slid as far to the side of the double seat as she could without falling off. Willard put the basket on the desk and tried to squeeze into the seat, but his legs were too long. So he sat on the floor by the desk and put the shoebox in his lap. Susan had put her head down on her desk and covered it with her arms, not daring to see what was happening.

Her mother patted her on the head and said, "Be nice now." Susan didn't move. "Come now. You're supposed to visit with the man." Susan started to sob.

Dale stood by his father and watched Willard tear off the bow and rip off the paper and open the shoebox. The bachelor farmer took the little chicken salad sandwiches, cut in triangles, and wolfed each of them down with one bite. He bit into a plum, squirting plum juice in all directions. Willard gnawed on a chicken leg until there was nothing but bone. He sucked on the bone, tossed it back in the box, and wiped his hands on his overalls. Susan's mother had kneeled down next to her daughter and had an arm around the sobbing girl.

Young Dale Henning had seen enough. He darted into the cloakroom, grabbed his coat, and ran outside.

Willard took out a wedge of blueberry pie. There was a fork in the box, but he didn't use it. He grabbed the pie with his big hand and munched it in three bites. He wiped his hands on his pants again and started rattling his false teeth in his mouth. He pulled out the upper plate and with a thick finger found a blueberry seed and flicked it away. He slapped his denture plate back in his mouth and looked over at Susan's mother. "I saved the Jell-O for her." He held up a small dish of cherry Jell-O topped with a dollop of whipped cream.

Susan's mother said, "No. I guess she's tired."

"Past her bedtime, eh?" said Willard. He licked the whip cream off the top and sucked up the Jell-O in slurps without using a spoon. He put the empty box up on the desk; he got up off the floor, and wiped his hands on his pants. He said, "Thank you." He let out a loud burp, coughed up a juicy gob of phlegm, and swallowed it. He wiped his mouth with his sleeve and said, "Just glad I didn't have to fix supper tonight." He went into the cloakroom, put on his winter coat, his cap, and headed for home.

Outside, Dale had joined a bunch of kids to play 'hide-and-seek'. "There he comes," said one of Dale's friends. They stopped playing to watch Willard Hoppstead come out of the school. He walked by the boys without saying a word. When he was well out of earshot, Dale said, "My pa said he's well off."

Inside, Eunice was sitting on the piano bench, thumbing through the *Golden Book of Songs*. She was looking for "Skip-to-my-Lou".

Vic was standing by her ready for another announcement. "Okay, listen here now. We have to work off some of that food we've stuffed ourselves with. Yes, indeed. We're gonna dance. You bet! It wouldn't be a Halloween Basket Social without doing a few rounds of 'Skip-to-my-Lou'. Now, we need a little help from the men. We have to move all the desks over by the window. Last year we stacked them on top of each other to give us plenty of room to dance."

The men cleared the area and started looking around for a partner. "Skip-to-my-Lou" is a partner-stealing square-dance done with four pairs. When the farmers and their wives were in place, Vic took charge. "Hey, Orvid, don't put any more wood in the stove, cause it's gonna get pretty hot in here once we start dancing. Okay, grab your partner and here we go." Vic sang out loud and clear.

Fly's in the buttermilk,
Shoo, fly, shoo,
Fly's in the buttermilk,
Shoo, fly, shoo,

178

Fly's in the buttermilk,
Shoo, fly, shoo,
Skip to my Lou, my darlin'.
Cat's in the cream jar,
Ooh, ooh, ooh,
Cat's in the cream jar,
Ooh, ooh, ooh,
Cat's in the cream jar,
Ooh, ooh, ooh,
Skip to my Lou, my darlin'.
Lost my partner,
What'll I do?
Lost my partner,
What'll I do?
Lost my partner,
What'll I do?
Skip to my Lou, my darlin'.
I'll get another one
Prettier than you,
I'll get another one
Prettier than you,
I'll get another one
Prettier than you,
Skip to my Lou, my darlin',
Skip to my Lou, my darlin'.

Yes, indeed, they were sweaty when they finished, and then, another set of partners moved in and they did it all over again.

By ten o'clock it was time to straighten things up and go home to bed. Some folks were almost out the door when Betty shouted out, "The blanket! The Indian blanket! We have to draw the winning ticket."

They all stopped in their tracks. Vic said, "Ernie, do you have the ticket stubs?"

"I'll get them." Ernie took an empty fishbowl from the top of the piano, put the stubs inside, and stirred them up. "The kids did a terrific job of selling tickets, and Marvin Newquist wins the prize for selling the most. He sold 29 tickets. Come up here, Marvin."

The sixth grade boy walked to the front of the room. "Now, your dad told me he gave you a BB gun for your birthday,

179

so here's some ammunition." Ernie handed the boy a tube of BBs. They shook hands and Marvin was a happy lad. "Good job, Marvin. I have another announcement. We added it all up, and the kids sold $51.25 in raffle tickets, and I'll bet with the money you all chipped in tonight we'll have more than eighty bucks." Everyone clapped.

"Okay, Marvin, since you won the prize," Ernie said, "I'm going to ask you to draw the winning ticket." Ernie stirred up the tickets, and Marvin reached inside. He grabbed a ticket and handed it to his teacher. Ernie held the ticket close to the lantern. "Okay, it says 'Ben Smierud' on the ticket.'"

Orvid piped up, "Like hell. Draw another one!"

Ernie said, "No, I can see his name on the ticket. Ben Smierud wins the blanket."

Orvid said, "He ain't here. Draw another one!"

Ernie objected, "No, that's not right. The students set the rules. You didn't have to be present for the drawing. I told them to make that clear when they sold a ticket."

Orvid blurted out, "Son of a bitch!"

Chub said, "Orvid, please! The children!"

Ernie tried to smooth things over. "We need to know who sold the ticket to Mr. Smierud." Little Pricilla raised her hand. "Pricilla, come up here. I'm going to give you a prize. It's a beautiful pair of mittens made by Mrs. Vic." Ernie reached into his desk drawer and pulled out the mittens for Pricilla. "Now, tell us how you sold it."

She was very nervous. "My pa took me in the tavern. Buck and Velma each bought a ticket. And then..." She turned to her dad and said, "You tell them, Pa."

Pricilla's dad put his arm around her and said, "Well, Ben was in there and I guess he heard Buck and Velma buying their tickets and I remember he said, 'Little girl, what are you selling?'

"Well, Pricilla was scared, but I held her hand and we walked down to the end of the bar.

"Ben said, 'You don't have to be scared of me, little girl.' He patted her on the head and she looked up and said, 'I'm selling tickets for an Indian blanket. It's for school.' Well, Ben reached for a quarter sitting next to his beer and gave it to Pricilla. She handed him a pencil so he could write his name on the ticket and that was that."

180

Chub Skime spoke up, "Well, that was nice." But Orvid was still shaking his head.

As the crowd left, Ernie stood at the door and thanked everyone for coming out. Vic and Ernie helped carry Tom's wheelchair down the steps. They carefully lifted him into the pickup. Ernie put his arm around Dale and said, "I'm sorry you didn't win Susan's basket."

Dale said, "Well, Pa said Mr. Hoppstead is well off. So, that's the way it goes." Dale lowered his voice. "Then Pa said, 'You still have your dollar. Spend it on something you really need.' I didn't know what he was talking about."

Ernie tried to explain. "Well, Dale, maybe your dad has forgotten what it's like to be a young boy in love."

"Gee, I wouldn't exactly say I'm in love." He stammered, "I don't know what it is. I just feel funny, sort of tingly and nervous all over when I'm around Susan."

Ernie said, "That sounds like love to me."

Carla stuck her head out the window and said, "Come on, Ernie, jump in!"

Ernie asked, "Do you need help getting Tom in the house?"

"No, we could call Kenny Torstad and his brother. What's up?"

"There's something I need to do."

"Okay, but don't stay too long now. You need your rest."

When Ernie came back in the schoolhouse, Betty Vic was taking the Indian blanket down from the wall. Iris was sitting in a front desk next to her dad. Vic said, "I don't know about you, but I'm pooped out."

Ernie said, "I'm tired, too. Didn't we have fun tonight?"

Betty was folding the blanket on Ernie's desk. "We'll drop the blanket off at Ben's tomorrow."

"No," said Ernie. "I want to do that myself. And if you can give me a lift, I'd like to do it right now."

Vic said, "Oh, I don't think you have to do that."

"I know, but I want to, and the sooner the better."

"Okay, suit yourself," said Vic. Betty carried the blanket, and Ernie and Vic each carried a lantern. They checked the stove, locked the door, and climbed into Vic's car. Betty sat by Vic and Ernie and Iris sat in the back.

As they came up Ben Smierud's lane, Betty noticed a dim, yellow light in the window. She spoke up, "Looks like he's home. His pickup is over by the barn."

They stopped near the front steps and Betty said, "Do you want us to come in with you?"

"No, it's better if you stay in the car. I want to talk about his boys and that's kind of personal."

Vic said, "We understand. And I don't think you have to worry. He ain't dangerous."

Ernie took the blanket and climbed out of the back seat. Vic kept the headlights on, so he could see his way up the steps. One of the boards was loose and Ernie had to reach for the post to catch his balance. He looked through the porch window and saw an old man, with a gray beard. Bunches of gray hair stuck out from under his cap. He was sitting in an old stuffed chair wrapped in a brown horse blanket. A kerosene lamp and an empty whiskey bottle sat on a small table near the chair. Ernie saw at least a dozen cats in the room. He tapped on the windowpane.

The old man yelled, "Go away, goddamn it!"

Ernie saw the cats scurrying around the room. One jumped up on the table. Another leaped into Ben's lap. Ernie yelled from the window, "Mr. Smierud, it's Ernie Juvland, the teacher."

"What the hell do you want? My boys are gone!"

"It's not about them. Can I come in?"

It was still, only the sound of the cats. Then he said, "What are you waiting for? The door ain't locked."

Ernie opened the door and said, "Mr. Smierud, I brought you this blanket. You won it in the school raffle."

"What waffle? I don't make waffles. I eat pancakes."

"No, I said, 'raffle'. We had a raffle for this Indian blanket to raise money. You bought the winning ticket. Here it is."

"I don't remember buying any ticket."

"It was in Buck and Velma's tavern. You bought that ticket you're holding. See. You wrote your name on it."

He stared at the ticket. He looked up. "The little girl."

"Yes. Her name is Pricilla. She's in my second grade class over at the school."

Ben looked down at the black cat he was holding. He stroked its fur. Then he spoke without looking up. "My boys were over there, Bobby and Neal. But now they're gone. Now I just have my babies." He lifted the cat and looked into its eyes. "Yes, sir. All my little poddies. I have 13 now and I've got names for all of them." He nuzzled the black cat in his beard and said, "This one here is Louise. Yes, sir. Louise likes me, doesn't she? Yes, she does. My cute little poddy."

"Okay," Ernie said as he walked over to a big table. "I can't stay right now, but maybe I'll come back and we can talk about Bobby and Neal."

Ben let out a laugh, "They told me you beat the stuffing out of them, first day of school."

Ernie managed to smile. "Is that what they said?"

"Yes, sir. And I said, 'Good for him!'"

"Well, I tried my best."

"Hey, you wanna snort?" Ben put down the cat and reached for the whiskey bottle on the little table. He held it to the light and saw it was empty. "Well, ain't that a kick in the balls!"

"I'll come back another time," said Ernie. He put the blanket on the big table and immediately two cats jumped on it and started clawing the fabric. Ernie stepped back and made his way to the door. "You take 'er easy now." He looked back at Ben and saw that he was nodding off. He left him there in his chair with his 13 cats. He carefully went down the steps and climbed into the back seat of Vic's car.

"How did it go?" asked Betty.

"Okay, I guess," said Ernie. "What can you say? He's a sad old man and his boys are in jail."

Vic started to back out. Then he stopped and yelled out in his booming voice, "Cheese and crackers got all muddy on the sunny beach! I smell cat piss!"

Chapter XII...The Blizzard

Ten days later on November 7, Ernie, Tom, and Carla sat up all night listening to the presidential election returns come in over the radio. Tom was a staunch Republican and was pulling for his man, Thomas E. Dewey, Governor of New York. Tom blamed Roosevelt for getting us into the war and complained about FDR being a Socialist, spending hard-earned tax money on giveaway programs like the CCC and the WPA. Carla remained neutral, though she had confided in Ernie that she was raised a Democrat by her parents. Just before dawn, it was clear that Roosevelt would win his fourth term. It had never been done before, and Ernie was happy. The Roosevelt-Truman ticket carried 36 of the 48 states. FDR received 439 electoral votes to 99 for Dewey.

A month passed and after Thanksgiving the weather in Jackson Township turned bitterly cold. Deer hunters complained about being out in below zero weather, facing a biting wind blasting down from Canada, with nothing between home and the North Pole but a strand of barbed wire fence.

But Tom wouldn't have complained. He would have gladly stood in 30 below weather, just for the chance to be hunting one more time. It made him angry to see his 30-30 lever action Winchester hanging over the front door. It reminded him of all the years he had hunted deer going back to his first year with a gun. He was twelve and drove deer for his dad. The next year, his pa let him post, and he shot his first deer, a small doe, with the very gun hanging over the door. Now he sat in his wheelchair and listened to the wind.

Winter had come like a nasty ogre from the North and would hold farmers in its icy grip until the spring thaw. There's an old saying, "We don't have summers in northern Minnesota, just three months of tough sledding."

One night Ernie heard sleet hitting hard against his west window from midnight on; by morning the window was coated with a thick glaze of ice. It was December 7, 1944, the war was three years old, and Ernie was thinking about his brother Andy. *He's done with basic training now. I'll bet he's counting the days till he gets his furlough. Sure will be good to see the kid.* Ernie dressed warm for school and went downstairs.

Tom was in his wheelchair near the stove with his feet resting on the opened oven door. With no expression, his tired eyes meandered from his slippers, to the ice-coated window, to Dale, who was sitting at the table hunched over his bowl of oatmeal. Carla stopped cranking the cream separator when she heard Kenny Torstad on the porch, kicking on the bottom of the door. She opened the door and the hired man came in with a huge armful of split wood for the kitchen stove.

He dumped the pieces in the wood box and took off his mittens. "Holy Moses, you can't hardly walk out there! You could skate between here and the woodshed. I've never seen such ice, and now it's turned to snow."

As Carla was sweeping out the snow that had blown in through the open door, she smelled burnt rubber and threw down her broom. The bottoms of Tom's slippers were smoking. She carefully removed them and examined the soles of his feet. They were warm, but not burned. She dressed him in wool socks and gently placed his feet on the footrests of the wheelchair. Tom stared at the ice on the window. He had never been in prison, but his house felt like it now, stranded, helpless, locked in a block of ice.

Ernie poured himself a cup of coffee and wondered how he'd make it to school. The temperature had dropped below zero, and the morning newsman over WDAY in Fargo was warning about a blizzard, heavy snow, and strong winds sweeping across North Dakota. Ranchers on the western plains were fighting three-foot drifts, trying to get hay to cattle stranded out on the range.

Kenny rambled on with nonstop chatter, "Good thing you had chunks that were split in the woodshed. The stuff outside is so thick with ice you can't pry the pieces apart. Holy Moses, what a mess out there! And now the snow is coming down sideways. You can't even see where you're goin'."

Tom looked over at Ernie. "Looks like you'll have the day off."

Ernie was quick to answer, "No, I have to go. I'm sure some of the kids will try to make it, and I want the stove fired up when they get there."

Tom said, "Well, you're the boss, but I think we'll keep Dale home. The way the snow is coming down now, who knows? The news says it could get a lot worse."

185

Dale put down his spoon hard, "No, Pa. I have to go. I have perfect attendance and I don't want to miss."

Ernie smiled. "I'm glad you said that, Dale, but maybe you should listen to your father."

Carla put a plate of scrambled eggs in front of Ernie and said, "I think we should let the boy go. My gosh, he hasn't missed a day, and that means a lot to him."

Kenny took over cranking the cream separator. "Heck, let the kid go. Heck, he's got his teacher, big strong guy to look out for him. What's the big deal? I remember back when my brother and I were in school. I was in the third grade and he was in the first. We were just little tykes, but Ma bundled us up and pushed us out the door. Heck, it was the worst blizzard in forty years. It was cold enough to freeze the nuts off a sulky plow!"

Tom cut him off. "Shut the hell up! We've heard that story a hundred times. Shut up with it!" He wheeled his chair over by the table and held Dale's hand. "You're our gift from God, son. We lost your little brother and now you're all we have." Kenny stopped cranking the separator and listened. Tom looked over at Ernie and said, "It looks like I've been overruled. Damn it! I hate to give in to anything a woman says, but if his mother thinks it's okay, well, I'm sure you know how we feel. I'm counting on you to get the boy to school and get him home again, safe and sound. Do you understand?"

"I understand," said Ernie. Then he added, "I wouldn't go myself, but I'd worry all day about some little youngster walking all the way to school in this awful weather and finding the door locked. I'd picture that child standing on the porch, knowing that the only thing to do was to turn around and start walking back home. I have to go, and if Dale insists on going, I'll take good care of him."

Carla was at the stove putting in more wood. She wiped her hands on her apron and walked over to Dale, putting her hands on his shoulders. "I think we sometimes forget what it's like for a teacher. We have one child here, but Mr. Juvland has 22 sons and daughters, who depend on him every day. And we parents depend on him to keep our children safe and out of trouble. We sometimes forget."

Tom was impatient. "You didn't need to make a speech." He rolled his wheelchair past her and headed for the front room.

He stopped at the door and whipped the chair around to face Carla. "There was a time when a wife knew enough to keep her damned trap shut. Just look at my wife! Standing there trying to tell me what's right and what's wrong! Sludder! I'm still the man of this house and don't you forget it!" He gasped for air, and with his strong hands on the armrests, he tried to lift himself out of his wheelchair. "If I could get out of this chair, I'd slap some sense into you, woman!"

Carla was silent. She started clearing the table.

Dale didn't know much Norwegian, but he knew enough to know his pa had used a cussword. It scared the boy. He was relieved when he and his teacher were out the door and on their way to school, slipping and sliding with each step. The strong wind was blowing the snow off the road, leaving glare ice on the packed surface. It was like walking on a skating rink. They soon found it was easier to walk in the ditch than up on the road. Dale was light enough to walk on top of the snow crust, but Ernie's boots punched through, making each step a struggle.

Ernie pulled on Dale's hand and said, "Look up there!" He pointed at the telephone wire overhead. It was thick with ice. Gusts of wind were swaying the line back and forth and tiny icicles were snapping off the wire and shattering on the snow crust.

The snow was coming down heavier, making it more difficult to follow the ditch on their one mile trek to school. Blindly, they came to a barbed wire fence and stopped just short of plunging into it. Ernie grabbed a fence post to steady himself.

He felt Dale tugging on his pants leg again, "Where are we?" The boy moved his head around looking in all directions. He had trouble seeing. Carla had wrapped his head in a flour sack, leaving just a small, open slit for his eyes.

Ernie kneeled down to look him in the face. The cloth was covered with frost from the frozen moisture of his breath. "How are you doing, buddy?"

Dale grabbed the ice-glazed strand of barbed wire and asked, "Are we lost?"

"No, we just came out of the ditch, and we've been walking on Ole Gangstad's field." He hit the icy fencepost with his fist and said, "This post is the corner of his pasture."

"Do you see his bull?" Dale asked in a muffled voice.

"No. I'm sure he's in the barn on a day like this."

Dale remembered something and tugged at Ernie's coat. He yelled over the howling wind. "I have to tell you something that happened right here by the fence."

"You have to wait, buddy. We need to make it to the schoolhouse."

"It's important," the boy said.

Ernie couldn't hear what he said. He looked through the blowing snow and said, "The road's over there. Grab my hand." Ernie had a brief notion of turning back, but the thought quickly passed. Judging by the fence line, he knew they were almost there. He kept thinking about freezing children out on the roads, trying to make it to school. He needed to be there, to unlock the door, and build a fire.

They trudged on, Dale slipping and sliding on the slick crust, and Ernie laboring with each step, plowing through snowdrifts up to his knees. He tugged on Dale's hand and shouted. "I can see the school. We're going to make it, pal. Just a little ways to go. Keep on chugging, buddy!"

He barely heard Dale say, "Good!"

When they got to the school, Dale plopped down on the porch and said, "I'm plumb tuckered out!"

"So am I," said Ernie, as he pulled the keys out of his pocket. But the key would not go into the keyhole. Ernie touched the door with his bare hand. It was coated with a layer of ice. He said, "Stay right here, Dale. I have to get the ax out of the woodshed." He came back with the ax and an armful of kindling wood and dumped it on the porch. He pounded on the door with the flat side of the single bit ax. The ice shattered off, and tiny pieces scattered across the porch. He tried the key again, but it still wouldn't go in. He used the small blade of his jackknife to clear the ice from the keyhole. The key slipped in and he heard a click. He tugged on the doorknob and it opened.

Dale gathered up the kindling and put the pieces in the orange crate next to the big wood stove. He touched the outside jacket of the stove and said, "It's still warm."

Ernie brought in another armful of wood chunks from the big wood box in the cloakroom. "Yeah, I stuffed it full last night and closed off the damper before I left." Ernie put his load of wood on the floor and opened the door to the firebox. "Yup. We still have coals in there. Brush all the snow off your coat, but leave it on until we get the fire going." Dale tried to unwrap the flour sack from around his head, but it was frozen into a block of ice. Ernie said, "Let it thaw out and then I'll help you."

Ernie stirred the glowing coals and teased the flames with small pieces of kindling. Soon the fire was roaring, and the long stovepipe overhead started making sounds, tink, tink, tink. Dale helped Ernie bring the recitation benches back to the stove. Ernie put in three more chunks of wood and left the firebox door open. They sat down on a bench in their coats. The flour sack around Dale's head thawed out, and Ernie helped him remove it. The boy's face was red and his hair was wet. They sat close together and watched the flames leaping inside the big stove.

Dale said, "I need to tell you now."

Ernie said, "Tell me what?"

"Remember when we were standing by the fence, I told you something happened there."

"Yes, I could hardly hear you with the flour sack over your mouth. What did you want to tell me?"

"Well, remember that day last fall when you sent me back to get your logbook?"

"Yes. Did something happen? I remember when you came back. You seemed upset about something."

"I'll tell you, but you can't tell Ma or Pa."

"I won't tell. Trust me!"

"Timmy Burstrom caught me and threw me in the ditch."

"Oh, my God! Did he hurt you?"

"No. Timmy saw Anders coming and let me go."

Ernie got down on his knees in front of Dale. He held both his hands and said, "You have to tell me. Did Timmy do anything bad to you?"

Dale started to cry, "He pulled my pants down and was gonna shove a stick of wood in my poop hole."

Ernie said, "Oh, God! You poor kid!" He reached out and hugged the boy tightly. "Why on earth didn't you tell me or your mom and dad?"

"I almost did, but I knew it would get you in trouble with Ma and mostly Pa."

"How would that get me in trouble?"

"Well, I figured, if they found out that you sent me home alone to get your logbook, they might think it was your fault. You promised not to tell, right?"

"Dale, I won't tell what happened in the ditch, but I'll make sure your mom calls Timmy's mother. I want this guy put away someplace where he can't hurt you or any other youngster.

"I don't want Ma and Pa mad at you."

"Don't worry about me. I have to look out for you. I have to look out for all the kids in this school." Ernie kept listening for noises from the front porch, wondering if more students would show up. He thought about frostbitten children out on the road, fighting the wind and snow. It wouldn't make sense to go out and look for them. He had Dale to care for. All he could do was sit and wait.

Dale suddenly thought of something. He said, "You have to mark me 'present'. Can we do that now?"

"Sure," said Ernie. He managed a little chuckle. He put two more chunks of wood in the firebox, closed the door, went up to his desk, and took out the register. The ink in his fountain pen was frozen, but he used a pencil, and with Dale looking over his shoulder, he put a check mark in the 'present' column next to Dale's name, Thursday, December 7, 1944. He was surprised to feel Dale's arms around him. The boy was hugging his teacher. He had never done that before.

Dale went back to the bench to take off his overshoes. Ernie stayed at his desk and opened his logbook to the **MISTAKES** page. He had quite a list of them now and was about to add another. *Should not have sent Dale back home for my logbook. That was stupid. Timmy Burstrom is dangerous. Never let Dale out of sight again.*

By 8:30 more light was coming through the windows, but still no more students. Dale was thinking he might be the only student in school that day. The notion pleased him—he would have his teacher all to himself. But he was wrong. Soon they heard stomping of feet on the front porch. Some of Ernie's children toughed out the storm and made it to school. By nine o'clock there were twelve of them, counting Dale.

The older students helped the younger ones unwrap their scarves and flour sacks from their faces, and Ernie gave them instructions, "If you brought a jar of cocoa, or a potato to bake,

190

put them on top of the stove now. Older students, help the younger ones who can't reach."

Ernie gathered them around the stove for opening exercises, and then he helped them move their desks to the back by the stove. Ernie shoved his own desk and chair back to the side of the stove and opened his register. The ink in his fountain pen had thawed out, and he began to take attendance. The following students were present:

Jane Alstad, grade one
Dwight Alstad, grade five
Pricilla Backlin, grade two
Peter Brunsvold, grade eight
Wendell Edberg, grade seven
Dale Henning, grade three
Marvin Newquist, grade six
Allen Rollag, grade one
Clyde Rollag, grade six
Susan Rollag, grade three
Eunice Skime, grade seven
Iris Vic, grade eight

He closed the register and said, "That's it. We have twelve students, an even dozen."

Wendell said, "Maybe the history books will call us 'The Dahl School Dozen'."

"Yes," said Ernie, "We made it to school on a stormy day, December 7, 1944." He looked into their faces. "Do you know what day this is? They've started calling this 'Pearl Harbor Day'. Does anyone know why? Something happened three years ago, December 7, 1941."

Dwight raised his hand and said, "It's the day the Japs bombed Pearl Harbor."

"Correct, Dwight," said Ernie. "Now, who knows where Pearl Harbor is?" No one had an answer, so Ernie said, "Let's have a look." They all went to the front of the room where Ernie lowered the globe hanging on the clothesline. "Can you all see this blue area? That's the Pacific Ocean. Now look where I'm pointing. Do you see these little dots out in the ocean? Those are the Hawaiian Islands. Okay, next question. Is Hawaii one of our states? You older students should remember this, because we covered it in your geography classes."

191

Peter raised his hand. "It's not a state. It's a territory."

"Good, Peter," said Ernie. "And on one of the islands, called Oahu, there's the city of Honolulu. On the edge of that city is Pearl Harbor. We had a lot of our Navy ships there. So what happened?"

Dwight spoke up. "The Japs bombed a whole bunch of ships and the airfield."

"Right, Dwight, and that's why your father is in the Pacific fighting the Japanese soldiers." Ernie looked at the older students. "Okay, Peter, here's a little job for you. Look up Pearl Harbor in our new encyclopedia and be ready to make a report on it after lunch."

Marvin came up to Ernie, "Since Janice Millrud isn't here, do you want me to handle the health chart?"

Ernie laughed out loud, "No Marvin. Let's forget about that today. Just think about it—anyone who can walk to school on a day like this is healthy enough!"

The day passed and Ernie continued with his lessons. He kept thinking to himself. *If I had only a dozen students to teach, it would make my day a lot easier.* After lunch Peter gave his report on Pearl Harbor and Ernie added more information about the Hawaiian Islands, how they were formed by lava oozing up from the ocean floor. They learned that there were still active volcanoes on one of the islands.

For music class, Ernie gathered the students around the piano. Eunice played and they practiced the carols they would sing at the Christmas Program, just two weeks away.

Through the afternoon the temperature began to drop, and the windows frosted over. "Okay," said Ernie. "Let's go over to the windows and we'll have art class." That excited them. They went to the windows and used tongue depressors, rulers, slivers of wood, bobby pins, and fingernails to scratch pictures on the frosty windowpanes. They drew pictures of Christmas trees, reindeer, and Santa Claus in the frost on the windows. Ernie let them use water colors to paint on the frost, but he told them they would have to wash down the window sills when the frost melted. While his students made pictures in the frost, he kept a close eye on the weather through his window peephole.

The room grew darker; the wind became stronger and rattled the windows. Ernie wondered if some of the parents might

192

be coming early, maybe with horses and sleighs to pick up their children. By 3:30 it was too dark in the room for the students to read their lessons. Ernie lit two kerosene lanterns and put them on his desk. He wondered how the students would make it home.

He went to the front door and pushed on it. The wind had covered the porch with more than a foot of drifting snow, making it difficult to open the door. He stepped out on the porch. A strong, bitter wind stung his face and turned his eyelashes to ice. The blinding snow swirled around the building, making it impossible to see the flag pole, just 20 feet away. He knew it was there, but he couldn't see it. He stood on the porch and thought of his children inside. *What am I going to do? It's almost four o'clock. Time for dismissal, but I can't let them go. Will any of the parents come to get them? Maybe not.*

He went inside to call Carla. He wanted to hear her advice, and maybe she could call the parents who had telephones. He picked up the receiver, but there was no buzzing sound. He cranked Carla's number several times, two longs and two shorts. He rattled the receiver hook again and again. One more time—two longs and two shorts. There was no sound. The phone was dead. He turned to look at his students. They had their coats on; some of them were holding their lunch pails.

"The phone is dead; it must be a line down. With that ice storm last night, it doesn't surprise me."

Dwight Alstad had lifted his little sister Jane onto a desk. She stood and held onto his shoulder as he helped her put on her thick snow pants. Clyde Rollag helped his little brother Allen with his four-buckle overshoes. Dwight said, "Me and Jane are going to give it a try. If we wait any longer, it will only get worse. Jane needs to get home."

Ernie put his arm around little Jane. "No. My mind is made up. We can't go out there. You can't see ten feet in front of your nose, and it's getting darker by the minute."

Eunice said, "So what do we do?"

"We don't have a choice. Boys and girls, it's getting dark. Listen to that wind rattle the windows. I have to think like your mothers and fathers now. I have to take care of each of you."

Peter said, "Does that mean we stay here overnight?"

"I don't see any other way out of this. We have plenty of wood. We'll keep the fire going and sleep here tonight."

193

There were mixed reactions. Jane hugged her brother Dwight and started to whimper. Allen had a long face and Pricilla looked scared, but the older students were excited. Iris said, "This will be fun. Sleeping over at the school. Who ever heard of that?"

Marvin said, "We are the famous Dahl School Dozen!"

Ernie put more wood in the stove and started planning ahead. He would not let them go to the toilets, so he put the slop bucket in the cloakroom and told the children that's where they had to go. He checked the water in the ten-gallon crock. It was running low. "Boys and girls," he said, "don't use any water for washing your hands. We have to save what we have for drinking."

They would be sleeping on the floor, which was cold. Eunice and Iris helped him drag out the white sheets, the curtains they had used at the Halloween Social. They folded them, making them thicker, and laid them out on either side of the stove. "Okay, everybody listen to me," Ernie said. "The boys will be on the north side and the girls will sleep on the other side of the stove."

Iris said, "Hey, Mr. Juvland, that's no fun! I want to sleep next to Peter." She and Eunice went into a fit of laughter, and Peter pretended he didn't hear them.

Clyde piped up, "So, what are we supposed to do all night? Sit around and pick toe jam?"

Ernie quieted everyone down. "Here's another job we can do." He pointed to the Christmas tree, which Orvid had delivered and set up in the front of the room. "Clyde, get the paper cutter out of the library and Dwight, there's some red and green construction paper. Bring out one pack of each." Ernie looked in his bottom desk drawer and brought out a jar of library paste. "I'll cut strips of paper and we can make some rings for wreaths. Then we'll drape them around the Christmas tree."

Clyde yelled from the library, "I found candles and candle holders. Should I bring them out?"

"Yes, we can put them on," said Ernie, "but we can't light them. We have to save them for the Christmas Program. And besides, I have enough on my mind. I don't need to worry about the tree catching on fire and burning down the schoolhouse."

Marvin said, "Aw, gee, Mr. Juvland. You're no fun!"

Ernie took one of the kerosene lanterns off his desk and said, "Now I'm going to do something my mother always made me do when we had a blizzard. She would tell me to hang a lantern on the front porch. She told me the story of a man, lost one night in a blizzard, and how in the morning, a farmer found him frozen to death only 100 feet from his front door. She said, 'If that man had seen a light on the porch, he might have made it to the door.' Sit tight. I'll be right back."

He took the lantern and pushed the door against the big snowdrift on the porch. By now, it was pitch-dark. Ernie hung the lantern on a hook near the door.

They spent the next hour working on the wreaths and singing Christmas songs. When they finished pasting the rings together in four long chains, Ernie, Iris, Wendell, and Peter draped the wreaths around the tree. Marvin and Dwight clamped on the candle holders, and then they placed a new white candle in each holder. Dale and Susan were putting on the tinsel.

Clyde had found the star in the top cupboard. Ernie reached up and put the star in place at the very top of the tree. Then he stood back and admired the work the children had done. "Eunice, can you see to play? I think we should all sing 'Silent Night'."

"I don't need to see," said Eunice sitting down on the piano bench. "I know that one by heart." She began to play and Ernie asked the children to hold hands and sing. Their clear voices rose and the wind whistled around the eaves and rattled the windowpanes of the old schoolhouse.

By seven o'clock they were all huddled around the stove. Ernie kept the door to the firebox open and the orange light of the flames flickered on their faces. He noticed Dale had moved over to sit next to Susan Rollag. She smiled and put her arm around her classmate.

Ernie sat in his big swivel chair with Jane on one knee and Pricilla on the other, all wrapped up in their coats and snow pants. Allen moved over to Ernie. They were quiet, staring into the firebox. "Did I ever tell you the story about these two sisters and their little brother? Allen, you sit on the orange crate by me here, because you're going to be the little brother."

The students turned their faces toward Ernie, eager to hear the story. They had grown to like the stories their teacher made up, even more than the stories in their *McGuffey Readers*.

Ernie began, "Once upon a time there was a little girl named Pricilla, who wanted to be an actress. She worked very hard in high school and college; she got all the leading parts. One day a stranger, a city-slicker from New York, came to her college and saw her play Laurey Williams, the farm girl in the musical play, *Oklahoma!* And when she and her cowboy boyfriend, Curly McLain, sang, "People Will Say We're in Love", the stranger from New York had tears in his eyes. So the man said, 'I want to take you to New York and make you a star on Broadway.'

"Pricilla was flattered, but said, 'If you take me to New York, you also have to take my baby sister, Jane, and my brother Allen.'"

Ernie tapped Allen on the head and continued, "But Allen said, 'You two can go, but I'm staying on the farm. I like my cows and I like my tractor and somebody has to stay home and take care of Ma.' So Pricilla and Jane got on the train in Minneapolis and went to New York. The stranger had lots of money, so he rented a large apartment on Fifth Avenue. He became Pricilla's agent, and he was able to get many leading parts for her in Broadway musicals. They ended up getting married.

"Jane started feeling left out. She had found a job working behind the counter in a jewelry store. The owner was one of the richest men in New York, almost as rich as the Rockefellers. One New Year's Eve, he took Jane dancing at the Rainbow Room and they fell in love.

"The sisters had more money than they knew what to do with. Every week, they sent money home to their brother Allen. He bought a fancy Oldsmobile, a new John Deere tractor, and they sent money to their ma, so she could buy new dresses and new Sunday hats."

The wind whistled around the corners of the schoolhouse and Ernie was about to say, "And they all lived happily ever after," when he heard someone yell, "Help!" At first he thought it was one of the older boys. He looked over at Marvin and Peter. "Did one of you guys yell?"

Marvin said, "No. It was coming from outside."

Then they heard it again, "Help me!"

Ernie put Pricilla and Jane down and got up. He went to the door and pushed it open. There in the dim light of the lantern he could just make out the form of a body dressed in black, lying in the snow at the foot of the steps. Ernie yelled back through the door, "Peter! Wendell! Get out here! I need your help!" The boys

196

appeared at the door. "Give me a hand." Ernie and Peter kneeled down in the snow. They each got under an arm and dragged the body up the steps. They managed to get the body through the door and into the cloakroom. The body was face down.

Peter said, "Is he alive?"

Ernie yelled, "Someone, bring the lantern!"

Marvin took the lantern off the desk and brought it into the cloakroom.

Ernie said, "Wendell, grab the broom and sweep the snow off him. If that melts, he'll have wet clothes. Ernie carefully rolled the body over on its back. "Bring that lantern here, closer." Ernie wiped the snow from around the man's eyes. His beard was a mass of white frost. Ernie took off his cap and saw the gray hair. It was Ben Smierud.

Ernie leaned down to listen to his breathing. He got a heavy whiff of whiskey. "Okay, he's still alive. Let's drag him to the stove." When they came through the cloakroom door into the classroom, the kids jumped back. Someone shrieked.

Iris asked, "Is he dead?"

Ernie said, "No. He's still alive." They dragged him near the stove.

The little kids huddled near the older students. Eunice said, "Who the heck is it?"

Ernie looked up. "It's Mr. Smierud."

"Mr. Smierud?" Eunice grabbed her head and ran for the library. "I'm not sticking around here!" The little kids screamed and followed Eunice, Iris, and Susan into the library. They slammed the door and Ernie was left with Ben and the older boys. He kneeled down and said, "Ben, can you hear me?"

He started to shake. "Yeah, I'll be okay. Can you get my bottle out of my coat? My hands are froze."

Ernie reached into his pocket and pulled out a pint of whiskey that was half full. He handed it to Dale and said in a low voice, "Here, put this in the bottom drawer of my desk." Then he turned back to Ben. "You're in the school, Ben. There are children here, who couldn't make it home in the storm. I can't let you have your bottle. We'll get you a drink of water. Dwight, grab a cup and fill it about half full." Dwight handed Ernie the cup. Ernie held Ben's head up and helped him drink.

The frost from around his beard had started to melt. "Wendell, hand me a dish towel." Ernie took the towel and wiped his beard and his neck where the water was dripping. "Ben, we're going to keep you here by the stove tonight. I don't want you to get up. Just stay on the floor and you'll be okay in the morning." Marvin and Peter helped Ernie slide Ben closer to the stove.

Then Ernie walked up to the library door and opened it.

Eunice said, "I'm not going out there with old man Smierud here." The girls were huddled together in the darkness.

"Okay, settle down. Come over here near the door, so I can see you," said Ernie. He took a deep breath and let it out. "I have to make decisions here and it was my decision to bring Mr. Smierud inside. I could not let him freeze to death on our front steps. Do you understand how awful that would be? He is a human being, and I am going to take care of him. We have him on the floor at the back side of the stove. I will sit by him all night.

"You must trust me. I will not let that man hurt any of you. Now come on out, find your place on the floor by the stove, and get ready to go to sleep. This has been a tough day for all of us, and we need our rest, because tomorrow morning, come hell or high water, I'm going to find a way to get you home. Now let's come on out. You'll freeze to death in here."

Ernie went back and shoved his desk between the sleeping Ben and the children. The girls slowly came out of the library and found places to curl up on the floor. Little Jane and Pricilla crawled between Eunice and Iris. Clyde kept his little brother Allen next to his side with his arm wrapped around him. Ernie put three more chunks of wood in the firebox and closed the door.

He went over to Ben and kneeled down. He was sleeping on his side and softly snoring. Ernie sat down on his swivel chair, placed his head on his desk, and listened to the wind outside the windows. The last thing he heard was little Jane sobbing and asking, "Where is my ma?"

Through the night Ernie would doze, wake up, quietly check the stove, and put in wood from time to time. Ben mumbled in his sleep, and through the night Ernie heard some of his students whispering to each other. The wind continued to whistle around the old school, and Ernie started thinking about what he would do in the morning. *The kids will be hungry and they'll need water.* He got up to check the ten-gallon water crock. He held the lantern over it. *Not much left, maybe an inch. I guess I could melt snow if we run out.*

He settled back in his chair and started to doze off. Then from somewhere he heard a strange voice speaking in a whisper, "You don't like me." He sat up and looked around, thinking it was one of the children, but they were all still and apparently sleeping. He looked at the frost on the east window, and he thought he saw a face. He got up and went to the window. But the face was gone. He must have imagined it. It couldn't have been a face from someone outside, because the window was completely covered with frost.

He sat back down and tried to forget what he had seen. *It was the face of a young man, very much like the face of Timmy Burstrom, the kid who attacked Dale last October. He said, 'You don't like me.'* Puzzled, worried, and strangely scared, the exhausted teacher eventually drifted off to sleep.

Morning could not come too soon for Ernie; it was a night of dozing, waking, and fearing he would have another nightmare. Finally he saw the windows growing lighter. He checked his watch and saw it was half past seven. The kids were all sleeping.

Ernie looked down at Ben, who was awake. He motioned to Ernie with his hand to come near. Ernie got off his chair and sat on the floor by Ben. The old man whispered, "What did you do with my bottle? I've got the shakes." He held out his hand to show Ernie.

"I hid it on you, Ben. I can't let you drink in the school."

Ernie thought he would get an argument, but Ben closed his eyes. The old man remembered lying in the snow and thinking he would die. His whole body began to shake. He looked up at Ernie and said, "You saved my ass last night. You know that, don't you?"

"It was the lantern on the porch, I'll bet."

Ben thought for a moment. Then he raised a shaking hand. "I just remembered. That was it. I saw that light."

"Ben, I'm going to need your help. I need to get these kids out of here. We're almost out of water and there's no food for them here."

Ben's voice quavered as he spoke, "Well, my place is the closest, but I don't have any wood in the house and nothing but some crackers to eat."

"No, Ben. We won't bother you with the kids. There's the Grundvig farm, where we get the water from their pump, but there's no one living in the house anymore."

Ben thought for a moment. "I think your best bet would be the Marum's place. They're about a half mile north of here."

"Yeah, I was thinking about them, but they don't have any kids in school, so I don't know them."

"Well," said Ben, "they never got married. Two sisters and a brother, I went to school with them right here. They're about my age."

"You think that's the best?"

"They're pretty nice people. They have a nice house and barn. They've always treated me square. And Wilber has a team of horses and a sled with a grain box. I've seen him out in the winter. Maybe once it lets up he could give the kids a ride home."

"You know the phone is dead, right?"

"No, I didn't know that. Well, the Marums are on the same party line, so I suppose their phone is dead, too."

The students were starting to stir. Ernie heard someone taking a leak in the slop bucket in the cloakroom. Ernie walked to the back south window near the science cabinet and scratched the frost off the windowpane. It seemed to have let up a bit. He could just barely make out the big birch tree at the edge of the playground. Its bare branches hung down, thickly coated with ice. He left the window and gathered the students in front of the stove.

Pricilla said, "I'm really hungry."

Ernie put his arm around her. "I'm sure we'll all get hungry pretty soon. Now I can't make you waffles and bacon and eggs, but I have something else to tide you over." He went to the library and came back with a box. He took out his jackknife and opened the top. "I ordered a box of Christmas candy to give out at the program, but it looks like we're having our Christmas early. Help yourself. The chocolate ones will give you the most energy."

Dale said, "Oh, boy, candy for breakfast! Wait till Ma hears about this!"

Ernie let Dale pass the box of candy around to all the students. "I have one more thing to say. Mr. Smierud is snoozing

200

here on the floor behind my desk. He's going to be okay, and he's going to help me get you guys out of here. We're going to walk to the Marum farm. I'm sure you all know where it is. Mr. Marum has a team of horses and a big old sleigh. I'm going to ask him to get all of you home safe and sound. I should say one more thing. If we had not been in the school last night, Mr. Smierud might have frozen to death in the blizzard. We saved a life last night, and that is something you will probably remember for the rest of your lives."

Ernie looked over at Ben. He had gotten up and was standing, hunched over, leaning against the washstand, looking down at the floor. In a low voice Ben simply said, "Thank you." He looked over at Ernie and added, "You kids have a good teacher. I hope you all know that."

Ernie carefully rationed the water so that each student got a sip. Then he took a clothesline from the library and gathered the children around him. "Okay, this is how we're going to do this. We have this long rope. I'm going to tie each of you to the rope. That way, we'll be sure not to lose anyone." He turned to Ben, "Mr. Smierud, you'll walk in the lead; I'll walk in the back.

"Allen, you will ride piggy-back on me and I'll carry Jane. Dwight, you will walk in front of me so your sister can see you. Peter, Marvin, Wendell and Clyde, I want you to take turns carrying Pricilla, and make sure you help Susan and Dale along the way. Okay? And Iris and Eunice, you're big enough to look out for yourselves. But we'll take it slowly, one step at a time.

"Now we're going to do one more thing before we wrap up and get tied to the clothesline." Ernie took a sheet of white construction paper and four tacks out of his desk. He took a red crayon and wrote in big letters. **WE ARE ALL ALIVE. WE HAVE GONE TO THE MARUM FARM.** Then he asked the students to sign their names. Ernie went outside and tacked the sheet of paper to the front door. He took the lantern off the nail and returned to his students.

They started making preparations to leave. Ernie decided to sacrifice one of the white sheets used for the program curtains. He ripped it into strips, and Eunice and Iris helped him wrap it around the faces of each kid. He gave them safety pins to secure the cloth, leaving just a slit for the eyes.

201

They all had their overshoes and mittens on. Mr. Smierud tied each student by the wrist to the long clothesline. Ernie closed the damper on the stovepipe, he blew out the kerosene lamps, and they made their way toward the door.

He loaded Allen on his back and he held Jane tightly in his arms. Mr. Smierud opened the door and led the way down the steps. Ernie closed the door behind, but didn't lock it. They had saved one life in this blizzard, maybe there'd be another lost soul in need of a shelter.

The toughest part was getting through the playground and up on the main road. The wind was so severe in places, it had blown the snow off the roads, but it was very icy. In stretches where trees sheltered the road from the wind, the snow was piled high. They plowed through drifts that were more than knee high. Ben Smierud kept a steady eye on the road ahead and managed to keep the train of children out of the ditch.

Ernie was worried mostly about the biting wind, which they were trudging directly into. He was glad he had remembered to wrap their faces up, or certainly there would be frostbites. Allen bounced on his back and Ernie could feel his breath close to his ear. Jane whimpered and called again for her ma. Her brother Dwight turned around and assured her they'd be okay. Ernie held her tightly, and they struggled on.

He looked up through the line of children and he saw Mr. Smierud pointing up the road and waving his hand over his head. Then Ernie saw it, the Marum's big red barn up ahead. Soon he could make out the house and he yelled out, "There it is, kids! We're going to make it!"

Wilber Marum was coming up from the barn. He stopped on the porch when he heard Ben Smierud shout, "Hello, Wilber!" He stood there and could not believe what he saw coming up the road. It looked to him like a long black snake with white spots on its back. It had a big head and a big lump on the end of its tail.

As they approached the house, Wilber shouted, "What in the heck is this now?"

Mr. Smierud said, "We brought you some company. Do you have the coffee pot on?"

And they surely did. Ernie smelled it as soon as he stepped into the Marum's kitchen. The sisters hugged each of the children and helped them off with their overcoats. One of the sisters said, "Now you go in the front room and warm yourselves at the stove. How about some hot cocoa?"

They were all very happy. The sisters made the cocoa and started working on scrambled eggs and pancakes. When the food was on the table, each student filed by with a plate. They filled up, sat on the front room floor next to the stove, and ate. They were all very hungry. Ben and Ernie sat at the kitchen table drinking coffee. The Marums wanted to know the whole story. When Ernie finished telling about their night in the school and rescuing Ben, he asked, "Is your phone out?"

Wilber said, "Yeah, it's been out since sometime yesterday morning." He got up and went to the wall phone. He took off the receiver and listened. "Yup, she's still dead."

Ernie said, "I'm sure the parents are worried sick about the kids. We have to try to get them home."

Wilber said, "Well, it looks like it's letting up a bit. I hate to take my team out when the roads are so icy, but we'll see what we can do."

It was just short of eleven o'clock when Wilber Marum pulled his team and the sleigh with the big grain box up to the front steps. The sisters had helped the children bundle up for their ride home. They all piled in the grain box. The kids sat on the floor, and Ernie and Ben stood in front on either side of Wilber. They started on their way with Wilber's big dappled Percherons stepping smartly on the icy road. They dropped Ben off first. Ernie shook his hand and thanked him for his help. Ben said, "Don't thank me. I'm the one that needs to thank you."

Except for Dale, the rest of the students lived south of the school. Parents were waiting at the windows and standing on the porches as Wilber Marum dropped them off. Finally, they came back north, swung east by the school, and headed for the Henning's farm. When they came down their lane, Carla was standing on the porch. She was all bundled up, having just come from gathering eggs. She broke out crying when Ernie carried Dale through the deep drift in front of the porch. "Thank, God! Thank, God. You're both alive!"

Dale reached up to hug his ma and then he went to hug his pa. Tom said, "The Lord has watched over you."

Dale took off his mittens and clapped his hands. He said, "I'm famous. I'm one of the Dahl School Dozen!"

Chapter XIII...The Christmas Program

Ernie hit the sack early Friday night and did not get up until noon on Saturday. The sun was out, and the blizzard was finally over. When Ernie came downstairs, he saw snowdrifts around the Henning house that went up to the windows. It was one of the worst blizzards he could remember. Ernie spent the rest of Saturday and all day Sunday, working with Carla and Dale to shovel out pathways to the toilet, barn, pump house, woodshed, and chicken coop. Kenny Torstad came over with his team of horses and a snow grader to clear the Henning's lane, and someone came out from town with a bulldozer to plow the township road.

The telephone was working by Sunday night so Carla was able to call parents to spread the word that school would be cancelled Monday. Orvid needed the day to plow out the schoolyard. Ernie walked up to the school with a snow shovel to help out. He dug out around the toilets and woodshed. When he shoveled off the porch, he saw the sign he had put on the door, dangling by one thumb tack. **WE ARE ALL ALIVE. WE HAVE GONE TO THE MARUM FARM.** It all came back to him, the fear of losing one of his students. He carefully folded it and put it in his coat pocket. *This is something I'll keep the rest of my life.*

On his way home, he saw a horse and rider coming lickety-split on the township road. Ernie stepped to the side of the road to let the rider pass. It was Marvin Newquist. He had a long rope tied to the saddle horn, and on the end of the rope was Wendell Edberg on a pair of skis. Ernie laughed and yelled at Wendell as he went flying by in the middle of the ditch, "Watch out for the mailboxes!"

By Tuesday, December 12, everything was back to normal at Dahl School. They would have only eight days to prepare for the Christmas Program. "I'll be expecting you to do a lot of work on your lessons at home on your own," he announced, "because we'll need all our afternoons to practice for the program."

Ernie created a number of lessons connected with the Christmas story. Each morning he read from the Gospels the story of the birth of Jesus. They learned the words, 'magi', 'frankincense', and 'myrrh'. They learned about the Star of Bethlehem and Ernie taught them about navigation before the invention of the compass. They learned about the origin of Santa Claus and how Christmas was celebrated in other countries.

Ernie raised a question that had everyone stumped. Why do we put up a Christmas tree? They learned that Germany was credited with starting the tradition of the Christmas tree, and Martin Luther might have come up with the idea of putting candles on the tree. Walking toward his home one night, he saw brilliant stars that looked like candles twinkling through evergreen trees.

Besides the readings from the Gospels, Ernie read a section of Charles Dickens's *A Christmas Carol* every morning. Seventh and eighth graders compiled a long list of Dickens's big words, benevolent, baleful, avarice, adamant, caustic, celestial. They discussed different social classes and how Scrooge didn't understand that in a democratic society, poor people need help. Janice Millrud and Eunice Skime wrote a rural version of *A Christmas Carol*. Bob Cratchit was a poor farmer about to lose his farm, because he couldn't pay the mortgage. Scrooge became the banker at the Farmer's National Bank, and Dale played Tiny Tim. Ernie was determined to turn the Christmas Program into another learning experience covering a host of subjects, from geography to mathematics, from history to literature to science.

On Wednesday, there was a letter for Ernie in the school mailbox. It was from Martha. When the children went out for morning recess, he stood by the window and read it.

Dear Ernie,

I miss you. Still working at the bank, but I'm bored. I haven't gone anywhere, I haven't done anything. I just go to work, come home, and go to work again the next day. My dad told me I have a bad case of cabin fever. So I've decided to take some time off for Christmas. I really want to see you. I thought maybe I could drive over for your Christmas Program on the 21st. Would you mind? Let me know right away. All for now. I'm writing this at work, so I don't want my boss to yell at me. Ha Ha.

Love,

Martha

Ernie looked out the window across the snow-covered fields and pictured Martha, the way she looked in her white dress the first day he saw her. As he rehearsed the students on their songs and skits that afternoon, he kept thinking about her. After dismissal time, he decided to write her back. "Dale, I have some things to do here. Sorry you have to wait, but I don't want you walking home by yourself."

Dale said, "That's okay. I'll do my homework."

Ernie said, "Good boy. This shouldn't take long." Ernie sat down to write.

Dear Martha,

Thanks for the nice letter. Sounds like you have the blues! Everything is fine here. Did you get hit hard with the blizzard? Twelve of the kids and I were trapped in the school and had to stay overnight. It was scary. I'll tell you all about it sometime. I hope you can make it over to see our Christmas Program on the 21st. We've decided to have it in the afternoon starting at two o'clock. It would be good to see you, and I'm sure the kids would be tickled to death.

If you can make it over, I have a favor to ask of you. I need a ride to my home place north of Thief River Falls. We have a big farmhouse and there'd be plenty of room for you to stay over. I'm sure my mom would like to meet you, and I'm hoping my kid brother Andy will be home from the Army.

I have your phone number. Maybe I'll give you a call one of these nights.

Love,

Ernie

On Friday, the students worked all day on finishing up their Christmas gifts for their parents. Iris and Eunice knew how to crochet, so they were able to help the other girls make doilies, hankies, and dish towels for the moms. The little girls strung weed seeds that Ernie had collected after threshing. They made colorful necklaces for their mothers. They made Christmas cards decorated with seeds to make them look like mosaic art.

Ernie spent his time in the library, which became the woodworking shop for industrial arts. The boys worked with coping saws, brace and bits, and wood chisels. For their gifts, mom would get a breadboard and dad would get a milking stool. There was a heavy smell of paint and varnish in the library, and a lot of sandpaper dust had settled on the books by the end of the day.

The songs were easy to rehearse because the students knew most of them, "Silent Night", "Jingle Bells", "Up on the Housetop", and "Come All Ye Faithful". Ernie was glad they had spent a couple hours working on songs the night of the blizzard.

On Friday, when Ernie and Dale came home, there was a letter addressed to Ernie on the kitchen table. It was from his mother.

Dear Ernie,

How are you? Did you survive the blizzard? I was thinking of you and your students. The Inderdal boys took their team to town to get groceries and a radio battery for me, so I was in good shape.

I received a letter from Andy. He will be home for Christmas. He is taking the train up from Minneapolis to Thief River and will be coming in Friday, the 22nd. He wants you to pick him up. I have to close now, and take this up to the mailbox before the mailman gets here. He's been coming early lately, and I can't figure that out.

I hope your Christmas Program goes well. Tell me all about it when you get home.
Love,
Ma

On Saturday, Ernie went up to the school to hang the curtains for the program. Carla had sewn a new side curtain together, to replace the one Ernie ripped up the morning of the blizzard. He noticed one of the big sheets had a yellow spot about the size of a dinner plate. Ernie shook his head and smiled. One of his youngsters had wet the bed the night of the storm. He washed the spot out in the dishpan and once the sheets were hung in place, they looked pretty good. Once again Dahl School became a little theater.

Before he left the school, he decided to call Martha in Bemidji. He wondered about the cost. *It's going to be a long distance call, but if I keep it short, it shouldn't be more than two dollars.* He rang the operator and gave her the number. Even before Martha answered the phone, Ernie heard a click. There was a rubbernecker on the line.

"Hello," said the voice on the other end of the line. Ernie knew it was Martha.

"Hi," said Ernie. "You probably know who this is, but watch what you say, because we have someone else on the line."

"Yes, I remember all about that. You're on a party line."

"Hey, do you live on Highway 2?"

"Yes, I do."

"Well, you'd better move, because there's a big truck coming!"

"Okay," she said, laughing. "Now are you going to ask me if I have Prince Albert in the can?"

Ernie laughed and said, "No, I want to ask you about our plans."

Martha said, "I'll be there at two."

Ernie asked, "And how about giving me a ride."

"Yes," she said, "I'm taking off Friday."

"Then how about our train ride to Hollywood?"

"What?" she was confused.

"We're going. I've already booked a Pullman."

"Oh, that will be marvelous!"

"Good," said Ernie. He dropped his voice down and said, "That should give them something to talk about."

Martha said, "You bet! And then we're going to New Orleans for Mardi Gras, right?"

"Of course," said Ernie. "See you soon."

Martha said, "I can't wait. Goodbye."

Ernie stayed on the line to get the charges from the operator. It was $1.24. Ernie wrote the price down in his logbook and added a note. *Remember to pay Vic.*

The next week passed quickly. Rehearsals went well, and everything was all set by the day of the program. When Ernie and Dale walked to school that morning, the boy was quiet. He was disappointed that his father decided not to come to the program to see him play Tiny Tim. Ernie tried to console the boy, "It has nothing to do with you, Dale. It's just hard for him to get in and out of the pickup."

Dale said, "I wanted him there to give him my milk stool present."

Ernie said, "I can understand how you feel. You surely did a good job on it. But it will be a nice surprise when he opens it for Christmas. I noticed you wrapped it nicely with a green bow on top."

Martha showed up on time and the students were surprised to see her. Ernie noticed the girls huddling around her, admiring her knitted red sweater with white reindeer leaping across the front in a flurry of snowflakes. The parents were also happy to see Martha. Even Orvid came up to her and said, "Good to see you. Just too bad you had to put up with those damned Smieruds. But they're gone now, and it makes a big difference." Then he moved close and whispered, "Are you and the teacher going out sparking tonight?"

Martha smiled and said, "Wouldn't you like to know?" She took her seat in the back corner, near the science cabinet. The children sang well and played their Tonettes without missing a note. They didn't drop a line in their skits and Ernie was pleased.

At the end, Ernie got off his stool behind the side curtain and walked to the front. "I want all your sons and daughters to come out and please give them a nice round of applause for a job well done." The students marched out in a straight line and formed two rows in front of the blackboard.

Ernie continued. "We have two eighth graders in our school and since this is their last Christmas Program at Dahl School, I want to honor them. Peter Brunsvold and Iris Vic, would you please step forward?" Everyone clapped. Ernie had two long, white candles, one for Peter and one for Iris. Ernie took a match and lit them. "Would some of you along the windows please pull

209

the top and bottom shades? There's one back there—the rope is missing; so we can't do anything about that. We want to get the room as dark as possible."

Ernie waited. Then he said, "That's fine. Thank you. Now Peter and Iris, carefully light the candles on the tree. Make sure the flames are not touching any needles. I'll do the one on top by the star. "

When the tree was lit, Ernie said, "I want to say a few words about the men and women around the world fighting for our country. Did you notice I said 'women'? We sometimes forget the women who are helping the war effort by working in factories making airplanes and working on assembly lines, turning out bombs and shells. I'm sure you know about Rosie the Riveter. And let us never forget the combat nurses working in aid stations just a few miles behind the front lines. I wish to tell you about one."

Ernie took a newspaper clipping out of an envelope and walked over to the tree to read by the light of the candles. "My mother sent me this newspaper article about a girl I went to high school with. It was in the *Thief River Falls Times.*" He showed the headlines. **Emma Anderson's Last Letter to Her Mother**. Ernie began to read.

Dear Ma,

I hope you're doing okay. I'm fine here so far, and too busy to worry about the bombs we hear exploding all the time. We are in the mountains somewhere in Belgium. We've had a lot of snow and it's getting colder every day. Good thing I come from Minnesota, because I'm used to it. They bring the wounded in here day and night, many with missing legs or arms. Our hospital, if you can call it that, is an old granary with an addition we made out of canvas. I can't complain, because I am better off than the poor boys who are carried in here.

Last night, I sat up and held the hand of an 18-year-old soldier from Lengby, Minnesota. He was delirious and calling for morphine. We talked about the

Gopher football team, and the first time he went off the top diving board at Lengby Lake. I tried to keep his mind off the pain. Poor guy. When they brought him in here, his intestines were coming out from an exploding grenade. All night I listened to the shelling and held his hand. The last thing he said to me was, 'Am I going to die?' I kissed him on the cheek and said, 'You'll be okay.' In the morning he was gone.

Sorry, Ma, they just called me. A truck pulled in and I have to help carry in more wounded soldiers. Don't worry about me. I have it good. At least I don't have to go to the front, with these poor boys.

Love, your daughter Emma.

Ernie wiped his eyes and put the clipping back in the envelope. "Emma was two years ahead of me in high school. She was a cheerleader and sang solos in the school choir. The article goes on to tell how Emma volunteered to go in a truck to pick up more wounded soldiers near the front. They were short on medics and she wanted to pitch in. The truck was hit with a shell and Emma was killed."

Ernie looked out over the parents and saw their stark faces. He heard some of his students sobbing behind him. "Christmas is a joyous time of the year, but none of us, not even the children, can overlook the sacrifices being made by these brave young soldiers like Emma.

"Please bow your heads. Heavenly, Father, we thank Thee for this school and these bright, healthy, and good children. Please protect their family members who are fighting in the war. Bless all those who are risking their lives this very moment. And please dear Lord, bring an end to this dreadful war. In the name of the Father, the Son, and the Holy Ghost, Amen."

Then in soft voices the students sang, "Silent Night".

At the end of the song, there were smiles of pride on the faces of the parents. They rose to clap loudly. Then, suddenly, from the cloakroom came a booming bass voice, "Ho, ho, ho! Merry Christmas!" Santa Claus burst into the room with a burlap feed sack slung over his back. Even though the jolly fat man wore a beard made out of cotton balls and angel hair, everyone knew from the voice it was really Mr. Vic. "Ho, ho, ho! Merry Christmas!" Eunice pounded the keys on the piano, the little kids grabbed their rhythm instruments, and the students of Dahl School sang loudly.

Up on the housetop reindeer pause
Out jumps good old Santa Claus.
Down thru the chimney with lots of toys
All for the little ones, Christmas joys.
Ho, ho, ho! Who wouldn't go?
Ho, ho, ho! Who wouldn't go?
Up on the housetop, click, click, click!
Down thru the chimney with good Saint Nick.

It was dark by the time Ernie and Martha got on the road. They stopped at a phone booth in Crookston; Ernie wanted to call his mother to tell her they might be late for supper. When they pulled into the farmyard, Ernie saw Blackie come running. "There he is," said Ernie, "my buddy, Blackie."

Mrs. Juvland greeted them in the kitchen with a big smile. She had fixed herself up. Her hair was parted neatly in the middle and pulled back tightly into a bun; she wore a new blue dress, with white polka dots and a white collar. Ernie noticed a few more lines around her eyes. She shook hands with Martha and said, "So this is the young lady I've been hearing so much about."

Martha looked at Ernie and giggled, "Uh-oh! Sounds like somebody's been talking out of school."

Mrs. Juvland smiled and said, "Yeah, he said you looked like a movie star, and he wasn't kidding either!"

Martha punched Ernie on the shoulder and laughed.

Ernie sat down at the table and played with Blackie. "He smells pretty good, Ma. He must have been out rolling around in the snow." Ernie ruffled up the fur behind the dog's ears. "You should smell this dog in the summer, Martha, after he's been slopping around in the sloughs or chasing down skunks."

Mrs. Juvland shook her head. "Ish-dah! I don't even let him in the house." She put a kettle of chicken and dumpling soup on the table. "You're probably hungry." She sliced up a loaf of freshly baked bread, and she and Martha joined Ernie at the table to eat.

After supper they went into the front room. Martha looked around the room and saw pictures on the china closet, five sons in uniform. Mrs. Juvland pointed to a small flag hanging in the window. It was white with a red border, and set in the middle were five blue stars, one for each of the Juvland servicemen. "There's some organization of women, who send out these flags to mothers who have sons in the war. I guess you would call me a 'Five-Star Mother'." She came over to Martha and picked up the picture of Andy. "This one is my baby, Andy. He's the one coming home tomorrow." Then she handed Martha a picture of Ernie in his high school baseball uniform. "And I guess you know this guy."

Martha held the picture and smiled. "Boy, were you ever skinny back then!"

Ernie laughed and said, "I was so skinny, my ribs were sticking out, and you could have used them for a washboard!"

Mrs. Juvland served coffee to Martha and Ernie, who sat together on the davenport. "Now, you two didn't end up getting married on the way up here did you?"

Martha almost dropped her cup. "No." She nudged Ernie. "Now what have you been telling your mother?"

Ernie said, "I haven't told her much at all."

Mrs. Juvland leaned forward in her chair and said, "Well, I want to know for sure. If you got hitched up, I'd let you sleep in Ernie's room. But since you haven't tied the knot, well, I'm sorry son, but we'll have to put your girlfriend in the spare room."

Ernie gave his mother a sly look and said, "It's your house, Ma."

They had a nice visit, but soon Mrs. Juvland started to yawn. Ernie started feeling sleepy himself. It had been another long day.

Ernie had trouble falling asleep. He hadn't given much thought to marriage, and Martha had not talked about it either. That was fine with Ernie, but he could not help thinking, as he heard Martha in the next room turning over in the squeaky bed, how nice it would be to have her lying next to him, naked and warm. He wondered if she was thinking the same thing.

The alarm clock rang at eight and Ernie woke up feeling elated. *I don't have to do the milking because the cows are gone. I don't have to grade workbooks, because I left them at school. I don't have to walk to school, because I am on vacation for two whole weeks.* He dressed and went down to the kitchen. Blackie was waiting for him at the foot of the stairs.

"So, did you sleep okay?" his mother said, pouring him a cup of coffee at the table.

"As snug as a bug in a rug," said Ernie, reaching down to scratch Blackie behind the ears. He took a sip of coffee. "Yeah, it sure was good sleeping in my old bed."

Mrs. Juvland leaned down close to Ernie's ear. "I'm letting her sleep in. I know she had trouble corking off last night. I heard the bed squeaking. For a minute there, I thought maybe you had snuck in her room."

"Ma! I'm surprised you'd even think that!"

"Well, I couldn't blame you. She's a good-looking girl with a nice figure."

"You're right about that, Ma."

"And she has a good sense of humor. Before she went up to the spare room, I told her, 'There's something under your bed in case you have to go in the middle of the night.'" Mrs. Juvland chuckled and whispered into Ernie's ear. "She said, 'You mean the piss-pot?' I was surprised and it made me laugh. When you told me she was from Bemidji, I started thinking, oh, boy, here comes another fancy pants girl from town. But she seems to be really down to earth. Real common."

"Well, you know she taught at Dahl School last year and stayed with the same farmers I'm living with now. I think she's lost some of her town girl ways."

"Good." She sat down and stared at Ernie. "So, when are you gonna make it legal?"

Ernie leaned back in his chair, "Boy, Ma, you sure have a lot of personal questions this morning, don't you?"

"I think you'd better snap that one up, before someone else gets her. I can just hear Andy saying, 'I wouldn't mind her shoes under my bed!'"

"Speaking of Andy, maybe we should get Martha up and get going here. And didn't you say the Inderdal boys are coming over today to butcher that last pig?"

214

"Yeah, sometime this afternoon. I'm gonna start boiling water for scalding as soon as you take off to get Andy at the train."

When Ernie went out to start his mother's car, Martha was still in bed. He let the car warm up and came back in. "She's a cold one out there. Eighteen below, if your thermometer is still right."

"Why don't you go on alone to Thief River? Martha can stay here and help me. And that will give us a chance to get to know each other a little better, too."

"Okay with me. Do you want me to pick up anything at the store?"

"Yeah, can you remember? A pound bag of sugar and a pound of coffee. The ration stamps are in the glove compartment."

"Okay," he said and went out the door. As he headed up the lane, he looked over at the Inderdal place, but he didn't see Bill and Roany, the two broncos. *Hmmm. Well, it's a cold day. They must have them in the barn.* He made the turn at the mailbox and headed for Thief River Falls.

It was ten o'clock before Martha came downstairs. She asked, "Where's Ernie?"

"Oh, he went to get Andy at the train," said Mrs. Juvland. "We decided to let you sleep." She poured Martha a cup of coffee and fixed her some pancakes for breakfast. Mrs. Juvland asked, "So are you teaching school now?"

"No, I'm working in a bank in Bemidji."

"I thought Ernie said you were a teacher. Maybe I didn't hear him right."

Martha took a bite of pancake and put her fork down. "I was a teacher last year at Ernie's school." They were both silent for a moment. "It didn't work out so hot for me." She wondered how much Ernie had told her. "It was my first job teaching, and I had trouble handling some of the bigger boys."

Mrs. Juvland sensed she didn't want to talk about teaching school. She said, "We've got work to do today. The boys are gonna butcher the last pig, and that's it."

"What do you mean?"

"We're all done farming. The cows went last summer, I gave the chickens away before the cold weather, and the neighbors have the horses. So, that's it."

"I see," said Martha. She noticed her expression and voice had changed. "I'll bet that's hard for you."

Mrs. Juvland sat down at the table. "Yeah, it is. We've always been farmers. That's all we know. And when my husband took off for good, I was stuck with the farm, me and the boys. They were good. They kept things going, but then the war came, and they had to leave, one right after another. When it came to Ernie, he probably could have qualified for a farm deferment. They called it 'essential farm labor'. But he never applied. He wanted to serve in the war like his older brothers. That's the way Ernie is.

"And once he was discharged and home working the farm, it made it unlikely that Andy could qualify for a deferment. I should remind you—please don't bring that up to Ernie, because I know he feels bad that his discharge put Andy in a bad spot."

She poured Martha a glass of tomato juice. "The war has really messed up the farm families. It's been hard, but I try not to complain. Some have it a lot worse than me.

"I'm gonna keep the place—one of the boys might want to farm it when the war is over. I'm almost 55 now and not as spry as I used to be. I can't farm on my own, so we'll see what happens."

Martha wondered why Ernie had never talked about his father, running off when he was so young. She decided not to pry into all that. She shook her head and said, "This darned war!"

"Yeah, it changes everything. And it ain't just me. A lot of families around here got thrown topsy-turvy once all the boys went off to war. But we'll manage. Ernie is very good about sending me money he makes teaching, and his brothers send me money, too."

Martha said, "I know Ernie worries about you here all alone. Have you thought about moving out?"

"Yeah. I haven't told Ernie yet, but I've found a place in town. There's an older lady, I think she's almost 80. Nice lady, she goes to our church. All her kids and grandkids have moved to The Cities, so she has this big empty house. Her name is Mildred Osterholt. She asked me to come live with her. She needs help getting around, so she'll let me stay there free of rent if I do the cooking, cleaning, outside yard work, and shopping. So, it's a good deal for both of us. She has a lot of books in her house, and I like to read. I think it will work out just fine."

"Good deal. I think Ernie will like that."

"Oh, yeah. They've all been after me to move into town. I've been the stubborn one, but now I have this deal with Mildred, and I'm gonna jump at it."

They spent the next two hours talking and getting ready for butchering. Mrs. Juvland gave Martha some work clothes and a big overcoat, so she could bring in pails of water from the pump. Ernie's mother watched the young woman working the handle of the pump. She was thinking what a hardworking girl she was.

Four big cookers sat on the old Home Comfort kitchen stove. Martha poured in pails of water they would boil for scalding the pig, and Mrs. Juvland kept the firebox stoked with wood. Steam rose from the cookers and the windows frosted over.

When they heard the car coming, they both stopped their work and waited for Ernie and Andy at the kitchen door. Mrs. Juvland began to cry. She had to stand on her tiptoes to hug Andy and kiss him on the cheek. Ernie introduced his brother to Martha. Andy shook her hand warmly and said, "You're too good-looking to settle for an old farm boy like my brother." Martha blushed and smiled. She noticed the aroma of shoe polish, moth balls, new fabric, and chewing gum as soon as Andy put his arm around her to give her a squeeze. "I think you'd better keep an eye on this one, Ernie. Somebody might steal her from right under your nose. Some rascal like me."

Ernie put a bag of groceries on the counter and said, "Don't listen to him. He's all talk."

They sat down around the table to visit. Andy had stories about training, and he wanted to know how Ernie was doing with his school kids. They dunked gingersnaps in their coffee and talked until they heard the Inderdal truck pull up. Ernie opened the door and saw them drag a big block and tackle off the bed of the truck. He yelled, "We'll be out in a minute! You can hang the block and tackle in that tree next to the flatbed sleigh."

Ernie closed the door and slapped Andy on the back, "There's a bunch of your old clothes up in my room. We're gonna put you to work, soldier."

Ernie went out to help the Inderdal boys. Soon Andy joined them, carrying a .22 rifle. Martha followed him and watched from a distance. She didn't know quite what to expect. She had never seen a big animal killed before, nothing bigger than a mouse.

Andy opened the gate to the pigpen and approached the pig with the gun cradled in his right arm. In his left hand he held a corncob. The pig bit hard into the cob. Andy held the corncob firmly and placed the end of the barrel against the pig's forehead.

Martha turned around and covered her eyes. She heard the gunshot and jumped. She peeked out from behind her mitten and saw Ernie and Andy drag the pig to the tree.

Ernie poked Andy, "I'm going to let you do this, buddy. I have to check with Ma to see how she's coming on the hot water."

Andy said, "Sure thing." He kneeled beside the twitching pig, slowly dying in the snow. Andy called to Martha. "Bring that dishpan over here. I'll need your help!"

She came near the pig's head. Andy straddled the pig and sat on its shoulders. Andy looked at Martha, "Sorry, I wasn't thinking. Does this bother you? I forgot, you're a town girl."

She shook her head, "It's sort of a shock, but I'm okay. Tell me what to do."

Andy said, "When I lift up the head, push the dishpan under the neck. You're going to catch the blood." Andy ran the long blade of a butcher knife into the pig's throat, and warm blood squirted into the pan. Martha turned her face away. Andy spoke to her. "Watch what you're doing, honey, and don't lose a drop." He bounced up and down on the pig and the blood came out in spurts.

Andy handed Martha a wooden spoon. "Keep stirring the blood or it will clot on you." Steam rose from the pan, and her hand shook as she moved the spoon through the warm blood.

When the bleeding stopped, Martha carefully carried the dishpan of blood to the house. Mrs. Juvland was waiting for her at the door. "Good girl." She took the pan from her and placed it on the table. She continued to stir. She looked up at Martha, "I like the way you're helping out the boys. Most girls wouldn't do that."

Martha wiped her nose with the back of her mitten. "Andy didn't give me much choice. I felt like a wicked hag stirring a cauldron of bloody witch's brew."

She laughed. "Have you ever had blod klubb?"

Martha shook her head, "I'm sure I haven't."

"It's a Norwegian blood cake. We always make it after butchering."

"My folks are German. That's a new one on me."

Ernie brought two ten-gallon cream cans into the house. He filled them with boiling water, and he and Martha carried them down the front steps to a toboggan. Ernie pulled the toboggan, and Martha walked along the side steadying the cans of hot water. Andy helped Ernie empty the cans of water into the scalding barrel.

The dead pig lay in the bloody snow under the tree. Andy cut a slit at the bottom of each hind leg, exposing the Achilles tendon. He wedged the ends of a singletree between the tendons and the leg bones. The singletree had an iron ring in the middle. He fastened the hook of the block and tackle to the ring and the Inderdal brothers hoisted the pig upside-down over the scalding barrel, which they had leaned against the end of the flatbed sleigh.

They dunked the pig into the hot water several times, and then they pulled it, steaming-hot, onto the flatbed. They scraped the loose hairs off with sharp knives.

When the pig was completely shaved, they hoisted it again with the block and tackle. Andy reached high up with the butcher knife and made one clean slit from the pig's anus down to its throat. The steaming guts tumbled out and plopped into a galvanized tub. Andy bent over and ran his bare fingers through the innards to find the heart, which he cut out and placed in a dishpan. He also took out the liver and kidneys. He handed the pan to Martha and she brought it to the house.

Andy wiped his hands on his pants, and put on his gloves. He said, "I think it's time for a little nip." He pulled a bottle of Old Grand Dad out of the snow and passed it around.

Ernie looked at the pig hanging in the tree. "Maybe we should take 'er up a little in case we get any dogs around here tonight, or even a timber wolf." The Inderdal boys pulled on the rope of the block and tackle. Ernie said, "That's good." He slapped Buddy Inderdal on the back and said, "Hey, Ma's gonna give you guys half of this pig. She told me this morning. We'll cut 'er up tomorrow and you can come over and get your share."

The Inderdal boys drove away in their truck, and Ernie and Andy went inside to wash up. The kitchen was steamy and warm. "Boy," Ernie said, waving the steam in front of his face, "all this steam could loosen your wallpaper, Ma. Remember the year that happened?"

"Yeah," she said, laughing. "And don't forget, I went back to the hardware store and told them they sold me lousy paste! I shot my mouth off and I got my money back, too! Remember?"

After supper Andy went into the front room. He noticed his framed picture on the china closet and said, "You make me feel like a grown man, Ma. There I am, next to my big brothers."

Ernie heard him and glanced at his own picture, dressed in his baseball uniform. He said, "We're all proud of you, Andy."

"Well," Andy said, "I haven't done much to be proud about. I've learned how to make my bed just right and shoot an M-1 rifle." He took off his boots and stretched out on the davenport. "Don't make me sound like a war hero. At least not yet."

Mrs. Juvland cleared the table and said, "If anyone wants to take a bath tonight, we're gonna need that tub."

Ernie said, "That's still down by the pigpen. I'll bring it up. Where's the lantern?"

"On the hook in the pantry."

Ernie brought out the kerosene lantern and lit it. Martha took her coat off the hook in the kitchen and said, "Let me go with you. There are some things in my car I want to bring in."

They went out into the frigid night air. Ernie carried the lantern, and Martha walked behind. She watched the shadows of Ernie's long legs against the snow banks along the trail to the pigpen. His moving leg-shadows were like a long black scissors cutting the snow.

She saw the pig, white and frozen, hanging head down in the oak tree. "Here," Ernie said, "hold the lantern." Ernie grabbed the handle of the galvanized tub and dragged it behind the pigpen. Martha stood alone next to the pig. She took off her mitten and felt the frozen white skin of its neck. She held the lantern up and saw the red meat inside the slit of the belly. Her eyes followed the opening down to the throat. The heart was gone, the lungs were gone, all was gone. She felt the small, frozen nipples on the sows belly and she began to tremble. She noticed a tightness in her body.

She jumped when Ernie touched her on the shoulder. She had not heard him come up behind her. She turned to him and said, "You scared me." She handed Ernie the lantern and said, "I guess this was the mother pig."

"Yup, she was the sow." Martha took one last look at the white pig hanging in the tree. The open slit down its belly felt like a wound in her trembling body. She was cold and reached for Ernie's arm to steady herself, as they made their way up the snow-packed trail to the house.

At her car she pulled out a bag of Christmas gifts for the Juvland family, and followed Ernie to the house.

It was warm inside, and Martha held her hands over the front room stove. They talked and played whist until midnight. Andy and Martha were partners and beat the pants off Ernie and his mother. Andy kept up a constant chatter about how good-looking Martha was until they all got sleepy and turned in. Martha enjoyed all the attention, but it made Ernie wonder. *Is that what every guy is gonna think about my woman? It's nice in a way, but it could end up being a real pain in the ass.* Those were his thoughts, as he listened to the squeaks coming from Martha's bed.

Martha left early the next morning. It was Sunday, Christmas Eve, and she was eager to get back to Bemidji to be with her parents. Ernie talked to her through the window of her car. "You drive carefully. Those icy patches can sneak up on you."

"You're sounding like my dad. I'll be okay."

"I didn't get you anything for Christmas. I'm sorry."

"Don't worry about it. Your gift was bringing me to meet your family."

"I hope you had a good time."

"Of course I did, silly. And just between you and me, I think your mom likes me."

"I know she does. And I certainly know Andy likes you!"

"What a flirt!"

"Yeah, he's okay. He's just been cooped up in a barracks too long. We'll take him out and dig up one of his old girlfriends for him. Then we'll send him on his way with a smile on his face."

She laughed. "How about you? Are you gonna dig up an old girlfriend?"

"Nope! I have one right here." He patted her on the arm.

She picked up his hand and kissed it. "Behave yourself now and don't forget to write."

"You can bet on it." She hit the gas, and pulled away. Ernie watched her car head up the lane. It suddenly dawned on him that he had not heard any voices and no laughter since leaving Dahl School. He wondered where the demons had gone. *Is it being away from that school and the demands of teaching? Is it being away from Tom and Carla? Why do I feel so relaxed? Maybe it's being with my mother and brother. Yes, I am comfortable right here on the farm where I was born. Or maybe it's being with Martha. When I'm with her, my fears just seem to melt away. Is that what love is all about? Chasing away the fears.*

The next morning Mrs. Juvland and her sons cut up the pig on the kitchen table. They packed the cuts in the meat barrel on the back porch. They put a lid on the barrel and a rock on the lid, making sure the rock was bigger than a cat. Buddy Inderdal stopped by to get his share.

Later that day, Ernie and Andy took the Swede saw and the toboggan to the tamarack swamp and cut a Christmas tree. That night, Mrs. Juvland and her sons put tinsel and popcorn garlands on the tree and carefully clamped on tiny candle holders.

Christmas Eve—they lit the tree and watched the flickering light for an hour. Mrs. Juvland said a prayer for her sons. Then Andy blew out the candles and they opened their gifts. Martha had knitted a scarf for Mrs. Juvland and socks for Andy and Ernie.

The boys made brandy eggnog, which was a favorite of their mother's. They listened to Christmas music on the radio.

Mrs. Juvland sat in her front room chair deep in thought. Finally, she said, "Turn the radio down a little; I have some news to tell you." She told the boys about moving into town to live with Mildred Osterholt. Ernie and Andy were relieved. Ernie told his mother he would borrow the Inderdal's truck to move her things to town. He assured her that he could get along without the car. She would need it, to go to the store or take Mildred for Sunday drives. They decided to leave all the furniture, because Ernie said he might want to live on the farm over the coming summer.

On Wednesday night Andy was due to catch the train. His military orders were cut. He was assigned to another Army base in Missouri for eight weeks of infantry training. Andy knew when the training was over, they would ship his outfit overseas—most likely to France. One way or another, the young soldier would be going to the front.

Snow started to fall late Wednesday morning. It came down heavily all afternoon, and by evening the road to the mailbox was drifted over. Andy was dressed in his neatly pressed uniform. He was all packed and ready to go. Two buddies from town were coming to pick him up and take him to Thief River Falls. They were going to tie one on before he got on the train. Andy went to the window and saw the headlights of a car turning around at the mailbox. He turned to his mother. She stood near the stove with her hands folded. "Well, this is it, Ma. They're here to pick me up." He hugged his mother and kissed her on the forehead. "You take good care of yourself now, Ma." His voice was strained; he wiped his nose on the back of his Army glove.

Mrs. Juvland was sobbing, "Yeah, you be careful now. We'll be praying for you and your brothers to get home soon."

Ernie waited at the door and Andy said, "Goodbye, Ma."

She said, "Goodbye, Andy," and turned her face away.

The two brothers stepped out into the howling wind, and Andy loaded his duffel bag on the toboggan. Ernie led the way with the lantern, and Andy pulled the toboggan behind, heading up to the mailbox. The drifts were so deep the lantern dragged in the snow, leaving a little trail, which was quickly covered over by the blowing snow.

They came to the mailbox and stood together in the headlights of the car. Andy moved close to Ernie and said, "For some reason, I don't feel like a big shot right now. To tell you the truth, I feel scared."

Ernie was surprised at the tone of his kid brother's voice. He tried to reassure him. "I think that's normal. Try to think of something that makes you happy."

"I guess," said Andy. He reached for his brother's hand and said, "Maybe I shouldn't have told you that, buddy. Don't let it get you down. I'll be okay."

"I'm sure you will." Ernie slapped his brother on the back. "Don't you guys get so drunk now that you'll miss the train."

"No," Andy said, "that would be a revolting development!"

Ernie stood alone in the bitter wind and watched the taillights of the car fade away. *Be careful, brother. Look out for yourself. Come home with all your arms and legs. I should be the one leaving. Not you. You're only 18 years old. What a crime to send a mere boy off to war.*

Chapter XIV...The New Year

Ernie's vacation was over, and when the bus pulled into Sparborg, he could see Orvid across the street, waiting for him in his Model A with the motor running. A thick stream of white exhaust came out of the tailpipe and met the bitter Sunday morning air. Ernie thanked Orvid for picking him up and climbed in. They drove by Bethany Lutheran Church as families walked from their cars to the church all bundled up in overcoats, caps, and scarves. Ernie could only see the heads of their children, the rest of them was lost behind the huge piles of snow that lined the sidewalks. It was January 7, 1945, the dead of winter in Jackson Township, Minnesota.

They drove by Dahl School, and Ernie noticed the snow had been plowed off the playground and the steps to the porch were shoveled off. Orvid said, "We were up here yesterday digging out. We also split up more wood for you, so you'll be all set for school tomorrow." Ernie realized it was the only thing Orvid had said since they left the bus stop. He gripped the steering wheel with both hands and stared ahead with a somewhat sad and distracted expression. Ernie sensed that something was wrong.

They turned into the Henning's lane and Ernie noticed the pickup wasn't there. "They must be at church."

"Yeah, there's nobody home," said Orvid as he brought the Model A to a stop by the front porch. Orvid got out and said, "I'll help you in with your stuff."

The kitchen was warm. Orvid put some small pieces of wood in the kitchen stove and felt the coffee pot sitting on top. He said, "I was over here early to start the fires. We wanted the house to be warm when you got home. He took two cups from the cupboard. He poured a cup of coffee for Ernie and one for himself. He brought the cups to the table, sat down across from Ernie, and cleared his throat. "I don't like doing this one bit—but I have to tell you something."

Ernie said, "I figured something was wrong."

Orvid leaned across the table, and in a strained voice he said, "Tom shot himself on Christmas Eve."

Ernie said, "What!"

"It was a real shock to all of us. We had no idea." He struggled for words. "Yeah, on Christmas Eve no less."

224

Ernie said, "Jesus!" He moved his coffee cup aside. He crossed his arms on the table and laid his head down. "Oh, mercy!" he said, his voice breaking and muffled in the sleeves of his coat. He felt Orvid's hand gently patting his head. "Oh, God!" Ernie blurted out.

Orvid left his hand on the teacher's head. "We were going to call you at your ma's place, but Carla wanted us to wait. She didn't want to ruin your vacation."

Ernie managed to drag his face off the table. It was wet with tears. He took a handkerchief from his pocket and blew his nose. "So, what about Dale and Carla?"

"They've been living over at Betty and Vic's place. Carla sold off the livestock and I don't think she'll be able to come back here very soon. She thinks living here would bother Dale. It hit them both real hard."

Ernie had trouble speaking. "Christmas Eve."

"Yeah. Carla and Dale drove into town for church. The boy was playing Joseph in the Sunday school play. Tom said he didn't feel like going. It was such a problem getting him in and out of the pickup, he mostly sat home here. After church Carla stopped by the Vic's, and our place, and the Rollags to give them cookies she had baked. Mrs. Rollag gave Carla some lutefisk. She had bought too much for her relatives that were coming for Christmas dinner. They're Irish on her side of the family, and they don't eat lutefisk."

Ernie looked up and saw Tom's deer rifle still hanging over the door. He turned back to Orvid and asked, "How did he do it?"

"Shotgun, his old single-shot 12-gauge." Orvid got up and went to the door of the front room and opened it. He walked in and Ernie followed him. "She found him right here." He pointed to a spot near the table. He was on the floor and the wheelchair was tipped over. The coroner told me the blast might have knocked him backwards. It took us a whole day to scrub down the place. It was a real mess." He put his hand on Ernie's shoulder. "I don't know how much of this you want to know."

Ernie took in a deep breath and let it slowly come out. "You might as well tell me." He sat down on the davenport and turned to Orvid.

"He must have been planning it, but Carla had no idea what was going through his head. He didn't leave any kind of note, but he laid out some papers on the table, the deed to the farm, some tax forms, and bank papers. The Bible was open and he had written something for Dale. Carla said it was something about, well, telling him to grow up to be a good man. Some advice like that."

Ernie looked at the table and saw the milking stool Dale had made his dad for a Christmas present. A green bow lay next to it. Ernie felt the tears coming again.

Orvid went on. "He figured out how to do it. There was a string tied around the trigger that went back around a notch he had carved into the stock. He put the end of the barrel in his mouth and pulled on the string."

Ernie shook his head and said, "This is awful!"

"The coroner told me that he damned near blew the back of his head off." Orvid got up and walked over to the wall by the stairway. "This whole wall was splattered with blood. We scraped off bits of his scalp and parts of his brain. We even found BBs in the plaster."

Ernie sat motionless on the davenport, his elbows on his knees and his head hanging down in his hands. Orvid walked over and sat down close to him and put his arm around his shoulders. "This is tough for all of us, Ernie." He tried to figure out what to say. "I've decided to stay in the house with you tonight and maybe tomorrow night, too, if you want me to. You're important to us, buddy. We had our differences at first." He shook his head and chuckled. "Hell, I even asked you if you were a queer! But that's all gone now. You proved yourself in more ways than one."

Ernie didn't want to listen. He stood up and raised both arms to the ceiling, "But I killed this man!"

Orvid got up. "What did I hear you say?" He grabbed Ernie by the arm and held him with a tight grip.

Ernie pulled himself free. "I did a stupid thing, Orvid. I took those kids out to the threshing rig, and this poor man ends up with a broken back!"

"You didn't kill this man. He killed himself. I ain't gonna let you talk like that! You just shut up, now!"

"You don't understand how awful I feel."

"I told you to shut up with that talk!" Orvid was out of breath. "Sure, I blamed you at first. I wanted to have you fired, but I came to my senses."

"But you didn't cause the accident. I did!"

Orvid yelled, "I'm not gonna listen to this! You're acting like a crazy man!"

Ernie stopped short. He turned on Orvid and slowly asked, "What did you say?"

"I didn't say nothing!"

"Yes, you did. You said 'crazy man' didn't you?"

"I don't know what I said."

Ernie walked slowly toward the stairway and stared at Tom's empty wheelchair standing in the corner. He said in a low voice, "Maybe you're right. Maybe I am a crazy man."

"If I said anything like that, I didn't mean it."

Ernie didn't answer. He climbed the stairs to his room. It was cold. He went to the floor grate and opened it. He took off his boots and crawled in bed under two quilts, pulled them tight under his chin and lay there, looking up at the ceiling. *Now I have to live with this hanging over my head. What was that I just heard? It sounded like laughter. But it wasn't Orvid. It sounded like Tom laughing at me.*

Then it all came back and it frightened Ernie. Tom isn't in his wheelchair, but he isn't dead either. He's inside Ernie's head. The bundle wagon is lurching forward. Tom is falling backwards; his body clears the back end of the load. His legs rise above his waist. His arms are flapping about. There's a thump! The horses gallop away. Over and over, the images played out in Ernie's head.

He stayed in bed all morning and late into the afternoon. When he woke up for good, just as it was getting dark, Tom was still there, but now he's in the barn. He grabs Martha from behind, his strong arms wrapped around her waist. He whirls her around. Her legs are kicking in the air. He drags her down to the hay and crawls on top of her. His hand goes under her skirt. She screams.

Ernie sprang up in bed and swung his legs over the side. His heart was pounding. He heard women singing. Was it Martha singing? He listened to the music. It wasn't Martha. Orvid had turned on the radio and the Andrews Sisters were singing, "Don't sit under the apple tree with anyone else but me." He smelled meat frying.

He put on his boots and went down to the kitchen. Orvid had two venison steaks frying in a large pan on the stove. He opened the oven and took out two baked potatoes. They ate, but they didn't say much. Orvid kept his eyes on his plate and Ernie's mind was racing.

After supper, they listened to *The Jack Benny Show*, but Ernie couldn't keep his mind on a word of what was said. "Train leaving on Track Nine for Anaheim, Azusa, and Cucamonga!" There was still laughter in Ernie's head. Tom was laughing, Martha was screaming and he thought he heard Timmy Burstrom whispering in his ear, "You don't like me." All the while Jack Benny was talking to Mary Livingstone as they waited for the train to arrive.

Orvid made up a bed for himself on the davenport. "I get up early," he said. "Usually, around five."

"That's okay with me." Ernie was also ready to turn in. Before he went upstairs to bed he said, "Thanks for everything."

"Glad I can help you out."

"I guess I should tell you." Ernie paused to set his mind straight. He didn't know how much he should tell Orvid. "I have bad dreams."

"Yeah, I heard something about that. You go to bed then. And don't worry about it."

"I just wanted you to know in case I come tumbling down the stairs in the middle of the night, screaming bloody murder."

Orvid rolled over on the davenport. He tucked the covers in tight and said, "I'll be at the bottom of the stairs to kick you in the ass."

Ernie said, "That's probably what I need." He climbed the stairs and was able to sleep the night through.

But when he awoke, the chatter in his head was still there. He tried to think about teaching, as Orvid served up a big bowl of Cream of Wheat. After breakfast, Ernie grabbed his leather satchel and put on his winter Army coat. Orvid drove him up to the school and said, "Just remember, we're here to help you."

The classroom had changed; Ernie sensed a difference in the way he felt about being a teacher in his little school.

Everything seemed dark and cold. He built the fire and sat at his desk with his coat and mittens on, waiting for the room to warm up, waiting for the students to arrive. He wondered if Dale would show up.

When Iris Vic arrived, he asked her about the boy. She told him Carla was going to keep him out for a week. She said, "I sit with him; sometimes we play cards or checkers, but he cries a lot."

The routine of the day played out like the ticking of the clock on the wall. Ernie did not mention Tom Henning and neither did the students. They went about their lessons, adding, subtracting, reading, and writing. The smell of cocoa warming and potatoes baking on top of the big wood stove, the sound of chalk scratching on the blackboard, writing spelling words, lunch came and went, recess came and went, the day crawled by until four o'clock.

Over the next two weeks, the students made great strides in learning. Since most days it was too cold to go out for recess, Ernie kept them inside and asked the older students to help the younger ones with their lessons. There was one warmer day, however, when Ernie let some of the big boys go out. Clyde Rollag's little brother Allen wanted to join the older kids. Ernie let him go, but he told Clyde to keep an eye on Allen, and if he got cold to send him in.

While the younger students played games inside, Ernie watched the older boys out the back window. They dug into the huge snowdrifts along the township road to the east, making a tunnel that was several feet long. Ernie was interrupted when he had to settle an argument over a game of marbles in the library. Ernie forgot about the boys outside until it was time to ring the big bell for the end of recess.

The bigger kids heard the bell, and when they came out of the tunnel, the entrance end collapsed, sealing it off. Ernie met his students in the cloak room with a broom and swept the snow off their coats, pants, and boots. The kids were all excited about their tunnel and they made Ernie promise that he would come out and crawl through it during the afternoon recess.

When Ernie called the first graders to the front for recitation, Allen Rollag was missing. "Where's Allen?"

Clyde Rollag jumped up and ran for the door without putting on his coat. He yelled, "My brother!"

Susan Rollag shouted out, "Where is he?"

Ernie threw his reading book on his desk and took off after Clyde. They ran at top speed to the entrance of the snow tunnel and started digging. They heard the little boy whimpering inside. "Hold on!" Ernie yelled, "We're digging you out!" Ernie reached the little boy's hand and pulled him out of the snow. The boy's face was white and he was too weak to walk. Ernie picked him up in his arms and carried him back to the school. Ernie swept off the snow, wrapped the boy in his big Army coat, and held him in front of the stove. Clyde took his jar of hot cocoa from the top of the stove and gave his brother a drink.

Ernie called for everyone's attention and spoke to the students in a stern voice. "That was a close call, boys and girls. And it was my mistake. I don't mind you making snow tunnels. That's fun. But next time, I have to be out there with you." Ernie held Allen on his lap and thought about what had happened. *Another five minutes and this little boy could have died. I have to watch everything they do. These are my children. All of them.*

Later that day, Ernie wrote in his logbook with a red crayon. *Terrible mistake! I let the older kids make a snow tunnel without supervision. Almost lost Allen Rollag. It can never happen again!*

On Saturday, January 20, Ernie was up early to grade arithmetic problems, spelling tests, and compositions. He made himself a big pot of coffee and sat at the Henning kitchen table until well past noon. He heated water for a bath in the galvanized tub. He turned up the radio loud to listen to music from WDAY. Dinah Shore was singing "I'll Walk Alone." Ernie listened and thought of Martha.

**There are dreams I must gather, dreams we fashioned the
night you held me tight.
I'll always be near you wherever you are
each night in every prayer.
If you call, I'll hear you, no matter how far.
Just close your eyes and I'll be there.**

When the song was over, the announcer said, "We now take you to the south portico of The White House for NBC's special broadcast of the swearing in ceremony of Vice President, Harry S. Truman and President Franklin Delano Roosevelt." Ernie had forgotten that this was Inauguration Day. He sat still in the tub and listened to Truman and Roosevelt taking the oaths of office. He thought of his mother, who worshiped the man who was entering his fourth term as President. Though severely handicapped with poliomyelitis, he stood at the podium and his voice rang out across a country weary of war.

As I stand here today, having taken the solemn oath of office in the presence of my fellow countrymen—in the presence of our God—I know that it is America's purpose that we shall not fail. In the days and in the years that are to come, we shall work for a just and honorable peace, a durable peace, as today we work and fight for total victory in war. We can and we will achieve such a peace.

After the speech, Ernie sat in the tub and soaked, mulling over the words of President Roosevelt. He thought of his brothers at war and wondered when they had their last bath, especially his older brother, Clayton, who had landed on Normandy last June. From the newspaper reports his mother shared with him, he was somewhere in the densely forested Ardennes Mountains of Belgium, advancing toward the German boarder, suffering a fierce Nazi counterattack and one of the worst winters on record for that part of Europe.

Then Ernie thought about Andy, not yet 19, going through infantry training, preparing to replace Army soldiers killed in battle. *Here I sit in a tub of warm water listening to the radio. There is nothing for me to feel good about. Did I just think that? Or was it someone speaking inside my head? Someone who wasn't me. Was someone talking to me through the radio?*

Ernie got out of the tub, dried himself, and dressed in warm clothes. He dragged the tub to the back porch and emptied it into the snow. The steam rose and disappeared; the water made a hole in the snow, the sides of which became an ice-walled canyon, dark and deep. Ernie looked at the thermometer. It read 28 degrees below zero, and the sun was still out.

Ernie put the empty tub back by the stove and went into the front room. He dialed the radio trying to find some music. There was static coming from a distant station, and Ernie thought he heard a voice saying, "You don't like me." He quickly turned the radio off and looked around the room. Tom's wheelchair still sat in the corner near the stairs. No one was sitting in it.

He looked at the wall where Orvid had told him they found bits of scalp and pieces of Tom's brain. He ran his fingers over the wall and felt the tiny dimples left by the shotgun BBs. *What was going through his mind when he pulled that string attached to the trigger? Did he feel any pain at all? Does the brain live for a moment, even when it's splattered on the wall?* He felt tears welling up in his eyes. He sat down on the davenport and held his head. *What is my brain doing right now? Why does it tell me that I was the cause of that gunshot? And where is that laughter coming from?* He went to the radio to check if he had actually turned it off. Yes, he had.

Ernie thought he heard the shotgun blast and went back to the wall. He pressed his ear against the place where he had felt the marks of the BBs. *There was the laugh again. Was it Tom's laugh?* Ernie stood back and stared at the wall. *Am I going crazy? No. I can't let it happen. I need to get out of this house.*

Ernie put on his coat and boots and went outside. He stood for a moment wondering where he was going. He wasn't quite sure. He looked up the lane toward the mailbox and decided to walk over to see Anders. He had not seen him since before Thanksgiving, and he thought he could help him sort things out. It was almost five o'clock and the sun had touched the horizon, leaving bright yellow sun dogs shaped like the tips of giant spears pointing toward the heavens. It was perfectly still except for the sharp crunching of Ernie's boots on the hard-packed snow.

The brisk air was good for him. But he was careful how he inhaled the frigid air, avoiding deep breaths that would burn his lungs. By the time he reached Anders's stairs he was feeling better. *I just needed to get out of that house. That's it. Anders will help me. I trust him.*

It was warm in Anders's new addition. Ernie heard the roar in the stovepipe over the potbelly stove, as he warmed himself, front and back. There were two leather chairs facing the stove, each with a footstool. Ernie sat down in one of the chairs and took off his overshoes.

"Make yourself comfortable," said Anders. "I'm going to fix us a hot toddy."

"That sounds very good." Ernie took off his shoes and felt his socks. They were cold and damp. He rubbed his feet in his hands, and then he propped them up on the footstool. "I'm sorry to barge in on you like this. But I hadn't seen you in—what has it been? A couple of months?"

"You are welcome here anytime, young man. I've been thinking about you, and wondering how you were getting on." He handed Ernie the hot drink in a coffee cup. "Here, try this. Let me know if it's too strong."

Ernie took a sip. "That's fine. Just the way it is."

Anders opened the door on the potbelly stove; he put in two more chunks of wood and sat down in the other leather chair. "I was very sorry to hear about Tom."

"Yeah, that was a real shock. I've tried to keep myself busy, but living in the house where he shot himself, it's always on my mind. It really bothers me." Ernie wondered if he should tell Anders about hearing voices and thinking it was coming from the radio. *No. I'm not sure how I would even explain that to him.*

Anders spoke. "I went to the funeral."

"Oh, yeah?"

"Yes, it was very sad. Young wife with a young lad. How is she coping with all this?"

"I haven't seen her. And Dale hasn't said much, when he's been in school. They're staying over at the Vic's place."

"So you're all alone over there?"

"Yeah, I've been batching since New Year's."

"Well, feel free to stop over anytime you need to talk to someone. I'm always here."

"Thank you."

The fire roared in the stovepipe, and they sipped their drinks. A minute passed and finally Ernie said, "I've been thinking a lot about Tom and what you told me about hearing that scream."

"Yes," said Anders, "so have I." He shifted his weight in the leather chair and leaned forward. "Especially at the funeral. You know he was a well-respected man around here. What they call a good, church-going Christian. I sat there and listened to the pastor deliver the eulogy. I could hear the sobs of his wife and other women. I found myself asking the question, 'Could he have actually attacked that young woman?' It's been playing on my mind ever since. The fact is—I made an assumption."

"Do you think you might have been wrong?"

"Certainly." He thought for a moment. "I told you what I heard and saw. I heard what sounded like a woman's scream. I saw Martha's car parked by the house. Then Tom came out of the barn and waved at me. That's it. The rest is all assumption. And as I sat in that church, with what appeared to be every living soul in this township paying respect to this hardworking farmer, it seemed ludicrous to think this man could have raped Martha Sampson."

"Yes, but maybe that's why he killed himself."

"That's another assumption. There is only one man who knows why Tom Henning killed himself, and that man is dead."

"And I caused all that," said Ernie.

Anders guffawed, "Ha! I knew that was coming!"

"Don't make fun of me, damn it!"

"If we are to respect ordinary logic and reason, I cannot sit here and listen to you blame yourself for his accident. It wasn't like you planned it. The man fell off a hayrack. Did you push him? Hell, no! It was not you who broke his back and put him in a wheelchair. Get over that!"

Ernie became agitated. He took his feet off the footstool and sat on the edge of the chair. "It all runs over and over in my mind." He took in a breath, let it out, and slumped back in his chair. "And then there's Martha."

"What about young Martha?"

"She stopped by the school one Sunday back in October. I think she came back to pick up her books and some clothes she had left at the Henning's. And then she found the doctor's report on the rape examination."

"Did you tell her you read it?"

"Yes, and she really flew off the handle."

"I can well understand that."

"Yeah, she was really upset, but after an hour or so she got over it."

"I'm glad to hear that. So tell me, how do you feel about this young woman?"

"I care about her a lot and she cares about me. We're getting to know each other better. She came home with me at Christmas to meet my mother and brother."

"That sounds fine. I don't see your problem."

"Oh, God, Anders! There's a very big problem. I can't get that rape off my mind!"

"Has she talked to you about it?'

"Not much. Only that she will never tell me who did it, and I guess that's what's driving me crazy."

"How will it help if you know?"

Ernie thought for a moment. "I'm really not sure."

"Are you looking for a place to fix your anger?"

"Maybe I am. But what good would that do?"

"I don't think it would do much good at all. In fact it might make things worse." Anders got up and walked over to a bookshelf. He took a book and opened it, "Have you ever read anything by Bertrand Russell?"

"No," said Ernie. "I never heard of him."

"He's one of my heroes, a British philosopher, who went through some of what I went through at St. Hallvard before they forced me out. He was refused a position at City College in New York because of his opinions on organized religion. Russell is a brilliant man, who has the courage of his convictions. I want to loan you this collection of his essays, but first, I want to read you a passage—if I can find it." He thumbed through the pages. "Ah, here we go." He sat down and began to read.

We want to stand upon our own feet and look fair and square at the world—its good facts, its bad facts, its beauties, and its ugliness; see the world as it is and be not afraid of it. Conquer the world by intelligence and not merely by being slavishly subdued by the terror that comes from it. We ought to stand up and look the world frankly in the face. We ought to make the best we can of the world, and if it is not so good as we wish, after all it will still be better than what these others have made of it in all these ages. A good world needs knowledge, kindliness, and courage.

Anders closed the book and handed it to Ernie. "There are a lot of good ideas in this book. Keep it as long as you wish."

Ernie thanked Anders and started putting on his boots. It crossed his mind to mention the voices he'd been hearing. *I'm not sure how he'd react. Would he tell me to see a doctor? But I don't want to do that. Seeing a doctor is like giving up. I need to handle this on my own. No one can know about it. Not even Anders.*

At the door, they talked about Roosevelt's speech. Anders expressed his admiration for the man who continued to give the country hope. "This has been a terrible time in our history, perhaps as difficult as the Civil War. We were a country gone broke in the 30s and faced with wars against the Fascists in the 40s. And this man, who spends his days in a wheelchair, but always manages to stand in public, has never wavered."

Ernie said, "My mother worships Roosevelt!"

"And well she should," said Anders. "Take good care of yourself, Ernie. And remember I am always here if you need help. Watch the ice on the steps going down."

The temperature had dropped a few more degrees, and Ernie heard the poplar trees snapping in the bitter cold. It was a clear, moonless night and his overshoes made crisp chirping sounds in the frozen snow. Cheep, cheep, cheep. Each step made the sound of a strange bird, left out in the cold. He thought about Anders and patted the pocket of his coat where he had put the Bertrand Russell book. *Anders is so kind. Yes, reason. He read about reason. Being reasonable. I have not used reason. I've been letting my mind run wild. I have to grab my mind and control it. If I don't, who knows? I might go stark raving mad. Can't let that happen. I am a teacher and I can't let my students down. When I think about those youngsters, the voices go away. Yes, my students and Martha will save me.*

As he approached the house, Ernie noticed a light in the kitchen window. The Henning's pickup was parked out front. Carla had come back. He walked up the steps to the porch and stamped the snow off his overshoes. He heard her voice calling from inside, "Ernie? Is that you?"

"Yes, it is."

"Can you stay out for a bit? I'm taking a bath."

"Sure," he said and stepped off the porch. He looked up at the north sky, and off the edge of the house, he saw a spread of northern lights, red, blue and green phosphorescence, a touch of magic from deep in space. He studied them as they appeared

236

behind the huge icicles that hung from the eaves at the corner of the porch. They undulated like gentle waves on a dark sea. Ernie followed their slow movement. How peaceful they looked, far from the battlefields and far from Jackson Township, beautiful colors rolling gently across a star-dotted sky.

I must send my thoughts outward. I can't keep thinking about what is happening in my brain. If I listen to Anders, I will be free of the laughter and voices. The answer is out there. Out there in the stars.

He heard Carla struggling to open the door. Ernie came up on the porch to help her. He put his shoulder against the door and pushed. She shouted, "It's iced up from all the steam!" When the door broke free and swung open, Ernie saw Carla standing in the steam. She was barefoot, wrapped in her black winter coat, with a white towel tied around her head in a turban.

Ernie closed the door tightly. "Sorry to barge in on you."

She said, "That's okay. I was done, anyway. I hadn't taken a bath in a week, and with all the people over at the Vic's place, I figured I would come over here." She sat down at the table and bent over to put on her slippers. Her coat came open and Ernie could see her breasts. She saw him looking and gave him a smile. She carefully closed her coat and leaned back in her chair.

Ernie took off his mittens and sat in a chair across the table from her. He noticed a bottle of brandy and an empty glass on her side of the table. Carla's eyes were red and Ernie thought she looked older. He reached across the table to hold her cold hands. He rubbed them gently and said, "I can't tell you how sorry I am."

She started to sob, "I know you are. And I'm sorry you have to be here, by yourself. We talked about finding you another family to live with, but we haven't had much luck."

Ernie said, "Don't worry about me. I'll be okay." He continued to hold her hands. "How's Dale doing?"

"Not good. Poor boy. First his little brother and now his father. He cries a lot. I have to give Iris a lot of credit. She helps him with his homework and they play games. She was teaching him how to play chess when I left. And maybe it's good for her, too. She has talked about wanting to be a teacher when she grows up."

"I'm glad to hear that. Iris is a remarkable girl. She cares about the younger ones." Ernie noticed Carla nodding and showing a smile. "We should all try our best to help you and Dale."

"Thanks, Ernie," she said and got up. "Betty sent a kettle of beef stew for you. It should be warm. Have you eaten supper?"

"No. As a matter of fact I haven't eaten all day."

"Shame on you. I'm gonna feed you right now."

After supper they sat together on the davenport in the front room. Carla opened another bottle of brandy and filled her glass. She offered Ernie a glass, but he declined.

Carla wanted to know how his trip home had gone. Ernie told her about his mom and Andy. She knew that Martha had gone with him and she asked him how she got along with his mother. Ernie told her that he was becoming sweet on Martha. Carla smiled and said, "Good. I'm happy for both of you." But as she said it, Ernie wondered how happy she really was. He changed the subject and talked about Andy, how he was assigned to infantry training, and would be soon sent to Europe.

Another half hour passed and Carla continued to drink. Ernie started to feel sleepy. He wondered if Carla meant to stay the night. *Orvid told me that she didn't want to be in the house. Had that all changed? Why did she smile when she noticed I was looking at her open coat? Did she really come back to take a bath? Or was there something else going on?* Ernie got up and said, "I'm about to doze off. I think I'm going to turn in."

Carla was disappointed. "I was hoping we could talk, but, yeah, you need your rest," she said. Then she added, "I think I'll sit here awhile, finish my drink, and see what I can find on the radio." She stood up and said, "Give me a goodnight hug, Ernie."

He held her in his arms. She ran her hand up to the back of his neck and kissed him on the cheek. Ernie pulled away, somewhat surprised and said, "Thanks for the supper."

"I was happy to feed you." She opened the top button on her coat. "I'll be awake if you get lonesome."

Ernie gave a nervous chuckle, turned and went up the stairs. He stripped down to his long johns and crawled under the covers. The room was fairly warm. He heard Carla putting more wood in both the front room and the kitchen stoves. When she walked by the bottom of the stairway, Ernie saw her shadow move across the wall at the top of the stairs. He heard her dialing the radio from station to station. Ernie remembered seeing her breasts when her coat came open. *She smiled at me. Why did she come back on such a cold night? Her husband shot himself in the room where she's standing. Only a month ago. What's on her mind?*

She had found some jazz music, a soft clarinet, maybe Benny Goodman. Ernie heard her slippers moving on the linoleum floor of the front room, and the shadow came back on the wall. Ernie watched it sway back and forth. She was slowly dancing. She took the towel off her head and fluffed out her long hair. Her coat dropped to the floor. He saw the outline of her naked body, her legs spread apart. The shadow turned in profile. She cupped her breasts with both hands and swayed to the soft music.

The shadow grew larger, larger, and the light went out. The music was gone, and he heard the door to her bedroom open, but he did not hear it close. Her bed squeaked.

Ernie lay silent. Then came her voice, soft and pleading. "Ernie. Are you still awake?"

"Yes."

"Would you come here, please?"

Ernie waited. Then he asked, "Is something wrong?

"I want you here, please."

Ernie sat up and reached under the bed for his slippers. It was completely dark in the room. He carefully felt his way toward the stairs and reached for the railing. The steps creaked as he slowly went down. He stopped at the foot of the stairs. He felt the handle of Tom's wheelchair and gripped it tightly.

"I'm in bed," she said.

Ernie had never been in the Henning's bedroom before. At the doorway, he smelled perfume.

"Over here," came her voice in a whisper.

Ernie moved slowly and found the bedpost. He ran his hand down to the quilt. She laid her warm hand over his. "I want you next to me, Ernie." Her hand left his and he heard the heavy quilts being thrown back. He smelled the soap from her body. "Don't worry," she said in a soft voice he could barely hear. "We don't have to do anything."

Ernie sat on the bed and slowly removed his slippers. She said, "Quick, I'm getting cold." He crawled in and pulled the covers up to his neck. His hand brushed against her naked thigh.

They both lay still, listening to the sound of their breathing. Ernie heard the snap of a poplar tree, the sap swelling in the frigid air, the thin skin of the bark cracking under pressure. "I don't like doing this," he said.

She moved her lips close to Ernie's ear and whispered, "It's okay." She touched his ear with her wet tongue. "I just can't be in this bed alone." She waited for him to answer, but he was silent and rigid. "I can't sleep alone anymore. I ask Dale to sleep with me every night." She undid the top buttons of Ernie's long johns and ran her fingers through the hairs on his chest.

He took her hand from his chest and said, "We really should stop. I'm feeling a little wild here."

She moved her hand down, stroking his belly. She opened the bottom buttons of his long johns.

He took her hand away and said, "Please, don't."

She moved back and settled her head on her own pillow.

"I'm sorry," he said. "It isn't right."

She was quiet and then, "Are you in love with Martha?"

The tone of voice bothered Ernie. "I'm not quite sure."

"She's very young."

Ernie wondered what she meant by that. "She's 20 now. That's only five years younger than I am."

Carla waited for more. Then she asked, "Did I ever tell you how old I am?"

"No, you never did."

"I'm pushing 40!" She raised her voice. "Do you know what that means to a woman?"

Ernie kept quiet.

"It means men don't look at you the way they used to. It means your breasts start to sag and your hips get lumpy and there ain't a darned thing you can do about it." She sat up and yelled, "And Lord, God, you know that each day it's gonna get worse!"

She waited for a reply, but he had nothing to say. She started again, "I know this is very personal. These are feelings I don't even talk to my women friends about. I just need you to listen." She took in a breath and blurted out, "The worst damned thing—and please don't think I'm awful—all I can think about is doing it! Every man I see—I want him to undress me and take me to bed. I want to feel his hands moving all over my breasts and up my legs. He can be young or old, it doesn't make a bit of difference. As long as he's nice to me. That's all I ask.

"Then I want to please him. I want to feel good about what we're doing. Most of all I want him to know I'm a woman with desires just like men have, a good woman and not some worthless whore!"

Ernie pulled away, "Please. You have to stop talking this way. You're making me crazy!"

"Well, damn it! Let's both be crazy!" She started to crawl on top of him, and Ernie started to get out of bed.

She started to cry. "Please don't go! I need you in this bed right now!" She was hysterical. Ernie reached over and touched her face. It was wet with tears. She grabbed his hand. Then she reached up and grabbed him around the neck and pulled him down on top of her. She kissed him on the mouth and ran her tongue deep inside. Ernie tasted the brandy. She squeezed him to her body and said, "Now I want you to be a man and make me feel good!" She was screaming. "And I hope you hear us, you bastard!"

Ernie struggled to sit up. "Who are you yelling at?"

"I'm yelling at my frozen husband in the attic!"

He shouted, "What the hell are you talking about?"

She was raging, yelling at the ceiling, "What a mean trick you played on me and our son! You shot yourself in the dead of winter when the ground was frozen like a brick! You awful man! Can you hear me up there? You didn't touch me for I don't know how damned long. And then you go and kill yourself! Well, you're gonna listen to me now! Ernie and I are gonna make love, and I'm gonna scream, and laugh and cry, and I hope you can hear us! I tried everything to help you, but you never listened and you never gave a damn about me!"

Ernie struggled to get free. He pushed Carla off his chest and started for the door without his slippers. She yelled at him, "Where the hell are you going?"

Ernie tried to answer in a calm voice. "Please listen. I can't do this. I can't stand to hear you yelling like this!" He stumbled toward the stairs and ran into Tom's wheelchair, sending it rolling across the floor.

She blurted out, "Ha! I've got you figured out! You're afraid your cute little girlfriend will find out?" Ernie started up the stairs without answering. "Okay, go to your room like a little boy."

Ernie crawled up the stairs and managed to find his bed. He stared into the darkness and listened to Carla sobbing. She had hurt him, and he was sure he would have a nightmare if he fell asleep. Each time he thought of lying next to her, naked and warm, he felt like he'd explode. *Little boy? Is that what she thinks I am? Maybe I should show her I can be a real animal!*

A half hour passed and Ernie heard Carla walking around in the front room. He saw a faint bit of light come up the stairway. He lay still, listening to the bottom steps creaking. Then he saw the candle, and then he saw her face. Steady and somber, she climbed the stairs, wrapped in her winter coat. She stopped at the top of the stairs and Ernie closed his eyes. *Will she crawl in bed with me? Then what? Maybe I'll show her I'm not a little boy. But her dead husband is in the attic. He's lying right over my head.*

He lay still with his eyes closed waiting for the sound of her slippers to approach his bed. He wasn't sure how he would do it. He started to unbutton his long johns. *I wonder what it will feel like. Will she tell me what to do?*

Then he heard a click. He opened his eyes and saw her opening the latch to the attic door. She closed the door behind her. Ernie heard the attic steps creaking, slowly. He lay still, listening to each step on the floor above him. He heard a faint squeak, like a rusty hinge, slowly opening.

He faintly heard her say, "I'm sorry." Then he heard a thump. It sounded like she had fallen to the floor. Ernie thought about the candle. He sprang out of bed, wrapped himself in his Army coat, and stumbled toward the door. She called, "Ernie?"

"Yes," he said, softly. "Did you fall?" She didn't answer. "I was worried about the candle."

"Will you come up here, please?" She was not sobbing now. She spoke in a controlled voice. "I need you by me."

Ernie slowly climbed the attic stairs. He saw her struggle to her feet and stare into the open casket. "Come stand by me, please." The candle shook in her hand, and Ernie saw the flickering light spread across the dead man's face. Ernie saw a deep sadness in his brow and in the corners of his mouth. The farmer's large hands looked useless, folded across his chest, as if he had lost some tool, a pitchfork, a shovel, or his ax.

Carla took Ernie's hand and began, "Forgive me, dear, for the things I said. I can't blame you. I know how unhappy you were, and I tried to help you. But I know it wasn't enough. I will try to be a good mother to your son. I love him very much, and I know he'll grow up to be a good man like his father. I'm sorry for the way I acted tonight. Please forgive me. And God forgive me. In the name of the Father, the Son, and the Holy Ghost. Amen."

Ernie said, "Amen." He took the candle from Carla and helped her slowly close the lid of the casket.

They stood silently together for a moment. Carla reached out and touched the lid again. "Goodbye, Tom."

Ernie held her hand and slowly led her down the attic stairs and down the stairs to the front room. She lit the lamp and spoke to Ernie with her head down. "I'm an awful, sinful woman."

Ernie wanted to hug her. "No. You're a good woman."

She turned toward the bedroom. "I'm gonna get dressed." She stopped and said, "I'm sorry for the way I acted. I probably drove you nuts, and that wasn't fair."

"That's okay. I'm glad we didn't go any further."

"I suppose. Who knows what's right or wrong?" She remembered something. "I want you to do me a favor."

"What's that?"

"I pulled the battery out of the pickup to keep it warm. It's sitting by the kitchen stove. Would you mind putting it in the pickup for me? There's a crescent wrench and a flashlight on the counter. Try to start 'er up for me and leave it running. If she won't turn over, the crank is under the seat."

"I'll do that," said Ernie.

"I appreciate it. Oh, one more thing, the hospital has been asking about Tom's wheelchair. Can you put it in the back of the pickup? Let me know if you need help."

"Don't worry. I can handle it."

"Thanks, Ernie. I brought canned food for you; it's in the cupboard." She reached for his hand. "I'm sorry to leave you alone, but I'm going back to the Vic's house to be with Dale. This place gives me the creeps."

Chapter XV...The River

Ernie moved out of the Henning's place the first week of February. He told himself he could deal with a frozen body in the attic, but then something happened one day that he wasn't prepared for. Tired and frustrated with the workload at his school, he came home and went upstairs to change clothes. He was lying on his bed exhausted, thinking he might just doze off for a while, when suddenly he heard footsteps coming from the attic. He sprang up and yelled out, "Who's up there?"

"Just me," came the voice. Ernie vaguely recognized the voice. *It couldn't be Kenny Torstad. Carla had sold off the cows.*

Ernie opened the door to the attic stairs and started up. It was Timmy Burstrom, the neighbor kid who had attacked Dale. Ernie shouted, "What the heck are you doing up here?"

"Tom is my neighbor and I wanted to keep him company. I talk to him and he can hear me." Burstrom had opened the lid of the casket and was holding the dead man's hand.

Ernie took Burstrom's hand away and closed the lid. He grabbed the kid by the arm and pulled him toward the stairway. "I can't have you up here." The kid was strong and he fought Ernie all the way down to the kitchen. Ernie finally muscled him to the front door and pushed him out. "Now, you go on home. And don't come back!" Burstrom started to whimper. Ernie yelled after him, "And if you ever lay a hand on Dale again, I'll kill you!"

He ran off. Ernie heard him laughing, "I'll get you!"

The next day, he sent a letter to Carla with Dale.

Dear Carla,

Last night I found Timmy Burstrom up in the attic with the body. I have decided to move out and live in the school. I can cook on the kerosene stove. But I'll need some kind of cot, maybe one I can fold up and put away during the day. I'll also need that galvanized tub from your place for taking a bath. I don't want anyone to worry about me. I'll be fine.
Ernie

It was the middle of March, and Andy Juvland bounced along in the back of a deuce and a half Army truck, north of Colmar, France. Ten young soldiers sat on benches along each side of the truck, as it lumbered up a muddy logging trail through the woods. The huge tires spun, swerving the truck back and forth, nearly hitting trees on either side of the deep ruts, and sending some of the infantrymen hurtling to the floor. Andy hung on and listened to the squad leader, a short corporal from Long Island, New York, ramble on. "You guys are lucky. You missed the fight we had in the Colmar Pocket. We lost a lot of men there, and that's why you're here, boys. You're replacements. We can hardly keep up with the casualties. That's the way it goes, boys."

Andy pulled the canvas flap back on the side of the truck and looked off through the woods. He saw a lean-to shed, the same shape and size as their chicken coop back home. Against the wall he saw a pile of cordwood stacked up to the edge of the roof. The truck took a bend in the trail, bringing the shed closer in view. It wasn't cordwood stacked against the lean-to. It was a pile of dead bodies. Andy wondered if they were our guys or Germans. But did it even matter? They were dead soldiers. He looked away.

The corporal continued to talk over the roar of the truck motor, "You guys look scared. That's normal. I was, too, before I got into combat. I can't give you a definite reason why, but when the shooting starts, the fear goes away. There are too many things to think about just to keep your tail from getting shot off."

Andy had already forgotten the date. He was on the ship crossing the Atlantic on March 7. He knew, because it was exactly a month after his birthday. Nineteen years old and going into combat. The training was over. To Andy those bodies stacked like cordwood were not actors in a movie pretending to be dead. They were real.

The deuce and half truck rumbled through the woods and came to a stop in a clearing. Andy climbed out of the truck and saw large tents, tanks, bulldozers, artillery guns, more trucks, and soldiers in battle gear, hundreds of them. He had no idea where he was—there was some talk about the Germans dug in at the Siegfried Line, a massive fortification the Germans had built as a last line of defense at the border of their Fatherland.

It was late afternoon of a sunny day, March 17, 1945. Warm days had melted the heavy snows of a terrible winter and there was mud everywhere. Andy stood in formation waiting to hear from his platoon sergeant, Staff Sergeant O'Carey, a quiet soldier, who spoke with a New England accent. Andy expected a pep talk like he had seen in war movies, but O'Carey passed by the young replacements, who had ridden with Andy in the truck. He was pulling out older men, late twenties or 30-years-olds, to go on patrol with him to the front as soon as darkness came. He found eight. They stood off to the side, and Andy noticed how tired they looked, bearded and grim, their uniforms covered with grime. These were hardened combat soldiers, who had made it through Anzio, Italy, landed on the beaches of southern France, and fought their way north to the Colmar Pocket. They were considered old veterans of war. Andy found out, if you were 30 years old, they called you 'Pop'. He wondered how long it would take before he looked like those guys.

Andy wished he had been picked for patrol. Waiting around made him think too much. He watched as the dead and wounded were carried into the command post, some struggling to walk, others on stretchers, their white bandages stained with blood. He saw a soldier with a leg missing staring up from the mud where he lay. A medic kneeled down beside him and removed a tourniquet from his thigh. He turned to a litter bearer and said, "This one is gone. Take one of his tags and stack him with the rest."

Sergeant O'Carey spoke with kindness to his young platoon, teenage soldiers, who looked more like high school boys waiting for a school bus. "It looks like you'll move out in the morning, just before it gets light. I'll see you when we come back from patrol. We're due back at 0300. Double check all your gear. Get help from the older guys if you need it. Get something to eat. Then you should try to catch some sleep. Tomorrow could be a long day." O'Carey left and joined his men chosen for patrol.

Early that evening they were called to formation again. They were addressed by a Lieutenant Benson, who had received a battlefield commission. Andy later found out that the guy was fearless. One of the combat veterans told him, "When we were dug in back at Ostheim, he would go out front with his rifle and shoot buzzards. Benson ain't scared of nothing!" He had a southern accent and everything he said made Andy feel like the man knew what he was talking about. He spoke to a few of the soldiers in the front row, and then he addressed the entire group in measured speech, choosing his words carefully. "It's good to see new blood out here. You're looking fresh and eager, and you smell damned good. I just got a whiff of shaving lotion! Looks like you brushed your teeth and combed your hair. That's good, but tomorrow we're gonna get you dirty. Some of you have asked me where you're going." He laughed and said, "I just told this guy up front here that you're all going to Hell. At least it might seem like that."

There was only slight nervous laughter from the green replacements. The lieutenant stopped joking around and said, "We'll know more after your sergeant comes back from patrol, but I can tell you this much, the enemy is dug in along a line of concrete slabs. If you know your geometry, they're tetrahedrons, four sides tapered toward the top like pyramids. They stick out of the ground about four feet high. They're made of four feet of reinforced concrete and placed about six feet apart, too close to drive a tank between them. We call them 'dragon's teeth'. Our objective is to smash through the 'dragon's teeth' and destroy the heavily fortified pillboxes set up nearby. The enemy is waiting for us with heavy artillery. They are dug into a long line of trenches in front of and between the fortifications. You can expect rows of barbed wire and mines in front of the trenches. Remember your training about mines and trip wires.

"They call it the Siegfried Line, men, and if we make it through, we've reached the German border. Now, Corporal Preston will check you out on all your combat gear. Then you should try to get some rest. Just before daylight, I want you saddled up and ready. If all goes according to plans, we'll be jumping off at 0545."

Neal and Bobby Smierud sat on the floor between their bunks in a long, dark dormitory. Bass Lake Juvenile Detention Center was set far back in the wilderness, ten miles north of Ely, Minnesota. The brothers had skipped going to the mess hall for supper. They needed to be alone to make their plans. Neal had made a knife out of a piece of metal he found in the woods behind the dormitory. Bobby played lookout as Neal cut a small slit in the bottom of his mattress. He reached in his pocket and took out four fishhooks and a length of fishing line he had wrapped around a stick of wood. He slipped the fishing gear and the knife back inside the mattress and whispered to Bobby. "We'll need lots of matches. Snoop around and we'll stash them in the mattress."

"Don't you think we should just find a road and try to hitch a ride," said Bobby.

"No, stupid!" said Neal. "You don't do that! We have to stay in the woods and keep moving. We need to get far away from here. Someplace where they ain't lookin' for us."

Bobby said, "When do we go?"

"Too cold yet. We need to wait. And we need matches." They stood up and Neal said, "Let's go. We might still catch the end of the chow line."

Andy found a patch of dry ground near a tree. He spread out his tent for a ground cover, but he didn't bother setting it up. He took off his pack and sat down with his back against the tree. He wrapped himself in his blanket and tried to fall asleep, dozing off and on. He noticed other soldiers stirring, so he got up and went through his pack one more time checking his gear, K rations, canteen, knife, small shovel, half tent, blanket, gas mask. He put four bandoleers of ammunition over his shoulders, six clips of eight rounds each. He strapped on his ammo belt with eight clips. He hooked on four grenades, three fragmentary and one white phosphorous. He carried an M-1 rifle and a bayonet. Dressed in heavy woolen shirt, trousers, boots, helmet liner and helmet, he was ready to march to the front. "This is it," he thought.

At 0300 the heavy artillery guns started firing at the German defenses. An hour later, Sergeant O'Carey's patrol returned to the command post. Their compass stopped working, and they had to find their way south by keeping their backs to the Big Dipper. O'Carey had not slept and was hoping he and his patrol unit could catch a break. But, no. They were ordered to join the rest of their outfit for the all-out attack. They had to turn around and retrace the same ground they had just struggled through in the dark.

The sky was just starting to lighten as Andy's outfit, Company B, First Battalion, Seventh Infantry Regiment of the Third Infantry Division moved out. Sergeant O'Carey led his platoon through the mud, heading north-northeast to the Siegfried Line, less than ten miles away. Of the 20 soldiers in Andy's squad, only four had been in combat, wounded in the Colmar Pocket, but patched up and sent forward to fight again. The rest, like Andy, had never been shot at. The casualties were running so high that every day dozens of replacements were brought to the front. Many of them would die on their very first day of combat.

Andy heard the friendly fire, heavy artillery shells whizzing over his head from their position behind him. And he heard the whining, screaming sound of the German 88s, big shells, coming his way. He soon realized that the enemy shells coming at him had a different sound than the rounds fired from the Allied artillery. They both exploded around him; the noise was deafening. He kept moving forward, sometimes running, sometimes stumbling, sometimes crawling, but always moving. He remembered his drill sergeant's commands from infantry training, "Keep moving. Don't be a sitting duck."

The sky had lightened more, and he could see rows of barbed wire, the dragon's teeth, and pillboxes ahead. He crawled on his belly, firing at the pillboxes. He was close enough now to hear his bullets bouncing off the solid concrete of the casements. Heavy mortars were exploding around them. Behind him a tank had run over a Teller mine and exploded. He kept moving.

Andy and three others made it through the barbed wire and somehow avoided the mines. Exhausted and wet, he slid down into a muddy trench. He recognized one of the soldiers beside him. It was Sergeant O'Carey. He put his finger to his lips, indicating quiet. Andy listened and he heard German voices. They were just up ahead, around a corner in the trench. One of Andy's comrades carried a bazooka. Sergeant O'Carey loaded it for him and connected the wire firing device. They waited. Two German soldiers stepped into view, and the bazooka fired, killing one. The other one disappeared. Andy and the three GIs pursued. He was in the rear and the last soldier to step over the dead German. The eyes were still open. Andy glanced at the corpse. *He looks just like one of us, pale, white, young, and scared. He's just wearing a different helmet.*

Andy's mother sat at the dining room table and worked on a jigsaw puzzle with Mildred Osterholt. They were almost finished. El Capitan was in place and so was Half Dome. The scene was Yosemite Valley, and Mrs. Juvland said, "I want to go there sometime. It looks so peaceful. Maybe one of my boys will take me there when the war is over." She was very content in her new home. Mildred had trouble getting around and she couldn't drive. Mrs. Juvland took her to church on Sundays, and they took drives out in the country on afternoons. They talked about taking a picnic basket to a park along the Red Lake River on summer days.

Living in town, Andy's mother had electric lights for the first time in her life. Mildred had an electric stove, refrigerator, and electric radio. She even had a wash machine with an electric motor. There was a pump in the basement, which ran on electricity. Mrs. Juvland had running water, a bathtub with a shower nozzle, and a flush toilet. All new to her.

She and Mildred finished the puzzle and stood up to admire the view. It was 6:45 and they were both quiet to listen to H.V. Kaltenborn deliver the news. But Mrs. Juvland liked Lowell Thomas better for his reports on the war. Halfway through the *Eddie Cantor Show*, Mildred was ready for bed, but Mrs. Juvland opened a box on the table and took out her pencil, envelopes, and stationary. She had letters to write. Five of them, one for each blue star on the war mother's flag, which now hung in Mildred's front room window.

Andy and the men of Company B fought all day from their position in the trenches. He saw things that terrified him. A soldier standing next to him rose up to fire and was hit in the eye. He turned and looked at Andy; blood was streaming down his face. He slowly slid down the side of the bank to the bottom of the trench. Andy thought he was dead, but then he heard him say, "Watch your head, kid."

A medic crouched down beside him and pulled a wad of cotton out of his kit. "Hold this against your eye, and we'll try to get you out of here." Andy saw that same medic running up and down the trenches all day, patching up bullet wounds and answering cries of pain with shots of morphine. They called him

Doc, and Andy tried to stay close to him. He later found out he was from a little coal mining town in Eastern Kentucky.

Darkness came, and they were able to sneak out of the trench. They crawled back to a temporary supply station to grab more ammunition and food. Andy heard the roar of bulldozers pushing dirt over the dragon's teeth, so the tanks could move forward. Andy crawled back in the trench where he would spend the rest of the night and two more days.

He had heard hardened soldiers talk about the sickening smells of combat. An old veteran back in infantry training had said, "In the movies, they can make bombs explode and blood spurt from a head wound, they can make the ratta-tat-tat sound of a machine gun, but they can't give you the smell." Now Andy was getting it, the stench of dried blood, burned flesh, gun powder, sulfur, exhaust fumes from the tanks and bulldozers, the smell of the sour bread the German soldiers carried as part of their ration, and the smell of his own dried sweat.

Ben Smierud slouched with his head on the bar of Buck and Velma's tavern, smelling of whiskey. "Wake up, Ben," shouted Buck. "We're closing up."

He lifted his head off the bar and started for the door. Buck raised his voice, "Aren't you forgetting something, Ben?"

Ben turned. "What's that?"

"Your coat," said Buck. "It ain't summer yet."

"Oh, yeah," said Ben and he returned to put on his long coat.

"One other thing, Ben."

"What's that?"

"You didn't pay up again."

Ben dug around in his pockets, but he came up empty. "Can you put it on the tab, Buck?"

Buck looked around. Velma had gone back in the kitchen. He lowered his voice, "Look, Ben. I can't carry you any longer. Look at this." He showed Ben a page from a notepad with a bunch of numbers on it. "I don't mind so much, but it's Velma. She does the books, and she told me tonight that I have to cut you off until I get some money from you."

251

"Well, I don't have it now, but I'll get it. I have three graves lined up to dig as soon as the frost goes out. You'll get your money." He turned, went out the door, climbed in his pickup, and drove home. He stopped at the mailbox and picked up a letter.

At home he lit the lamp on the table, shooed the cats away, and sat down to read a letter from Bobby.

Dear Pa,

How are you? How many cats do you have now? Me and Neal are doing okay, but we sure will be happy when they let us out. We play cards and have wrestling matches. Neal is good. He can beat anyone in our dorm. We go to classes, but none of the teachers are as good as Mr. Juvland. I really liked him. Tell him hello for me if you ever see him. We take classes that are like high school subjects. I am getting better at reading. They also make us write. That's why I am writing this letter. I have to show it to my teacher before I send it. I guess you could say that this is my homework.

I feel bad about what me and Neal did with those guns that night. When I think about that, it was pretty stupid. When we came here, all the other jailbirds wanted to hear about it. Neal did most of the talking, sort of bragging about how we shot up the town. But now I just think it was dumb. I promise when I get out, I'll be different. I want to go to high school and maybe get on the baseball team or the football team. I might enlist in the Army or Navy. I don't want to ever go back to jail. Don't worry about me. I'm doing okay.

Love,

Bobby

A cat jumped up on Ben's lap and put his paw on the paper. Ben moved the paw away and read the letter again. It was still in his hand when he drifted off to sleep.

Andy's time in the trenches was a nightmare. It seemed to be endless, but actually, it was about two and a half days. The penetrating sounds of war, the smells, and the utter confusion wore on Andy, and yet he was still alive. He wondered about that. Why had he survived, when another soldier, equally trained, standing within a couple of feet of him could be struck down by an enemy bullet? It made no sense to him. He was no better a soldier than those who died, and yet he was alive.

By the time they crawled out of the trenches, avoided the mines, and made it through the German Westwall, he was numb. The Battle of the Siegfried Line was over. Andy was too tired to feel any joy or a sense of accomplishment. He was breathing, his heart was beating, and he could stand on two good legs.

On March 20, 1945, Company B walked into Zweibrucken, a German city that was almost flattened by incessant bombing. It was quiet except for occasional sniper fire, and they were able to catch a break. But the orders soon came to pack up and head east. They were told that their next objective would be the crossing of the Rhine River, supposedly the last natural barrier, as the Allied Powers moved steadily into Germany.

It was a 70 mile stretch from Zweibrucken to the Rhine. Between March 21 and 22, Andy's First Battalion cleared six towns without firing a shot. They moved into an assembly place named Frankenstein. They spent a day cleaning equipment, going to religious services, and trying to rest up for the next battle. Andy had not written home since he arrived in Europe.

Dearest Ma,
Somewhere in Germany
I guess it's about time I'm writing you a letter. I imagine you're getting worried about me. Well, I'm feelin' O.K. Having a wonderful time. Yes, I am over in the land of the "Kraut." So you can draw your own decisions as to what I'm doing. It's not fun, but I'll take care of myself. I at least have learned to pray. I hope you're doing the same. So please don't worry about me. I think the Krauts

are about ready to "hang up." I'm stayin' in a German house. The German people treat us just swell so far. When we go through their towns searching for Krauts, they offer us coffee and bread and most anything they have. We of course aren't supposed to accept anything from these people. In fact we aren't supposed to talk to them. But the German I learned in school sure comes in handy. I'm the unofficial interpreter in my platoon. Sorry, they just called us to muster. Gotta go. Don't worry about me. They say the war will be over soon.

Love,

Andy

Sunday, March 25, Ernie slept late. It was 10 o'clock when he sat up on his cot in the library of Dahl School. He didn't bother building a fire because the schoolroom was fairly warm. He dressed, grabbed two milk pails, and walked to the Grundvig farm for water. The ditches along the road were filled with water from the melted snow. The fields were mostly bare, with only patches of snow on the north side of banks and willow thickets. When he returned, he heated water on the kerosene stove. He washed up and shaved, looking in the mirror over the washstand. He noticed lines in his forehead he had not seen before.

He hadn't experienced any nightmares since moving out of the Henning house. He thought about that. *The voices and laughter have gone away. It could have been Tom's suicide, that house, the dead body, and that crazy night with Carla. Maybe that's what brought it on. Maybe I just needed to get away.*

He spent the day grading workbooks and essays his older students had written. It pleased him that their writing had improved over the school year. Late in the afternoon he filled a pitcher of water from the ten-gallon crock. He went to the south windows to water the plants and flowers the students had started three weeks before. The children had brought vegetable and flower seeds from home and tin cans filled with dirt. They sat in a row along the window sills. Ernie liked how green and healthy they looked. The beans and peas had come up first. *This is life beginning from the earth. I need to explain that to the students.* He walked along the windows watering the green shoots one by one. *Life depends on water. The sun, the soil, and the water create life.* He looked out the window and saw the tiny streams of water seeping out from the snowdrifts under the window. Soon the playground would be green, and they'd be playing softball again.

Ernie became tired in the late afternoon. He decided to lie down on his cot in the library, while it was still light enough to read. He lay on his back and opened the book Anders had given him, the essays of Bertrand Russell. He soon found out it was not like reading the sports page. Many passages he had to read twice to understand the author's message. He came to the chapter titled, "What I Believe." Toward the bottom of the page Ernie noticed that Anders had underlined a sentence. **The good life is one inspired by love and guided by knowledge.** He thought about that message. *Words from a wise man, deeply troubled by the stupidity of war. I should put that passage over the top of the blackboard. Make sure my students see it every day.*

While Ernie lay reading, across seven time zones to the east, the First Battalion of the Seventh Infantry Regiment had arrived at a military staging area near a place called Frankenthal, Germany. Andy's outfit had received their orders. They would cross the Rhine River commencing at 0200.

Under the cover of darkness, Andy and five other men gripped the side handles of a 16 foot aluminum and plywood boat. The soldiers carried the boat through the trees, moving toward the river. At 2200 hours the Germans started shelling them from their defensive positions across the river, heavy machine guns, and big 88s. One of the big shells hit a barn and set it on fire. The orange firelight spread through the trees and helped the soldiers find their way, carrying the boats. Andy could see on either side of him dozens of men from the First Battalion struggling to move their boats to the river. The enemy knew the Allies were coming. Someone in Andy's outfit had heard 'Axis Sally' talking about it on German radio two days before. So much for a secret plan!

The Americans answered the heavy German barrage with their own fire. Ten thousand rounds of artillery shells were fired at the German positions in preparation for the crossing. Andy's outfit moved closer to the river with their boats. Many soldiers were hit by enemy fire even before they made it to the river. But Andy was still moving. He had thrown some of his gear away, the gas mask, the half tent, and his blanket, just to lighten the load. But he still carried his pack, the four bandoleers of ammunition across his shoulders and his heavy ammo belt. He wore heavy wool clothes and combat boots. He was carrying more than 40 pounds of gear.

He gripped his rifle slung on a strap over his left shoulder and grasped the handle of the boat with his other hand. Shells were exploding in the woods all around them. The roar of the big guns was deafening. Up ahead, he could see the bank in front of the river. They were close now. At the foot of the bank, they set the boat down and waited.

At 01:45 on the morning of March 26, the order was given to launch. They dragged the boat over the bank and down to the river at a place near Worms, Germany. There was a bridge for a big highway to their right, about a hundred yards downstream. The Germans had blown it up. From the light of the moon and the glow of the tracers, Andy could see the remains of the bridge, huge concrete pillars sticking out of the black water.

Andy watched a Navy engineer clamp a small outboard motor on the back of the boat. The men were ready to launch. They slid the boat into the water and 12 soldiers climbed in. Andy was the last. He was knee deep in cold water, when another soldier grabbed his arm above the elbow and pulled him in. Andy was close to the engineer who was cussing the outboard motor. He pulled on the starter rope several times, but it wouldn't start. The river was high and swift, flowing eight feet per second. The boat was drifting downstream. The men leaned over the edge and started to paddle with their hands. They had 984 feet of river to cross to get to their objective on the other side, the town of Sandhofen, just downstream.

Finally, the engineer managed to start the motor, and they were moving. Shells were hitting the water on all sides. Men were hit and boats were going over. Andy crouched low in the boat, trying to make a smaller target of himself.

Then came the screaming sound of an 88 shell. It exploded near the bow of the boat, ripping it open. Andy felt water rushing over the top of his boots. The boat was going down. The motor sputtered and died. Andy felt something soft under his feet. He was standing in mud at the bottom of the river. His rifle was gone. Fighting to hold his breath, he pulled off his pack and started ripping off his bandoleers. He struggled with the buckle of his ammo belt. It came free and he pumped his arms frantically, trying to swim to the surface. He started to feel dizzy; he felt his boots being dragged by the swift current over the silt at the bottom of the river. He pumped his arms with all his strength. Then he bumped into something hard, something made of concrete. It was one of the pilings of the destroyed bridge. He grabbed it and tried to pull himself up, but he could not hold his breath any longer. He opened his mouth. The cold water rushed into his lungs.

Monday, March 26, Andy's mother was up early helping Mildred Osterholt take the sheets off the beds and the curtains off the windows for washing. She took out a flour sack of overalls and shirts her sons had outgrown. A neighbor family of Mildred's was very poor. They had three boys, two in high school, and one still in grade school. Mrs. Juvland had met the mother and her sons after church one Sunday and told her she had some hand-me-downs from her sons off at the war. She planned to wash them, iron them, and give them to the neighbor woman. Mildred Osterholt was frail and could not stand up for long without getting tired, but she managed to stand by the washing machine and catch the clothes that Mrs. Juvland fed through the wringer.

It had warmed up over the past week. The snow had melted in the backyard by the clothesline. Mrs. Juvland hung the sheets on the line and waited for the *St. Paul Pioneer Press* to come in the mail. She had not heard any war news for a couple of days. All she knew was the Germans were pulling back. She had heard Lowell Thomas interview a combat reporter, who said, "The boys at the front are telling me we've got 'em on the run."

Andy's body tumbled over and over at the bottom of the river.

It was just past noon when Ben Smierud wandered into Buck and Velma's Tavern. He sat down, put two bits on the bar, and asked for a Grain Belt Beer. Buck said, "The preacher stopped in this morning and told me to tell you that there's a grave for you to dig on the Henning's plot. Then Velma wants you to settle up your bill."

Ben said, "Yeah, as soon as they pay me." He finished his beer and drove over to the preacher's house.

The preacher was on a ladder outside, taking off a storm window. "Hello, Ben," he said, climbing down off the ladder. He leaned the storm window against the side of the house and said, "You feel like working today?"

"Yeah, Buck told me to stop over. What do you have?"

"Carla Henning called me. She wants to get Tom out of the attic. I guess she's thinking about selling off the place."

Ben stomped his foot on the ground. "I don't know. Might still be frost down a ways. Maybe we should wait a couple of weeks."

"We don't have a choice, Ben. It's starting to get warm in the Henning attic. That's what Carla said, anyway."

"Well, I'll see what I can do."

"Carla was up at the cemetery to mark out the spot for you. She wants him on the north side of their son Kent."

"Okay," said Ben. "I'll give it a try, but it ain't gonna be easy. I need to go home and get my pick and shovel. I might need a crowbar, too. Do you have one?"

"Yeah, there's one in the garage."

Ben went to the preacher's garage to get the crowbar and then he drove home to get his pick and shovel.

Andy's body lay at the bottom of the river,
forced against a boulder by the powerful current.

Ernie had gathered his older students by the south window of the classroom. The water from the melted snow was running in little rivulets away from the schoolhouse. "Do you all know the word 'erosion'?" He walked over to the blackboard and printed out the word. "Erosion is the wearing away of the land. On our planet we have both wind and water erosion. The wind blows the sands across the land. The tiny grains pepper the rocks and mountainsides and wear the boulders away. Wind erosion is a slow process, but water erosion works faster and we can actually see some of it right out the window. Watch carefully and you can see the trickling water pick up bits of dirt and tiny pebbles and carry it all downstream.

"Here's another word for you, 'tributary'." He wrote the word on the blackboard. "Notice straight down by the building, in front of that little patch of snow. Tiny streams trickle out from under the snow. Do you see them? They are like tributaries. Now look further down the bank. Do you see where they gather to join the larger stream? That would be the main river.

"Now way out there at the bottom of the bank, do you see that little pile of silt carried down by the moving water? That would be called a 'delta'. When we finish, I want you to write these words in your notebook. Now, at the bottom of the Mississippi River the delta is several miles long and more land is added each day, carried by the rushing water from as far away as here in Minnesota. Let's pull down the map of the United States and I'll show you the Mississippi Delta of Louisiana. Have you heard of the city New Orleans? Well, maybe some of the dirt from your farm will pass through New Orleans and add to the delta right here." Ernie tapped on the map with his pointer.

Andy's body washed ashore three miles south of the crossing at Worms.

Martha Sampson sat with her father on their back porch, looking out at Lake Bemidji, eight miles long from the north to the south end. "I really like him, Daddy," she said.

Mr. Sampson had thinning gray hair that he parted in the middle and combed straight back. He wore dark, horn-rimmed glasses. An intelligent man, dressed in his suit, he had just come home from teaching his afternoon class at Bemidji State Teachers College, four blocks north on Birchmount Avenue. "Are you thinking of getting married?"

"We haven't talked too much about it, but I feel like he's getting serious."

"I'd like to meet him sometime." He looked out across the lake and took a sip of iced tea. "You say he received a medical discharge from the Army. What was the matter with him?"

"He hasn't said much about it, but I got the feeling from talking to his mother that it was some kind of nervous condition. She didn't say anything specific."

"Do you see any signs of anything wrong with the guy?"

"Not really, Dad. I'd say he's very sensitive. He's just a very nice man."

"Well, go slow. And I'd like to meet him."

"I think you'll like him, Dad."

Andy's body lay in the sun. A deer came down
to drink at the river's edge.

Mrs. Juvland was working on the last load of hand-me-down clothes for the mother who lived next door. She leaned over the washer and pulled out a pair of white trousers she had sewn for Andy. She held it over the tub and let the water drip. She wrung the trousers out with her hands and then she fed them through the wringer.

Two litter bearers carried a stretcher down
to the river and placed it beside the body.
One of them pulled the dog tags out
from under the soldier's shirt.
He read the name, "Andrew Gerald Juvland,"
and tucked the tags back under the shirt.
They rolled the body onto the stretcher
and carried it up to a dirt road,
where a deuce and a half truck waited
with the motor running.

Chapter XVI...The Telegram

Ben Smierud swung his pick into the hard ground of the cemetery. He was nearly finished digging Tom Henning's grave. The first two feet had thawed out, but then he hit almost a foot of frozen ground. Timmy Burstrom had just been released from the Fergus Falls State Hospital, and his mother gave him permission to help Ben. He sat on a pile of dirt keeping up a continuous string of chatter, which amused Ben from time to time, but usually was a distraction. Ben liked to work alone, but when the kid showed up to help dig Tom's grave, he didn't have the heart to send him home. Burstrom was trying to hit a squirrel with chunks of dirt, but the furry bugger was too fast and the kid's aim was off. "Will Tom rot in the casket, Ben?"

"Sooner or later, I suppose."

"How does he get from this hole all the way up to Heaven?"

"I don't rightly know how the Lord does that, Timmy. Hand me down that shovel."

Timmy got up and held the shovel for Ben to grab. "Maybe he grows wings."

"Maybe," said Ben, throwing out a shovelful of dirt. "The Lord works in mysterious ways. Hand me that water, Timmy."

Timmy handed him a quart Mason jar of water and said, "Ma told me he might go to Hell because he shot himself."

"I don't believe that nonsense." Ben drank a half dozen glugs of water and handed the jar back to Timmy. "A man that works hard all his life and goes to church should go to Heaven."

Timmy snickered, "Even if he gets drunk, Ben?"

"Depends on what he does when he gets drunk, Timmy." Ben managed to smile. "If he's a mean drunk, he should probably go to Hell. I've told a few of them to go there myself over the years, if they pissed me off."

"But it's the Lord who decides who goes to Hell and who goes to Heaven, right, Ben?"

"I suppose," said Ben. "He's the boss."

Timmy watched Ben dig. Then he asked Ben, "Did you ever see Tom's pecker?"

Ben threw down his shovel, "Jesus H. Christ, boy! What are you talking about?"

261

Timmy said with a grin, "I asked Carla how big it was, and she told me to shut up."

"Good for her."

Timmy threw another clod of hard dirt. "Did you know I've seen Carla naked? I used to sneak up to her bedroom window at night when Tom wasn't home."

Ben had heard enough. "If you don't shut your goddamned trap, I'm gonna come up there and beat the stuffing out of you!"

They heard the sound of the hearse coming up the road to the cemetery. Timmy yelled, "Here they come, Ben." Ben handed his tools up to Timmy. He climbed up his short wooden ladder to the top of the grave and carefully stepped out. He pulled out the ladder and laid it off to the side. He and Timmy laid three short 4X4 planks across the opening of the grave. Between the planks, Ben stretched two long leather straps that had been harness reins; they would be used now to lower the casket into the ground.

The undertaker backed the hearse in close to the grave. Pop Andrews climbed out from behind the driver's seat. Two helpers, Kenny Torstad and his brother Slim climbed out of the other side. They walked over and looked down in the hole. Pop said, "Looks good, Ben."

"Yeah," said Ben. "It was a real bugger there about two feet down, like digging in concrete."

Kenny Torstad said, "We had a hell of a time trying to get Tom down from the attic. We finally had to take him out of the casket. It was too heavy with him in it. You should have been there, Ben. Ha! We left the body on the front porch and went back to get the casket. Ha! Get this, Ben. A stray dog shows up! Oh, boy! We're trying to get the casket down the stairway, and this mangy old mutt is down there chewing on Tom. He had him by the hand. It was a hell of a note!" Kenny slapped his leg and bent over laughing. "The dog chewed off one of the fingers! Then we put Tom back in the casket and folded his hands on his chest, but we made sure the bad hand was on the bottom. Ha!"

Pop Andrews cut him off, "Shut up, Kenny! That ain't something to go blabbing around and laughing about. What's the matter with you anyway? Just keep your mouth shut for once! This is a graveside ceremony. Shut up now and try to look serious!"

The men turned and saw the pastor's car coming up the hill. The pastor, dressed in a black suit, got out of the car, holding a small prayer book. Carla and Dale climbed out of the back seat. Carla held a geranium plant that was in a clay pot. Dale held her other hand. Carla glared at Timmy Burstrom and wondered why he was there. Timmy got up off the dirt pile and went over to Dale. He put his arm around the boy, but Dale pulled away and stood behind the pastor. Ben yelled at Timmy, "Get over here and give us a hand." Ben and Timmy helped the men pull the casket out of the hearse. They carried it over to the grave and carefully placed it across the 4X4 planks. The pastor, Carla, and Dale moved closer, as Pop Andrews and the other men stood back.

The pastor spoke in a quiet voice. "We had a nice memorial service for Tom at the church just before New Year's. So many people were there to pay their final respects to Tom and comfort his wife and son. Let us bow our heads in prayer. Dear Heavenly Father. We gather here to pay our last respects to Mr. Henning. We ask Thee to comfort Carla Henning and their son Dale in their time of grief." He opened his prayer book and read, "In sure and certain hope of the resurrection to eternal life through our Lord Jesus Christ, we commend to Almighty God: Thomas Edward Henning."

The pastor took a handful of dirt and tossed it on the casket. "We commit his body to the ground, earth to earth, ashes to ashes, dust to dust. The Lord bless him and keep him, the Lord maketh His face to shine upon him and be gracious unto him and give him peace. Amen."

Carla stepped forward with Dale at her side. She placed the geranium plant on the casket. She stood up, took Dale by the hand, and slowly walked to the pastor's car without looking back. Pop Andrews and the crew waited by the grave until the pastor's car was out of sight. Then the four men grabbed the harness reins, lifting the casket a few inches. Timmy pulled out the three planks and the four men slowly lowered Tom Henning into the ground.

It was a cloudy Thursday, April 5, 1945. A cold rain had tapered off to a drizzle by noon. The depot agent turned his car onto Mildred Osterholt's street and parked in front of her house. He took the yellow telegram and walked up the sidewalk. The neighbor lady was out in her yard raking leaves. She recognized the depot agent and thought it could be bad news for Mrs. Juvland.

"My Lord," she thought. "Maybe one of her boys is lost in the war."

The depot agent noticed the war mother's flag with five blue stars hanging in the front room window, and figured he had the right house. He knocked on the door and waited. He looked over at the blue star flag and thought soon another flag with one gold star would be hanging in the window. He had delivered these telegrams twice before, and he didn't like doing it. Mildred Osterholt walked slowly to the door and opened it. She recognized the depot agent and leaned on her cane. "Good morning, Mildred," he quietly said. "I understand Olga Juvland is living with you. Is she here?"

Mildred said, "Yeah, I'll get her." Soon Mrs. Juvland appeared at the door.

The depot agent said, "I have a telegram for you. You need to sign here." He handed her a pen. She managed to sign her name and thanked the man. She closed the door, went to the front room, and stood by the table. The jigsaw puzzle of Yosemite Valley was still there in the middle of the table with a small basket of decorated Easter eggs resting on top. Mrs. Juvland placed the telegram on the table and went over to turn off the radio. They had been listening to *Ma Perkins*. She sat down at the table and held the yellow envelope. She remembered seeing a mother in a movie receiving a telegram from the War Department and wondered at the time if it would ever happen to her. Now it had.

She asked Mildred for a paring knife. Mildred brought her a knife and sat down beside her. Mrs. Juvland took the knife and carefully made a slit in the envelope. She removed the telegram and read the first line. Mildred reached over and put her arm around her. **We regret to inform you that your son, Andrew Gerald Juvland, was killed in action...** She could not read the rest. She got up and patted Mildred softly on the shoulder. "Thank you for being here with me." She spoke in a voice that was weak and beginning to break. "I have to lie down now." She left the telegram lying on the table and climbed the stairs to her room.

The next day was a Friday, and Ernie was holding the weekly Dahl School spelling bee. It was boys against the girls, and there was only one standing for each side, Pricilla Backlin, a

264

second grader and Marvin Newquist, a sixth grader. "Okay," said Ernie, "it's almost dismissal time. If we don't have a winner by four o'clock, we can stay late or we can finish up Monday morning."

The students stamped their feet and shouted, "Stay late! Stay late!"

"Okay, Pricilla, it's your turn. Now don't be nervous." Ernie picked up the second grade spelling book and said, "Your word is 'stamp'. The lady put a stamp on the envelope."

Pricilla touched her chin with her fingers and said, "Stamp, S T A M P, stamp."

"That's right," said Ernie, and the girls shouted and squealed!

Pricilla was grinning from ear to ear. "I'm shaking," she giggled.

"Okay, Marvin," Ernie said, "This is getting exciting. Don't let the girls beat you now. Your sixth grade word is 'incessant'. The incessant rain continued all night."

Marvin said, "Oh, Mr. Juvland, couldn't you find a harder one? That's so easy. Incessant, I N C E S S E N T, incessant."

Ernie looked down at his book and then looked up at Marvin. "Are you sure?"

Marvin said, "Yes."

"Sorry, Marvin, you missed it." The girls went wild. They sprang out of their seats and started yelling and jumping up and down. They hugged little Pricilla. She was so happy—she had tears coming down her cheeks.

Ernie said, "Okay, settle down, settle down. Marvin, you missed one letter. It's spelled I N C E S S A N T." The phone rang, three longs and one short. "Okay, settle down. That's our ring." Ernie went to the phone and picked up the receiver. "Please, students, quiet down. I need to hear." The students settled down and Ernie said, "Hello."

The voice said, "Ernie?"

Ernie recognized his mother's voice. "Yeah. How are you doin', Ma?"

She didn't answer right away. "Not so good." It was obvious to Ernie that she was having trouble speaking.

"Can you hold on a second, Ma? Let me dismiss the students." He put his hand over the speaker and said, "Students, you're dismissed. Please be very quiet on your way out. This is an important call." He waited until the last stragglers had left the classroom. He took his hand off the speaker and said, "Ma, are you still there?"

"Yeah," she said. Ernie could hear her take in a breath. "It's Andy. He's gone."

"Oh, my goodness!"

"Yeah, the telegram came yesterday. I should have called you last night, but I was pretty shook up."

"How did it happen?"

"Well, it didn't say much. They found him in the Rhine River on March 28.

"Ma, I'm coming home."

"Well, that would be nice. I've been crying a lot."

"I'll leave first thing in the morning. I'll get someone to drive me up there."

"That would be good. I don't know how they heard about it, but the Thief River Falls newspaper called. They wanted to write an article for next week's paper. I don't feel up for that. I thought you could write it for me."

"Sure, Ma. Don't worry about that. You try to rest now, and I'll be there before noon."

"Thank you, Ernie."

"Take care of yourself, Ma. I'll see you tomorrow."

"Okay. Goodbye."

"Goodbye, Ma." Ernie hung up the receiver and looked around the room. He walked to the window and looked at the students' plants growing green on the window sill. He looked out the window and saw the old birch tree. The branches were drooping. He pictured his mother reading that telegram. He thought of his kid brother dying in a river thousands of miles away. It made him feel cold. He went into the library and put on his heavy coat. The classroom had changed. It looked dull and gloomy.

He went outside and sat on the porch steps. He heard low voices, like a male chorus singing a funeral dirge. No, it wasn't that. It was a tractor off in the distance. A farmer had started in the fields early. He heard the squeaking of the swings. It sounded to Ernie like babies crying. He looked across the playground and saw Dale, moving slowly back and forth in a swing. The boy waved.

"Hey, buddy. Come see me," Ernie said in a voice loud enough for Dale to hear.

Dale ran up to Ernie and sat down on the steps beside him. Ernie put his arm around him and said, "How come you're still here?"

"Ma is picking me up," he said. "We're going to town. I need new tennis shoes."

"So you can run fast, right? So you can beat me in a foot race, right?"

Dale smiled and looked at Ernie. "Something's wrong with you. We noticed when you were on the telephone. I heard Iris telling Eunice that you looked sad."

Ernie held his arm tightly around the boy. "Yes, it was my mother and she had some very bad news."

Dale waited for more. Then he said, "You don't have to tell me."

"That's okay. My mother told me my brother Andy was killed in the war."

Dale grabbed his teacher's hand. "Now we both have brothers that died."

"Yup," said Ernie, "Kent and Andy are gone."

Dale was puzzled. "God has taken our brothers away. Does that mean we've been bad? Pa used to tell me that God will punish me for being bad."

"No, we're not bad. We're both good and we aren't being punished. My brother drowned in a river and your brother died from polio. And I believe God hates war and disease as much as we do. No, I think it's something else. It could be just bad luck."

They listened to the roar of the farmer's tractor across the field. Then Dale stood up and said, "I've been waiting all day to tell you something, but Iris said I should wait, and not tell it in school."

"Are you going to tell me now?"

"Yes, I want to, because it might cheer you up."

"Good, I need that."

"Okay, last night Mr. Vic took us all to the movies. It was *The Gang's All Here*. It was all kinds of dancing. Ladies dancing and holding these big bananas. One of the ladies was singing. And get this. She had a big bowl of fruit on her head, apples, pears, peaches, bananas, and even a pineapple. Iris knew her name. Carmen somebody."

"Carmen Miranda"

"That's it." Dale started to laugh. "So she's dancing around singing this song about Brazil."

"Yes, I've heard her sing it on the radio."

"Okay," Dale was laughing so hard, he had trouble speaking. "When we got home, Iris and I made up new words for the song and put on a show for Ma and the Vics."

"Oh, boy. I'm sorry I missed that one."

"You would have laughed. Iris was holding this dishpan full of potatoes and onions and cucumbers on her head and she was dancing around. I was singing, 'Brassiere! Are you wearing a brassiere? Brassiere! Are you old enough for a brassiere?'"

Ernie suddenly jumped up and started singing. "Brassiere! I'm not wearing a brassiere!" Dale fell over laughing and started rolling around on the ground.

They both looked up when they heard a pickup coming. "It's Ma," said Dale, and they both hurried over to meet her. She pulled into the schoolyard and turned off the engine. She rolled down her window and said, "Hi, you guys. Dale, jump in, we've got to get to the store before it closes." She looked at Ernie. He was standing with his weight shifted on one leg, his hands in the pockets of his coat. "You look cold. Are you feeling okay?"

Ernie said, "I don't feel good at all, but Dale has been cheering me up."

"Are you sick? Do you have a fever?"

"No, it isn't that. My mother called with some very bad news."

"Oh, no!"

"My kid brother Andy. Ma got the telegram yesterday. He was killed in Germany."

"Oh, Lord," she said and put her head down on the steering wheel.

"I wish it had been me instead," said Ernie. His voice was breaking.

She looked up. Ernie could see the tears in her eyes. "Don't talk like that." She got out of the pickup and gave Ernie a big hug. "Looks like we're in the same boat," she said. "I feel so bad for you."

Ernie held her and said, "I need a big favor. I need a ride up to see my mom tomorrow. She's in real bad shape."

"Of course," she said. "I'll drive you myself."

"It's about a two hour drive."

"Don't worry about that. The tires will make it. When do you want to go?"

"First thing in the morning."

"I tell you what. Why don't I pick you up when we come back from town? Then I'm gonna take you over to the Vic's for supper. I told Betty that I would cook tonight. If you don't mind sleeping on their davenport, I think they would want you to stay over. None of us would want you staying alone here in the school tonight. You need to be with your friends now. That's what we're here for."

"I'll think it over. Stop by when you come home."

She got back in the pickup and started the engine. "Please don't stay here alone. Vic and Betty will put you up for the night." She turned the pickup around and headed for town.

That night Ernie tossed and turned on the Vic's couch, but he was glad to be there and not alone at Dahl School. Ernie's mind was on Andy. *It should have been me, not Andy. I escaped the Army for something a couple of doctors found out. But what was it? And now the laughing has come back. There it was again. No. Maybe the wind blowing through the spruce trees.*

In the morning Ernie and Carla were underway by nine o'clock. They stopped in Bly, and Ernie insisted on paying Carla for the gas. Carla had a 'T' gas ration sticker on the 'farm pickup', so it was not a problem to fill 'er up.

Ernie was quiet on the way up, long stretches of straight road up the flatlands of the Red River Valley. They arrived at Mildred Osterholt's house before noon. Olga Juvland teased Ernie about having a new girlfriend. He was glad that his mother seemed to be feeling better. Carla sat with Mildred Osterholt in the kitchen, while Ernie sat with his mother on the davenport. She showed Ernie the telegram, and he read it over and over. He looked up at his mother, "So they were crossing the Rhine River? But they sure don't say much more."

"Yeah," said Ernie's mother. She went over to the table and picked up a copy of the *Pioneer Press*. "The neighbor lady brought over the paper from last week. There's an article on the second or third page." Ernie found the article and read the headlines. **Seventh Infantry Regiment Crosses Rhine River near Worms.** His mother waited while Ernie read the article. When he was finished, she asked, "Did you see the picture of those little boats they were in?"

"I can't believe it," Ernie said. "They look like row boats. They're so small. No bigger than the kind we use for fishing."

"Yeah," she said. "The poor soldiers. And I suppose they were all young like Andy." She dabbed at her eyes with a handkerchief.

Ernie went back to the telegram. "It says there were no wounds on his body."

"Yeah," she said, "how about that? How did he die, if he wasn't shot?"

"He drowned, Ma."

"Yeah, but Andy was such a good swimmer. He was the best swimmer of all you boys."

"But he was wearing his heavy boots, maybe his winter combat fatigues, and all the gear, his pack and ammo belt. He was weighted down, Ma."

"I suppose," she said. "It's hard to think about. I just hope your other brothers make it home okay. I'm sick of this darn war!"

Ernie sat at the table and wrote the article for the Thief River Falls newspaper. He gave a little family background on Andy, his mother, and his brothers off in the war. He used some of the details from the *Pioneer Press* and the telegram from the War Department. When he finished, there were tears on the paper.

Late in the afternoon, Ernie and Carla said their goodbyes and started for home. Carla wiped her eyes and said, "It must be so tough for your mother."

"Yes, it is. But she is one tough cookie, I can tell you that."

"Five sons in the war? I don't know how she does it."

"Well, I'm glad she has Mildred. I worried about her a lot last fall when she was still on the farm alone." Ernie looked out his side window. The sun was just touching down at the edge of the prairie. "Did it bother you that my mom teased me about having another girlfriend?"

"No. Goodness! I didn't mind that."

They were driving through Crookston and came to a stop sign. Carla brightened up. "There's a tavern up ahead. You know what I want more than anything right now?"

"I'm guessing you're thirsty."

"I want to go in that tavern and have a beer. I haven't done that for ages. Tom and I used to do that before we were married, and then it all stopped. He didn't want me out drinking with him. He only wanted to drink with the men."

"Okay, we can stop for a beer if you want to."

"Oh, gosh, wait a minute. I didn't bother to think. Maybe I shouldn't have asked to stop. You've just lost a brother. You're probably not in the mood to sit in a tavern. I can understand that."

"Yeah, I was thinking about that, too. But what can I do? I can't bring Andy back. So, damn it! I'm ready for a beer!"

"Good," she was pleased. She parked under a green sign, **Jack and Connie's Irish Pub**, and they went inside. The place was noisy and smelled of stale beer. A row of tired men sitting at the long bar turned to stare at Carla and Ernie. The place went quiet. Carla sat down in a booth by the jukebox, and Ernie said, "Let me get you something."

"You bet. I'll have a Hamms."

"Good enough," said Ernie and he walked up to the bar. Again the men stopped talking and looked down the bar at Ernie. "Two Hamms," said Ernie.

The bartender had been arguing politics, but he stopped yammering, as he reached into the cooler and pulled out two beers. He glared at Ernie and said, "You must be new in town."

"Just passing through," said Ernie. He paid for the beers, walked back to the booth, set the beers on the table, and sat down across from Carla. They clinked bottles and Ernie said, "Here's to better days."

Carla said, "You bet! They might get better right here."

They finished their beers and Ernie went back for two more. Carla had loosened up and wanted to talk. She reached across the table and held his hand. "I think about you all the time."

"Yeah, what do you think about?"

"Oh, I don't know. Mostly about that night when I asked you to come to bed with me."

Ernie managed to laugh. "I've tried not to think about that night." He turned his eyes away from hers. "I'm just glad it didn't go any further."

"Yeah, I thought the same thing, but I've changed my mind about that. I just think it would have been real nice." She sipped her beer and added, "It's been a long time for me since, well, you know what I mean."

"Come on, Carla. Your husband had just died."

"No, you forget something." She leaned forward and gripped Ernie's hand. "He ran out on us. He ran out on me and Dale. He left us, Ernie. Don't get me wrong, I'm not angry with him. I've gotten over that. I feel sorry for him because he turned out to be a coward."

"But you loved the man."

"I'm not so sure about that. I didn't hate him, but I'm not sure if I loved him. I wanted to please him. I did everything he wanted me to do. I followed orders, like I was in the Army and he was some kind of general. Do this, do that. Is that what I was supposed to be?"

"Well, that's the way most husbands treat their wives."

"I suppose, but I got sick and tired of it." She took a long swig off her beer and wiped her lips with her fingers. "And then you came along. A nice man. Okay, so you're what, maybe 15 years younger than me. But I didn't care. You were nice to me. You paid me some attention, and then I saw you in front of your students, the way they loved you. They worshipped you. I wanted to be one of those girls, in love with their big handsome teacher."

"Oh, come on, Carla. I'm nothing special."

"Yes, you are. To me you are." She took another swig. "Remember that night when you had that bad dream? What was it, the second night in our house? I came up the stairs and you were on the floor, kicking and thrashing around. I got down on top of you to hold you down, and you know what I was thinking?"

"Carla, I don't want you to talk about that."

"Tough," she said. "This is something you should hear, because I think I'm going crazy. I need to tell you these things." She finished her beer and said, "Would you get me another one, please? And bring me a shot, too. Blackberry brandy. Don't worry. I'll let you drive home." Ernie wasn't moving. "Please, Ernie. I need to do this."

Ernie got up and returned with a shot and a beer for Carla. "Thanks, sweetie." The shot went down in one swig. She said. "I want a cigarette. Do you have a cigarette, sweetie?"

"No, I don't smoke."

"Okay, that's okay." She took a long pull on her beer. She reached under the table and grabbed Ernie above the knee. She started stroking his leg back and forth. "That night when you were having that bad dream, it felt so good to feel your bare chest squirming under me. I wanted to open my nightgown, so you could feel my breasts on your skin."

"That's enough, Carla. Let's talk about something else."

She took her hand away and sat back in the booth. She stared at Ernie with a frown. "It's little Martha, right? You're thinking about your girlfriend. Well, I have something to say about little Martha. She's a flirt, Ernie."

"How can you say that?"

"Oh, I can say it, all right. Cause I watched it every day with my husband. You should have seen her shaking her little ass around him. Bringing him pie. Bringing him coffee. I would get so upset and I had to hold it all back. And Tom was eating it up. Yes sir, I saw a whole lot."

"I don't want you to talk about Martha anymore."

"Okay, suit yourself." She had become agitated. Ernie watched her jerking her head around. She blurted out. "Give me a quarter. Do you have a quarter? I wanna play the jukebox."

"Are you sure you want to do that? Maybe we should go."

She stood up and leaned over with both hands on the table. Her breasts were inches away from Ernie's face. "You ain't goin' nowhere until you dance with me."

Ernie found a quarter in his pocket and put it on the table. Ernie realized the bar had grown quiet. The men at the bar were looking over their way. Ernie got up and followed Carla to the jukebox. She punched in three buttons and Dinah Shore started to sing, "You'd be so nice to come home to." She put her arms around Ernie's neck and they started to slow dance. She kissed him on the neck and pushed her breasts tightly against his chest. She pulled her head back and smiled into his face. Then she kissed him long and hard on the lips. In a whisper, she said, "I'm crazy about you, Ernie." She buried her face against his shoulder and stroked his back with both hands.

When the song was over, she said, "Let's get out of here. I don't like these bastards staring at us. I want to tell them to go straight to hell!" She grabbed her purse. They put on their coats, and Ernie followed her out the door. The sun was down, the sky was completely dark, and the streetlights had come on. She gave Ernie the keys and kissed him on the cheek. "That was fun, damn it! We deserve to have some fun! Right, buddy?"

Ernie opened the door for her. Her skirt came up over her knees when she climbed in. She kissed him again before he closed the door. Ernie got behind the wheel, and after two beers, he was cautious. Carla slid over close to him. She put her arm around him and gently fondled his ear. Ernie noticed her head was jerking around. He figured she was pretty drunk.

They came up on an implement dealer outside of town. "Pull in here," she said, "I have to take a leak. I should have done it back at the tavern."

Ernie pulled in and stopped, leaving the motor idling. "Let me take you back to the tavern."

She opened the door and started laughing, "Don't you think I know how to squat?" She got out and went behind an International combine. The headlights were pointed in her direction and Ernie could see her legs under the machine. She took off her panties and put them in her purse. When she came back to the pickup, she said, "Pull back there behind that combine."

"Oh, come on, Carla. Let's get going."

"Just pull back there and don't worry about it. Let a woman give the orders for once. I've waited way too long for this, Ernie. Try to understand me, just this once."

Ernie didn't answer. He was aroused.

She dropped her voice down low, almost a whisper, "Now, just drive back there and we're gonna see what happens."

Ernie drove back behind the combine. It was away from the road and dark. He turned off the engine. She held his head gently with her hands and kissed him softly on his mouth. She pulled back and said, "You know, this has been going on in my head since the first time I saw you. Do you know that? Do you know how much I want you?" She spread her legs and said, "I took off my panties for you." She took his hand and ran it up between her soft legs. He felt her hair and warm flesh. She whispered in his ear, "I'll make it easy for you."

274

Chapter XVII...The Celebration

The following week, Ernie had difficulty talking to Dale. Something was missing that was there before, a genuine, buddy-buddy friendship. The boy was the same; he looked the same, sitting at his desk doing his arithmetic problems. Ernie realized that Dale hadn't changed, but he had. Carla had come between them, and Ernie was hearing laughing again. This time it was a woman. *The laughter sounds like Carla. I wonder if I should have told her that I had never done it before. I'll bet she figured it out anyway. Is that what she's laughing at? I might have done better if we were in a bed.*

It was Thursday, April 12, the students had gone home, and Ernie sat on the steps of the porch watching the flag fluttering in the breeze. He thought of his brother Andy and wondered if they would send his body home. He had seen newsreels of caskets carried off ships. They were draped with American flags. He had seen wives and mothers receiving flags, folded neatly in a triangle, honoring their loved ones lost in the war.

Raising and lowering the flag at Dahl School was a monitor job for two older students. Ernie thought about that as he listened to the sound of the flag flapping in the breeze, wondering why it sounded like laughter. Somebody forgot to do their job. Ernie got up and lowered the flag. He carefully folded it, making sure it didn't touch the ground.

After he put the flag in the cupboard of the library, he sat down at his desk. He had not written to his other four brothers since Christmas. He wanted to tell them about Andy. When he finished the letters, he walked out to the mailbox to mail them. He looked to the west and the low clouds were blood red. The sun was below the horizon, but it was splashing red light on the belly of the western clouds. He stood by the mailbox and admired the sunset. He heard a crow cawing from somewhere. Then he saw it pass overhead, heading into the blood-red clouds.

When he came back in the classroom, he lit the kerosene lamp and placed it on his desk. He had just started to grade arithmetic tests, when the phone rang. He got up and answered it, "Hello."

"Ernie?" He recognized his mother's voice. She was crying. "Did anyone tell you the news?"

275

"No," said Ernie.

"President Roosevelt died this afternoon."

"Oh, no!" Ernie heard his mother sobbing heavily.

"What will we do now?" She was having trouble speaking.

"I'm so sorry to hear that, Ma."

"First Andy is gone, and now this. It's just awful."

"Is Mildred there with you?"

"Yeah, don't worry. We'll be okay. She has the radio on and there's more news coming in."

"How did he die?"

"I'm not sure. I just wanted to call you because I knew you didn't have a radio at the school. It's so sad. He's the one man who has kept this country going. Every time I hear him speak or see his picture in the papers, it gives me something to go on. That good man has given me hope that we will win this war, and your brothers will come home. I don't know what we'll do now. Our leader is gone."

"I feel the same way, Ma, and so do millions of others around the world." Ernie tried to think of something more to say. "Well, school will be out in another month, and then I'll be home with you. Just hang on and take care of yourself."

"Yeah. I guess we'll survive." She hung up.

All night, Ernie tossed and turned on his cot wondering about the death of the President. The sound of his mother's voice played over and over in his mind, and then he saw her. Her sad face was pressed against the dark window. Ernie heard her speak. *They might all die now. My sons will all die in the war.*

Ernie went to the window to touch his mother's face. He placed his hand against the cold glass and wiped the tears from her eyes. He pulled his hand away and felt his fingers, cold and wet. He whispered, "Don't cry, Ma," and then she disappeared. Ernie stared into the blackness beyond the window. He listened for her voice, but it was silent.

In the morning he awoke on his cot and could not remember falling asleep, but he remembered his mother's face. *Was I dreaming? No. I remember leaving the window and going back to the cot. What's happening in my brain? I must think about each little task that has to be done.*

When the students arrived, they were all talking about the death of Roosevelt. Ernie was glad to see them. Being with his

276

students, teaching them, listening to them, would always scare away the voices. He needed them now, more than they would ever know. After opening exercises, Ernie said, "Before we start our lessons, I think we should talk about the passing of President Roosevelt. I don't have a radio here, so can you tell me what you've heard? Did any of you listen to the news broadcasts? How did he die?"

Marvin said, "He had a stroke and died real quick."

Susan said, "I heard that, too. What's a stroke?"

Ernie said, "Well, Susan, let me put that word on the board, and maybe one of the older students will look it up in the encyclopedia. I've heard a stroke happens in the brain, when a blood vessel breaks. A patient can survive a minor stroke, but in worse cases, he may become paralyzed or suddenly die, like President Roosevelt."

Iris said, "I wrote it down, last night when I heard it on the news." She read from her notebook. "They said it was a massive cerebral hemorrhage."

Ernie wrote those words on the board, and stood back to see what he had written. "I hope I spelled that right. Dwight, go to the dictionary and look up those words."

Eunice raised her hand and said, "Well, my ma and I listened to the news, but Pa went to bed early. He never liked President Roosevelt. He blames him for everything."

"Well, Eunice," said Ernie, "this is a free country and we all have a right to our opinions."

She corrected herself. "Maybe I shouldn't have told you that about Pa. It wasn't like he was happy he died. He just never voted for him." She shook her head and continued, "Anyway, Ma and I heard that he wasn't in the White House when it happened. He was in Georgia."

Ernie pulled down the map. "Okay, that would be Warm Springs, Georgia—right here. That's where he would go to rest. They called it the 'Little White House'."

Dale raised his hand, "President Roosevelt had polio, like my brother Kent."

"Yes, Dale," said Ernie. "And he had to wear heavy iron braces on his legs."

The students continued to talk about President Roosevelt for most of the morning. They finished up with a prayer for

President Harry S. Truman, asking God to help him continue to lead our country to an early end of the war.

In the coming days, students brought in newspaper clippings about the death of Roosevelt, stories about his life and career, the funeral, and burial at Hyde Park, New York. They found stories about President Truman, a man who had worked on a farm in Missouri, and had been a captain in the First World War. They made a whole bulletin board full of pictures and news clippings on the passing of the President, and in big letters, cut out of construction paper, they had placed over the top, a quote from a reporter. **Men will thank God on their knees a hundred years from now that Franklin Delano Roosevelt was in the White House.**

Warm weather brought changes to Dahl School and the farm life of Jackson Township. Ernie hauled the ashes from the big wood stove for the last time and the wood box was cleaned out of all the remaining chunks and chips. Just beyond the southwest corner of the schoolyard was a small slough, which filled with water in the spring. Ernie let the students take off their shoes and roll up their overalls to wade in the warm water during recess. The older students carried buckets of water from the slough to gopher holes. They poured water in one hole and watched the gophers pop out of another hole maybe twenty feet away.

With the coming of warm weather Ernie was not surprised to see a certain rambunctiousness in the older boys. There had been minor classroom pranks and playground fights that he had to break up, but nothing that was out of the ordinary until sometime around the first week of May. It all started in the boys' toilet.

One day during recess Ernie noticed first grader Allen Rollag standing outside the boys' toilet. Ernie called him over to home plate for a little batting practice, but the boy shook his head. Ernie walked over to him and said, "Come on, Allen, you need some work on your swing."

Allen whispered, "The big boys in the toilet told me not to move."

Ernie crouched down and whispered back, "So, how come they told you not to move?"

Allen continued to whisper, "They told me I'm the lookout."

Ernie smiled, "That's just what I figured. So, are you going to tell the big boys that Mr. Juvland is coming?"

The boy was starting to whimper, "I should, because that's my job. But now I'm scared."

Ernie put his arm around the boy and told him to go play 'red rover' with some of the other kids. He added, "Don't worry. I won't tell on you."

Allen said, "Thanks. It really stinks in there. They're squirting on the wall." Then he ran off to play.

Ernie was mentally preparing his speech before he went into the toilet. He had drilled into them that the boys' toilet was also the teacher's toilet. It was to be kept clean all year long. He had read about toilet behavior in his teachers' training manual. It clearly stated, "Forbid urinating contests and any urine-squirting combat." Ernie thought of those terms and said to himself, "Sometimes you just can't go by the book." He burst into the toilet and yelled out, "Okay! Who pissed all over that wall?"

Five boys stood in front of the urinal like choir boys, heads down and hands folded. Peter buttoned up his pants and sheepishly raised his hand. The rest followed with their hands, Wendell, Clyde, Marvin, and Dwight.

Ernie asked, "and who made that black line with a crayon up at the top?'

Peter raised his hand, "I did, Mr. Juvland."

"I should have guessed that, Peter. I see your initials 'PB' next to it." Ernie looked at the urine splattered wall again and said, "Well, boys, I guess Peter has set the high-water mark, something for you all to shoot for. And judging by the looks of the wall, I can't blame you for not giving it your best shot. Now tomorrow, you'll pay the price. You're going to take buckets of water from the slough and scrub down this entire, stinking toilet. Top to bottom!"

Dwight asked, "Are you gonna tell our moms?"

Ernie answered, "I'll make a deal with you boys. I won't tell your moms if you don't tell them the bad word I just used. Fair enough?"

They all nodded.

Ernie continued, "I thought I made it clear to you fellows the first day of school. There would be no monkey business in the boys' toilet. And I don't even think monkeys do what you guys have been doing!"

Marvin spoke up, "Mr. Juvland, it was a lot worse last year."

Ernie was curious. "Oh yeah?"

Wendell said, "Yeah, the Smierud boys were here, and Torstad. Boy oh boy! That was something!"

Ernie said, "I'm afraid to ask."

Clyde said, "I can tell you, but I'd have to use that bad word you just used."

Ernie let out a breath. "Go ahead. I'm listening."

Clyde was smiling. "The Smieruds started piss fights. We even had teams."

Peter chimed in, "Neal was a champion. He could shoot from one end of the toilet to the other. No kidding!"

Dwight said, "He hit me in the eye once. I couldn't even see."

Ernie had heard enough. "Okay. Stop it! I shouldn't even be hearing this!" He looked them each in the eye. "Look, boys, I have a job to do here. My duty is to train you to be good students and good citizens of our country. I have to teach you lessons about how to be civil toward your fellow Americans. Who knows? One of you might grow up and be a senator one day, and it's my job to prepare you for that. My gosh, I can't send you off to Washington worried that you'll squirt on another senator just because you didn't like the way he voted. No way!"

The next day, the five squirters spent all their recess time scrubbing down the boys' toilet. They had learned their lesson. They figured, why misbehave when there were just too may fun things to do that were legal and didn't raise the ire of their teacher?

Spring was a season to enjoy, celebrating warm weather after a winter of deep snow and howling winds. The red-winged blackbirds had returned and sat on fence posts, staking out their territory with melodious trills. The boys opened the top buttons of their shirts when they played softball, and there were no signs of long underwear buttoned to the neck. The girls dressed in cotton skirts that fluttered in the breeze when they ran the bases.

From everywhere came the sound of tractors working the fields, the plowing, the harrowing, the dragging, and finally the seeding. Another growing season had begun.

Tuesday, May 8, was a clear, warm day. The thermometer outside the schoolhouse window reached 70. At the end of the day, Ernie dismissed his students and decided to take a walk. He had not seen Anders since moving out of the Henning's farmhouse and thought it would be nice to sit down for a visit. He also wanted to return the Bertrand Russell book Anders had loaned him and deliver letters his students had written acknowledging his gift of encyclopedias.

Anders was in his garden transplanting tomato plants he had started inside by the windows a month earlier. When he rose up to greet Ernie, he looked bigger than ever, in his railroad worker's overalls, short sleeved shirt and straw hat. "Mr. Juvland, how good to see you. I thought you had run off to join the circus. Come; let me give you a bear hug. I know Norwegian men aren't noted for hugging, but what the hell." They hugged and Anders gave Ernie a few hearty pats on the back.

"Here's the book you loaned me."

"Ah! My hero, Dr. Russell. The man who inspired me to stand behind my beliefs. Or I could say, the guy who got me fired from St. Hallvard College. Did you read about how he was hired by the Board of City College in New York, and then some bishop got his feathers ruffled and went to the press?"

"Yes, it was hard to believe how they were able to overturn his contract."

"Public pressure with smear tactics, my boy. Very effective when dealing with college administrators in positions of authority, but with the spines of earthworms."

"And here are some letters the kids wrote to you thanking you for the encyclopedias. I didn't bother correcting them."

"Shame on you, Ernie. I suppose you want me to get out my red pencil."

"I would never ask you to go through that punishment."

"You are a kind humanitarian, my man. I wouldn't do it even if you asked me. One thing I don't miss about the classroom, the drudgery of grading papers."

"I know what you mean."

"I hope you can stay—I'll fix us something to eat. How about some leftover pheasant? It won't be under glass, but then again we aren't a couple of swells. We are basic Norwegians! To honor our Fatherland, you'll get your pheasant covered with white gravy. How does that sound?"

"That would be a treat after eating canned food up at the school."

"Yes, I heard you were living there. My, what a dedicated young teacher! He's so wrapped up in his pedagogy, he sleeps in his schoolhouse."

"Believe me, it's not by choice."

"Yes, I heard about that mess over at the Henning's place. Tell me, did you actually sleep alone in that house with frozen Tom in the attic?"

"I lasted through January, and then I had to get out. I guess they couldn't find another family to put me up."

"Hmmm...they never asked me. But then again, they probably surmised that I would corrupt your morals with all kinds of heathen gibberish. You didn't show anyone the Russell book, I hope."

"Well, as soon as I started reading about his views on organized religion, I started hiding the book as if it were a girlie magazine."

Anders laughed. He had been gathering up his tools as he talked. "I'm about done here; that's the last of my lovely tomato plants. Tomorrow I'll put in the stakes for the vines. I'm ready to call it a day. How about a beer?"

"That sounds real good." Anders went up the steps to the front porch and returned with two opened brown bottles of beer. Ernie noticed there were no labels on the bottles. "What kind of beer is this?"

"Homemade, my friend. I made a whole batch of it last fall. It doesn't have a name, so you may name it what you wish. How about Anders's Amber Beer?"

"That has a nice ring to it."

"I must warn you about this beer, Ernie. Go slow. It has the kick of a mule that stepped in a hornet's nest. One will be just fine. But if you drink two really fast, it will knock you on your arse."

"Thanks for the warning." Ernie took a short swig of his beer. "I like it."

"I'm glad, just go slow. The taste turned out to my liking." Anders took a swig. "Have you ever had German beer, Ernie?"

"I'm afraid not."

"When I've met German tourists, they are quick to characterize America as, 'White bread and weak beer'. So what I made here is more like the beer they drink over there." Anders put his tools in a little shed and when he returned, he asked, "Would you care to take a walk?

"Fine," said Ernie.

"Let me get a couple more beers and we'll cross the creek and go up on the ridge. I built a bench up there. It's a lovely place to watch sunsets across the prairie."

Anders had built a narrow swinging bridge out of planks and cables. It was rigged with ropes and pulleys and counter-weighted, so that he could raise it up into the trees during flood-times. Anders led the way across the little bridge and up the path through the woods to the clearing on the ridge. They sat on a large wooden bench Anders had hewn out of logs, enjoying the stillness and watching the low-lying sun, streaking the dry grass along plowed fields with orange light. Anders heaved a sigh and broke the silence, "I heard about your young brother, Ernie. I offer my deepest condolences. I know that sounds like something printed on a sympathy card, but there really aren't words that adequately express the sorrow of losing a brother in war. I'm just terribly sorry for you and your mother."

"Thanks. Yeah, it's been pretty rough. Actually, it's been good that I'm so involved with my students. They're a good distraction."

"Yes, and it's a distraction that's positive. You are nurturing your young charges, and you are also nurturing yourself. You are absorbing them in all the beauty that is in the world, and we need much of that. And that's why I come up here. We are connected with all we see before us. That sun, which has warmed this beautiful day, brings life to all that grows around us. And we are connected to each atom in the leaves of these trees and each mineral which lies in this plowed field. We are brothers of those earthworms under the sod, and one day they will feed on our rotting flesh."

"That sounds depressing."

"No, it shouldn't. You see, it's all an almost magical process and once you understand that nothing is stasis, everything is developing—it becomes beautiful and satisfying. Just like our sun. It is a great and powerful engineer, driving a process."

Anders opened a second beer for each of them. "Remember what I said, Ernie. Go slow, or this conversation will quickly go from Buddhist philosophy to barroom blather." They both laughed and drank their beers.

Ernie remembered something. "Oh, before I forget to tell you, I wrote a quote from Bertrand Russell on the top of my blackboard."

"Oh, boy! You're in hot water now. May as well pack your bags and hope to find a job digging ditches."

"Ha! It's the one from the essay, 'What I Believe'."

"I know some of it by heart, but go on. What did you write on your blackboard?"

Ernie wanted to get it exactly right. "The good life is one inspired by love and guided by knowledge."

"Bingo! It's the one line I would have chosen myself," said Anders.

"Yes, I noticed you had underlined it in your book. It kind of says it all, doesn't it?"

"Indeed it does."

They sat and talked until the sun was gone and darkness had started creeping into the trees. They made their way back to Anders's kitchen. Anders served Ernie a hot plate of pheasant covered with white gravy, thick slices of bread and corn he had canned himself. Ernie asked, "Did you shoot this pheasant?"

"Yes," said Anders. "In fact it was up on that field where we were just sitting. Lovely bird."

"I'm puzzled about that." Ernie tried to collect his thoughts. "I see you as a man who admires all living things. Okay, the pheasant was walking around up there and you shot it."

"I can understand that impression. But I look at it this way. I only kill what I need to eat, just as the pheasant only eats the seeds that it needs to survive. And that philosophy doesn't come from Aristotle or Kierkegaard. It comes from our native tribes that walked the land we live on and fished this very creek below my shack. On the plains, the Indians only killed enough buffalo to provide food, shelter, and clothing. Contrast that harmonious and conservative way of life with the white buffalo hunters, who slaughtered buffalo by the thousands for their hides and left the carcasses to rot on the prairie. Massive profits were made and they destroyed that good way of life, practiced by our first Americans."

Ernie was riveted to Anders's message. "Thank you for explaining that. Once again, you've given me something to discuss with my students. In fact we'll talk about this tomorrow. I'm sure their dads hunt. It would be interesting to hear what they say. I also need to talk more about how our native tribes were treated."

Anders laughed, "You know, Ernie, that's one of the things I like about you. You are a born teacher. I believe you could find a pebble in your shoe, pass it around from one student to another, and make a whole lesson out of it." Anders got up to clear the plates off the table. Ernie helped and offered to wash the dishes. Anders said, "Be my guest. Mind if I turn on the radio? I found this station from Minneapolis that plays classical music; you can only get it at night." Anders dialed around, from station to station, but they were all news broadcasts. Some he could tell were short-wave reports coming from London. Ernie heard the word 'surrendered' and put down his dishrag. "At 3:30 this afternoon, Nazi Germany announced its unconditional surrender to the Allied Powers."

Anders let out a whoop. "Do you think you can handle another beer, my man? This is cause for celebration!"

They drank beer and listened to more radio reports. It had turned chilly. Anders started a fire in his fireplace. He cranked up his record player and they listened to Sousa marches and Tchaikovsky's "1812 Overture". Anders danced around the room. He grabbed a wooden spoon and beat on the bottom of a wooden bucket when it came to the cannon shots at the end of the overture. They sang war songs, drank more beer, and started telling dirty jokes.

Anders blurted out, "Maybe you've heard this one. This young lad wanted to have sex with his girlfriend, but each time she said, 'You must ask the Heavenly Father.' And each time the boy prayed, he received no answer. He told his buddy about the situation, and his buddy possessed a genius for scheming. He said, 'Do you still park under that big oak tree by the lake?' The boy answered, 'Yes.' His scheming buddy said, 'Okay, you park there tonight and I'll be there to help you out.' So that night the young lad parked with his girlfriend and asked if he could do it to her. She, like always, said, 'Oh, you have to ask the Heavenly Father.' So the boy said,

'Heavenly Father up above,
Is it alright if I diddle the girl I love?'

285

And the answer came back…
'Blessed son, down below,
Put it in as far as it will go,
And if there's any room left for me,
Help me out of this goddamned tree!'"

Ernie laughed until he fell over on the davenport. He laughed so hard he thought he would throw up. Anders realized he was in no shape to walk back to the school in the dark. He took a blanket and covered him. "You're going to stay put here tonight. I get up early, so I'll get you off to school in time. The master teacher can never show up late for school—heaven forbid!"

"Thanks, Anders. I was just thinking—I haven't had much fun this year. I really needled this."

Anders laughed, "Did you say 'needled', Ernie?"

There was no answer. He was about to fall asleep.

The party was over and Anders's face grew grim. He found a pillow for Ernie and slipped it under his head. He sat down at the table, and opened a calendar book. He asked Ernie, "What day did your brother die?"

Ernie mumbled, half asleep and very drunk, "The telegram said March 28, I think I'm right on that, but who knows? My head is buzzing and the room is spinning around."

"Reach over and put one hand on the floor. That's an old trick I learned in the Army, and it usually makes the room settle down." At the table Anders turned the pages in the calendar book to March 28. He counted until he got to the present date, May 8. He looked up and said, "Your brother was killed 41 days before it was all over. What a shame!" He looked over at Ernie on the davenport, but the teacher was sound asleep.

He closed his book and walked to the fireplace. He stared into the dying embers and spoke to the last stubborn flame. "Perhaps the Japanese will quit now. But maybe not. Sons of ancient Samurai warriors, they will fight to their last breath. You might run your bayonet through his gut, but he'll meet you again in Hell with his sword drawn!"

Chapter XVIII...The Rumors

Ernie made it to school on time the next morning, a little woozy from his night of drinking with Anders. But he needed to shake it off. The school year was winding down, and there were deadlines to meet. Mother's Day was coming on Sunday, and the students planned a tea for their mothers on Friday. Ernie asked the children to design and print out their personal invitations.

You are cordially invited to a special tea in honor of our mothers to be held in the classroom of Dahl School. At 2:00 p.m., Friday, May 11, 1945.

Ernie had a meeting, "Okay, everyone, I'm an old farm boy and I don't know too much about hosting a tea. Iris, did you do this last year?"

"Yes," she said. "Miss Sampson made us decorate the tin cans we grew our flowers in, and we gave them as gifts to our moms."

"Okay," said Ernie. "The marigolds are blooming and looking good. So we'll get out some paper to wrap the tin cans in, and you can do decorations with crayons, watercolors or some of the weed seeds you've been using for mosaics." Ernie looked around the room. "Now, how about this tea business? If this is an afternoon tea, we have to serve tea, right?"

Eunice said, "My ma never drinks tea. I don't think we have it in the house."

Clyde added, "My ma and pa only drink coffee."

"Okay," Ernie said, "How about the rest of you? Do you drink tea in your house?" Nobody raised a hand. "Okay, that stands to reason. We're not English; we're a bunch of Swedes and Norwegians. We'll serve coffee at 'the tea'. Case closed!"

Eunice said, "Miss Sampson also made Kool-Aid for us kids, and she made date bars."

Ernie shook his head, "Okay, now we have a problem. I can make Kool-Aid, but I don't know the first thing about making date bars. We'll need some help from a mom on that one."

287

On Friday all the mothers arrived, nicely attired in summer dresses. A few of them even wore hats. The girls put placemats out on the desks and a greeting card for each mom, which included a short poem. Allen wrote, "Roses are red, violets are blue. Even when you spank me, I still love you." The afternoon tea was a huge success, and Iris, being the oldest girl, had the honor of 'pouring'.

After the moms left, Marvin was closing the south windows and noticed something. "Mr. Juvland, there's one more flower can left over here."

Dale got out of his seat and said, "It's mine." He walked over and Marvin handed him the flower gift. Ernie watched the boy carry the plant to the cloakroom with his head down. Dale's mother had not come to the tea, and Ernie felt deeply sorry for the boy. He heard snickers coming from the cloakroom. Then he heard Dale say, "Why don't you buggers shut up and leave me alone!"

Over the next few days Ernie spent his evenings correcting spelling tests, workbooks, and compositions, preparing for final grades and filling out report cards, which were to be handed out on the final day of school, May 25. There would be an entire day of activities, what was traditionally known as 'field day'. The students would bring rakes and garden tools, to clean up the schoolyard. The woodshed would be organized and the toilets scrubbed. In the afternoon, Ernie had invited another nearby country school to come over for a softball game. All the parents would be invited. Awards would be given out, and the children would receive their report cards.

On Thursday, the day before closing day, Ernie dismissed his students, with last minute instructions about the big event. He walked around the room thinking about his first year as a teacher. His visit with Anders came to mind. *The man is so brilliant. He knows so much, and I know so little. How can I call myself a teacher when I don't know much more than a high school graduate?* He started to get depressed. He decided to go out and sit on the front porch; maybe it would settle his mind.

Outside, he thought he heard someone calling him in a low voice. It wasn't that. It was a pickup and Carla was driving. Ernie had not spoken to her since the day they went to his mother's place almost two months ago. He felt uneasy as she walked toward him.

She looked tired and sad. She offered her hand and Ernie said, "Long time, no see."

"I'm sorry about that. I guess I should explain. Are you busy right now?" she asked in a flat voice.

"Not really; I have most of my work done."

She looked down the road to the east, and then she looked back at Ernie and said, "You probably wonder where I've been the last two months."

"Yeah, I was wondering why you didn't come to the tea we had for the mothers."

"I'm sorry about that, mostly for Dale's sake." She looked up and down the road. "I need to talk to you, and I don't want to do it here. You know—people driving by."

That surprised Ernie and gave him something more to worry about. "Okay," he said.

"I'm on my way to the farm. Wanna ride along?"

"Sure," he said. He locked the door to the school; they got in the pickup and started down the road.

She was quiet for the first half mile, but before they came to the mailbox, she started to talk. "This is so dumb, and I shouldn't bother you with it, but maybe you should know—so you'll understand why I've been staying away from school."

"What's the problem?"

"It's about that night we got drunk in Crookston." Ernie waited to hear more. "I'm really sorry I got so crazy. I hope you don't think I'm some kind of whore."

"I'd never feel that way."

"I want to ask you something. Please forgive me, but was that your first time?"

Ernie smiled at her. "I guess you could tell, eh?"

"I figured it was, and that even makes me feel worse." They had pulled into the farmyard. Carla wiped her eyes. "And you're so young, and you have a girlfriend. I just feel awful sometimes. I feel like dirt!"

"Don't worry about it." He started opening the door. "I left some clothes in your wardrobe upstairs; I should get those out of there."

She grabbed his arm. "Wait! There's more."

Ernie turned and looked at her. "What's that?"

She grabbed her head and leaned her elbows on the steering wheel. "People have started to talk."

"Talk? About what?"

"About us. They're spreading all kinds of rumors about you and me carrying on."

"Oh, Jesus!"

"Yeah, it's so stupid. They're making up lies, and it really hurts me that I dragged you into this."

"How did it start?"

She burst out laughing, "Poor Dale. I guess he let the cat out of the bag, but it was really my fault."

"Dale? How would he know anything?"

"It's so ridiculous; I hate to even think about it. That night coming home from Crookston, I was still pretty drunk when I let you off at the school. I drove over to the Vic's place and I clipped their mailbox pulling into the driveway. They were all waiting up for me when I came in the house. I must have looked like a wreck.

"Anyway, the next morning, I stayed in bed, and the Vics were taking Dale to church with them. He asked me for a quarter for the collection. I told him my purse was probably on the front room table. I got up later and dressed before they all came home from church. I went downstairs and there it was."

"What was it?"

"My damned panties!" She covered her face "They were lying there, right next to my purse. Remember I took them off and stuck them in my purse?"

"And that was it?"

"Yeah, that started it. They all must have seen it." She looked up toward the house. "That's why I had to talk to you. The rumors have spread like wildfire, and the women aren't even talking to me. And that's why I didn't show up for the tea you had for the mothers. Can you imagine? They would have been watching us like a hawk. They're all talking, even the men. Orvid Skime was over at the Vic's house one day, and I guess he didn't know I was upstairs. I heard him say, "I'll bet she was shackin' up with the schoolteacher, even before her husband died."

"It doesn't surprise me that he would say something like that." Ernie paused. "You know, there's something about that guy that rubs me the wrong way. Why is he on the school board in the first place?"

"Okay, I haven't wanted to say anything about him while I'm still on the board, but right now, I just don't care. People are scared of him, because he's a backstabber! Tom had him figured out and he warned me about him. Orvid is on the board because he makes money selling and sawing wood, plowing snow—any chance he has to make a buck off Dahl School, he jumps at it. Watch out for him, Ernie. And now he doesn't have anything better to do than smear us.

"Here's the best one. Vic told me Orvid had this theory— right from the start—that I shot Tom. Yeah! It gets worse. He thinks we might have planned it together. And that's why he wanted to spend the night with you in the house when you came back after Christmas. It was Vic's idea that someone should be with you. Vic had wanted to be here himself, but Orvid was acting like a big shot. Orvid told Vic, 'I'll take care of it. I want to go over there myself and see how he reacts when I tell him the news.' Pardon my French, but Orvid Skime is one sneaky son of a bitch."

Ernie was upset. "That bastard! I wondered about that night, and why he took such an interest in me. And all the time he was playing me like a fish on a line. Yeah, I get the picture."

"Now you know." She started sobbing. "And poor Dale. The kids have started teasing him. The day of the tea, he came home crying. When he handed me the flower he had grown in his tin can, he could hardly talk. Susan asked him why his mother wasn't at the tea. He heard one of the boys say, 'She's probably home having a baby.' I just don't know..." Carla struggled to explain. "And I've dragged you into this mess. I feel so awful!"

"I don't know what I can do to help you. Really."

She reached over to hug him. "Just don't hate me. Don't think I'm bad." She pulled away and said, "I'm gonna sell this damned farm and get the hell out of here!

Martha showed up early for the last day of school, wearing overalls and a sweatshirt. She brought a rake and pitched in, helping her former students clean up the yard. Ernie noticed how his students were drawn to her. *Sweet Martha will be a good teacher in the right school. Especially younger kids. She's a natural.*

291

After the yard was cleaned, the children from the neighboring country school showed up for the softball game. Martha knew the teacher from the other school, and the two of them worked together to supervise the game.

Ernie had other things to do. He started the fire in the grill and brought out chairs and benches for the parents to sit on. He carried out the little-kid-table for serving and arranged paper cups, paper plates, and napkins.

Finally he sat at his desk and went over what he planned to say to the gathering of students and their parents. He double-checked the report cards and the awards he planned to hand out. He opened the logbook to his **MISTAKES** section. He wrote, *Be careful. Do not become too close to any particular parent.* He thought about Orvid and added, *Be careful whom you trust. Look out for your own skin.*

By two o'clock the softball game was over, and the parents started to arrive. Carla brought a bowl of potato salad. She made small talk with Martha for a few minutes and then moved back and stood alone behind the crowd. The parents helped themselves to the picnic food and sat down. The students sat in the grass in front of the porch.

After everyone ate, the students stood up and sang two songs: "America, the Beautiful" and "Flow Gently Sweet Afton". Ernie had placed his stool on the porch, which now served as a stage for the end of the year doings. He rose to speak, "Students, thank you for those songs. And I want to thank all the mothers who brought food and helped with this wonderful picnic. Let's give them a round of applause."

Ernie looked at his notes and continued. "Well, it's been a heck of a year and I want to compliment all these Dahl School students for working hard and making me and their parents proud. Thank you for your patience with me. After all, this was my first year as a teacher, and I know I made a lot of mistakes. Maybe I shouldn't bring it up, but I think I should apologize for the terrible injury Mr. Henning suffered as a result of my bringing you youngsters out to see the threshing. That showed poor judgment on my part, and I'll live with that for the rest of my life. You will never know how bad I feel about that."

Ernie took his handkerchief out of his pocket and blew his nose. "Excuse me. I get emotional every time I think about that day." Ernie looked out over the audience and saw Carla. She was still standing in the back, all alone. Her hands were folded and her head was bowed.

Ernie tried to be cheerful. He opened a paper bag and spoke in a brighter voice. "I guess the main event of the year was the blizzard we had in December." Ernie looked down at his students sitting in the grass. "I shall never forget that night. I am so proud of those students who spent the night with me here in the school and then braved the storm in the morning to walk to the Marum farm.

"Now, I'm sure you've all heard about something else that happened the night of the blizzard. By being in this school, we saved one of your neighbors from freezing to death." Ernie looked out and saw Orvid Skime whisper something in his wife's ear. Ernie paused and almost asked Orvid if he had something to say. But he stared him down and went on. "We saved Ben Smierud's life that night. And the next morning, Ben helped me walk your children to safety. I won't forget how much I needed him that morning, and he came through for me."

Ernie looked down at the students and said, "That whole experience showed me what tough kids you are, but more importantly, it showed how you worked together, how the older students helped the younger ones. And I didn't hear one single person complain."

Some of the students were beaming and laughing. Peter said, "Heck, it was the most fun I ever had." The kids and parents chuckled.

"Okay, it might have been fun for you, Peter, but it was no fun for me." Ernie laughed, "I'm just glad you older kids didn't ask me if you could play 'spin-the-bottle'. I would have put my foot down on that one." Ernie took out a white ribbon from his bag. "All twelve of you, who went through that night in the school, should be proud to have been part of that adventure. In fact, even before Mr. Marum brought you home safe and sound, you had started calling yourselves, 'The Dahl School Dozen'. So I made special ribbons for you." Ernie held up the ribbon. "It says, 'Member of the Dahl School Dozen'."

Ernie came down the steps of the porch. "Now I want those twelve students to stand and let's give them a big cheer." The Dahl School Dozen stood up and Ernie pinned a ribbon on each member. Everyone clapped, and Ernie went back up on the porch.

He continued, "There are two students I would like to recognize with a couple of gifts I bought. First, would Eunice come up here?" She came up to stand by Ernie. He put his arm around her and said, "Ladies and gentlemen, let me introduce the Dahl School music teacher." Everyone loudly clapped. "I can't play the piano, so Eunice took over that job like a real professional, and so I have something for you." He reached in his bag and took out a music booklet. "This has all the songs from the new musical, *Oklahoma!* I'm sure Eunice will be able to sit down and play all those tunes in a very short time." He turned to her, "You're a real genius, young lady." Eunice thanked him and sat down.

"Okay, it is a tradition to honor students with perfect attendance. This year, we had only one, Dwight Alstad. Now you might remember," Ernie continued, "back at the Halloween program, we had a wonderful solo sung by Dwight, whose dad, Marine Corporal Robert Alstad, is fighting right now in the Pacific. Dwight, would you come up here?" Dwight rose and stood by his teacher. "I hope you have a phonograph at home, Dwight." The nervous boy nodded that he did. "Good, then I hope you enjoy this." Ernie handed Dwight a record of Bing Crosby singing "Only Forever" and "Do You Care?" Ernie patted him on the back. "Let's give him a nice hand."

"And finally," Ernie said, "We want to honor our two eighth grade students, who will be going on to high school in the fall. Iris Vic and Peter Brunsvold, will you two come up here?" Iris and Peter went up the steps to stand by their teacher. "Iris and Peter, you have been our leaders this year, assisting me and helping our younger students with their lessons. Remember in our writing lessons, I talked about using the right word. Well, now you have lots of words to choose from." Ernie handed Iris and Peter each a large, hardcover dictionary. "Let's send these two fine students on their way to Sparborg High School with a big cheer!"

Ernie reached for the report cards. "Okay, I want all the students to line up with the first graders in front and the eighth graders last. Here comes your big moment." The students all formed a line and faced their teacher. Ernie smiled and said, "Some of you look a little nervous out there. You're probably wondering if you passed or if you'll be held back. Well, maybe I should tell you right now, so you don't worry yourselves to death.

Everyone from Dahl School passed!" The students let out a whoop and a holler!

Ernie called each student's name as he handed out the report cards and at the end he said, "Parents, let's give your children a standing ovation!" The parents stood and clapped. "One more thing, folks. I was happy Miss Sampson came over from Bemidji to help us out today. She even pitched in and helped her former students rake the yard. Thank you, Miss Sampson. Let's give her a nice hand." Martha smiled and gave one of the students standing by her a big hug.

When the noise died down, Ernie said, "Well, that's about it. There are more hot dogs left and salads if anyone is still hungry. Anyway, that wraps up the festivities. Students, I hope you have a nice summer vacation. And if your dad asks you to pick mustard on a hot day, it isn't the end of the world!"

"Hold on there, everybody!" Vic's booming voice came from the back. "Everybody sit down. We've got something else to do here." Vic waddled up to the front, climbed the steps, and stood by Ernie. He held a large paper bag. "Now we have something for you, Mr. Juvland. Really now, Orvid Skime should be doing this, but Orvid doesn't like to get up in front of people, so that's why I'm here." He turned to Ernie and said, "Last winter we noticed you were wearing a pair of overshoes that had a buckle missing. So we thought you should have a new pair. Here you go. A pair of four-buckle overshoes, like we all wear around here. Yessiree! Not a bit of manure on them either. Wear them with pride, Mr. Juvland!" The kids and parents laughed and clapped.

"Well, thank you very much. You really didn't have to give me anything at all." Ernie admired his new overshoes; he looked out and saw Carla in the back. Dale had joined her, and she was looking at his report card. His mind was racing, the rumors, and Orvid sitting out front, acting like a big shot. It all came rushing over him and he figured he may as well do it right now. "Okay, I have one more thing to say. I was thinking of waiting until later, but since my mind is made up, I might as well tell you now, while you're all here." Everyone stopped talking. The students held their report cards and looked up at their teacher. "I've given this a lot of thought since my brother Andy was killed in the war. It hit my mother really hard." Ernie felt tears building up. "She needs me to be close now. So, here's the deal—I won't be coming back to be your teacher next year." The only sound was a distant tractor and the rope slapping against the metal flag pole. "Orvid, I haven't had time to write out a letter of resignation, but I'll take care of that. I know I'll miss you all, and students, always try to do your best. Now you'll have to excuse me. As most of you know, I have trouble controlling my emotions."

Ernie managed to make it into the classroom without crying, but once he was in the library with the doors closed, it all came out. He sat on the counter and cried out loud. Time passed and he kept crying. He heard cars starting up. He heard tires on the gravel road. He continued to cry. He just couldn't stop. Then he heard knocking on the door.

"Ernie, please let me come in." Ernie recognized Martha's voice. He held his head in his hands and continued to cry. He could not control his wailing. He heard the door open and close. He felt Martha's arm around him, and he cried even louder.

"Hush," she said. "It's gonna be okay. I'm here, Ernie." She sat next to him and held him tightly. His body heaved in convulsive wails. "Hush, now. I won't leave you."

It was more than a minute before Ernie could speak to her. "Thank you, sweetheart. I really need you now. I feel all alone— just me and my weird thoughts. Voices and laughing come and go, and there's no one there. Sometimes I think I'm going crazy."

Martha was startled. She had wondered about his so-called nervous condition, but she was shocked to hear him talking about hearing laughter and voices. She held him tightly and started piecing things together, his sudden change of moods, the way he would stare off into the distance, and how his eyes would tear up over the slightest thing. She knew she had to say something. "You're not going crazy. Don't talk like that. You've just gone through a tough first year. I know what that's like, believe me. I thought I was going crazy, too."

"Just don't leave me, Martha."

"I don't want to ever leave you."

Time passed and Ernie started to come out of it. Martha wanted to spend the night with Ernie in the schoolhouse. After everyone left, they came out of the library and checked around the schoolyard for anything left behind. The parents had cleaned everything up and put the chairs, benches, and little-kid-table back in the classroom.

Ernie and Martha sat on the front steps watching the sun go down. A car went by that neither one of them recognized. Martha patted Ernie on the knee and said, "People are going to see my car here and know I spent the night with you. What do you think?"

Ernie looked down the road at the trail of dust behind the car and said with a smile, "What was that thing Clark Gable said in *Gone with the Wind*?"

Martha laughed and dramatically said, "Quite frankly, my dear, I don't give a damn!"

Ernie said, "That's it. That's exactly the way I feel."

Martha recited, "No more pencils, no more books; no more teacher's dirty looks." She put her arm around him and said, "Can you give me a dirty look, teacher?"

"What kind of a dirty look do you want? A dirty, mean one or a dirty, sexy one?"

She slapped him on the knee, "Shame on you!" She looked out across the fields, "Let's go inside. I'm getting chilly."

They went inside and Ernie lit the kerosene lamp. He brought it into the library and made up the cot for Martha. "I'm going to give you my fancy bed, my dear." Then he remembered something he had seen that morning when he was cleaning out his desk. "Oops, I almost forgot." He went to his desk and came back with Ben Smierud's whiskey bottle. "How about a nightcap, my dear?" Ernie told Martha how he had taken the bottle away from Ben the night of the blizzard. They sat side by side on the cot and passed the bottle between them.

Martha said, "I think you're trying to get me drunk, naughty teacher!" She looked around and asked, "So, where are you going to sleep?"

"I'll sleep on the counter." They sat on the cot and finished the bottle. They hugged and smooched until Ernie got sleepy. He climbed up on the counter and covered himself up with his winter coat.

Martha lay on the cot staring up at the ceiling. "I want to ask you something. How come you didn't tell me you were quitting?"

Ernie didn't answer right away. "Well, I hadn't made up my mind."

"So, when did you make up your mind?"

"I've been thinking about it since yesterday. I don't think I'd be happy here anymore."

"What are you talking about? They love you."

"I'm not so sure about that." He thought for a moment. "That whole thing out on the porch was like playacting. I was acting and the parents were acting. But the kids are real. They are genuine because they know me better than anyone around here."

"I don't understand what you're trying to tell me."

"Rumors."

"Rumors? What?"

"I'm surprised someone didn't bend your ear out there today. They've started rumors that Carla and I have been carrying on. Seems that Orvid Skime has been stabbing me in the back."

"I'm sorry to hear that, but it doesn't surprise me. He did the same thing to me. How did you find out?"

"Carla told me yesterday. Orvid and others have smeared both of us, and it has really hurt that very good mother and friend."

Martha was quiet, waiting for Ernie to say more. Then she said, "I was wondering about that. Carla wasn't herself today. She seemed distracted." She waited. "We don't have to discuss it, but I can tell. She really likes you."

Ernie said, "Can we just leave it at that?"

Martha said, "Sure. It doesn't change the way I feel about you."

Ernie said, "Good. I really appreciate that." He sighed, "I'm tired. It's been a busy day. And tomorrow I have to face Orvid. I'm not quite sure what I'll tell him."

Martha said, "You'll be okay." She thought about being in the school with Ernie. "When I left here a year ago, I never wanted to come back. But thanks to you, this day was very good for me. It has been a valuable lesson about forgiveness. Goodnight, Ernie."

"Goodnight, sweetheart," he said. A barn owl called out from the woodshed.

"What's that?" she asked.

"Barn owl. Lonesome sound, eh? I'm glad you're here." They listened to the owl. Then Ernie said, "I sometimes have bad dreams."

"Yes," she said softly, "I know all about that. Don't worry." They both drifted off.

In the morning Martha helped load all his things in her car for the drive up to his home. Ernie took out a sheet of composition paper and began to write.

May 26, 1945
To: The Jackson Township Board of Education
From: Ernest O. Juvland
    Kindly accept my resignation as teacher at
Dahl School, Dist. # 128, effective this date.
    I have enjoyed working with your children,
and greatly appreciate the help given to me by the parents.
    I know I made some mistakes, primarily due to my
inexperience. But I tried my best.
Respectfully yours,
Ernie Juvland

Ernie performed one last act in Dahl School. He took down the Indian Thanksgiving prayer, which he had hung over the blackboard between Washington and Lincoln. A precious gift given to him by Lisa Olson, the Ojibwa midwife who helped bring him into the world, he carefully wrapped it in tissue paper and put it in his satchel.

He locked the front door and climbed into Martha's car. "The mail," said Ernie. "I forgot to check it yesterday." Martha stopped by the mailbox and Ernie pulled out a letter addressed to him. The return address showed, **Bobby Smierud, Bass Lake Juvenile Detention Center, Ely, Minnesota**. Ernie put the letter in his satchel and said, "We need to swing by to see Orvid. I have to drop off this letter of resignation and give him the keys to the school. I've decided to be civil, Martha, and part on good terms. Somewhere down the line, I guess I'll need a recommendation from him. That's the way it goes."

They headed out to the Skime farm and Martha parked on the side of the road. They saw Orvid on his Minneapolis Moline tractor pulling the grain drill, seedtime in Jackson Township. "That's where I met Orvid, when I came for my interview, out on that field. That day it was muddy, and I was pretty damned nervous. A lot has happened since that day."

Orvid saw them and waved. He stopped his rig at the edge the field and let the tractor idle. Ernie went down into the ditch and up the other side, meeting him halfway. "Well," said Orvid, "you sure threw us for a loop. We still can't believe you're gonna quit."

Ernie handed him the envelope with his resignation and gave him the keys. "It wasn't easy." He tried to figure out what more to say. "I should have stuck around outside, but I started to choke up and I didn't want the kids to see me that way."

"Yeah, we knew you were pretty shook up. We hate to see you go, Ernie. You did a hell of a job with our young ones. I was hoping you'd stay another year for Eunice."

"Well, I'll miss Eunice and the rest of the kids, but I had to think about my mother. She lost a son and that's tough. Now she has four more to worry about, especially the two in the Navy."

"Yeah, this damned war has been rough on all of us. Let's hope those goddamned Japs give up. Let's get the boys home."

"That's what we're hoping for."

Orvid looked up at the car. "I see Martha gave you a lift."

"Yeah, she's giving me a ride up home."

Orvid moved close to Ernie and said, "I saw her car was still at the school late last night. Are you gettin' some from her?"

Ernie felt the rage coming. It started in his neck and moved down his arms, into his bare fists. "I wouldn't tell you if I were."

He laughed and slapped Ernie on the back. "Well, I can't blame you. I wouldn't mind some of that myself. Real nice piece of tail, I'll betcha. Come on—you can tell me. How is she?"

Ernie started to walk away, but he froze and turned around. He pointed a finger in Orvid's face, trying to control his anger. "What I really should do is throw you in the dirt and stomp on your stupid head. But I don't have time for that right now. So I'll leave you with some friendly advice. Why don't you go piss up a stiff rope!" He turned and walked back to the car.

What a jackass! I should have hit him in the snot locker! Maybe should have kicked him in the balls for good measure!

When Ernie got back to Martha's car, he was still steaming. He decided not to talk about it and tried to forget the whole scene. They drove on. He opened Bobby's letter, and read it to himself.

300

Dear Mr. Juvland,

How are you? I'm good. But Neal gets into a lot of trouble. They make him sleep in a locked room now by himself, because he bothers a couple of the other guys. He did bad things to me on the farm, and now he's doing it here. I don't want to write about it. I just wanted to tell you that I'm sorry for all the bad things I did at school. You're a good teacher and I liked you. I'm going to classes every day. They tell us we are learning high school stuff. I had to write a letter for my English teacher. So that is why I'm writing to you. I hope you're happy. You are a good man and I'd like to be a good man like you some day. I'm trying my best. Please write me a letter.

So long,

Bobby Smierud

He put the letter back in his satchel. "That was from Bobby Smierud. He seems to be surviving the best he can. He's taking high school classes up there."

Martha thought for a moment. "Bobby was okay. It was mostly Neal, and I think Bobby just went along with Neal to show him he was tough. There might be hope for Bobby, but not Neal. I guess a teacher shouldn't say this, but Neal is rotten to the core."

"Bobby says he's getting in trouble up there."

"That doesn't surprise me" said Martha.

They drove in silence for several miles. Ernie looked out his window at the tractors working the big fields along the Red River Valley. They drove by the implement dealer outside of Crookston where he and Carla parked. He remembered something. *I never had a chance to say goodbye to Dale and Carla. Maybe I'll borrow Ma's car and drive down to see them this summer. I'll have to see how her tires are holding up. I should also go back to see Anders. I wonder what he'll think about my resigning and wanting to go back to college. I'll bet he'll approve.*

Chapter XIX...The Return

Ernie and his mother lived on the home farm that summer. Mrs. Juvland was getting monthly payments from Andy's military insurance, and with the money Ernie was able to pick up working on the Inderdal farm, they were able to make ends meet. They planted a garden together and brought their two broncos, Bill and Roany, back home. Blackie was happy to be back on the farm, nosing out his old haunts, sloshing around in the sloughs on hot days and chasing woodchucks down burrows.

Martha continued to work at the bank in Bemidji, but she came out to the Juvland farm most every weekend. She pitched in with work around the place, helping Mrs. Juvland wallpaper the front room. She helped Ernie repair fences and replace windowpanes in the barn. They were fixing up the home place. Maybe one of Ernie's brothers would want to farm it when the war was finally over.

Ernie thought Martha had lost most of her town girl ways, until one day she came out of the outhouse shaking her head. She buckled up her overalls and announced, "I'm going to town for toilet paper. The Sears Roebuck Catalog just isn't working out."

Ernie laughed, "Not even the index pages?"

Martha huffed and went to get her keys and purse.

Ernie thought about a future with Martha and what he would do for a living. He wanted to teach, but not before he went back to college. The time he spent with Anders told him how lacking he was in the knowledge of history, literature, science and the arts. Martha was hoping he would start classes at Bemidji State Teachers College in the fall. She wanted to leave the bank, get her bachelor's degree, and maybe teach first or second grade in a town school. They grew closer. Ernie sang to her out in the field; Martha's favorite song was "It Had to be You".

Ernie was happier than he had been since high school days. He was in love, and this wonderful young woman had chased away the demons. No more voices, no more faces in the windows, only Martha's sweet smile. Ernie started thinking about popping the question.

Down on the Henning farm, another pair was spending time together, though they were many years younger than Ernie and Martha. Dale Henning and Susan Rollag were playing farm in a patch of dirt near the splitting block. They were using a pair of clamp-on roller-skates for tractors. They pretended they were neighbor farmers with a fence between their pastures made out of sticks for fence posts and binder twine for barbed wire. Dale pumped a pail of water and poured it into a hole they had dug for a muddy slough, complete with weeds around the edges. Dale helped Susan make a house out of an empty box of Blue Diamond Matches. He carefully cut out doors and tiny windows with his jackknife.

Carla was cleaning out the last items in the Henning house, built by Tom's homesteading father in 1875. The auction had been a success—she had sold all the furniture and machinery. Only two beds, clothes and a few personal items remained. Tom's sister Wilma had been back, trying to claim a share of the property she always felt was hers. But Tom had made out a will before he committed suicide, leaving everything to Carla and Dale.

Carla came out on the porch with a box of letters and old photographs. She saw an unfamiliar car moving slowly down their lane, past the granary, past the barn, and into the yard. When Carla saw the tall, young man behind the wheel, she set the cardboard box on the porch and yelled out, "Ernie Juvland, you son of a gun!" Dale and Susan heard her yelling and they came running. They were all there when he climbed out of his mother's car. Carla hugged him tightly. Ernie bent down to hug Dale and Susan, who were happy to see their old schoolteacher.

"Looks like I surprised you." Ernie laughed.

"Surprise us?" Carla was out of breath. "You almost gave me a heart attack! I'm weak in the knees!"

Dale said, "You ran off before I even had a chance to say goodbye and thank you." He and Susan giggled. "We're playing farm. We're neighbors. We even have a slough. You wanna see it?"

Susan said, "Dale just made me a house out of a match box."

Ernie put his arms around Susan and Dale. "Okay, you go work on your farm, and I'll be over in a while to see what you've done. Right now I need to talk to your ma."

The kids ran back to their farms in the dirt, and Ernie followed Carla up to the porch. They sat down and Carla put her arm around Ernie. She was holding back the tears, "I never thought I'd see you again. This is such a gift, just seeing your smiling face. Thank you, Ernie. You'll never know how much you've meant to me."

"I don't think I did that much." He paused, "I tried to call you, but the operator told me the line was shut off."

"Yeah, we did that a week ago."

"So, what are you going to do now?"

"We have the farm up for sale." She sighed, "I could almost hear Tom turning over in his grave when we had the auction. It was hard to see his plow, his disk, and his tractor go— everything he and his father had worked for." She looked over where the kids were playing farm in the dirt. "He dreamed that Dale would own the farm one day, free and clear. But I have no choice. We have to sell."

"I know how my ma felt when we sold the cows."

"But it's done now. And if the war ends soon, there'll be a lot of boys coming home, looking for a place to live. We shouldn't have any problem selling it."

Ernie looked closely into Carla's eyes and could not believe how suddenly she had aged. It was just short of a year, when he first saw those sparkling blue eyes and rosy cheeks. Now her eyes seemed to be looking at something 500 miles away, and the color was gone from her face. When he first saw her, she reminded him of his high school girlfriend, now she made him think of his mother. "So, I guess you'll be moving?"

"Yes, I have a dear aunt in St. Paul, with a big house on Fairmont Avenue, very close to Augsburg College, and guess what?"

"Tell me."

"I'm finally going to college to get my nursing degree. If things work out, my aunt told me we could stay there until I start working. We have a balance to pay off at the hospital and some doctors' bills, but the auction covered most of that. And we have no loans on the farm, so we should be all set."

Ernie kissed her on the cheek. "I'm happy for you."

"Thank you, sweetheart. Yeah, things are working out pretty good so far. Even the rumors about you and me have died out." She chuckled. "It seems they have someone else to pick on."

"Who's that?"

"You won't believe this. They've all turned on Orvid Skime because he claimed ownership of Tom's horses for keeping them through the winter. A week before the auction, he wouldn't give them up. Vic told Orvid he didn't understand that farmers help their neighbors during a crisis. But you know Orvid, stubborn as always. I finally went over there with a pair of halters and Orvid tried to stop me. I led the team out of his barn, right by his nose and said, "These are Tom's horses and you can kiss my ass!""

Ernie burst out laughing, "Good for you!"

"Yeah, now I'm the big hero around here; they're all saying, 'Finally someone had the guts to stand up to Orvid!' It felt good to tell him off, but that didn't change my plans to move out."

Ernie said, "You'll be a great nurse, Carla."

"Thanks." She laughed, "I'll be an old nurse for sure— twenty years older than my classmates. But I don't care. This is something I always wanted to do." She looked at him. "So tell me, what have you been up to?"

"Well, Martha and I have been seeing a lot of each other this summer, and I might be going back to college at Bemidji to get some more book-learning."

"I hate to ask you this, because I'm jealous. But are you kids gonna get married then?"

"Well, I've been thinking about it."

"Good for you."

"Yeah, so far, so good." Ernie felt uneasy talking to Carla about Martha. He sensed it bothered her. "Sorry, I can't stay long. Let's go over and see this farm Dale and Susan are working on."

She grabbed his hand and stopped him. "Don't get up yet. There's something I figure you should know about. I didn't want to bring it up while you were teaching, because you had enough on your mind as it was."

"You're right about that. So, what gives?"

She reached for the box of letters and photos and pulled out an envelope addressed to Carla. Ernie recognized the handwriting. It was his. "Here, I've kept this hid, and I want to give it to you,

305

because I don't want anyone, not even Dale, to read what you wrote me that day."

Ernie skimmed the letter. *Last night I found Timmy Burstrom up in the attic with the body. I have decided to move out and live in the school.* "Okay, I wrote that when I found Timmy sitting by Tom's casket in the attic."

"Right, but there's a problem with that, and I never told a soul. When people asked me why you moved out, I just told them it was easier for you to live at the school."

"I don't understand what you're getting at."

"I didn't want to tell you, and it hurts me now." She put her arm around Ernie and pulled him close to her. "I decided you have to know this, because I worry about you. Timmy was not in the attic with Tom's body."

"What?"

"Yeah, it's true, Ernie. I had called his mother to tell her he was bothering Dale, and then I guess he started forcing himself on his younger sister. His mother told me she couldn't leave them alone together. He was even bragging to his sister that he had seen me naked through our bedroom window. Right here. Can you imagine?" Ernie was shaking his head. "She had him committed again in the Fergus Hospital the day after Thanksgiving. He was there from December until March. They didn't let him come home until the week before Tom was buried."

Ernie was shocked. "Oh, God. I can't believe this!"

She took his hand. "It had to be part of a dream."

He squeezed her hand, "But damn it, there's more! He showed up once at the school window late at night. I saw him with my own two eyes. He was pressing his face against the glass and whispering, 'You don't like me!' I've heard voices and laughter. Sometimes, I think people on the radio are talking about me. One night, I thought I saw my mother in the window!"

"If it was at night, well, maybe those were all dreams."

"Oh, Christ! Am I really crazy?"

"Of course you aren't. But if you're crazy, I must be strongly attracted to crazy men. You drove me up the wall—you know that, don't you?"

"I'm sorry, Carla. Let's not talk about all that."

She looked over at the kids, who were still playing. "There's one more thing I should tell you, because I don't know if

I'll ever see you again." Ernie started to get up. "No, Ernie, please. This is about me and Tom, and I'd feel better if you knew the whole deal. Not for you, but for my own peace of mind."

She waited until Ernie turned his face to her. "Tom developed this problem, I guess about two years ago. It was between haying and harvest. Kenny Torstad quit on the job, right before harvest. They had it out one day right here in the yard, and it almost came to blows. Kenny didn't come back to work for us until a year later. So Tom was left without a hired hand when he needed him most. He was working himself to death and came down with a terrible cold. He had these pains in his chest, but he kept working. That's when it all started."

She paused. "Gosh, this is tough to explain. Okay, I'll tell you straight-out. He couldn't perform in bed. And what really made it tough—he blamed me. He started beating me, and that aroused him. I could never figure that out. He would attack me, force himself inside me, and hurt me. He wasn't making love. He was showing his anger, and crazy as it sounds, he thought I enjoyed it. But I wasn't, and when I tried to explain how I felt about his anger and his rough stuff, it just made matters worse.

"Finally, Tom gave up on sex completely. As soon as we crawled into bed, he would kiss me on the cheek, say goodnight, and roll over. He had no idea what I was going through. When I told you that night—it had been almost two years since I'd been with a man, I wasn't kidding." Then she sat up straight. "But I wish people would give me some credit. I didn't leave him, and I never cheated on him. I was patient with his moods and jumped when he barked. I even let him slap me around when we were in bed. I took care of him until the day he died."

She took in a deep breath and let it out. "And then you came along. Dear God, I never knew a man could be so gentle and kind. I couldn't hold back."

Ernie leaned over and kissed her on the cheek. They sat in silence. Carla had spoken her piece and there was not much more to say. Finally Ernie said, "Yeah, I figured you had gone through some bad times with Tom." He patted her on the knee. "I'm glad you told me, but I want you to know something. I never for once thought that you were a bad woman. You are one of the strongest, most decent persons I have ever known. Second only to my mother."

Carla looked up. "Shush, here come the kids."

Dale and Susan came running up to the porch. Dale was laughing, "I got my tractor stuck in the mud by the slough, but Susan pulled it out with her tractor."

Ernie was still thinking about the way Tom treated Carla, but he managed to smile, "Good for you, Susan. I have to see this big farm operation you kids have." The two youngsters led the way and Ernie and Carla followed behind. Dale was on his knees pushing his roller-skate tractor up to his shoebox barn. He dipped a rag into the pail of water and started washing the mud off the wheels of his tractor.

Ernie smiled, "It's good to see you kids having fun and using your imaginations. I remember playing farm in the dirt when I was a kid. We didn't have any toys, so we made our own, and it looks like that's what you're doing here. I like your fence, Dale. Will it keep out Ole Gangstad's bull?"

"I hope so." He said with a laugh. But then he turned serious. He stood up and took Ernie's hand. "I want to thank you for being such a good teacher, Mr. Juvland. We had fun."

Susan said, "Thanks, Mr. Teacher. We all liked you, and I'll never forget how you took care of us the night of the blizzard."

"That's right, Susan. I almost forgot. You were one of the Dahl School Dozen."

"Yes, I was," she said. She started to laugh and gave Dale a shove. "Now I have to tattle on Dale."

"Don't you dare tell him that, Susan!" Dale glared at Susan. The smile had left his face. Susan laughed and Dale took off for the icehouse. He jumped inside and slammed the door.

Susan was laughing as she yelled, "I'm gonna tell. You bet I am!" She looked up at Ernie and giggled. "Remember, when we got down on the floor to sleep? You filled the stove with wood and told the boys to sleep on one side and the girls on the other."

"I remember very well, Susan," said Ernie.

"Well, Dale waited until you dozed off in your chair, and then he sneaked over to me and kissed me goodnight. But it was only on the cheek."

The door to the icehouse flung open and Dale came running out. Susan took off and Dale ran after her. "I'm going to get you, Susan!" He chased her around the yard.

Carla and Ernie watched and laughed. Then Carla hugged Ernie and said, "I'm so glad you came back. You will always have a place in my heart. Forever and ever."

"I had to come back, Carla. You helped me through a tough year. I can't thank you enough." Ernie walked toward his mother's car, and the kids came up and grabbed him around the legs. Ernie kneeled down to speak to them. "I'm so glad I had a chance to say goodbye to two of my favorite students. Susan, don't be too rough on Dale now." The little girl started to cry. "And Dale, you're the man of the house now. Take good care of your mother."

Dale hugged Ernie and was crying too hard to speak.

Ernie got in the car and slowly drove up the lane, glancing out the rearview mirror—the mother and two children at her side were waving goodbye. He came to the mailbox, crossed the township road, and drove down Anders's lane, hoping the dear old man was home. His truck was there, but he wasn't in the yard. Ernie got out of the car and as he climbed the stairs, he heard the radio. It sounded like a news broadcast. Ernie came up to the screen door and then he could see Anders. He was sitting in a chair close to the radio, listening intently. Ernie knocked.

Anders turned and got up. "Lord, mother of mercy! The shining knight has returned to the field of battle! There must be one more dragon to slay. Are you ready to go into the cave and wrestle with Grendel's mother? Come in!"

Ernie opened the screen door and walked in laughing, "Dummy me. I have no idea what you're talking about."

"*Beowulf,* my man, if you haven't read it, you should."

"There are a lot of things I haven't read, and thanks to you, I'm going to get at it this fall."

Anders gave Ernie a big bear hug and slapped him on the back with both paws. "I want to hear all about it."

"I actually came back for another glass of dandelion wine."

"You shall have it, my good friend, but first, have you heard the news about Japan? I just heard it on the radio."

Ernie blurted out, "Is the war over?"

"No, but it could happen any day now. Seems we had a secret weapon. A very powerful bomb. Truman didn't even know how much damage it would do."

"Have they used it yet?"

"Yes, they did. Yesterday, August 6. They dropped it from a B-29 bomber on Hiroshima, Japan. They are calling it 'Little Boy'. Unimaginable destruction!" Anders's voice was grave. "They estimate as many as 20,000 civilians were killed instantly."

"Does this mean Japan will surrender?"

"They haven't yet. The War Department is threatening another bombing if they don't."

"It sounds like good news to me." Ernie said.

"Well," said Anders, "it is and it isn't. I'll tell you my initial reaction, but first things first. You came for a glass of wine." Anders went out on the back porch and pulled up his bucket of wine. He uncorked the bottle, poured two big glasses, and gave one to Ernie. "Cheers, good friend. I'm so glad you're here."

"I had to come back to see you."

"Glad you did." They walked over to the radio and stood silently listening to the news reports coming from the BBC. When it was over, music came on and Anders turned the radio off. Anders sat at the table and Ernie climbed into the canvas swing. Anders sipped his wine and gathered his thoughts. "The good news is perhaps this will force Emperor Hirohito to surrender. And the Russians are gearing up to invade from the north.

"But I am deeply troubled by the annihilation of a large city and the killing of thousands of innocent people. It all happened in an instant, and it was done with one single bomb. That, my friend, is something we'll be dealing with for a long, long time. Without control, it will change the nature of international conflict. Perhaps it could be the end of all civilizations, and those who manage to survive will take to the woods, hunting and gathering roots. Back to the Stone Age. And here we're telling the Japanese Government, 'How did you like that one? Better give up or we have another one coming.' Do you see how casually we are treating the destructive power of this weapon?"

Ernie moved back and forth in the canvas swing. "But if it ends the war, isn't this bomb a good thing?"

"Granted. We all want this awful war to end. But I'm thinking about what we have unleashed as a species. Remember in one of our conversations, we talked about how we have perfected more efficient ways of killing each other. Well, when I hear these news reports, it looks like we've hit the jackpot in Hiroshima!"

"You're saying it depends on how we use this weapon."

"Exactly. And today people are thrilled, because it can kill a whole bunch of people in one shot. It angers me." Anders got up to fill Ernie's glass. "Perhaps we should talk about more pleasant things." He took in a deep breath and let it out. "So, tell me, Ernie, what's on the horizon? I was surprised to hear you had quit Dahl School, and so were the parents. Surprised and disappointed that you up and left. They are talking as if you were the Lone Ranger. You came into a bad situation, took care of business, left a silver bullet on your desk, and rode off on your horse. Now they're saying, 'Who was that masked man?' So, tell me your plans. You hinted at going back to college."

"Yes, I am. At Bemidji State. I'm thinking about asking Martha to get hitched, and I think we could live with her parents until I get my bachelor's degree."

"Good for you, Ernie. You and Martha, eh? I'm happy for both of you. Do you see another one-room school in the future?"

"I'm not sure. I've been thinking I might do well as a high school teacher. And I'd like to coach baseball."

"Sounds good."

"But the main reason I want to go back to school, and you were the one who opened my eyes—I feel like I don't know much of anything."

"Oh, dear. Are you telling me I made you feel inadequate?"

"Not exactly. I just admire you for your education, your knowledge of history and books, stuff I don't know much about at all. To be a good teacher, there is so much I'm lacking."

"Well, if I inspired you to go further in education, I'll take that as a compliment." He sipped his wine, "You're young, Ernie. You might have noticed a few deficits in your background, but turn it around and use your feelings of inadequacy as motivation to learn. It appears you're on the right track."

Ernie walked over to the table and put down his empty wine glass. Anders offered a refill, but Ernie said, "No, I'm fine. But I do have a question that's nagging me."

"Fire away."

"What do you know about mental illness?"

"Wow!" Anders frowned and slapped the side of his head. "Where did that come from?"

"Okay, let's start with my medical discharge and what the Army doctors found out about me. I've had terrible nightmares."

"Yes, you mentioned that once, briefly."

"Okay, can they lead to something worse, like hearing voices and seeing people who aren't really there?"

"You're talking about hallucinations." Anders paused for a moment. "Have you had them?"

Ernie said in almost a whisper, "It seems I have."

Anders wanted to be reassuring. "It could be stress, Ernie. You went through a horrific year as a beginning teacher. Quite frankly, I don't know how you survived. There's a toughness about you that I admire, and I believe you have to use it to your advantage. Do you know the word, 'paranoid'?"

Ernie thought for a moment. "I've heard it used, but I'm not exactly sure what it means. Is it some kind of fear?"

"Yes, it is an unfounded fear. And it most often manifests itself in feelings that people are talking behind your back or people are out to get you."

"Okay, but what does that have to do with my nightmares or hearing voices?"

"Look at it as a warning, Ernie. If you become paranoid—sometimes a person doesn't even realize it's happening—go to a doctor and talk about it."

"Are you saying that I might be going crazy?"

"No. I am not saying that. But I think you should be aware of your perceptions, especially of people close to you. And it will be very important that you and Martha understand the symptoms of paranoia. She is a kind and sensitive person, but unless you build a solid trust that you would never hurt each other, there might be serious problems down the road."

"I really love her." Ernie said.

"That's good. But try to understand the nature of your love. Kindness is more important than love in the long run. Kindness builds trust and well-being."

Ernie felt better. He began to piece together what he had just heard. *Anders has given me a warning and a challenge. The rest is up to me and Martha. And, yes, maybe I should see a doctor.*

It was hard for Ernie to say goodbye to Anders, but he promised that he and Martha would come back to see him. Anders gave Ernie one more bear hug at the door and said, "I should add one more bit of advice to you, Ernie. I doubt if you have a problem with alcohol right now, but beware of heavy drinking. I have known drunks, who have marshaled booze as a defense against their deepest fears. But liquor never does the trick. In fact it sends the demons into dark dungeons, where they plan and plot new ways to steal your mind. Be careful, good friend, paranoia and alcohol are a deadly duo that has wrecked many a good man."

Anders stood, holding his young friend by the hands and said softly, "I'm glad you're going back to college. I don't know when I shall see you again, but allow me to send you on your journey with a Rilke poem I memorized years ago, because it seemed to touch something stirring inside me at the time. Now, I pass it on to young Ernie." Anders recited in a dramatic voice.

I live my life in growing orbits
which move out over the things of the world.
Perhaps I can never achieve the last,
but that will be my attempt.

I am circling around God,
around the ancient tower,
and I have been circling for a thousand years,
and I still don't know if I am a falcon,
or a storm, or a great song.

"That's beautiful. Thank you, Anders," said Ernie as he opened the screen door.

"Be the captain of your ship, young man, and the master of your soul." Ernie started down the stairs and stopped as Anders shouted, "Come back and see me anytime you wish. I'm always here and I'll tell you about my new passion."

"What's that?"

"Making furniture. It's good for anything that ails you!"

Ernie slowly drove up Anders's lane to the township road, wishing he could have stayed longer to visit with this remarkable friend. As he made the turn and started toward Dahl School, he spotted Ole Gangstad's Black Angus bull watching him from the corner of the fence. He stopped the car and decided to get out. He stood by the front bumper and watched the bull digging in the dirt with his front hooves. Ernie went into the ditch and up to the fence. The bull shook his head as the tall man stared him down, eyeball to eyeball. The bull backed up, turned around, and walked away.

313

Chapter XX...The Long War Ends

Ernie felt a whole lot better after his talk with Anders, but there were important warnings in the wise man's words. On the drive back to the family farm he thought about what was happening in his head. It especially troubled him that seeing Timmy Burstrom next to Tom's frozen body in the attic was something his mind invented. *How could that be? It was so real. I can picture him standing over the casket. I can hear his voice. I can feel his arm in the grip of my hand when I dragged him down the stairs. And then he starts showing up at the school. In the dark of night, with his face pressed to the window. I need Martha's help. But is that fair? How can I ask her to bear the burden of my mixed up mind?"*

He tried to distract himself by looking at the combines harvesting winter wheat on the big fields along the highway south of Crookston. There were three of them in tandem, straight-combining on a field as big as the Juvland's entire farm. He noticed the wind reels turning slowly, bending the tall wheat strands over the sickle bar. This was the way the rich farmers did it, not the way the little farmers in Jackson Township struggled, with binders, shocking, and old threshing machines.

Suddenly, Ernie was back there in Mr. Dahl's stubble field, kneeling down to comfort Tom. *What was it he said? 'I'm shot now. My father's farm is lost.' And this morning, there were Susan and Dale playing farm in the dirt, on the land that Torkel Henning homesteaded, making fence posts out of twigs and stringing binder twine for wire.* Ernie flashed ahead to his own mother, the day she sat on the porch crying, as the truck carried the last of the cattle off to slaughter. *It is all changing and it saddens me. How far back do family farms reach? Since the beginning of our country and certainly back to the Old World and further. I see the day coming when farms will be big business, like factories producing food. Maybe I'll write a poem some day about the death of family farms.*

When he got home, there was another letter from Bobby Smierud lying on the kitchen table. They had exchanged letters all summer, and Ernie noticed Bobby's writing was getting better, clearer sentences and fewer spelling errors. He eagerly opened the envelope and read.

Dear Mr. Juvland,

Sorry I haven't written in a while. Something happened and I need to see you. I'm not doing o.k. Could you come up and visit me? I really need to talk to you. I told my counselor what a nice man and good teacher you were and he thought it would be good if you came for a visit. I'll draw a map for you on the back and put the phone number down. You have to call first if you are coming to see me.

I hope you're o.k. and I hope you can come see me. I need your help.

Bobby

Ernie put the letter down and wondered what the problem was. He had planned to spend a day or so with Martha and her parents over in Bemidji. He had not met her folks and Martha had told him over and over, "It was about time." He asked his mother if he could borrow the car again for a few days. He told her about visiting Martha's parents and going up to the Bass Lake Juvenile Detention Center to see Bobby, maybe during the following week.

Mrs. Juvland said, "Yeah, I should have warned you before. I had to put the spare tire on the right front and she's a bologna-skin. That's a long drive all the way to Ely, so take 'er easy on the highway. Take me back to Mildred's and I'll be okay."

Ernie called the number of the center and spoke to a receptionist. She said he could see Bobby on the coming Tuesday, August 14. Ernie asked about Bobby and the receptionist said, "We've had some trouble with Bobby, but mostly with his brother. It would be better if we don't discuss it over the phone."

Ernie said, "Okay. Put me down for the 14th. I'll be there."

The receptionist said, "How about at two o'clock?"

Ernie said, "Good. Please tell Bobby I'm coming."

The receptionist said, "Okay, I'll do that."

Ernie packed a few clothes in a small bag and left for Bemidji shortly after noon on Monday. He was a little nervous about meeting Martha's parents, but when Mr. Sampson met him at the door and gave him a warm handshake, he felt better. Mrs.

315

Sampson was a small woman, with beautiful white hair she had cut short. She was quiet, where Mr. Sampson was rather boisterous. They sat on the back porch looking out over Lake Bemidji. Mrs. Sampson served them ice tea and tuna salad sandwiches. Ernie had the feeling he was sitting down for a job interview. Mr. Sampson wanted to know all about him and his family life on the farm. He asked him a number of questions about his first year of teaching at Dahl school, and finally the subject turned to religion.

"What church do you go to, Ernie?" Mr. Sampson asked.

"We're Lutheran."

"Well, we're Catholic here," said Mr. Sampson.

Martha sat quietly listening. Her mother spoke up. "Well, Lutheran is okay. We have some friends who are Lutheran. They're nice enough."

There was a moment of silence broken by Mr. Sampson. "I save newspapers telling of major events." He handed Ernie a copy of *The New York Times,* dated August 9, 1945. "I'm betting this one will be in my file until the day I die."

Ernie was puzzled by the abrupt change of subject. He looked at the headlines. **SOVIET DECLARES WAR ON JAPAN; ATTACKS MANCHURIA, TOKYO SAYS; ATOM BOMB LOOSED ON NAGASAKI.** Ernie said, "Yes, I heard on the radio, they dropped a second bomb." Ernie looked up from the paper. "Maybe now they'll give up."

Mr. Sampson said solemnly, "I believe they will. But it's terrible that it has come to this."

No more was said about the war. The conversation shifted from one subject to another, and Ernie wondered if it would drift back to him and Martha. He needed to tell them he wanted to marry their daughter. He mulled it over, thinking of ways to say it, but nothing seemed right. Most of what he thought of sounded like something Jimmy Stewart would say in a movie, awkward and corny. He decided to wait for another time.

The next morning was August 14. Ernie and Martha took their coffee down the stairs to the lake shore where Mr. Sampson had built a small dock for his boat. They sat on a bench at the end of the dock and watched the sun rise over the lake and spread a path of yellow on the glassy water. Martha wanted to know about Ernie's visit with Carla, Dale, and Anders. Ernie started, "Yeah, I'm really glad I did that. Carla is selling the farm. She and Dale are moving to St. Paul. They'll be living with her aunt, and Carla is going back to nurse's training school."

"Good for her." She added, "Did you tell her about us?"

"I told her we were getting mighty serious."

"So, what did she say?"

"She told me she was jealous."

Martha let out a big laugh. "Lucky me, eh?" She paused. "I always liked Carla. We had some lively gabfests when I stayed there. She was always trying to figure out Tom. I don't know how you felt about him, but he treated Carla like an old dishrag. I tried to be nice to Tom, but he treated me like a child, like I was some little toy in the house, just for his amusement."

Ernie said, "I thought he was a hard man to get close to. He was the boss, and he let everyone around him know it." Ernie wanted to change the subject. It made him uncomfortable talking about Tom and Carla. "And then I went over to see Anders."

"And how was my old buddy doing?"

"Great, as always." Ernie thought this would be a good time to tell Martha about the dreams, the hallucinations, and how Martha needed to understand. "Okay, we need to talk about these bad dreams I've been having. Anders suggested what might be happening, and he told me that I should be open with you about it."

Martha was puzzled. She tilted her head to the side and asked, "Is this going to be bad news?"

"No, not really. But we both have to realize what's going on in my head and how it might get worse. He said if we get married, it will be very important that we trust each other in everything. We must be open and honest."

Martha felt nervous. "How might things get worse?"

"Carla told me something pretty shocking." Ernie wondered how to explain it. "Remember I told you I saw this neighbor kid, Timmy Burstrom, in the attic by Tom's casket?"

"Yes, and you told me that's why you moved out."

"Right. But here's the strange part. The kid couldn't have been there. Carla told me he was in the hospital in Fergus Falls."

"Well, that's interesting." She looked out across the lake. "But maybe it was just part of a dream. And don't forget—you were going through a lot of problems." She patted him on the arm. "I don't think you should worry about it."

"I felt I had to tell you about that, just to be honest."

317

"I understand, and it doesn't change the way I feel about you." Ernie held her tightly. They sat in silence. And then Martha said, "Mom and Dad really like you."

Ernie was pleased. Then he asked, "Do you think it matters that I'm Lutheran?"

Martha thought for a moment. "You know, my folks aren't all that religious. Especially dad. They just want us to be happy."

"Okay, I guess that's settled." Ernie rubbed his hands together. "So, do you want me to get down on my knees like they do in the movies?"

Martha laughed, "I'd ask you to do that, but you don't have a bouquet of flowers."

"Shucks! I knew I forgot something!" They hugged and Ernie whispered in her ear, "Hey, girlie, you wanna make it legal?"

Martha drew her head back and looked Ernie square in the eyes. "So what if I said, 'No!' What would you do then, big boy?"

"Well, I would maybe jump in the lake and drown myself."

"So, that's your game, eh? You'd want me to live the rest of my life in guilt?"

Ernie had a sly grin. "Something like that, I guess."

"Then I'd better take you up on the deal, right?"

"You know what I like most about you, Martha?

"Tell me."

"You are so very, very romantic!" He held her tightly and laughed. They talked about the wedding, and both agreed they shouldn't rush into things. Ernie wanted to start classes at Bemidji State Teachers College, and Martha felt good about that. They continued to talk about the future, but Ernie was thinking he should be leaving for Ely soon. And then he had an idea. "Say, I want to ask you, would you like to ride with me up to Ely to see Bobby?"

She tilted her head to the side. "I have to think about that."

"I just figured it would give us more time to be together. I'll have to get back home first thing tomorrow morning. If the weather is nice, we'll be cutting wheat over at the Inderdals."

"I really don't want to see those boys. I've tried to forget about them."

"You wouldn't have to see them. I'm only going to be there for half an hour or so. I'm sure we could find you a place to wait."

"I guess I could even wait in your car."

"We'll try to do better than that."

At nine o'clock Ernie and Martha started out on their 175 mile drive to Ely. They finally found the place stuck way back in the woods, off a gravel road. Bass Lake Juvenile Detention Center. They pulled up to the window of the guard house.

"You're on the list, sir," said the guard. "I'll need to keep your driver's license until you leave." He placed the license in a drawer and handed Ernie two passes. "The visitor center is straight ahead." He pointed, "It's that long building on the left. See it? And don't forget to pick up your license on your way out."

Ernie thanked the guard and drove on. He parked in the shade of a big Douglas fir and said, "Let me go in and see if there's a place for you to wait inside."

"Don't worry. I'll be okay here." She took a *Look Magazine* out of her bag.

Ernie checked in with a guard at the reception desk. He was a big man with a crew cut, tall and husky. "Bobby is waiting for you. Did you bring anything with you? Food, gifts, other items?"

Ernie said, "No, sir."

The man came out from behind the desk and said, "I'll have to pat you down." Ernie raised his arms and the guard frisked him. "Fine," he said and pointed to a door. "Go through that door to the porch and we'll bring him out. There'll be a guard in the room with you during the visit. And you'll have to keep it short."

Ernie thanked the guard and went out on the porch. He sat down in an Adirondack chair and looked out through the long line of screened windows facing the north. In the yard were a flag pole, volleyball net, and a basketball basket.

Beyond the yard loomed the jack pines, white spruce, and Douglas firs that stretched for miles across the border and deep into Canada. They called it 'The Boundary Waters', giant granite and greenstone outcroppings, peat bogs, sloughs and thousands of pristine lakes set in the endless forest. Ernie was raised on the prairie and now these woods placed him in a different world. The forest made him feel trapped. The prairie gave one an open view of what's coming. Here there were mysteries behind every tree.

Ernie heard a door open at the end of the porch, and a guard led Bobby into the room. The boy had changed; he was more of a man now, dressed in an olive drab T-shirt, and khaki trousers, neatly pressed. His brown hair was cut short and he looked clean.

The guard, a tired, older man, with a huge beer belly took a seat at a table near the door, and Bobby walked up to greet Ernie.

"Hello, Mr. Juvland. I'm glad you made the trip." He reached out to shake Ernie's hand.

"Hi, Bobby, you're looking good." Ernie squeezed one of Bobby's biceps.

"Yeah, we get a lot of exercise and I've been lifting weights." They sat down next to each other.

Ernie heard a teacher's voice coming through an open window further down the long porch. He was talking about Lincoln and the "Emancipation Proclamation". Ernie said, "That's a history class, right?"

"Yeah," said Bobby. "That's Mr. Kiersky. He's a very good teacher. All the teachers here are good."

"I was just thinking—you haven't mentioned Neal in your letters lately. Is he still here?"

Bobby looked out across the yard. "Well, I guess I could say he is, but he really isn't." He pointed to three white crosses on the far side of the yard. "My brother is out there." Ernie was not quite sure what he was talking about. Bobby continued in a flat voice. "That cross on the end. You can tell—it's freshly painted white. I painted it myself and put his name on it."

Ernie was stunned. "Neal died, and that's his grave."

"Yeah, I could be there next to him, too, if I hadn't chickened out and turned back."

Ernie turned to Bobby. "Can you tell me about it?"

"Yeah, that's one of the reasons I wanted you to come up here. When they called Pa and told him the news, I don't know, he might have been drunk, but he told them he didn't want anything to do with the body. But when I get out, I want to bring my brother back home, so he can be buried next to my mother. And if Pa doesn't want to dig the grave, I'll dig it myself. Neal had a mean streak, but he was still part of our family. I think Pa will get over his hate for Neal in time. He just gave up on my brother, and doesn't want to hear his name mentioned. But I'm hoping that will change."

"I'm so sorry." Ernie studied Bobby's eyes and waited for him to say more.

"We were so dumb! Neal had this idea that we could break out of here. We made plans to live in the woods. We started

320

stealing stuff like fish hooks, fishing line, and that. Neal said if we could stay in the woods and not walk down any of the back roads out there, they would give up looking for us."

"So you broke out of here."

"Yeah, it was right after the Fourth of July. We walked and walked through the woods. We swam in lakes and fished. We had plenty of matches, so we made a fire at night and ate fish. But I started to get scared. Then we ate some mushrooms. They were probably poisonous, because I felt like I was going crazy. Neal started beating me, trying to make me move deeper and deeper into the woods. But I ended up, well—I just couldn't take it anymore. I left him one night when he was sleeping and started back. I came across a road and someone picked me up and brought me back here. It was so stupid. If I hadn't broken out, I might have been paroled by now. As it is, they tacked on more time to my sentence. I don't know when I'll get out now. I'm mad at myself, and my brother is dead."

"How did he die?"

"Mosquitoes."

"Really?"

"That's what the report said. I saw the body when they brought it out of the woods. I had a hard time looking at it. He was all bloated. His skin had turned a bluish black and he had these blisters all over his body. I knew he would swell up from bee bites, but I guess mosquito bites did the same thing, if there were enough of them."

"I'm very sorry for you, Bobby." Ernie leaned over to put his arm around the boy.

"The mosquitoes were so bad, that's why I turned back. Sometimes we had to go into a lake and sink down so the water was just under our noses. But they would still get us. They'd crawl in our ears. My face started to swell up." Bobby looked down at Ernie's arm. "There's one now." He slapped a blood-filled mosquito off Ernie's arm, leaving a streak of red. "Yeah, they get in here, too."

Ernie changed the subject. He told Bobby about the night of the blizzard and how they had found his dad in the snow outside the school, nearly frozen to death. Bobby smiled when Ernie told him how his dad had helped him in the morning, walking the children to the Marum farm.

Ernie looked at his watch. The time had flown by. "Well, I suppose I should be getting back on the road. Martha is waiting in the car."

"Martha?" He started to get up. "You mean Martha Sampson, the teacher?"

"Yeah, we've become real close this past year. We're planning to get married."

Bobby sat back down again and heaved a sigh, "That's good, I guess."

"Yeah, I asked her to come along for company, but she decided to stay in the car."

Bobby looked out across the yard. "Well, I might as well tell you. I was going to wait, but I might as well get it out right now."

Ernie waited. Bobby wiped the sweat off his face. He looked over at the guard and saw that he was busy doing a crossword puzzle. He whispered to Ernie, "I don't want the guard to hear. Me and Neal did a very bad thing to Miss Sampson, and as far as I know, she never went to the cops. Has she told you anything about what happened in our barn?"

"No, she never told me anything. I heard about the snake in her car."

"No, this was much worse." Bobby held his head in his hands and started to sob. His voice came out in a whimper, "Neal raped her. I held her down and he raped her." He sat up and looked over at the guard. He continued, "She kept us after school one day, but we snuck out and hid in our barn. She drove over and found us. Neal was hiding behind the door when she came in. He jumped her from behind and threw her down on the floor. I yelled at him to stop, but he told me to hold her arms down or he would beat the hell out of me."

Ernie reached over and grabbed his arm. "You don't have to tell me anymore, Bobby. Just try to pull yourself together."

"It was Neal, Mr. Juvland. Please! I never would have done a thing like that. I just did what Neal told me to do. I held her down."

Ernie hugged him and said, "It'll be okay, Bobby."

The guard got up and started their way. Bobby was close to Ernie's ear. He whispered, "Tell her for me. Tell her how bad I feel. I'll apologize to her one day, but I feel so bad. I just can't face her right now."

"I understand."

The guard said, "Sorry, sir, Bobby has a class now."

Bobby held Ernie tightly and blurted out, "I'm all alone and scared. Please don't forget me! You're the only person I have!"

Ernie softly patted him on the back and said, "I won't forget you, Bobby. I will do whatever I can to help you. I give you my word on that."

Ernie and Bobby said goodbye to each other and promised to write. Bobby left with the guard and Ernie went back to the car where Martha waited. He thought about the scream Anders had heard coming from Tom Henning's barn. It struck him how stupid he was to assume that Tom had raped Martha. He recalled what old Anders had said about perceptions making that leap to truth.

They drove in silence for several miles. Martha noticed there was something troubling Ernie. "So, how are the Smierud boys doing?" There was a touch of regret in her voice, like it was difficult to even speak their name.

Ernie gripped the wheel and looked ahead. "Neal died in the woods. He was trying to escape. As for Bobby, he's all alone now and pretty shook up."

"He died in the woods." It was not a question, just a simple statement of fact.

"Bobby wants to talk to you some day. He wants to apologize."

"Okay," she said flatly and took in a breath. "We'll see." She looked out the side window. "So I guess Bobby told you what happened in the barn."

"Yes." Ernie wondered if he should say more. "He told me it was Neal, and he's very sorry he couldn't stop him. He feels so bad about the whole thing, and now he's alone. I promised I would not forget him. I'm determined to help that kid get through life one way or another."

Martha was holding back her tears. "I can't tell you how awful it was, and it didn't get any better when I went for help. I wanted to get home to my mom and dad and never come back. I managed to get out of the barn and start my car. I was weak. It hurt and I was bleeding. The first person I thought of was Carla. I drove to the house, but she and Dale had gone somewhere. I left the keys to the school on the kitchen table, grabbed a few clothes, and threw them in the car.

"I heard Tom yelling at the cows in the barn. He was doing the milking. I thought I should tell him I was leaving. I went in the barn and he said something like, 'What the hell have you been doing? You look like you've been playing football in the mud.'

"I went crazy. I screamed at him and started punching him in the face with both fists. He grabbed me by the arm and threw me on the floor. Then he said, 'I don't let any goddamned bitch lay a hand on me!' Then he stormed out of the barn.

"I was a raging maniac, screaming bloody murder! I drove over to Anders, and you probably know the rest. Thank God there was one human being who cared about me. I was a wreck!" She looked out the window and then continued, "It was late Friday night when the doctor examined me. That was another dreadful experience.

"I drove home to Bemidji and told my parents I was quitting, but on Sunday night Orvid Skime called and demanded I come back until they could get a substitute. Can you imagine my spending three more days in the Henning house and three more days at Dahl School after what happened? Fortunately, the Smierud boys never showed up for school.

"On Wednesday of that week, one of the students brought in the mail. I read the doctor's report at my desk, while the students were out for recess. My purse was in my car, so I just stuck the letter in the desk drawer, locked it, and forgot all about it. I had already decided I wasn't going to the police. Orvid came by after dismissal and told me they had a substitute. He also told me that they could not pay me anything for the first week of May. By that time, I was so damned mad; I just wanted to get home. The last thing I said to Orvid was, 'Why don't you go jack off!' Eunice was standing by her dad. She let out a giggle and said, 'Oops!'" Martha managed to smile and so did Ernie.

They were coming over a rise, and they could see the long, straight road through the forest. They drove for several miles in silence. Finally Martha said, "It's a nice day and we're here together. That's all that matters to me right now."

Ernie said, "I love you, Martha."

"I love you, too. Sorry you had to hear all that."

They drove on. Martha had moved close to Ernie and she draped her arm over his shoulder. They were on Highway 169, coming into Grand Rapids. They heard a train whistle. Then they heard another one. Then they heard a train whistle that would not stop. They pulled into town and they heard fire sirens wailing. Three fire trucks were parked at an intersection, with their bells clanging and sirens blasting. The firemen had brought out fire hoses and were shooting great streams of water up over the street lights, high in the air. Martha leaned forward, her chin almost on the dash to see the bursts of water. "What's going on here? Is it a fire?"

Ernie looked out his window. A lady was hanging out of a second story window waving an American flag. On top of the building he saw two teenage boys, with a huge flag stretched out between them. They were hooting and hollering. The traffic was completely stopped at the intersection of Highway 2. Another train went by across the highway on the Great Northern Line, the whistle wailing out to the people on the sidewalks; they were spilling into the streets. Ernie saw a tavern with the door thrown open. Half a dozen men were outside the tavern drinking beer. Ernie yelled at them. "What the heck is going on here?"

A short guy, built like a fireplug raised his beer and yelled, "Haven't you heard? The Japs surrendered!"

Another guy yelled, "The war is over!"

A clock on a bank stood at 6:45. It was August 14, 1945. Martha grabbed Ernie around the neck and kissed him. "Whoopee!" She shouted, "Let's park and get out!"

Ernie looked at the line of stalled cars ahead of him and said, "May as well, we aren't going anywhere anyway." He cut down an alley and parked. They got out and Martha was dancing. They heard music coming from everywhere, mixed with radio broadcasts of the news. Martha and Ernie did the jitter-bug right out on the sidewalk. Men in work clothes and farmers in overalls had come to town. Total strangers wanted to dance with Martha. They hugged her and kissed her, but Ernie didn't care. He was hugging every woman who came down the sidewalk. Ernie told one old woman, "The war is over and I don't give a hoot. I'm gonna give you a kiss!"

Ernie found a phone booth to call his mother at Mildred's. The phone rang and rang, but there was no answer. Ernie hung up

325

and figured his ma and Mildred were downtown celebrating. He told Martha, "They might be in a tavern getting rip-roaring drunk!"

It was eight o'clock, and the sun was hanging low over Highway 2, when Ernie and Martha pulled out of Grand Rapids. Martha laughed and said, "I was looking around for Judy Garland. Heck, this is such a big deal, you'd think she'd come back to her hometown to celebrate with the common people."

Ernie laughed. "I'm afraid she's out in California right now celebrating with all her Hollywood swells."

"Grand Rapids can brag all they want. Whoop-de-do! They have Judy, but we have Jane Russell, the pride of Bemidji."

"That's right. Last summer I took my mother to see her in *The Outlaw*."

"So what did you think?"

"I loved it, but my mom said, 'Why did you take me to a dirty movie?'" Ernie laughed. "Then Ma said, 'If a girl crawls in a haystack looking like that, she's just asking for trouble!'"

They headed west, and the train whistles where blowing on the Great Northern Line just off to the left of the highway. Passing through each little town on the way to Bemidji, joyous people were out on the sidewalks, Cohasset, Deer River, Ball Club, Bena, Cass Lake—they were all celebrating. In Bemidji, the high school band was playing down by the statue of Paul Bunyan and Babe, the Blue Ox. They had set up a beer stand, and people were walking along the lake shore with bottles of Grain Belt, Hamms, and Blatz Beers in their hands. There was singing, dancing and drinking. Several people jumped in the lake with all their clothes on. Some folks got very drunk!

Back at the Sampson house, Martha and her mother prepared a special dinner. Mr. Sampson brought out a bottle of champagne he had been saving. He slapped his wife on the butt and said, "I told you, honey, we weren't going to open this until the war was over."

Martha tapped on her glass with her spoon and spoke up, "Before you open that, we have an announcement to make." She looked over at Ernie and took his hand. "Do you want to tell them, or should I?"

Ernie said, "You have the floor."

"Okay then. Here goes. This wonderful man has asked me to marry him."

Mr. Sampson was about to twist the cork. "So, what did you tell him?

"I told him I'd take him up on the deal."

Mrs. Sampson chuckled, "You make it sound like buying a used car."

Ernie was laughing so hard he could barely speak, "I told her she really knew how to be romantic!"

"Pop," went the cork and it hit the ceiling. Mr. Sampson poured the champagne and then he raised his glass. "Here's to our two wonderful teachers in the family, Ernie and Martha." They sipped their drinks and then he added, "Oh, goodness, I almost forgot. Here's to the end of this terrible war."

After dinner they sat in the front room and listened to the news broadcasts until everyone started to feel sleepy. It was after midnight when Ernie got up and said, "I'm so happy to be here. Thank you for everything. And especially, thanks for raising such a wonderful daughter." He put his arm around Martha. "I'd like to stay up, but I want to get up early and get on the road. We're cutting wheat tomorrow." He shook hands with Mr. and Mrs. Sampson and gave Martha a kiss on the cheek. He said goodnight and started up the stairs to the spare room.

Mrs. Sampson called after him, "I put an extra blanket in your room if it gets chilly. The windows are open; you might want to close them before you turn in."

"Thanks," said Ernie. He waved to them at the top of the stairs, went into his room, and closed the door behind him.

Martha sat down by her dad and put her arm around him. "Isn't he a real sweetie pie, Dad?"

"I like him." He thought for a moment. "Have you set a date?"

Martha shook her head. "No, we want some time to think about that. He just asked me to marry him this morning out on the dock."

Mrs. Sampson said, "He's very polite, and I really don't care if he is a Lutheran."

Mr. Sampson said, "But he quit his job, Martha."

"He wants to go back to college, Dad."

Mr. Sampson said, "Well, that's good, I guess."

Mrs. Sampson said, "Well, maybe he could stay here and go to Bemidji State."

Mr. Sampson said, "I suppose we could work something out." He put his arm around Martha. "I just want the best for you, and frankly, he seems like an honest man."

Ernie slept well. He got up before dawn, dressed, and slipped out without waking anyone up. As he headed north from the Sampson house, he saw the main college building on the right. *Beautiful place for a campus. Right on the shores of a big lake. Maybe I'll be there in a couple of weeks. I love this town and Martha's family.*

Just east of Erskine on Highway 2, Ernie heard a pop coming from the front of the car. Then she started to pull to the right. He pulled into a farmer's driveway, got out and walked around the front of his mother's car. The right front tire was flat and he didn't have a spare. He opened the trunk and pulled out the jack, the tire pump, two tire irons, a lug wrench, and a round patch kit. When the tire was off, he found a nail that had punctured the 'bologna-skin' tire. He pulled out the nail with a pair of pliers and put it in his shirt pocket. One little nail had found his tire.

He scuffed up the rubber around the hole in the inner tube, using the raspy surface of the cap from the patch kit. He applied the cement, put a small patch in place, and pressed it down by rolling the edge of the cap over the surface. He put the tube back in the tire and used the tire irons to get it back on the rim. He pumped up the tire, mounted it, tightened the lug nuts, lowered the jack, and in 30 minutes, he was back on the road. After making the turn to head north out of Erskine, he took the nail out of his shirt pocket and felt the sharp point with his thumb. *You little bugger! You thought you could ruin my trip, didn't you? I'll bet you didn't figure I'd carry a patch kit. Well, now you know. I always do.*

The Sampson family slept late, especially Martha. She was still sound asleep, when her mother went into Ernie's room to strip the sheets off his bed. She was leaving the room with an armful of bedding, when she looked back to see if she had missed anything. Her eyes caught something white on the floor under Ernie's bed. She bent down to pick it up. It was Martha's brassiere. She said to herself, "Those rascals!"

Chapter XXI...The 2012 Reunion

Dale Henning sat at a bar in the Atlanta Airport drinking a glass of orange juice and watching the TV screen behind the bar. They were showing clips of a speech President Obama had given at the House of Blues in New Orleans the night before. The bartender came over and said, "Can I give you a refill on that?"

"Sure," said Dale. "A little less ice if you don't mind."

The bartender said, "No problemo."

"You're a good man." Dale put a twenty on the bar and went back to watching the President.

The bartender set his drink on the bar, took the money, and returned with the change. "So, where are you heading off to so early in the morning?"

"Minneapolis."

"Minneapolis. I see where the Twins are having another bad season."

"Yeah, so what else is new? What is this? July 26 and they're in last place, 13 games out. I'd say it's all over." Dale sipped his orange juice. "Twins and Vikings will drive you nuts!"

"Do you live back there?"

"No. I grew up back there, but I've lived here in Cobb County since 1960. I took a teaching job out here when I graduated from college."

"You still teaching?"

"No. I've been retired for a number of years." Dale sipped his drink. "Speaking of teaching, I'm going back to see two teachers I had years ago, a husband and wife. I went to an old one-room country school north of Moorhead, Minnesota."

"So how far back was that?"

"The last year of World War II."

"Really? How old are you now?"

"I'm 75 and my third grade teacher is either 92 or 93. Not sure how he's doing. I haven't seen him in 67 years. He and his wife Martha—she was my second grade teacher—they're now the only living persons who taught at that school."

"Wow! That's quite a story."

"Funny you say that. I'm meeting a reporter, who's doing a feature article for the *Minneapolis Star Tribune* on this big event coming up. A lot of good folks back there have raised money to move my old schoolhouse into town. The building is in good shape, even though it's over a hundred years old. They're going to turn my Dahl School into a museum. It's a big deal for a little town."

"That's amazing."

"Yeah, I was talking to the reporter on the phone. She's the granddaughter of my old teachers, by the way. She told me that the school is jacked up. They have the wheels on, and it will roll out at noon tomorrow."

"And you and your old teachers will be there."

"Yes, we will, and I'm hoping some of my schoolmates will be there as well." Dale continued to talk to the bartender as he finished his orange juice. Then he heard his plane called. He left a three dollar tip, climbed off his stool, and grabbed his bag.

"Have a good trip, buddy."

"I will," said Dale, "and you take care."

The reporter's name was Samantha Juvland Becker, the granddaughter of Ernie and Martha. She drove a Prius with a GPS screen on the dash. She had a Bluetooth in her ear and a Droid in her right hand. She punched in their destination and sped out of the Minneapolis Airport. Heading north on I-94, they were on their way to Moorhead.

"I'm going to record our chit-chat on the way up, so everything you say is (she dropped the wheel to do air quotes) 'on the record,' LOL." Samantha was dressed to the nines, looking very professional in her dark blue business suit. She had long blond hair with subtle highlights. "Excuse me a sec. I have to check on my son before we start the interview. He's on a high school orchestra trip to Kansas City, by bus of all things! I want to check where he is." She took her gadget out of her Kate Slade purse and punched in her son's number. "You have the 'Latitude app' on your cell phone, right?"

Dale said, "No, I've never heard of it."

"How about Farmville? I play it on my Droid."

"What's Farmville?"

"I'm totally surprised you don't know Farmville. You grew up on a farm, right?"

"Yes, I did."

"Farmville is a Facebook social game app. You set up your own farm and sell chickens and cows and stuff. You make 'farm coin'. I've just added a second farm out in Hawaii. I'm gonna start growing pineapples out there."

"So, do you play Farmville in the dirt?"

"No, silly! You play it online. And check out 'Latitude'. Here, look!" She held the gadget in Dale's face. "See that star? That's my son. Wow! I can't believe this! They're just now going around Des Moines, and they left early this morning! I'd be going nuts by now!" She put her gadget in her purse. "Okay, may I call you Dale?"

"You may call me anything you want to."

"Fine." She pulled a small recording device out of her Kate Slade. "I want you to tell me about going to Dahl School. What was that like? Grandma Martha told me you didn't have electricity and no indoor bathrooms. Were your outdoor toilets like those dreadful Port-a-Potties? Yikes! My husband had tickets to an outdoor Billy Joel concert. He ended up taking a buddy of his from the office. When I heard they had Port-a-Potties, I said, 'No way is this girl goin' in one of those!' The smell! I would rather pee in my pants! I'm thinking—how on earth did you survive?"

She pressed her finger against her Bluetooth, which was sticking out of her ear. "Oooops, it's the office. Sorry, I have to take this. Hi there! Yeah we're out here on the prairie, playing Farmville, literally. LOL. Yeah, WTF? He-he-he!" She rambled on and said, "Yeah, I'll text you on that right now." She picked up her Droid and started working her thumbs, while passing a UPS semi pulling double trailers. "Hey, that place in Motley that sells the best fresh salmon." She waited for a reply. "Yeah, Morey's. Am I near there? Okay, I'll punch it in and hit it on the way back." The prairie miles flew by, and the interview was forgotten. Samantha was locked into her gadgets.

Dale was happy to arrive at the Motel-8 in Sparborg. With new buildings, a wider highway, even a traffic light, he hardly recognized his old hometown. Samantha had things to do, more people to interview, calls to make, a trip to the Fargo Airport, and she needed to check out a farmer's market that sold reed baskets, made by a Pennsylvania woman, who had actually been written up in *The New York Times*. She left Dale in the lobby and told him that Ernie and Martha would be arriving shortly.

331

Dale checked in at the desk, went to his room, turned on the AC, took off his shoes, and lay down on the bed. He could not tell how long he dozed; it didn't seem long before he heard a knock on his door. A small woman, older than Dale, stood in the doorway. She was neatly dressed in a light brown skirt and a green blouse with a double strand of pearls. Her curly hair was a mixture of gray and light brown. Dale noticed she tilted her head to the side when she spoke. "Is that you Dale?"

"That's me and I'm sorry to ask, are you Miss Samson?"

"Well, I have to correct you, Dale. I'm Mrs. Martha Juvland and I've been that since 1946."

"Of course, Ernie's wife. Wow! You're looking so good!"

"Not bad for an old lady, right? Let's have a hug."

Martha took a seat by the window and Dale sat on the bed. "So tell me—is Ernie around here somewhere?"

"Well, he left with Bobby in his pickup to get something for you. They'll be back soon. You remember Bobby, don't you?"

Dale frowned, "You don't mean Bobby Smierud, do you?"

"That's him. We've been friends with Bobby and his wife, going back to when we got married."

Dale was trying to think back and picture Bobby from school days. "That's a surprise. I seem to remember, Ernie told me in a letter that his brother Neal died. Am I right on that?"

"Yeah, he died in the woods trying to escape." Martha looked out the window. "Lucky for Bobby, he had enough sense to come back, and serve his time. He lived with us and went to high school in Thief River Falls. Ernie and I both taught in the Thief River District. Bobby was a heck of a football player, and we helped him get a scholarship at the University of North Dakota. Then Ernie got him a job teaching phy-ed at Thief River High. He coached football and Ernie coached baseball, for a couple of years.

"That is so fantastic! What an amazing outcome! You, Ernie and Bobby. I never would have dreamed it."

"Yeah, it was wonderful." She paused and looked down. "But then things started going bad for Ernie."

"Really? I'm sorry to hear that."

"You might recall—he had those nightmares."

"I certainly do. I remember the one he had in our house."

"Well, they got worse. Then he started seeing people who weren't there and he heard voices. You know—hallucinations."

332

"Yes, I remember my mother told me a little about that."

"Ernie started having problems with his high school students. He thought they were plotting behind his back and then he started to drink too much. He finally ended up in a veteran's hospital in St. Cloud. He was diagnosed with schizophrenia, and he became very violent. And you know how big and strong he is. Uff da! He became dangerous. He almost killed one of the orderlies."

"That must have been about the time he stopped writing."

"Probably. I guess I should have stayed in touch with you, but those days were pretty rough for me. Good thing Bobby was around to help me out. I was trying to teach and take care of our little boy, Bernie." She glanced out the window. "By the way, he's coming today from Seattle. He's a big shot with Boeing, but he still talks to us." Martha tossed her head back and laughed. "His daughter Samantha is picking him up at the Fargo Airport. You met Samantha, right?"

"Of course. She drove me up from The Cities."

"So what did you think of her then?"

"Well," said Dale, "Samantha is very modern."

"That's a diplomatic way of saying she's full of bull, eh?"

Dale laughed and said, "I was trying to be civil." Then he turned serious. "So how did things work out for Ernie?"

"Well, we took a chance. I still don't know if it was the right thing to do, but we had to do something. One of his doctors heard about this neurologist who claimed to have a lot of success doing what he called 'transorbital lobotomies' on schizophrenic patients. This man travelled around the country and used a technique that avoided cutting into the skull."

"Right! I remember seeing a documentary on this guy."

"Well, he showed up at the State Hospital in Hastings, and Ernie's doctor took him there for the procedure. That was 1953, Ernie had just turned 34. We had no idea what was coming. The operation wasn't even done in an operating room. I was there and saw the whole thing. They put Ernie on a table and induced an epileptic seizure using electric shock. That way they could do the procedure without anesthesia." Martha stopped. She reached for a tissue on the bedside table.

"This neurologist used a ten inch needle—it looked like an ice pick. He raised Ernie's eyelid and inserted it into the eye socket through the tear duct. Then he tapped on the end of it with a

333

surgical hammer to get through some bone. It went almost two inches into my husband's brain. He moved the instrument back and forth. And then he did the same thing through the other eye socket. The idea was to sever the neural tissue between the prefrontal lobe and the thalamus. I think I'm right on that. I used to know all the right medical terms, but I've put most of it out of my mind."

Dale said, "I'm afraid to ask how it worked out."

"Well," said Martha, "it was good for the most part. He stopped all that violent behavior. He became very calm, which was good. He was able to come home, but we both knew, he would never teach again. And that hurt, because teaching was his passion." Martha wiped her eyes, "He has trouble with his balance, and it affected his speech. His words come out all mumble-jumble, and he gradually stopped speaking, even to me. But he writes. He has dozens of notebooks of stories and poems he wrote to me, and they all start with, 'To my beloved Martha, who taught me about kindness.' I just love them!"

Dale said, "Now I need the Kleenex." He reached for a tissue and wiped his eyes.

Martha continued, "And I really kick myself, because shortly after they did the lobotomy, they came out with drugs that helped control the behavior of schizophrenics. Thorazine was approved—I think it was 1954 or maybe 1955. So maybe if we had waited, things would have worked out better for Ernie."

Dale said, "You must have gone through hell."

Martha smiled, "Oh, I don't know how bad it was. I've forgotten a lot of it. I always loved Ernie, and after the lobotomy, I just had to learn how to love a different Ernie. And old Anders was so helpful. You recall Anders, right?"

"How could I ever forget him? He lived across the road from us in that funny house."

"Right," said Martha. "He was always our best friend. He taught us how to be patient with each other. In fact he was Ernie's best man at our wedding and he read a favorite poem of his that we have both memorized. It is so fitting for Ernie, because he came out of a poor background. But one thing for sure, he never gave up on his dreams. And Anders taught me to respect that."

Dale looked into her wet eyes, "I'd like to hear that poem, if you remember it. Would you recite it for me?"

She smiled and sat up straight, "Oh, I suppose I could. It was written by Yeats, titled, 'We Wish For the Cloths of Heaven'. Anders really had the voice and passion for reciting it, but I'll do the best I can. Don't laugh if I mess up." Martha began.

Had I the heavens' embroidered cloths,
Inwrought with golden and silver light,
The blue and the dim and the dark cloths
Of night and light and the half light,
I would spread the cloths under your feet:
But I, being poor, have only my dreams;
I have spread my dreams under your feet;
Tread softly, because you tread
on my dreams.

Martha smiled, "I'm sometimes surprised that my old brain can remember those words. I guess it's stuck with me, because those were my instructions, to tread softly on Ernie's dreams."

Dale said, "You are a remarkable woman, Mrs. Juvland."

"Oh, I don't know. It just comes from love. And Ernie is an easy man to love."

"Amen to that," Dale nodded.

"I should tell you one more thing about our wedding. When Anders read that poem, it had such an effect on one of the women, it started a romance. You will never guess who that woman was."

"I have no idea."

"Ernie's mother, Olga Juvland. This is such an amazing story, and Samantha has talked about writing a book on it. After our honeymoon, Ernie and I planned to come down here to visit Anders. Ernie's mom asked if she could ride along. When she walked into Anders's house and saw all his books, she said, 'Next time I tag along, I'll bring my suitcase.' Anders said, 'Very good. I was just thinking about making a big four-poster bed.'"

Dale was laughing, "Yes, that is an amazing story!"

"They became active in the Bethany Lutheran Church here in Sparborg. Anders started going to church on Sundays and he directed plays with members of the congregation. They both spent a lot of time with the Dahl School students. Anders invited them over on field trips. They did all kinds of hands-on science projects until the school closed in 1958." Martha smiled. "I once heard Anders tell Ernie, 'I discovered the hermit life was not for me'."

She laughed. "Here's where it gets good—Anders built a little house on the back of his truck and they hit the road. They spent a month camping at Yosemite National Park and they ended up in Berkeley, California. They were hanging out with a bunch of beatnik poets in the late 50s. Anders was reading his poems in coffee houses and Mrs. Juvland was doing storytelling in schools."

Dale added, "And I remember Ernie writing to me about his four older brothers, who all made it safely home from the war."

"Yes, all but Andy. She was so thankful the rest survived. She lived a long life, and Anders was very good to her. She called him 'Papa Plato' and Anders called her his 'Little Chickadee'."

Then Martha leaned forward. "So that's the deal with our family. How about you? How did things work out for you and your mom? I remember some of it from your letters to Ernie. You went out to teach in Georgia, right? I notice your southern drawl. You don't sound like a Norwegian from Minnesota anymore."

Dale said, "Yeah, I'm retired now, but I taught high school biology for many years. I really enjoyed it. We have an adopted Native American son—he's more than half Cherokee. He's done very well in television production in Atlanta, set design, lighting, and that. I owe so much to my mother. Carla got her nursing degree and worked hard to get me through college. She was an incredible woman. She never got remarried, but she had a lot of friends and lived a long life. She was 87 when she passed away."

Martha nodded and said, "She was a good woman, who had a tough life. I'm happy things worked out." She flashed an impish smile, "I'm sure you know, she fell in love with my husband back then, but we won't go there, right?" Martha looked out the window and stood up. "Oops. Here they come. Don't look. Go in the bathroom until they get in here with your present. Bobby gave me strict instructions. This has to be done just right or he'll scold me."

"Okay," said Dale. "This is exciting. I feel like I'm in a play." Dale went into the bathroom and looked in the mirror. He somehow thought he would look like a third grade farm boy. Martha had brought him back to his youth. He heard them whispering outside the door, and then he heard Martha say, "Okay, Dale, you can come out now."

Dale slowly came out of the bathroom and saw the three of them standing in a row by the window. Ernie steadied himself with a cane. His hair and neatly trimmed goatee were completely white. When he smiled at Dale, his lower lip quivered and his mouth opened as if he wanted to speak. Bobby was husky with a trim waist. He wore a T-shirt with a picture of Dahl School on the front.

Dale's voice broke, "I never thought I would live to see this day. Look at the three of you. Alive and grinning at me. Come on, let's have a group hug." After a long and hearty hug with much laughter, Dale stepped back to look at them again. "We're going to have so much fun this weekend. I might not want to go back to Georgia." He reached out to grab Bobby's hand, "So good to see you, buddy. Martha told me that you've had a good life."

Bobby was holding back his tears. He was 82 years old now, and he spoke in a hesitating manner, searching for the next word. "Yes, I have, Dale. And I...owe it all to Martha and Ernie here. I asked them for help, and they never gave up on me."

Dale said, "I recall your dad. He dug my father's grave."

Bobby laughed, "Yeah, he dug a lot of graves...and lowered a lot of caskets. He used to tell...guys in Buck's Tavern, 'I'll be the last man to let you down.'" They all laughed and Bobby went on. "You know he drank a lot...but he cut back, and the bugger lived to be 80. They should have put his liver...in a museum. I spent my summers with him. We got rid of most of his cats...and I helped him fix up the place. I think I made him proud. He even came...to a few of my football games."

Dale said, "I'll never forget the night of the blizzard, and how we found him in the snow outside the school."

Bobby laughed, "Oh, yeah, gee, he told that story over and over. It got better with age, but he always...used the same punch line. 'But the damned teacher stole my bottle of whiskey!'"

Dale hugged Bobby again, "I'm so happy for you, buddy."

Martha spoke up, "We are very proud of Bobby." She paused. "Well, Dale I see you've been looking over here at this big thing with a sheet on it." Dale saw Ernie pointing at it and smiling.

Dale said, "You mentioned a present. I'm guessing that's it under the sheet. How the heck am I going to get it on the plane?"

Martha said, "Samantha has made all the arrangements. It will be shipped to your home. She's good at stuff like that."

337

Bobby walked over and was about to remove the sheet. "Wait," said Martha. "I should tell Dale something. When Ernie had to leave teaching, we came down here often to see Anders and Mrs. Juvland. Anders took up woodcarving and taught it to Ernie."

Dale looked over at Ernie. He saw him smiling and nodding his head. It was obvious to Dale he heard every word Martha was saying and he was proud. She continued, "Okay, Bobby, let's have the official unveiling." Bobby reached over and slowly lifted the sheet.

"Oh, my God!" Dale shouted. "That is the most beautiful thing I have ever seen!" Dale snapped his fingers trying to think of the Norwegian name. "It's a—oh, Jeeze, I used to know that word. They make these in Norway. Big chairs carved out of a tree trunk."

Martha said, "Kubbestol."

Dale said, "Right. Kubbestol. Why couldn't I remember?"

Bobby said, "We're getting old, Dale." He pointed to the painted figures on the dark brown wood. "Look at all the pictures."

Dale said, "I see that. It's amazing! Just look at that!"

Across the back to the kubbestol were colorful illustrations. At the bottom Dale saw a farmer and his wife, standing on the porch of a farmhouse, waving goodbye to a small boy, carrying a gallon pail, holding the hand of a tall man in a black suit and hat. To the right was a Black Angus bull by a barbed wire fence. In the distance was Dahl School, with the flag flying out front. There was a husky football player with **Thief River** printed on his jersey.

And over the top, forming a canopy for the painting, was a large tree, and nestled in the spreading branches was a house made of weathered lumber. At the top of the steps stood a tall, dignified man wearing a straw hat. He was passionately embracing a gold-star mother. Behind her stood four sons in military uniforms, and by her side was a pretty young woman wearing a white dress with lilac blossoms. They were waving and each held a glass of wine.

Dale looked up at Ernie. He was moving over to the kubbestol. He shuffled his feet on the carpet and Bobby held his arm to steady him. Dale heard him say something that sounded like, "Look." Ernie gently tapped with his cane on the seat. There was a passage written in beautiful lettering. Dale read out loud, "The good life is one inspired by love and guided by knowledge."

338

The author in fifth grade, outside his country school in northern Minnesota, December, 1946.

AUG 2 0 2014

CPSIA information can be obtained at www.ICGtesting.com
Printed in the USA
LVOW07s2122130614

390051LV00014B/183/P

9 780615 817316